WORDS IN THE BLOOD

WORDS IN THE BLOOD

Contemporary Indian Writers of North and South America

Edited, with an
Introduction and Notes, by
JAMAKE HIGHWATER

A MERIDIAN BOOK

NEW AMERICAN LIBRARY

NEW YORK AND SCARBOROUGH, ONTARIO

MERIDIAN TRADEMARK REG. U.S. PAT. OFF. AND FOREIGN COUNTRIES
REGISTERED TRADEMARK—MARCA REGISTRADA
HECHO EN WESTFORD, MASS., U.S.A.

SIGNET, SIGNET CLASSIC, MENTOR, PLUME, MERIDIAN, AND NAL BOOKS are published *in
the United States* by New American Library, 1633 Broadway, New York, New
York 10019, *in Canada* by The New American Library of Canada Limited, 81
Mack Avenue, Scarborough, Ontario M1L 1M8

Library of Congress Cataloging in Publication Data
Main entry under title:

Words in the blood.

1. Literature—Indian authors.   2. Literature, Modern—
20th century.   I. Highwater, Jamake.
PN6069.I53W67   1984   808.8'9897   84-4905
ISBN 0-452-00680-5

First Printing, June, 1984
Designed by Barbara Huntley
1 2 3 4 5 6 7 8 9
PRINTED IN THE UNITED STATES OF AMERICA

ACKNOWLEDGMENTS

❖❖❖

Copyrights for works published from manuscript for the first time in this anthology are held by their authors and all rights are reserved by their authors.

Permission to reprint the following previously published and copyrighted works is gratefully acknowledged:

Chapter 21 of D'Arcy McNickle's *The Surrounded*: copyright © 1936, 1964 by D'Arcy McNickle. Reprinted by permission of the Estate of D'Arcy McNickle.

The Epigram, Prologue and Part I, Chapter One from the novel *The Names* by N. Scott Momaday: copyright © 1976 by N. Scott Momaday. Reprinted by permission of Harper & Row, Publishers, Inc.

Pages 30–51 from *Seven Arrows* by Hyemeyohsts Storm. Copyright © 1972 by Hyemeyohsts Storm. Reprinted by permission of Harper & Row, Publishers, Inc.

"A Wounded Knee Fairy Tale," "Red Beauty," and "White Brothers From the Place Where No Man Walks" from a collection of stories entitled *Dreams That Burn in the Night* by Craig Kee Strete. Copyright © 1982 by Craig Strete. Reprinted by permission of the author. "Every World With a String Attached" from a collection of stories entitled *If All Else Fails* by Craig Kee Strete. Copyright © 1980 by Craig Strete. Reprinted by permission of the author.

Pages 1–22 inclusive from *Winter in the Blood* by James Welch. Copyright © 1974 by James Welch. Reprinted by permission of James Welch.

Pages 101–213 inclusive from *Ceremony* by Leslie Marmon Silko. Copyright © 1977 by Leslie Marmon Silko. A Richard Seaver Book. Reprinted by permission of Viking Penguin, Inc. "Humaweepi, the Warrior Priest," "Yellow Woman," and "Tony's Story" from *The Man to Send Rain Clouds*, an anthology by Kenneth Rosen. Copyright © 1974 by Kenneth Rosen. Reprinted by permission of Viking Penguin, Inc.

Pages 181–187 from *Blue Highways* by William Least Heat Moon. Copyright © 1982 by William Least Heat Moon. Reprinted by permission of Little, Brown and Company.

Juan Rulfo, "Luvina," pp. 111–121, from *The Burning Plain and Other Stories*, translated by George D. Schade. Copyright © 1967 by Fondo de Cultura Economica, Mexico; Pan American Paperback Edition, 1982. Reprinted by permission from the University of Texas Press.

◈◈◈

*The final belief is to believe in a
fiction, which you know to be a
fiction, there being nothing else,
the exquisite truth is to know that
it is a fiction and that you
believe in it willingly.*

—Wallace Stevens, *Opus Posthumous*

CONTENTS

WORDS IN THE BLOOD

INTRODUCTION

The Word Was Born in the Blood

> The Word
> was born in the blood,
> grew in the dark body, beating,
> and flew through the lips and the mouth.
> —Pablo Neruda

❖❖❖

The brilliant Native American painter, T. C. Cannon, died in a senseless automobile accident in 1978 at the age of thirty-two, leaving us only a dozen major paintings and some splendid recollections. One luminous conversation I had with him in Oklahoma a few months before he died has special relevance to the subject of Indian writers today.

"I have something to say about experience that comes out of being an Indian, but it is also a lot bigger than just my race. It's got to do with my *own* mythology—the one I make up myself. That's what I want to express in my art," he said.

That is a remarkable statement for a traditionally raised Indian to have made. It focuses upon exactly what made Cannon's ideas and art so culturally revolutionary and vivid: it is an articulation not only of his profound regard for tradition, but also of his strong need to become a unique creative personality with his own "reality." For a traditional Indian, this assertion of cultural independence and individuality was not as easy nor as acceptable as it would be for other people living in the various democracies of the late twentieth century. Self-assertion, originality, and "a myth of one's own" were startling and new ideas in the rural world of Native Americans.

Many of the Indian writers represented in this anthology traveled the arduous journey that T. C. Cannon traveled in his search for a personal style which reflected both his own mythology as well as the culture of his Native heritage. Many of these writers have faced, to some degree,

1

the scrutiny, dissatisfaction, and sometimes the outright disdain of both Indian conservatives and non-Indians who are uncomfortable with the idea of sophisticated or learned Indians. It is specifically this new Indian individuality that marks their works with an unmistakable tone and texture, a vision that is at once communal and highly original; both ancient and ultramodern. To enter fully into the remarkable worlds of tales and poems of this anthology we must attempt to understand the tribal mentality that underlies the lives of traditional Indians of all the Americas. For it is the delicate blending of tribal traditions with modern and personal inventiveness that gives contemporary Indian literature its unique power and character.

The modernist trend among twentieth-century Indian authors is unprecedented in tribal life. In the Indian world the pervasiveness of *progress*—at least as it is understood by non-Indians—does not exist. Of course, change exists for Indians, but it is change unconnected with the ideals of "progress" and unallied with the romantic European idea of the inventive and exceptional *individual*. For instance, the invention of agriculture in pre-Columbian America brought about great, widespread changes in the lives of Indians all over the Western Hemisphere, but these changes did not come about from the personal energies or convictions of a particular individual.

Such individuality, such rebelliousness is unheard of among highly traditional and tribal peoples who live in an exquisite unity that puts them directly in touch with their cultures and with their carefully prescribed and perpetuated customs and artistic conventions. To depart intentionally from these forms and taboos is to be considered highly self-centered and unacceptable. And though these social restrictions may seem stultifying and repressive to people who value personal initiative, the harmony of tribal living is exceptionally useful and productive to Indians—now and as it was for many centuries before the coming of Europeans to the Americas.

The literature of Indians is an intrinsic part of the long history of the Americas, but its twentieth-century emergence is not well understood as an inventive and individual form because Native American traditional literature is so little-known. Such a predicament seems unthinkable when we realize that the same landscapes, the same uniquely American passions, and the same mystic idealism that inform the works of Walt Whitman—that bulwark of modern poetic imagination—are also intrinsic to Indian writing.

Indians are the very core and essence of the American spirit, not simply because they were here first, but because the transformation of European settlers into Americans was impelled by exactly the same sublime land and rivers, the same environmental influences that shaped America's aboriginal peoples. Just as Indians are now Americans, so, too, in a peculiar and meaningful way, Americans are now Indians.

Exploring this cross-culture *Indianization* and *Americanization* can give us access to the unique visions that emerge in contemporary Indian literature—even if the spiritual bond between us lies somewhere hidden from our memories. Long before the invention of writing, an ancient literature already existed for all people of the world in oral literature: the singing of words, the chanting of prayers, the recitation of histories and tales and religious songs of destiny. In this we are all primal, all of one mind. And even when writing was later used to record chants and tales, most of us agree that among our greatest writers there is still found in the written word the voice that speaks within the words.

Among North American Indians, the use of written languages is relatively recent, and so it's reasonable that we discover in Indian poetry and prose a human voice that is still singing inside the words now trapped on paper and in books. How natural it is that contemporary Indian writers of North and South America should reawaken the voice that slumbers within their remarkable heritage, giving the words back to the throat that uttered them.

The reservoir of Indian oral literature is immense. Every tribe of the Americas has numerous songs, tales, histories, poems, and incantations. With the exception of the still undeciphered glyphs used long ago in Mexico and parts of Central America, there were no written languages among Indians. As a matter of fact, most Native people of the Americas seemed to be in no hurry to commit their literature to the written word. As a holy woman put it when I asked her about the failure of North American Indians to produce a written language: "When you write things down you don't have to remember them. But for us," she said proudly, "it is different . . . all that we are, all that we have ever been, all the great names of our heroes and their songs and deeds are alive within each of us . . . living in our blood." These are the *words in the blood* of which the mestizo Chilean poet, Pablo Neruda, wrote so eloquently.

With the coming of Europeans in the fifteenth and sixteenth centuries, Indians began to speak Spanish and English. As much as they resented the intrusion by strangers upon their carefully sustained customs, these new languages made it possible—for the first time—for Indians of vastly different regions and languages to communicate with one another. Thus Indians began the slow process which has resulted in the recent discovery of the use of written language as a political and artistic weapon. Yet Indians did not immediately seize upon literature as a vehicle of expression. To the contrary, it was primarily white people who tried to preserve Indian traditions in writing.

A renaissance of interest in Indian literature and arts gradually began to take shape during the nineteenth century. Anthropologists sought the assistance of Indians in collecting and translating songs and ritual dramas. By the early 1900s ethnologists like Frances Densmore, Natalie Curtis, and Alice Fletcher had succeeded, if only tenuously and imperfectly, in transcribing a massive number of Native North American tales and songs. Such dedicated ethnological interest in Hispanic Indian culture, however, was almost nonexistent in the nineteenth century, a neglect which is peculiar considering the initial surge of ethnological activity by Spanish padres in the sixteenth and seventeenth centuries.

Yet Latin Americans were not entirely impervious to their Indian heritage. A large group of non-Indian, Spanish writers were producing a so-called *Indianist* literature: novels and poetry that, when sympathetic, was focused upon the romantic idea of the Noble Savage. The most notable of such literary works were produced by Clorino Matter de Turner, Aleides Arguedas, and Juan Leon de Mera. These writers were the Latin American counterparts of authors of the United States such as James Fenimore Cooper, Henry Wadsworth Longfellow, and Herman Melville, who produced some of the most famous works depicting Indians. Charles M. Russell, William R. Leigh, and Thomas Moran were among the numerous white sculptors and painters of the nineteenth century who were obsessed with Indian themes in their works.

These artists and writers had an important impact—consciously or unconsciously—on the way people thought of Indians, even on the way Indians came to think of themselves. Their efforts represented a drastic revision of the highly biased and unsympathetic chronicles and drawings of early visitors to the Americas, such as Bernal Diaz of Mexico and John Vanderlyn in the United States. And their depiction of life among Indians—if highly romantic—was strikingly more affirmative than the so-called *captivity narratives* written by whites who presumably had lived among Indians after being taken prisoner: *A Narrative of the Captivity and Restoration of Mrs. Mary Rowlandson*, written in the 1600s, and *John Tanner's Narrative of His Captivity*, published in the early 1800s. Likewise, the paintings of early artists/explorers of the Americas, such as George Catlin, Albert Bierstadt, Karl Bodmer, and Paul Kane, were distinctly different from the Europeanized or frankly racist art of painters like Theodore De Bry in the 1500s, Benjamin West in the 1700s, and Robert Smirke in the 1800s.

What was emerging with these written, sculpted, and painted images of Indians was an alternative to the unsavory and unsympathetic way Native Americans had been depicted for centuries. The results were hardly more realistic, but the enthusiastic interest of whites in aboriginal American culture made it possible for the first time for Indians themselves to begin to use English and Spanish as languages in which to make their own voices heard, offering a view of Native American life from the vantage point of Indians themselves.

The first efforts toward a Native literature in the Americas were largely collaborations between Indians and non-Indian writers, such as *The Autobiography of a Winnebago Indian, Black Elk Speaks, The Autobiography of Geronimo*, and *Sun Chief*. Though many of these collaborations resulted in important social documents, and some of them are even significant as American literature, on the whole they persist in presenting the Indian from a remove—from a romantic distance—which matches the white expectations of Indians: a terminal people who are usually referred to in the past tense, stoic, proud, impervious to physical pain, incapable of feeling, children of an unreal concept of nature, and living as fossils forever residing in the seventeenth or eighteenth centuries.

Such books often fail to provide an authentic Indian perspective, meaning that they impose a European reality upon the Indian, which lacks the very qualities (values, perceptions, attitudes, life-styles, diversities, etc.) that make Indians unique and worthy of attention. This missing Indian perspective—Indian life as actually lived and experienced by Indians *themselves*—could not begin to surface as a Native American literature until Indian writers became comfortable with their complex identities as an ancient people living in both the world of their forebears and in the "new world" of European settlers. They could not undertake a truly Indian literature until they became confident of their literary powers in the new languages they were learning: English, Spanish, and (though we sometimes overlook it) Portuguese. And the ease with which they made this transition was largely determined by the relationship of the dominant cultures to Indian culture itself.

Hispanic America is so predominantly Indian that its "Indianness" tends to be overlooked. Today it is taken for granted that Latin American literature has strong Indian qualities even when it is produced by non-Indians. Though Indians are socially and economically depressed, their cultures have been thoroughly assimilated by Latins. In fact, the nations of Latin America are so completely Indianized that even the rare person without Indian blood is familiar with the customs, dress, dialect, and mannerisms of Indians. This curiously imbalanced situation results in a predicament that could not easily exist in the United States or Canada: Indian culture belongs to every Latino, and writers, authors, intellectuals, and business people think nothing of drawing from the Native American world whatever will benefit them. Indians are part of the Latino psyche, even if they are not part of its social consciousness.

Thus, despite the Anglo domination of Indianness in Latin America, mestizo writers soon produced a literature which defined their uniqueness as Indians. For generations it was the custom in Latin America to send children to Europe for their education. It was an expensive undertaking, but some Indian families acquired sufficient wealth to permit them to give their children the kind of training that resulted in a profoundly urbane mentality, an acquaintance with several languages, a freedom from social and tribal restraints, and a grasp of European culture.

Such long-standing and rarified educational experience outdistanced the relatively provincial training available to English-speaking Indians until World War II. It is not surprising, then, that the mestizo writers represented in this anthology developed a sophistication, literary control, and a finesse not often discovered among Indian writers of the north. And it is no wonder that Latin American fiction and poetry by writers of Indian origin have achieved international acclaim and awards of the highest order. In fact, the literature of mestizo Latin America has entered the mainstream to such an extent that one does not normally hear Pablo Neruda, Octavio Paz, Miguel Angel Asturias or Juan Rulfo referred to as "Indian writers." They are simply writers!

The literature of Latin America has even managed to reach a mass audience despite its peculiar and remarkable styles. I am thinking particularly of *One Hundred Years of Solitude* by the Colombian author Gabriel Garcia Marquez. There are numerous Indian elements in Marquez's worldwide best-seller, but I have not chosen this author for inclusion in this anthology simply because he does not recognize himself as an Indian.

I have decided instead to use an arbitrary standard as the basis for including mestizo authors in *Words in the Blood*: I have selected works by writers who simply claim to be Indian. Of these, Cesar Vallejo was the first and most revolutionary. In 1920, he made a break with tradition and created an original style that placed him at the lead of mestizo literature. A Peruvian who came from a modest *cholo* (part Indian, part Spanish) background, Vallejo was jailed as a political dissident and spent his time in prison composing some of his finest poetry: such as *Trilice, 1922*.

The mestizo authors whose works are included in *Words in the Blood* have provided an inspiration for some of the most interesting writing produced in recent years by Indians of the United States. We see among the less racially self-conscious Hispanic Indian authors a wider variety of attitudes about themselves and their art than we find in the United States. We encounter Indians untroubled by the fact that many of their influences come from Europe's avant-garde. We find writers who are not criticized because they have spent most of their adult lives in France or England, rather than within an Indian community. And we discover a wide range of political persuasions. In short, we find individuals with sufficient personal liberty and experience to produce great, international literature.

Because mestizo writers have been working at their art with utter individuality since the turn of the century, they have become more relaxed as artists, less rattled by criticism that presumes upon their authenticity as Indians, less bridled by the stereotypical expectations of both Indians and non-Indians, and more inclined to produce great works because they allow themselves the essential artistic liberty to be themselves.

We should, however, be aware that our evaluation of mestizo writing is based on the fact that only the foremost Hispanic authors are available to us in English, whereas our access to the writings by Indians composing in English—as this collection makes clear—is far wider and includes the works of young authors whose efforts are just emerging into mainstream literature. The Indian writing of Latin America is an established, internationally acclaimed genre which already possesses a large body of criticism. For English-speaking Indians, the passage toward a Native North American literature has been more complex.

An insecurity among Indians about their personal and creative identities and the processes by which experience becomes literature has been complicated further by the relative indifference of the intelligentsia, the public, and publishers to Indian writers. This indifference to Indian writing was based partially upon the peculiar belief that good Indian stories could only be written by non-Indians, and partially on the extent to which Indians had not yet achieved a literary method that allowed them to transcribe their own linguistic styles and imagery into effective European prose.

It is not surprising, therefore, that the first novels in English to be published by Indian writers were emphatically non-Indian in texture, technique, and tone. In fact, they were really non-Indian books based upon the effort to *reshape* Native American experience so that it would successfully fit the mode and mind set of the realist novel of the time.

The first of these non-Indian Indian novels was by Potawatomi chief, Simon Pokagan, and was entitled *Queen of the Woods*, a sentimental tale of 1899, which helped to popularize the ridiculous use of words like *queen*, *king*, and *princess* to describe Indian leaders, though such appellations are completely unsuitable politically and linguistically.

Shortly after the Pokagan novel, the writings of the Sioux author Charles Alexander Eastman (Ohiyesa) began to appear, namely, his book of recollections of 1902, entitled *Indian Boyhood*. This book perfectly represents twentieth-century Indian literature in English in its initial period, reflecting the tendency of Indian writers to reconfirm the expectations of non-Indians. This is usually described as "an assimilationist stance." It reinforced the dominant white culture's views that Indians are somehow inferior until such time as they learn the white man's ways and become quickly and quietly part of the so-called American melting pot, rather than remaining distinctive in culture and languages and values—not a very pleasing picture of Indian literature, and a dismal description of several hardworking Indian writers of the early 1900s.

"When we leave the first group of Native American novelists and pass on to their successors, we begin to notice a sharp change in perspective—in their concern with their 'Indianness.' Increasingly, as these novels are read in the order in which they were written, we see the writers themselves become aware of their own ethnic consciousness, moving away from assimilation, through the equally frustrating period of cultural syncretism, and finally toward a separate reality," as Charles R. Larson notes in *American Indian Fiction* (University of New Mexico Press, 1978).

D'Arcy McNickle (Flathead) and N. Scott Momaday (Kiowa) reflect that shift. The thirty-two years that separate the active careers of McNickle (whose first novel was published in 1936) and Momaday (whose first novel was published in 1968) suggest that these authors would have very little in common, yet their books essentially are concerned with the same issues: the stressful efforts of Indians to combine in their minds and works different life-styles, beliefs, cosmologies, and world views—in short, very different realities—from the ones people of white America and Europe take for granted. This syncretism, as it is called, has been part of the process by which all minorities, as well as many white people who are outside the power systems of the West, have attempted to carry themselves and their arts into a relationship with dominant cultures, which essentially deny all realities and all belief systems except their own. What such Indian efforts to make Native reality visible and, possibly, tolerable to whites often revealed was the self-defeating inclination to accept the imagery and values that mainstream society fabricated to describe Indians, rather than aggressively changing such stereotypical ideas and images. I must admit, this is not surprising.

Although our customs and languages may insist upon one kind of reality, when we talk about them or put them down on paper, they almost inevitably change into something else—something that fits the expectations of the dominant culture. It's the same thing that often happens to us when we try to talk about a vivid dream. We have to change what we clearly know about the dream—how it felt and what it emotionally meant to us—simply because the language we speak will not accommodate our dream experience. To talk about the dream we have to change it . . . and so we're left with the nagging feeling that we really haven't said what we wanted to say. We haven't expressed in words a vivid experience we wanted to share with others. And that's very frustrating. Yet most of us take for granted that curious and frustrating feeling as a fact of life. By extension we may be able to grasp the frustration of possessing an ethnic awareness—a private world inside ourselves—that we cannot express because we have no words with which to turn these unique aspects of ourselves into a conversation or a poem or a book.

Indian authors like McNickle and Momaday were trapped in just such a predicament. They were denied the expression of the separate Indian reality upon which their identities as Indians greatly depended. They could not be any kind of writer except a realistic writer, even if realism did not serve the ideas or images they had in their minds. The novels of McNickle and Momaday valiantly serve two irreconcilable mentalities at the same time: allowing the standards of the realistic novel to dictate their style, content, and even their literary vision.

Yet McNickle and Momaday are clearly not apologists in the manner of Charles Alexander Eastman. *The Surrounded* and *House Made of Dawn* are iconoclastic works: novels of renunciation that express an emphatic rejection of the white man's world. "These two works illustrate a new ideological stance: repudiation of the white man's world coupled with a symbolic turn toward the life-sustaining roots of traditional Indian belief" (Charles R. Larson, *American Indian Fiction*, University of New Mexico Press, 1978).

The styles of McNickle and Momaday represent a curious contradiction: in perpetuating the white man's literary realism and at the same time clearly repudiating the white man's world view. As such, the novels of McNickle and Momaday are more strongly political than artistically daring. McNickle and Momaday filled realistic novels with long-repressed cries of outrage, like the novels of John Dos Passos, Upton Sinclair, Frank Norris, and John Steinbeck. The themes of repudiation and social justice coupled with *a symbolic return to traditional Indian belief* long remained the major thrusts of Native American literature.

Published in 1972, Hyemeyohsts Storm's episodic novel *Seven Arrows* seemed to be continuing the genre of McNickle and Momaday. There is, however, in Storm's writing one stylistic deviation that has marked several other recent Indian novels. Storm is less concerned with the politics of Indian issues than with the history of his whole race of people. As such his novel represents the *symbolic revival of Indian tradition*. It is a novel of nostalgia, for Storm is interested in the same recovery of the idealized Indian past as Kiowa/Comanche painter Blackbear Bosin, who once said: ". . . in my paintings there is absolutely no recognition of our defeat. I am painting the Indian as if 1492 simply never happened!" (Highwater: *Song From the Earth: North American Indian Painting*, New York Graphic Society, 1976).

This kind of nostalgia and revivalism has produced some exquisite paintings and some profoundly moving literature. The painting style is called "traditional."

As a literary style, this same traditionalism is visible in the writing of Hyemeyohsts Storm and is reminiscent of *Black Elk Speaks*. Storm, however, does not write in the manner of Black Elk—an elder recalling a succession of historical events. What Storm has invented is something which might be called "a cultural autobiography" in which there is no central narrator or character whose life and times we follow through a series of adventures. Instead, Storm has created a group of protagonists who represent, as a whole, the Native American experience. His style and even the lavish visual presentation of his novel (broken columns of text interspersed with numerous photographs and full-color plates of medicine wheels) combine two widely separate schemes of literature: anonymous and ancient tribal folk-history; and modernist graphics from the era of the McLuhanesque book. Hyemeyohsts Storm apparently outgrew the realistic novel when he switched his focus from the individual's survival to the survival of a whole way of life. What Storm wanted to say did not fit into the techniques, the rationale, or the structures of realism; and Storm therefore reinvented the Indian folktale. He had no other choice.

Realism works very well for novels of social justice, but it cannot successfully contain the visionary view of the reality of Indians, nor can it convey the unique spirituality implicit in the Indian experience of the world. The folktale and fantasy, on the other hand, provide an immediate access to other worlds. Closer to poetry than prose, the literature of fable is concerned with dream and with structuring a world in which imagination is a significant power. This is the world of post-realist writers like Hyemeyohsts Storm. Their works have often been assigned to children and adolescents, since they are often regarded as being the opposite of adult novels. Adult readers have not easily come to terms with the literature of fable, which is, doubtlessly, one of the reasons that recent Latin American writing has taken so long to make an impact on European and, especially, on American sensibility.

Yet *Seven Arrows* was not a landmark book. It did not launch a new style for the Indian writers of the late twentieth century. What made *Seven Arrows* significant was its transitional nature: withdrawing from social realism and moving closer to the folktale, an idiom that captures the special sensibility of Indians.

Storm pointed toward what was coming; he did not achieve it. That distinction was left to a group of writers whose manner was far more daring and urbane. Following Storm, a succession of brilliant Indian authors who were not simply dissatisfied with the limitations of realism (like Storm) but who also had experience with modern literary forms, dared to combine them with the traditional aspects of Indian fable. Like the Indian painters of the late 1960s, these young Native writers agreed with T. C. Cannon's observation: "I have something to say about experience that comes out of being an Indian, but it is also a lot bigger than just my race." And so writers such as Craig Kee Strete, Leslie Marmon Silko, and James Welch began to expess in their art a myth of their own making. That expression of individualism and modernism seems blatantly arrogant and immodest to people accustomed to the romantic folk-history which has long been the stereotype of Indian literature; and it seems equally self-centered and disengaged to political activists accustomed to novels of repudiation. Without social outcry and without the Noble Savage, many conservative readers believe that there is nothing left of Indian literature. Actually, it is just beginning. It is, however, not an "Indian literature," but a literature created by writers who happen to be Indians!

Their works range from the radically experimental to the folkloric and sublimely poetic. They provide a spectrum of style from Storm's turning point to Strete's point of no return. There is always an element of racial lamentation in these works, but they are not specifically political. The revolution these new writers seek is a revolution of technique. Their heresy is the inclination to absorb the most daring potentials of worldwide literature and to write out of a personal vision. The result is a style similar to the "magic realism" invented by Latin American writers thirty to thirty-five years before the publication of *Seven Arrows*. In magic realism the combination of the full range of human experience— the fantastic, naturalistic, bizarre, ambiguous, linear, intuitive, rational, and imaginary—needs no explanations or apologies.

Seven Arrows and *The Names* by Storm and Momaday, respectively, have as their primary purpose the instruction of readers in the spiritual mentality of Indians and the clarification of a troubled Indian identity. Though the viewpoint is totally immersed in the traditional world of Indians, such books are nonetheless *about* those traditions and are not extensions of Indian mentality into a distinctive literary form. The difference is important. The fictional writings of many authors included in this anthology represent an urge to break away from the "traditional style" and to produce an idiosyncratic style, an unapologetic extension of tribal mentality into a new and innovative personal form that combines Indian history, avant-garde European and American artistic values, and absolutely anything else that provides ideas and forms capable of supporting the imaginations of Indians. As a result, a few exceptional Indian authors, like Silko, have succeeded in writing directly *out* of their cultures, rather than simply writing *about* them. Again, the difference is very important.

I must hasten to add, however, that throughout this depiction of Indian individualists in search of personal literary idioms, let us recall that none of them are denouncing the validity of the traditional Indian world or attempting to escape from it into some other world. To the contrary, most of these writers are highly traditional people whose works focus on vital aspects of Indian culture. The major difference between this new breed of writers and prior Indian authors is that they insist on presenting whatever they personally envision as "reality," and they do so with or without tribal consent or peer sanctions or popular approval because the very core of their unprecedented motivation is to assert themselves not as Indian writers but as writers who happen to be Indians.

◆◆◆

Although the history of Native American writers in the theatrical media has not yet been written, and in our own era there has been surprisingly little activity in Indian drama despite the long heritage of Native ritual forms that could contribute greatly to the making of an Indian theatre, from the evidence of the dramatist represented in this anthology—Hanay Geiogamah—the artistic concerns and technical issues confronting playwrights are not much different from those of the Indian prose writer. Geiogamah uses a complex combination of ritual Indian devices, Brechtian influences, and activist purposes. His writing is emphatically nonromantic—modernistic and filled with populist images, rock music, and camp illusions. It rises on an authentic Indian vernacular voice, both in diction, which captures distinctive elements of Indian speech in English, and in the forms and the content of his dialogue.

A futuristic aspect of Native American theatrical art is found in the fact that a startling number of young Indians are now working in film. Writers like Sandra Johnson Osawa, a Makah Indian living in Seattle, Washington, are creating their own cinematic style. In showing the life of people on reservations, Osawa could readily involve her scripts in political rhetoric, but she is more interested in the interpersonal conflicts of Indian people themselves, than in confrontational racial situations. Her manner and her purpose are straightforward: the use of naturalistic drama to express what it is like today to be an Indian living on a reservation.

Like prose writers, Indian dramatists have been grappling with tough questions: How do contemporary Indian artists retain their cultural identities and also discover their individual voices? How do you remain an "Indian" in the traditional sense of keeping alive your customs, your world view, your values—and at the same time give birth to yourself: to a unique, expressive, assertive individual with the courage not only of his or her tribal (societal) convictions but also those self-made ideals and aims that make us real to ourselves?

In the writing of poetry, Indians found answers to these questions more readily, or at least more quickly, than in other literary forms. There are probably good reasons for this dichotomy: In poetry it is far easier to depart from the standards of Western realism.

The popular view of poetry is exceptionally liberal. Poetry is less restricted, less linear (B does not *have* to follow A), less factual and commonsensical (the world *isn't* exactly what it appears to be). On the other hand, fiction is supposed to be logical and realistic; it's supposed to take us by the hand, step by step, day by day, mile by mile, minute by minute, room by room, through a sequence of events. It's all right to get a bit dreamy in a poem, but fiction is supposed to keep its eyes wide open: no nonsense, no messing around with words or objects. We have invented a phrase—"poetic license"—which conveys the notion that poetry may make wild leaps of the imagination while prose, apparently, is supposed to keep its feet flatly and firmly on the ground.

Of course, the realistic conventions in prose are also purely arbitrary, as demonstrated by James Joyce, Virginia Woolf, Franz Kafka, and William Faulkner. These great heroes of experimental prose had their own well-documented problems getting into print, getting reviewed, or being read by more than a select and small public. They did, however, have a powerful intellectual network behind them. By contrast, the constrained artistic atmosphere into which twentieth-century Native American literature was born was so unfriendly that Indian writing went virtually unnoticed. Publishers, critics, and most readers did not seem to be hospitable to the Indian's separate reality and were largely indifferent to the way in which Indian reality found its way into verbal expression.

Native American poetry begins in an older tradition, which we do not usually consider to be "literature." Its roots, as N. Scott Momaday has said, "run into the very origins of language." Indian poetry was born out of a largely nonwritten tradition: an oral literature of songs, charms, prayers, chronicles, and tales. And, as I have already pointed out, by the end of the nineteenth century, a great many dedicated anthropologists had succeeded in collecting and transcribing an immense repertory of such oral literature. They published it in countless volumes; they held conventions and conferences for the study of these Indian texts; and they went to great lengths to learn Native languages so that their translations into English, Spanish, and Portuguese might truly reflect the character of the original pieces. They helped to make some of the "literary" genius of the Indian world visible to non-Indians. They also unwittingly suggested that Native American culture was capable of producing things worthy of study, preservation, and admiration. And this praise raised Indian self-esteem and aroused the interest of young Native people in their own cultures (an interest which had begun to falter badly in the 1900s). As we learn from the works of the poets of this anthology, poetry became a major means of keeping Indian tradition alive. And, just as European scholars and ethnologists had studied Indian languages in order to deal effectively with Native oral literature, a new generation of young Indian poets began to use European languages to transform their oral traditions into a written literature. The interaction between the non-Indian documentation of oral literature and the creation of a written literature by young Indians is more important than many Indians are willing to admit, for without these documents, many significant aspects of Indian oral traditions that now find their way into the works of Indian writers would have been lost.

The public interest in Indian culture in the early twentieth century was almost entirely the achievement of ethnologists and the massive literature they made available to readers. Unfortunately these early, published translations were often appalling, for there were many intentional and unintentional liberties taken with the texts, inflating them with non-Indian ideas, inferring European values where none was intended, and generally interpreting Indian poetry as if it were European. Almost as soon as translations of Indian oral literature were published, a debate arose in regard to the failures of such transcriptions. That discussion has greatly accelerated during the last two decades, resulting in new approaches to the presentation of oral literature, approaches that are more imaginative and at the same time more cautious about authenticity. As a consequence, many new translations have appeared, although they are no longer called "translations." Instead they are usually called "versions"—suggesting that they are not definitive, nor exacting, literal translations (which are impossible when translating from one mentality to another). These so-called transliterations aim to capture the spirit rather than the word of the Indian oral texts.

Brian Swann and John Bierhorst are heirs of the ethnologists who first studied Indian poetry. At the same time they are part of the generation of translators who want to minimize the anthropological value of their material and to regard it as true literature of the highest order. Swann's version of the Iroquois song of the northeastern United States and Bierhorst's version of *Cantares Mexicanos* from Mexico provide a glimpse into the immense repertory of songs, chants, prayers, tales, and histories that were kept alive in the living languages of Indian people, told from generation to generation and cherished as prized personal and tribal possessions. They also mark the curious divisions that were set up when European languages were introduced to the Americans. And since this anthology includes the works of mestizo writers as well as Indian writers of the United States and Canada, these two examples of oral literature give us some familiarity with the roots of both branches of Native literature.

◈◈◈

An anthology is a collection of writings built upon a premise. During the 1960s and 1970s, that premise was often a matter of racial, sexual, or national focus. Such anthologies served an essential purpose: to provide alternatives from the dominant culture's perspective. Today it seems to me that we need a different motive and a different objective when assembling anthologies. Alternative voices must not be kept in an artistic ghetto. Literary specialization in a racial, sexual, or national mentality too often results in a reinforcement of a subtle segregation. This kind of presentation of literature can be counterproductive and insular. Today I strongly believe that alternative voices need to enter the mainstream and attain a prominence based upon nothing but merit.

An anthology of contemporary Indian literature is unquestionably a political concept. For this very reason, such anthologies are normally highly inclusive, giving *everyone* some degree of visibility. I have, however, declined to produce such an anthology on the grounds that when it comes to the arts I believe in artistic rather than political motives as a reasonable basis for making decisions and selections. The procedure I have chosen may be crushing to everyone concerned; but no other premise seems valid or honest to me. As a result, *Words in the Blood* is a collection of only a few of the excellent writers who are Indians; not an assemblage of works by writers who are included simply because they are Indians. For me that difference is essential, although I realize that some readers will note the absence of some fine writers (that is a predicament of all anthologies; partially due to matters of taste and partially because some writers were simply unavailable).

One of my major motives for including mestizo writers in *Words in the Blood* is to deny the numerous barriers about race, language, and Indianness that are founded upon the erroneous notion that Indians are only found in the United States and Canada. And since I felt it imperative to include in this collection a few works of oral literature by unknown authors, I have naturally credited the non-Indian translators who achieved such exquisite results in rendering nonwritten Indian literature in forms that make them accessible and meaningful.

Finally, like that outstanding translator from the Chinese, Amy Ling, I hope to see in some distant rosy future a universal literature. And like Joyce Carol Oates, I hope to see "novels by women that are not women's novels; novels by minorities" that are not minority novels. When society recognizes a book as being "interesting" because it is by a minority person, the condescension is palpable. As Ms. Ling affirms: "Only if a work is recognized simply for being a good book . . . will we have all gotten somewhere."

PART I

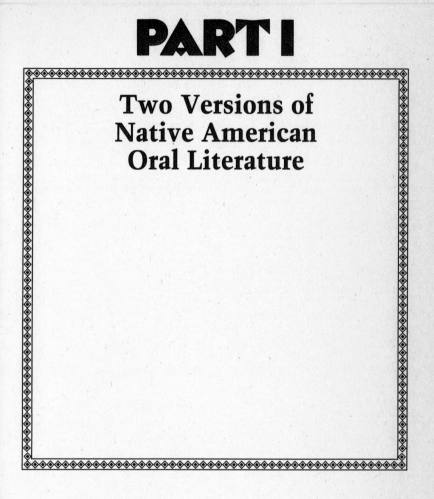

Two Versions of
Native American
Oral Literature

ROUND DANCE:
AN IROQUOIS SONG

◇◇

ADAPTOR'S NOTE: The mere translation of *words* cannot convey the meaning of these "poems." The words are abstracted from a matrix of music, song, dance, story, religious ritual. . . .

In this adaptation (and others I am working on) I have tried to utilize the silence of space. I have tried to allow the shape of that space to enact a meaning. I have used a "concrete" approach, using shape to create tension and movement. The poem does its own dance in the shape it creates for itself.

I make no pretense at being able to provide "easy entry into a strange world." The versions cannot stand alone. The originals cannot be translated into simple American poems, because the basic assumptions between the two cultures are not the same. There is no idea of self-expression in Native American "literature." Their songs, legends, ceremonies seek to "embody, articulate, and share reality, and bring the isolated private self into harmony and balance with this reality," as Paula Gunn Allen has told us.

To understand my version, some notes are necessary.

The *yeidos* ceremony is also called the Society of Medicine Men and Mystic Animals. There are two men who are head singers and chant the dance song. In addition, each member of the society has a song to sing. Hence the length of the ceremony depends on the number of people present. There can be no such thing, then, as a complete "text."

The *yeidos* ceremony is a curative ceremony, which takes place at night. There is a section in the ceremony, I am told, when the individual medicine men sing their personal songs. Some of these refer to feats of magic that are no longer performed—tossing hot rocks, casting the sharp point (whatever it was), and so on. At some point the Iroquois singers "put the songs on high, overhead." According to Fenton the old longhouses had a shelf over the bunks (as in the old Pullman cars), where they stored gear. In the Round Dances there is use of masks, those belonging to the so-called False Faces, the society that cured disease and sickness, especially diseases of the face and head. They would perform shamanistic acts, such as juggling live coals, and blew hot ashes over the sick person or the affected part. Their rattles were made of the shells of snapping turtles.

I have only worked with one part of the large ceremony.

Adaptation by Brian Swann

19

The song,
the great Sharp Point
ceremony
goes on
I see it walking
the song
I see it walking
I went there too
all the others came in
during that song
now they're dancing
the whole length
of the longhouse

we will try too
it is dancing here
my song
we will fill the house with noise
of the pounding of feet
it is well under way
we are turning our bodies
from side to side
we are stirring
we turn our faces
from side to side
we peer about

it has started
we have sung the songs
we have repeated the songs
we have passed through narrow valleys
the bodies of all the dancers are swaying
you are a lucky woman
you shall recover
I know why she took sick
I will cure her
I will make her well
our songs are getting mixed up
our songs are confused
the songs are clashing
our songs

they are walking beneath the hillside
they make a small stick stand on end
by itself
like antlers

their rattles held up
the masks are butting
it is peering about
the great sharp point

the great yeidos ceremony
now it has gone home
our songs are dead
now he has gone
above the sharp point
let us put the songs high up
turning his head from side
to side

one mask is peering about
sparks are scattered
ashes are flying about
red hot coals
the man blows from the mask
their two faces are together
each other
our two faces are against
each other
their two faces are against
mask and man
everyone is saying
the embers are ready
the maskers say to each other
the embers are ready
the embers are ready she says
they enter dancing
the two masks peer in at the door

the last song
so now
now she is dancing
I will try to make her dance
of the lodge
I made her stand up in the center
I made her stand up in a certain place
I made her stand up
he is carrying it low down
they erect a twig
in the middle of the lodge
they erect a small stick
at a certain place

WORDS IN THE BLOOD 21

THE *CANTARES MEXICANOS:*
FIVE SONGS AND A FRAGMENT

TRANSLATOR'S NOTE: *Cantares Mexicanos* is the Spanish title of a 169-page Aztec-language manuscript shelved at the Biblioteca Nacional in Mexico City. Compiled by a native scribe in the mid 1500s, this codex preserves the texts of 89 songs, or poems, many of which were composed before the Conquest. Although a number of short songs are to be found in other 16th-century manuscripts, the *Cantares*, with its large-scale poems and its rich variety, is unquestionably the principal source.

The lovely but inaccurate translations of D. G. Brinton, published in 1890, made the *Cantares* instantly famous. Since then, excerpts from Brinton, or from the later versions of Angel M. Garibay, have been quoted again and again. Upon hearing an Aztec poem, even in the garbled renderings of Brinton or Garibay, audiences have the sense of stumbling into one of literature's locked rooms. Here, we feel, is something new.

But in spite of the effort expended upon it, Aztec poetry has remained undeciphered. nor has anyone yet produced a complete edition of the *Cantares.* My own conviction that the time is now right derives from the increasing sophistication of Aztec language studies during the past twenty years. It seems clear at last that the necessary equipment is available for an assault on this highly unusual and difficult codex. . . .

The English versions that follow are not final. Almost certainly they contain stylistic errors, or at least inconsistencies. And there may be linguistic errors as well. The process of translation, in this case, is self-correcting. As the lexical concordance grows, rules of syntax and even vocabulary items slowly make themselves apparent. When an error or an infelicity is discovered it is weeded out wherever it occurs throughout the whole translation. An example of a problem yet to be disposed of is the term *quechol,* which I give as "spoonbill" in some places, "swan" in others. It is gradually becoming clear to me that "swan" (sensu Webster II, swan 2) is more correct than the pseudo-Linnean "spoonbill." But the final decision must be saved for later.

Inasmuch as the following versions are here presented without commentary, it may be useful to provide a few general observations. When we speak of Aztec poetry we mean poetry of the type preserved in the *Cantares*—an elegant genre produced by the warrior poets of a militarist state for the entertainment of its noble elite. We know little or nothing of the lullabies, corn-grinding songs, healing songs, and other (mainly folk) genres that must have existed. War is the pervasive theme of the *Cantares*. Yet superimposed upon this basic thread, which may be referred to through puns only, are songs that treat worship, immortality, the origin of poetry, truth, sodality, courtship, and homosexuality. These are the songs with which the emperor Montezuma entertained his guests and with which he himself was regaled at dinner by his favorite poets.

Translated from the Nahuatl by John Bierhorst

MEXICO-OTOMI SONG (SONG NUMBER 4)

I smooth the remembered song-root like a sunshot jade, adding bits of trogon down, I, the singer, refining the pure-song with troupial plumes, mixing it with jadelike riches, bringing out a flower brilliance to entertain the Ever Present, the Ever Near.

With treasured feather-bits of troupial, trogon, and with spoonbill, I design a little song: gold jingles are the song, the gilded corn-warbler's tinkling song I sing as flowers sprinkle down before the Ever Present, the Ever Near.

Delicious is the song-root, as I the gilded corn-warbler lift it through a conch of gold, the sky song passing through my lips: like sunshot jade I make the pure-song glow, lifting fumes of flower fire, a singer making fragrance before the Ever Present, the Ever Near.

The spirit spoonbills answer as I sing, shrilling like bells from the Place of Pure-Song. Like a mat of jewels, spreading hues of green, the Green Place flower songs lie shot with jade-and-emerald sun ray: a flower incense, flaming all around, spreads sky aroma, filled with sunshot mist, as I the singer come within the flower dew to sing before the Ever Present, the Ever Near.

I work the Place of Pure-Song with my colors, mixing in my flowers. Like a mat of jewels, spreading hues of green, the Green Place flower songs lie shot with jade-and-emerald sun ray: a flower incense, flaming all around, spreads sky aroma, filled with sunshot mist, as I the singer come within the flower dew to sing before the Ever Present, the Ever Near.

As I exalt Him, rejoice Him, with heart-pleasing flowers in the Place of Song, the poyon fumes content my heart: my heart grows dizzy with the fragrance, drinking in pure flowers in the Place Where One Knows Joy. My heart is drunk with flowers.

ANOTHER SAD OTOMI SONG (SONG NUMBER 9)

To you the Ever Present, You the Ever Near, I call in sadness: I lay my
signs before Your face, I that am wretched here on earth: I wail, I that
am poor, I that am never touched by joy or riches. What but vainly
was I born to do? Its growing season this is not. Here indeed the
wretched person sprouts or blossoms not at all and yet serenely in
Your presence, by Your side. Let this be soon. May You desire it. In
Your presence may my soul be calm. I will dry my tears beside You,
in Your presence, You By Whom All Live.

How fortunate are they?—they who come to praise themselves on earth
and wail to no one, reveling in arrogance, while yet indeed they fool
themselves, they that do not wail to You the Ever Present, the Ever
Near, believing they will live forever here on earth. Seeing them, I
begin to get hold of myself. Indeed they drink the thornapple, the
castor bean. Though I am poor, my spirit strengthens in that one
may go and be esteemed beyond, in the Place Where One is Shorn:
no matter what we are, all hearts will then be full.

Let no one's heart be troubled here on earth, though we are sad, though
we are weeping. Truly, in but a moment it will end, and we will go to
do the planting, like the princes who were rulers. Copy them, my
friend, you that are discontent and joyless here on earth. Adorn yourself with sad flowers, weeping flowers: praise Him with flower-
sighs: offer them to Him the Ever Present, to Him the Ever Near.

I adorn myself with sad flower-jewels, sighing shield flowers lie in my
hand: I raise a sad song. I offer up good song as though it were jewels
of jade. With dewy flowers I whirl my jade drum, I, the singer, prop-
ping up my little song against the sky: indeed I take it from the sky
dwellers, the troupial, the quetzal-green mountain-trogon, and the
spirit spoonbill, the singing spoonbill who regales the Ever Present,
the Ever Near.

FRAGMENT FROM SONG NUMBER 18

We merely come to stand sleeping, we merely come
to dream. It is not true, not true that
we come to live on earth.

We come to do as herbs in spring: and though our
   hearts come sprouting, come green, those few
   flowers of our flesh that open wither away.

UNTITLED (SONG NUMBER 35)

He spreads a crown of jade upon the city. He abounds in plume light here
   in Mexico. Beneath Him lords are shaded: a flower mist spreads over
   all.

This, then, is Your home, O Life Giver. Here, then, is where You sing, O
   Father, O Only Spirit. Your song is heard beside the waters, spreading over all.

To the white willows, where white rushes grow, You, Blue Egret Bird
   come flying, You, O Spirit, O Spiritu Santo!*

So that You might open out, unfurl, Your tail and wing upon Your vas-
   sals, You are singing here in Mexico beside the eternal waters.

May no one walking forth be captured! That which rises shall be Your
   sadness, O Monteuczoma, O Totoquihuaztli! Who provides slaves
   for Life Giver? Indeed, they come to earth in order to support the
   sky.

As though a blaze their words are stirring. From the four directions they
   arrive and speak, giving Tenochtitlán City its place within the dawn.
   They are Monteuczoma and Acolhuacan's Nezahualpilli!

And it is shaded by this fan of plumes, as He is sighing, grieving. How
   else is Tenochtitlán City to endure? What sings *our* God, even here?

A SONG OF GREEN PLACES, A SONG FOR
ADMONISHING THOSE WHO SEEK
NO HONOR IN WAR

Clever with a song, I beat my drum to wake our friends, rousing them to
   arrow deeds whose never dawning hearts know nothing, who lie
   dead asleep in war, praising themselves in clouds of darkness. Not in

*Spiritu Santo: in Spanish in the original.

vain do I say, "They are poor." Let them come and hear the flower dawn-songs drizzling down incessantly beside the drum.

Sacred flowers of the dawn are blooming in the rainy place of flowers that belongs to Him the Ever Present, the Ever Near. The heart pleasers are laden with sunstruck dew; come and see them: they blossom uselessly for those who are disdainful. There is no one who does not crave them, O you friends of ours! Not useless flowers are the life-colored honey flowers.

They that intoxicate one's soul with life lie only there, they blossom only there, within the city of the eagles, inside the circle, in the middle of the field, where flood and blaze are spreading, where the eagle shines, the jaguar roars, and all the precious bracelet stones are scattered, all the precious lordlings are dismembered, where the princes lie broken, lie shattered.

These princes are the ones who greatly crave the dawn flowers. So that all will enter in, she causes them to be desirous, she who lies within the sky, she, Ceollintzin, the noble one, who makes them drizzle down, giving a gift of flower brilliance to the Eagle-Jaguar princes, making them drunk with the flower dew of life.

If, my friend, you think the flowers are useless that you crave here on earth, how will you acquire them, how will you earn them, you that are poor, you that gaze upon the princes at their flowers, at their songs? Come look: do they rouse themselves to arrow deeds for nothing? There beyond, the princes, all of them, are troupials, spirit spoonbills, mountain trogons, roseate spoonbills: they live in beauty, they that know the middle of the field.

With shield flowers, with eagle-trophy flowers, the princes are rejoicing in their bravery, adorned with necklaces of pine flowers. Songs of beauty, flowers of beauty, glorify their blood-and-shoulder toil. They who have accepted flood and blaze become our black-mountain friends, who rise warlike on the great road. Offer your shield, stand up, you Eagle-Jaguar!

UNTITLED (SONG NUMBER 37)

In grieving may I call to You, O Father, O Life Giver. Be a friend to us, and let us tell Your good words to each other, let us say the ones by which I suffer, I who seek Your flower pleasure, Your song glory, Your riches.

He says that in the Good Place in the sky all live, all glory, stands the drum, lie songs that are real, our tears, our suffering, alive within His home. Believe it, O princes!

With shields you paint, with javelins you paint nobility and blaze. And then at once, Beyond, you are feathered. By dint of chalk you are plucked, O Tlacahuepan, you that in this way departed for the Place Unknown.

You are then a payment for the lords, O Tlacahuepan—singing with your mouth! He answers you, he the eagle swan, the bird, the dancer, the whistle caller, there Beyond, then, in the Place Unknown.

Your songs are painted as jaguars, your flowers shaken down as eagles, O my child, O Dancer! The drum you beat so well is roaring with the sound of shields.

As eagles do you flower-whirl the noble comrades, O Dancer. This cacao wine makes drunk, bedecking all. Their songs arise, their flowers rise: with these they've gone away, created, to the Place Unknown, and they that rise are Mexicans.

You are hesitant and fearful, O my hearts. You dare not go where God is pleasured.

But you are not to go beyond where all are shown. Move on Beyond, where God is pleasured!

PART II

The Emergence
of a Native American
Literature

CHARLES ALEXANDER EASTMAN (OHIYESA)

Evening in the Lodge
FROM
Indian Boyhood

I had been skating on that part of the lake where there was an overflow, and came home somewhat cold. I cannot say just how cold it was, but it must have been intensely so, for the trees were crackling all about me like pistol shots. I did not mind, because I was wrapped up in my buffalo robe with the hair inside, and a wide leather belt held it about my loins. My skates were nothing more than strips of basswood bark bound upon my feet.

I had taken off my frozen moccasins and put on dry ones in their places.

"Where have you been and what have you been doing?" Uncheedah asked as she placed before me some roast venison in a wooden bowl. "Did you see any tracks of moose or bear?"

"No, grandmother, I have only been playing at the lower end of the lake. I have something to ask you," I said, eating my dinner and supper together with all the relish of a hungry boy who has been skating in the cold for half a day.

"I found this feather, grandmother, and I could not make out what tribe wear feathers in that shape."

"Ugh, I am not a man; you had better ask your uncle. Besides, you should know it yourself by this time. You are now old enough to think about eagle feathers."

I felt mortified by this reminder of my ignorance. It seemed a reflection on me that I was not ambitious enough to have found all such matters out before.

"Uncle, you will tell me, won't you?" I said, in an appealing tone.

"I am surprised, my boy, that you should fail to recognize this feather. It is a Cree medicine feather, and not a warrior's."

"Then," I said, with much embarrassment, "you had better tell me again, uncle, the language of the feathers. I have really forgotten it all."

The day was now gone; the moon had risen; but the cold had not lessened, for the trunks of the trees were still snapping all around our teepee which was lighted and warmed by the immense logs which Uncheedah's industry had provided. My uncle, White Foot-print, now undertook to explain to me the significance of the eagle's feather.

"The eagle is the most war-like bird," he began, "and the most kingly of all birds; besides, his feathers are unlike any others, and these are the reasons why they are used by our people to signify deeds of bravery.

"It is not true that when a man wears a feather bonnet, each one of the feathers represents the killing of a foe or even a *coup*. When a man wears an eagle feather upright upon his head, he is supposed to have counted one of four *coups* upon his enemy."

"Well, then, a *coup* does not mean the killing of an enemy?"

"No, it is the after-stroke or touching of the body after he falls. It is so ordered, because oftentimes the touching of an enemy is much more difficult to accomplish than the shooting of one from a distance. It requires a strong heart to face the whole body of the enemy, in order to count the *coup* on the fallen one, who lies under cover of his kinsmen's fire. Many a brave man has been lost in the attempt.

"When a warrior approaches his foe, dead or alive, he calls upon the other warriors to witness by saying: 'I, Fearless Bear, your brave, again perform the brave deed of counting the first (or second or third or fourth) *coup* upon the body of the bravest of your enemies.' Naturally, those who are present will see the act and be able to testify to it. When they return, the heralds, as you know, announce publicly all such deeds of valor, which then become a part of the man's war record. Any brave who would wear the eagle's feather must give proof of his right to do so.

"When a brave is wounded in the same battle where he counted his *coup*, he wears the feather hanging downward. When he is wounded, but makes no count, he trims his feather and in that case, it need not be an eagle feather. All other feathers are merely ornaments. When a warrior wears a feather with a round mark, it means that he slew his enemy. When the mark is cut into the feather and painted red, it means that he took the scalp.

"A brave who has been successful in ten battles is entitled to a warbonnet; and if he is a recognized leader, he is permitted to wear one with long, trailing plumes. Also those who have counted many *coups* may tip the ends of the feathers with bits of white or colored down. Sometimes the eagle feather is tipped with a strip of weasel skin; that means the wearer had the honor of killing, scalping and counting the first *coup* upon the enemy all at the same time.

"This feather you have found was worn by a Cree—it is indiscriminately painted. All other feathers worn by the common Indians mean nothing," he added.

"Tell me, uncle, whether it would be proper for me to wear any feathers at all if I have never gone upon the war-path."

"You could wear any other kind of feathers, but not an eagle's," replied my uncle, "although sometimes one is worn on great occasions by the child of a noted man, to indicate the father's dignity and position."

The fire had gone down somewhat, so I pushed the embers together and wrapped my robe more closely about me. Now and then the ice on the lake would burst with a loud report like thunder. Uncheedah was busy re-stringing one of uncle's old snow-shoes. There were two different kinds that he wore; one with a straight toe and long; the other shorter and with an upturned toe. She had one of the shoes fastened toe down, between sticks driven into the ground, while she put in some new strings and tightened the others. Aunt Four Stars was beading a new pair of moccasins.

Wabeda, the dog, the companion of my boyhood days, was in trouble because he insisted upon bringing his extra bone into the teepee, while Uncheedah was determined that he should not. I sympathized with him, because I saw the matter as he did. If he should bury it in the snow outside, I knew Shunktokecha (the coyote) would surely steal it. I knew just how anxious Wabeda was about his bone. It was a fat bone—I mean a bone of a fat deer; and all Indians know how much better they are than the other kind.

Wabeda always hated to see a good thing go to waste. His eyes spoke words to me, for he and I had been friends for a long time. When I was afraid of anything in the woods, he would get in front of me at once and gently wag his tail. He always made it a point to look directly in my face. His kind, large eyes gave me a thousand assurances. When I was perplexed, he would hang about me until he understood the situation. Many times I believed he saved my life by uttering the dog word in time.

Most animals, even the dangerous grizzly, do not care to be seen when the two-legged kind and his dog are about. When I feared a surprise by a bear or a grey wolf, I would say to Wabeda: "Now, my dog, give your war-whoop;" and immediately he would sit up on his haunches and bark "to beat the band" as you white boys say. When a bear or wolf heard the noise, he would be apt to retreat.

Sometimes I helped Wabeda and gave a war-whoop of my own. This drove the deer away as well, but it relieved my mind.

When he appealed to me on this occasion, therefore, I said: "Come, my dog, let us bury your bone so that no Shunktokecha will take it."

He appeared satisfied with my suggestion, so we went together.

We dug in the snow and buried our bone wrapped up in a piece of old blanket, partly burned; then we covered it up again with snow. We knew that the coyote would not touch anything burnt. I did not put it up a tree because Wabeda always objected to that, and I made it a point to consult his wishes whenever I could.

I came in and Wabeda followed me with two short rib bones in his mouth. Apparently he did not care to risk those delicacies.

"There," exclaimed Uncheedah, "you still insist upon bringing in some sort of bone!" but I begged her to let him gnaw them inside because it was so cold. Having been granted this privilege, he settled himself at my back and I became absorbed in some specially nice arrows that uncle was making. "O, uncle, you must put on three feathers to all of them so that they can fly straight," I suggested.

"Yes, but if there are only two feathers, they will fly faster," he answered.

"Woow!" Wabeda uttered his suspicions.

"Woow!" he said again, and rushed for the entrance of the tepee. He kicked me over as he went and scattered the burning embers.

"En na he na!" Uncheedah exclaimed, but he was already outside.

"Wow, wow, wow! Wow, wow, wow!"

A deep guttural voice answered him.

Out I rushed with my bow and arrows in my hand.

"Come, uncle, come! A big cinnamon bear!" I shouted as I emerged from the teepee.

Uncle sprang out and in a moment he had sent a swift arrow through the bear's heart. The animal fell dead. He had just begun to dig up Wabeda's bone, when the dog's quick ear had heard the sound.

"Ah, uncle, Wabeda and I ought to have at least a little eaglet's feather for this. I too sent my small arrow into the bear before he fell," I exclaimed. "But I thought all bears ought to be in their lodges in the winter time. What was this one doing at this time of the year and night?"

"Well," said my uncle, "I will tell you. Among the tribes, some are naturally lazy. The cinnamon bear is the lazy one of his tribe. He alone sleeps out of doors in the winter and because he has not a warm bed, he is soon hungry. Sometimes he lives in the hollow trunk of a tree, where he has made a bed of dry grass; but when the night is very cold, like to-night, he has to move about to keep himself from freezing and as he prowls around, he gets hungry."

We dragged the huge carcass within our lodge. "O, what nice claws he has, uncle!" I exclaimed eagerly. "Can I have them for my necklace?"

"It is only the old medicine men who wear them regularly. The son of a great warrior who has killed a grizzly may wear them upon a public occasion," he explained.

"And you are just like my father and are considered the best hunter among the Santees and Sisetons. You have killed many grizzlies so that no one can object to my bear's-claws necklace," I said appealingly.

White Foot-print smiled. "My boy, you shall have them," he said, "but it is always better to earn them yourself." He cut the claws off carefully for my use.

"Tell me, uncle, whether you could wear these claws all the time?" I asked.

"Yes, I am entitled to wear them, but they are so heavy and uncomfortable," he replied, with a superior air.

At last the bear had been skinned and dressed and we all resumed our usual places. Uncheedah was particularly pleased to have some more fat for her cooking.

"Now, grandmother, tell me the story of the bear's fat. I shall be so happy if you will," I begged.

"It is a good story and it is true. You should know it by heart and gain a lesson from it," she replied. "It was in the forests of Minnesota, in the country that now belongs to the Ojibways. From the Bedawakanton Sioux village a young married couple went into the woods to get fresh venison. The snow was deep; the ice was thick. Far away in the woods they pitched their lonely teepee. The young man was a well-known hunter and his wife a good maiden of the village.

"He hunted entirely on snow-shoes, because the snow was very deep. His wife had to wear snow-shoes too, to get to the spot where they pitched their tent. It was thawing the day they went out, so their path was distinct after the freeze came again.

"The young man killed many deer and bears. His wife was very busy curing the meat and trying out the fat while he was away hunting each day. In the evenings she kept on trying the fat. He sat on one side of the teepee and she on the other.

"One evening, she had just lowered a kettle of fat to cool, and as she looked into the hot fat she saw the face of an Ojibway scout looking down at them through the smoke-hole. She said nothing, nor did she betray herself in any way.

"After a little she said to her husband in a natural voice: 'Marpeetophah, some one is looking at us through the smoke hole, and I think it is an enemy's scout.'

"Then Marpeetopah (Four-skies) took up his bow and arrows and began to straighten and dry them for the next day's hunt, talking and laughing meanwhile. Suddenly he turned and sent an arrow upward, killing the Ojibway, who fell dead at their door.

"'Quick, Wadutah!' he exclaimed; 'you must hurry home upon our trail. I will stay here. When this scout does not return, the war-party may come in a body or send another scout. If only one comes, I can soon dispatch him and then I will follow you. If I do not do that, they will overtake us in our flight.'

"Wadutah (Scarlet) protested and begged to be allowed to stay with her husband, but at last she came away to get re-inforcements.

"Then Marpeetopah (Four-skies) put more sticks on the fire so that the teepee might be brightly lit and show him the way. He then took the scalp of the enemy and proceeded on his track, until he came to the upturned root of a great tree. There he spread out his arrows and laid out his tomahawk.

"Soon two more scouts were sent by the Ojibway war-party to see what was the trouble and why the first one failed to come back. He heard them as they approached. They were on snow-shoes. When they came close to him, he shot an arrow into the foremost. As for the other, in his effort to turn quickly his snow-shoes stuck in the deep snow and detained him, so Marpeetopah killed them both.

"Quickly he took the scalps and followed Wadutah. He ran hard. But the Ojibways suspected something wrong and came to the lonely teepee, to find all their scouts had been killed. They followed the path of Marpeetopah and Wadutah to the main village, and there a great battle was fought on the ice. Many were killed on both sides. It was after this that the Sioux moved to the Mississippi river."

I was sleepy by this time and I rolled myself up in my buffalo robe and fell asleep.

D'ARCY McNICKLE

◆◆

FROM
The Surrounded

EDITOR'S NOTE: As *The Surrounded* opens, Archilde Leon has just returned from the big city to his father's ranch on the Flathead Indian Reservation in Montana. From that beginning, the novel unfolds the intense and varied conflicts that already characterized reservation life in 1936. Educated at a federal Indian boarding school, the main character, Archilde, is torn between the white and Indian world as well as his love for his Spanish father and his Indian mother—a marvelous elder who in old age has rejected white culture and religion and returned to the ways of her people. For Archilde the tragic life on the reservation is temporary, for he intends to return to urban life after visiting his family. But his growing awareness of the annihilating pressure that faces his people and a series of personal entanglements delay his departure until he faces destruction by the white man's law.

◆◆◆

When Mike and Narcisse returned from the Mission school something was wrong.

Mike was quieter. He showed no desire to clip a horse and ride breakneck across the meadow, he had given up shouting and blustering. The change showed itself in another way. Mike was afraid of the dark. He couldn't be dragged from the house once night had fallen. When the family laughed, he hung his head sullenly but said nothing. Narcisse appeared to be normal—that is slow, easy-going, and maybe a little dull-witted; but he was his brother's best friend and would not talk about his secrets.

One night at bedtime, when Mike refused to go outside, Archilde teased him.

"If you don't go outside you'll make a puddle in the bed, then we'll have to get a pot for you."

Instead of flaring up Mike hung his head.

That very night, after midnight, Mike woke up screaming. He frightened everyone in the house. It was a piercing cry, and it had a peculiar "lost soul" sound. This description flashed upon Archilde's mind at the instant he awakened. He found himself sitting in the dark, frightened and, to his amazement, crossing himself! He stopped in the middle of the act.

The cry came a second time, muffled, but still fearful. Then he located the sound as coming from his nephews' room.

When he turned back the covers he found Mike with his fists dug into his eyes, his knees drawn up, and his body rigid. It was several minutes before he would relax, and then shame kept him from removing his hands. Narcisse had jumped out of bed and was squatting in a corner, his face hidden.

Agnes came upstairs with a flaring lamp in her hand, her eyes wide, and found Archilde sitting on the edge of the bed with Mike's head in his lap.

Mike had wet the bed. Agnes saw it and looked wonderingly at Archilde. He too had been looking at it and recalling how he had teased the boy. He was sorry.

"The old lady shakes like a wet dog," Agnes whispered. "I sent Annie to her. The devil is after her she thinks. You must talk to her. My talk does her no good."

Archilde brought the boys into his room to share his bed. Then he went to see the old lady. She sat upright in bed, moving her lips. As he talked quietly, explaining that Mike had had a bad dream, he felt her watery eyes searching his face. And he knew that mere words were of no use to her.

In the breast of everyone, as the family went back to bed, strange emotions lingered, strange beings encumbered the night. The lamp in the kitchen, where the old lady slept, was not extinguished.

Mike was no longer teased but was rather looked upon in awe. It was clear that something had gone wrong inside. Agnes looked at her son and shook her head. She could not make it out. Archilde set about to discover what had happened.

He went to every boy who he knew had been at the Mission school and asked; "Why is Mike afraid? Why does he wake up and yell?" Sometimes the answer was no more than a shrug of the shoulders, but at other times he saw eyes shift uneasily and he put other questions, with cautious indirection.

Much of the story he was able to supply from his own experience, once he had been given certain hints. And in time he pieced together what had happened.

Mike had been frightened at school.

It seemed that he had been incorrigible. He had started out by refusing to have his hair cut off, but he was unruly in worse ways. During grace at table, in the class room, or in bed at night, he was always whispering; in marching two-by-two he would trip up his marching partner. Also he had wet the bed three times, although punished and warned each time, and in this too he was thought to be acting defiantly. And to all that he had added a bit of defiance which had made everyone quake.

On a morning after he had again wet the bed and was to have been punished, he bet one of the boys that he was not afraid to chew the host which the priest put on his tongue at Communion. The several boys who knew about the bet saw him turn from the Communion rail and chew, and this, as they knew, was sacrilege. He was reported by someone before they reached the refectory for breakfast. Mike was taken out of line just as it was filing into the dining quarters. No words were said, the prefect simply took him by the collar and marched him away. By that time every boy knew what had happened in church and there was silence all through the meal. They wondered what would happen to Mike and were sobered.

In one corner of the dormitory was a small room of unpleasant reputation. As the door was always locked, no one ever saw the inside except those committed to it, but there was much whispering among the boys. Some said that it contained a crown of thorns—the *real* crown of thorns—and some bones, a skull. Some went so far as to say that who-ever was put in the room was forced to wear the crown of thorns and kiss the skull. It was apparent that none of the boys who had ever been placed in the room had remembered, or cared to describe, its furnishings.

Mike was locked up and no one saw him again that day. Since the dormitory was closed in daytime, it was impossible even to whisper through the keyhole. That night, when the boys had prayed and gone to bed, the prefect took unusual care to see that all beds were occupied. He marched up and down the center aisle telling his beads long after the lights had been turned off. In the dark they heard the clicking of his beads and the rustle of his cassock as he passed. It made the hair prickle on their heads.

At midnight everyone was sound asleep. Mike's friends tried to stay awake but weariness closed their eyes at last. Sometime after midnight they were awakened by screaming. The first cry merely awakened them, it was the second that set them trembling. The cry ended suddenly, just as it reached its shrillest point. It was that sudden breaking off, and the silence that followed, that seemed most terrible. They could not imagine what had happened. The cry echoed in their heads and made them feel weak.

The prefect appeared, they could not tell from where, because none dared sit up in bed. He entered the solitary chamber, closing the door firmly behind him, and a moment later they heard him praying. It was half an hour before he reappeared. Mike was with him, supported on the prefect's arm. He was pale and, as everyone could see, as limp as a rag, as if he had been restored from a faint.

The prefect remained at Mike's bed through the remainder of the night, praying over him. Mike's friends thought he stayed so they couldn't talk to him.

The next morning, at breakfast, the prefect made a short announcement. "The Father Superior has ordered that a week of prayer be observed, beginning today. In keeping with this order, it will not be seemly to play any rough or loud games. Accordingly, your recess periods will be given to prayer and at all times you are to deport yourselves with humility." There was no explanation of this action, but the boys needed none.

They needed no explanation either of what had happened to Mike. He had been placed in the infirmary and had talked to no one, but they knew that he had been visited by the Evil One. That was why they had to pray. They discussed this in whispers and looked about uneasily. Their active imaginations could perfectly well visualize good and evil spirits flying through the air; they were prepared to see the earth crack open at any moment and reveal the fires of hell, as the large painting on the church wall showed it. They knew that the devil had appeared to Mike because there was a tradition that such a thing had happened before in that room, to a boy who later was dragged to death by his horse.

"Something will happen to Mike, now, you see," they whispered. "The devil's mark is on him."

Some would not discuss it at all. "God can hear when you whisper. Take care what you say! Something will happen."

❖❖❖

Meantime, Mike continued to be afraid of the dark, only he tried to hide it now. He had to be urged to go fishing, but nothing could induce him to ride a horse. He knew the story of the boy who had been dragged to death. Archilde stayed close to the boys. He fashioned spears and sling shots and tried to make fishing and hunting as exciting as it used to be, but Mike would walk through the woods and have no eyes for a squirrel sitting at close range. If the woods were deep and shadowy he would never walk in the lead.

One day when he was alone with Narcisse he tried to get close to the trouble. "Will Mike get better? What d'you think?"

Narcisse shrugged his shoulders.

"Listen. You must tell him—" He didn't know how to reach Mike through words. But he would try it. "Tell him it's all lies, what the priests say. It's all lies about the devil. Tell him to look at the birds. They fly around, and they don't know nothing about the devil. Look at them fly!"

Narcisse watched some birds fly past. Then he contemplated the earth again. He frowned to show that he was thinking. "But the hawks!" His face cleared with the words. "They're afraid of the hawks! Maybe the hawks are devils!"

"Pshaw! The hawks—" Archilde frowned in his turn. "We shoot the hawks, and they die. If they were devils, could we kill them? Not the way the priests talk."

Narcisse was taken with the idea. When birds again flew by he watched them until they were out of sight. "I'll tell that to Mike," he promised.

Archilde did not expect anything to come from his theological argument. Something more than words was needed to lift Mike out of his dark mood, but he didn't know what. He thought hard, in bed at night and while walking through the woods on a spring day, but no ideas came to him.

These efforts to bring peace and order into the lives of his relatives before he left them forever did not please him greatly. Whatever he did, he felt that he remained on the outside of their problems. He had grown away from them, and even when he succeeded in approaching them in sympathy, he remained an outsider—only a little better than a professor come to study their curious ways of life. He saw no way of changing it.

N. SCOTT MOMADAY

<><><><><><><><><><><><><><><><><><><><><><><><><><><><><><><><><>

FROM
The Names

EDITOR'S NOTE: *The Names* is a memoir about Momaday's Indian fore-bears and his own life. The names in this book—animals, plants, places, and the names that Indians give to each other ritually—have a special significance. Momaday's own name was given to him by an old story-teller who believed that a person's life proceeds from a name, in a way that a river proceeds from its source. Momaday makes powerful use of his strong interest in the oral tradition of Indians in bringing to life the flow of his own life and that of his family.

❖❖❖

My name is Tsoai-talee. I am, therefore, Tsoai-talee; therefore I am.

The storyteller Pohd-lohk gave me the name Tsoai-talee. He believed that a man's life proceeds from his name, in the way that a river proceeds from its source.

In general my narrative is an autobiographical account. Specifically it is an act of the imagination. When I turn my mind to my early life, it is the imaginative part of it that comes first and irresistibly into reach, and of that part I take hold. This is one way to tell a story. In this instance it is my way, and it is the way of my people. When Pohd-lohk told a story he began by being quiet. Then he said *Ah-keah-de,* "They were camping," and he said it every time. I have tried to write in the same way, in the same spirit. Imagine: They were camping.

PROLOGUE

You know, everything had to begin, and this is how it was:
the Kiowas came one by one into the world through a hollow

*log. They were many more than now, but not all of them got
out. There was a woman whose body was swollen up with
child, and she got stuck in the log. After that, no one could
get through, and that is why the Kiowas are a small tribe in
number. They looked all around and saw the world. It made
them glad to see so many things. They called themselves*
Kwuda, *"coming out"*

—Kiowa folktale

❖❖❖

They were stricken, surely, nearly blind in the keep of some primordial
darkness. And yet it was their time, and they came out into the light, one
after another, until the way out was lost to them. Loss was in the order of
things, then, from the beginning. Their emergence was a small thing in
itself, and unfinished. But it gave them to know that they were and who
they were. They could at last say to themselves, "We are, and our name
is *Kwuda*."

CHAPTER ONE

The names at first are those of animals and of birds, of objects that have
one definition in the eye, another in the hand, of forms and features on
the rim of the world, or of sounds that carry on the bright wind and in the
void. They are old and original in the mind, like the beat of rain on the
river, and intrinsic in the native tongue, failing even as those who bear
them turn once in the memory, go on, and are gone forever: Pohd-lohk,
Keahdinekeah, Aho.

*And Galyen, Scott, McMillan, whose wayfaring lay in the shallow
traces from Virginia and Louisiana, who knew of blooded horses and
tobacco and corn whiskey, who preserved in their songs the dim dialects
of the Old World.*

The land settles into the end of summer. In the white light a whirlwind moves far out in the plain, and afterwards there is something like a
shadow on the grass, a tremor, nothing. There seems a stillness at noon,
but that is illusion: the landscape rises and falls, ringing. In the dense
growth of the bottomland a dark drift moves on the Washita River. A
spider enters a small pool of light on Rainy Mountain Creek, and downstream, at the convergence, a Channel catfish turns around in the current
and slithers to the surface, where a dragonfly hovers and darts. Away on

the high ground grasshoppers and bees set up a crackle and roar in the fields, and meadowlarks and scissortails whistle and wheel about. Somewhere in a maze of gullies a calf shivers and bawls in a tangle of chinaberry trees. And high in the distance a hawk turns in the sun and sails.

Gyet'aigua. Where you been?
'Cross the creek.
'S'hot, ain'it?

The angle of the Washita River and Rainy Mountain Creek points to the east, and the thick red waters descend into the depths of the Southern Plains, as if they measure by means of an old, organic equation the long way from the Continental Divide to the heart of North America. This angle is a certain delineation on the face of the Great Plains, an idea of geometry in the mind of God.

The light there is of a certain kind. In the mornings and evenings it is soft and pervasive, and the earth seems to absorb it, to become enlarged with light. About the noons there are edges and angles—and a brightness that is hard and thin like a glaze. There is something strange and powerful in it. When you look out across the land you believe at first that it is all one thing; there appears to be an awful sameness to it. But after a while you see that it is not one thing at all, but many things, all of which are subject to change in a moment. At times the air is thick and languid, and you imagine that the world has grown very old and tired. At other times the air is full of motion and commotion. Always a hard weather impends upon the plains. In advance of a storm the plains are a strange and beautiful thing to see concentrated in random details, distances; there are slow, massive movements.

> There in the hollow of the hills I see,
> Eleven magpies stand away from me.
>
> Low light upon the rim; a wind informs
> This distance with a gathering of storms
>
> And drifts in silver crescents on the grass,
> Configurations that appear, and pass.
>
> There falls a final shadow on the glare,
> A stillness on the dark, erratic air.
>
> I do not hear the longer wind that lows
> Among the magpies. Silences disclose,

Until no rhythms of unrest remain,
Eleven magpies standing in the plain.

They are illusion—wind and rain revolve—
And they recede in darkness, and dissolve.

Water runs in planes on the earth, in ropes in the cuts of the banks the wind lunges; lightning is constant on the cold, black hemisphere; and everything is visible, strangely visible. Oh Man-ka-ih!

Some of my earliest memories are of the storms, the hot rain lashing down and lightning running on the sky—and the storm cellar into which my mother and I descended so many times when I was very young. For me that little room in the earth is an unforgettable place. Across the years I see my mother reading there on the low, narrow bench, the lamplight flickering on her face and on the earthen walls; I smell the dank odor of that room; and I hear the great weather ranging at the door. I have never been in a place that was like it exactly; only now and then I have been reminded of it suddenly when I have gone into a cave, or when I have just caught the scent of fresh, open earth steaming in the rain, and I have been for a moment startled and strangely glad in the presence of the past, the mother and child. But at times as I look back I see the fear in my mother's face, a hard vigilance in the attitude of her whole body, for hail is beating down upon the door, and the roar of the wind is deafening; the earth and sky are at odds, and God shudders. Even now, after many years of living in another landscape, my mother will not go into that wide corridor of the Great Plains but that she does so with many misgivings and keeps a sharp eye on the sky.

The terrapins crawl up on the hills.
They know, ain'it? The terrapins know.
A day, two days before, they go.

Carriers of the Dream Wheel

This is the Wheel of Dreams
Which is carried on their voices,
By means of which their voices turn
And center upon being.
It encircles the First World,
This powerful wheel.
They shape their songs upon the wheel
And spin the names of the earth and sky,
The aboriginal names.
They are old men, or men
Who are old in their voices,
And they carry the wheel among the camps,
Saying: Come, come,
Let us tell the old stories,
Let us sing the sacred songs.

❖❖❖

Rainy Mountain Cemetery

Most is your name the name of this dark stone.
Deranged in death, the mind to be inheres
Forever in the nominal unknown,
The wake of nothing audible he hears
Who listens here and now to hear your name.

The early sun, red as a hunter's moon,
Runs in the plain. The mountain burns and shines;
And silence is the long approach of noon
Upon the shadow that your name defines—
And death this cold, black density of stone.

HYEMEYOHSTS STORM

FROM
Seven Arrows

Nine Moons had begun Crescent, become Full, and had Passed. Winter Man had been Lazy with his Cold and there had been many Days of Sunshine. The Wings of Thunderbird Stirred the Air and brought the Gentle Southern Breeze to the Camp of White Shield.

Day Woman stopped her work at the edge of the creek and untied her braids, letting the gentle Medicine of the south bathe her face and hair.

The camp circle was waking up. The voices of children beginning to play mingled with the excited barking of the camp dogs, happy to see their young masters. The camp crier was making his round of the lodges, crying the news of the night.

Day Woman returned to her work, secure within the familiar sounds and scenes. She only half listened to the crier singing his news to the camp. She began to daydream about her little sister, Morning Star Woman. The doeskin she was working on would be whiter and softer than any she had ever made and it would soon become the most beautiful dress in the whole camp. In her dream, she could already see Morning Star Woman smiling shyly for all her admirers and spinning around for everyone to see the new dress. It was a magical morning, one made for the daydreams of a young woman. The sun danced and sparkled on the water in the creek, helping her dream to grow.

Her whole family would be there to see the new dress. Day Woman saw herself braiding her baby sister's hair while she tied the last feathered plume in it. Morning Star Woman wiggled in excitement to be outside showing off her new dress.

"Hold still, little rabbit, or you will wriggle right out of your new dress and we will have to begin all over again," Day Woman laughed in her dream.

Finally the last touch was finished and the little girl was released. She ran for the lodge door, stopped and added her own small touches to her appearance, and then walked outside for the world to see her.

47

Lame Bear and Standing Eagle, two of her uncles, saw her first. Lame Bear stalked around Morning Star Woman, snapping the string of the bow he had been working on.

"By the Power, Standing Eagle, we have a Spirit Woman here!" he said, pretending to be overcome by Morning Star Woman's beauty.

Day Woman smiled with the perfect success of her dream. Good, tall, Lame Bear, her favorite uncle, would have spoken in just that way, and kindly, round-tummied Standing Eagle would have joined in the pretending with a little more reserve, but just as enthusiastically as her other uncle.

"Day Woman! Day Woman!" someone called.

The girl let the dream dim quietly as she looked up and saw her best friend, Prairie Rose, running towards her. Her friend's excitement made her get to her feet.

"What is it? Is something wrong?" she asked as Prairie Rose reached her, grabbing her hand.

"Come on!" Prairie Rose said, dragging her friend after her. "Have you not heard the crier? Dancing Water has returned to the camp! She is in Flying Cloud's lodge, and she had her baby last night!"

Day Woman was excited and pleased by the news of her aunt's return to the camp, but she was unable to fight down the uneasiness that touched her stomach. They had visited not long ago when their camps had been together on the Powder River. The five miles that had separated the two camps then had been an easy walking distance, and Prairie Rose and she had visited Dancing Water almost every day. Now Dancing Water had come so suddenly to their camp, and the possible reasons for her abrupt arrival crowded into Day Woman's mind.

There was no joy upon the faces of the people outside Flying Cloud's lodge. Both girls were silent as they approached. Suddenly their thoughts were interrupted by the muffled thunder of pony's hoofs, as the warriors of the camp galloped past Flying Cloud's lodge. A young warrior named Stinging Eyes was mounted in front of the lodge, holding Flying Cloud's war pony. Flying Cloud ran from the lodge, bow in hand, leaped upon the waiting horse, and both men raced off after the other riders. Prairie Rose ran to watch the party of men as they disappeared over the hills, and was nearly knocked down by Lame Bear's horse as he rode by after the others at a full gallop.

Day Woman turned to enter the lodge.

◈◈◈

"The Wars! The Wars! Has the whole world gone mad?"

It was Standing Eagle speaking. The group of men with him lounged in the shade, some of them busy repairing their camp equipment. A camp dog snapped at what it believed to be a fly. Whining and growling, the dog bit at its tail and began to run in circles.

"Look at that dog," Standing Eagle continued. "All of us are like that dog. The poor fool still does not understand that it has bitten a bee and been stung. It runs in circles just as we do."

Falls Down called the dog to him and began to soothe the animal.

"It is all right, old fellow," he said, rubbing the dog's jaw. "You will live and so will we. We will not let that old man scare us. We will. . . ."

"Scare us!" Standing Eagle roared, jumping to his feet. "You young fool, do you not realize that our whole world is falling to pieces? That the People are being exterminated like rabid camp dogs?"

"How do you know?" Falls Down struck back. "All we know is that there have been two or three camps ravaged by packs of mad wolves. These unnatural white wolves can be fought and beaten. All we have heard of their power has been just hearsay. How do you know that the stories we have heard have not been stretched out of shape? Have you seen any of these broken camps? Were all the People truly murdered as we heard, or were the stories of this only the whinings of frightened women?"

"The stories we heard were from no frightened women, my brother." It was Grey Owl who answered, getting to his feet. His dark, handsome face gave no sign of the fury that was in his heart. Falls Down's words and actions seemed to be typical of all young men in the last few years and Grey Owl hated them. He walked to a pole that supported a rack of drying meat and leaned against it. Taking a piece for himself, he threw the remainder to Falls Down. The two young men ate in silence. Grey Owl let much of the anger die inside him as he ate.

The man who had carried word of the broken camps to them had been his clan brother. Their two camps had come together on the Medicine Wheel River for the Sun Dance, Grey Owl's first.

❖❖❖

It was the eleventh moon and the summer sun was hot. Grey Owl lounged in the shade of an arbor that he and his father had made near the lodge, and watched his mother embroidering his Sun Dance belt with porcupine quills. All the lodges had been put up in a common circle along with those of the Sioux, the Brother People. He lazily watched a few Sioux women, latecomers who were just now putting up their lodge. A pretty girl was tending their children and talking to Prairie Rose.

"Who are those people, Mother?" Grey Owl asked, indicating the direction with his eyes. "That is the lodge of Painted Elk," she answered without looking up. "He is your clan uncle, and the girl you are so interested in is Morning Song, his daughter."

"*Zahuah*, Mother!" Grey Owl bleated, shuffling nervously. "That thought is a ragged feather."

"Ragged feather thought?" his mother laughed. "You remember what you said when she went for water at the river?"

"I remember," Grey Owl answered, getting to his feet and leaning his arm against the arbor, hoping the subject was ended.

"By the thunder, Mother, where is my father? I thought we were to hunt together this morning."

"White Shield left before the sun was up, long before you stopped your dreaming."

"*Zahuah*, Mother!" Grey Owl whined. "Owls sit on your head! Why did you let me sleep?"

"My sleepy son, I tried to wake you. . . ." Their conversation was interrupted by the arrival of Painted Elk and his family.

Grey Owl turned to look at the visitors. Prairie Rose was pulling Morning Song along by her hand. She was laughing and pointing to her brother. Morning Song was trying her best to maintain her gait and keep her balance with the little girl tugging at her.

Morning Song was even more beautiful than Grey Owl had thought, and he felt a tension grow inside of him that was totally new in his experience. "By the Power!" he thought, "Why did I sleep so late this morning instead of going hunting!"

"Peace, my sister. I wish to borrow my nephew from your camp. He will hunt with his uncle if he wishes," Painted Elk said as he approached the shade.

"All I have seen here all morning is a lazy green lizard. You may have to cuff him awake to get him to go hunting with you," Grey Owl's mother answered as she hugged Painted Elk's wife.

A few minutes later, Grey Owl led his horse to Painted Elk's lodge. A young man the same age as Grey Owl was standing beneath the arbor and was tying four quivers of arrows to his horse. Another horse that was tied to the arbor snorted and pulled nervously against its reins. A painted and quilled robe was draped over the horse's back, and an ornamented sheath with a strange weapon in it was also tied there. Even though Grey Owl had never seen a thunder stick before, he recognized it by the stories he had heard of them. The carved wooden butt of the thunder iron was decorated and tied with hawk feathers. It was beautiful.

The three of them rode in silence together onto the broad, rolling prairie. While they rode, Grey Owl studied his companions. Painted Elk was almost as lean and tall as his son, but more muscular. Hung loosely from his back was his Shield, on which was painted a black bear with elk signs over the bear's eyes. The seeker band that cut diagonally across the

Shield was painted in rainbow colors, with four white eagle feathers at its middle. Painted below the band was the symbol of the water, his Clan Sign.

Painted Elk's son turned in his saddle toward Grey Owl, and began to speak to him in sign language.

I am your Clan brother, he signed. *This will be my first Sun Dance. Will it also be yours?*

Yes, it will be, Grey Owl quickly signed back. *I am called Grey Owl.*

And I am called Lame Buffalo, he signed with a broad smile.

What is the meaning of the four white eagle plumes upon your father's Shield? Grey Owl asked.

These were given to him at the Sun Dance by White Wolf. I think that White Wolf's tongue is that of the Little Black Eagle, the Crow. My father was given these signs to seek wisdom within his Medicines, Lame Buffalo answered.

What are his Medicines? Grey Owl asked. *Does he know them all yet?*

My father knows of three. They are the Grey Stands Alone Wolf, the Orphaned Yellow Buffalo Calf, and the Red Robed Bat, Lame Buffalo answered, then turned to his father and said something in his own tongue.

Painted Elk rode on for a moment in silence. Grey Owl was just about to ask Lame Buffalo what he had said, when suddenly Painted Elk stopped his horse and dismounted. The two young men looked around quickly and then they also dismounted.

The older man made signs for the young men to sit with him. He pointed to where an eagle was feeding upon the carcass of an antelope. Four or five she-wolves were lying near the half-eaten animal, some of them suckling their pups. *Do you see that bird?* Painted Elk signed. *That eagle will stuff himself until he cannot fly up from the ground. That is Vihio, surely a knowledgeable fool. Very few of the creatures of this world see as much and as far as he does, but he foolishly comes down to blindness and gorges himself. What have you to say about the meaning of this Way of the Eagle?*

Their talk was all with sign language, so that each could understand and take part in it.

Lame Buffalo signed first. *This foolish thing seems to be a common weakness among all People.*

Grey Owl said nothing, wanting a little more time to think before answering.

You have asked about my Medicine Ways, Painted Elk signed to Grey Owl. *When Lame Buffalo spoke to me just now, he was asking about the name I had been given by the same old man who had given me the four white eagle plumes. The name he gave me was Lame Eagle. This means one who is lame in what he wants to do, because of his way of gorging himself too full to fly.*

Painted Elk had hardly finished his signing before he broke out in laughter. Grey Owl and Lame Buffalo were laughing as hard as he. Painted Elk began again.

I will seek my colors in this Sun Dance. It will be your first, and I will be dancing with you. I have asked White Wolf of the Little Black Eagle People to paint me and also to paint both of you. He will be here soon and we will have the Give-Away. I already have asked White Shield's approval to Give-Away for you too, Grey Owl. I will Give-Away this horse, my robe, my tobacco pouch, and this iron that speaks.

When he had finished signing, he mounted his horse, kicked him into a run, and yelled in Cheyenne to Grey Owl, "Come, little green lizard, or I will cuff your ears."

That evening nearly all the young men of the camp played arrow and hoop games. The women visited together and tended their children, letting their daughters watch and cheer at the games and, of course, meet young men.

Morning Song was watching with Dancing Water, Grey Owl's cousin. Grey Owl had performed pitifully at arrow throwing and was being teased unmercifully by Stiff Arm. Grey Owl was as tight as a bowstring because of the teasing, and because he had noticed the presence of Morning Song. He had also noticed that at each chance Stiff Arm got, he went and stood next to Morning Song. For some reason Grey Owl burned inside when he saw this, which made him all the more clumsy. It was not long before Lame Buffalo joined in Stiff Arm's teasing of Grey Owl. Grey Owl grinned, but it hurt his face to do it.

Finally his turn came again during the hoop game, and he was determined to prove himself. He took careful aim, pulling the bowstring taut, but just a second before the hoop was rolled the string broke. Lame Buffalo doubled over with laughter. Morning Song was laughing and so was Dancing Water. In fact, everyone was. Grey Owl's patience was at an end. His wooden smile disappeared and he reached for another bow, jerking it from a young Sioux's hand who stood next to him. He fitted an arrow into the bow, pulled it half-way back, and took one step backwards. But luck was not with him. Turtle, his faithful dog, was lying stretched out on the ground just behind him. When Grey Owl stepped back to shoot, it was squarely onto his dog. The dog yelped and squirmed from under his foot. Grey Owl went down into a heap of angry boy, dog, and bow. He was humiliated, and he avoided the laughing eyes of Lame Buffalo and Morning Song.

In the days that followed, Stiff Arm grew intolerable. He became fast friends with Lame Buffalo. Lame Buffalo had taught Stiff Arm some of his language, and whenever Grey Owl found himself with them in small groups of boys, the two would look at him, say a few words in Sioux, and laugh.

One morning, while Grey Owl hunted with his father, they came upon a small herd of buffalo. As soon as they sighted the riders, the buffalo ran and scattered into ravines. Grey Owl rode by himself into one of the ravines and suddenly came upon a second herd. He rode straight into their middle, scattering them. The herd milled frantically around and tried to climb the steep banks. Many failed in the attempt, and retreated to run in other directions. Grey Owl picked out a two-year-old bull, and set out to bring him down.

He failed to notice that he had also been joined in the chase by Lame Buffalo, Stiff Arm and his own father. The other riders smashed into the herd, driving their arrows into the buffalo nearest them. Lame Buffalo was about to bring down a fat cow when suddenly his horse collided with Grey Owl's, who still had not seen him. Grey Owl's horse was knocked to the ground, spilling him from the saddle. Lame Buffalo's horse, staggered by the blow, lost its footing for a second and then righted itself with a quick jump. Barely keeping his seat, Lame Buffalo turned his horse to regain control and to see what had happened. He could dimly see Grey Owl through the dust and frenzied animals. Grey Owl had caught his horse and was trying to mount, but the horse jerked and bucked, trying to run. Grey Owl had his back to the bull he had wounded and did not see it start to charge him. Lame Buffalo kicked his horse into a run, putting himself between the bull and Grey Owl. The bull hit Lame Buffalo's horse, snapping ribs and spilling him into the dirt.

Grey Owl had remounted and saw Lame Buffalo's wounded horse trying to get up. When the bull charged again, Lame Buffalo was still trying to get to his feet. Grey Owl never moved. Everything seemed to be happening in a dream, with the bull charging, Lame Buffalo running, and then the sudden appearance of White Shield, who jerked Lame Buffalo to safety on the back of his own horse.

That evening Grey Owl sat by his mother, fuming.

"What happened?" his mother asked. "Lame Buffalo seems to have broken his leg."

"Lame Buffalo! Lame Buffalo! That mouse-minded fool. . . . *Zahuah*, Mother, forget it!"

"Forget it!" His father had entered the lodge almost spitting the words at his son. "Forget it! He saved your life. He put his horse between you and the buffalo bull. He. . . ."

"He what?" cut in Grey Owl. "*Mahka-Zaughan,* no! I never knew!"

The boy jumped to his feet and ran into the night. His mother jumped up and started to run after him.

"Leave him alone!" White Shield said, throwing the lodge flap back and leaving. Grey Owl's mother sat down and began to cry.

Grey Owl had run from the lodge, his mind and heart a blinding confusion of pain and sorrow. A double and triple shame was his, because he had shamed himself, his parents, and his People. The tears in his eyes blinded him just enough that he did not see the three young people who were walking towards him. They were Morning Song, Dancing Water, and Stiff Arm.

"Hello, Grey Owl," Morning Song said.

Her gentle voice cut into Grey Owl's brain like crippled lightning. He jerked his eyes from the ground and saw Stiff Arm. Stiff Arm grinned and said something he didn't hear. Grey Owl's mind exploded with hate and he grabbed for his knife. Morning Song screamed as the two young men locked themselves in a death struggle. Stiff Arm slipped and fell to the ground. Grey Owl kicked his knife from his hand and stood over him.

"Please, oh please, do not harm him!" someone pleaded. It was Bear Woman. The girl grabbed Grey Owl's arm and was crying. "Please, my beautiful cousin, do not harm him!" she begged, looking into his eyes. "Your jealousy is for nothing! Morning Song has slept with him and they were not of one song! Please listen to me!" she begged. "Morning Song loves you!"

Grey Owl's knife was scarcely a half-inch from Stiff Arm's throat.

"I . . . I am sorry, my cousin," Stiff Arm's voice wavered. "Forgive me."

"I cannot kill you, Stiff Arm," Grey Owl said through tears. "You must also forgive me." His knife fell from his hand as he stood up.

The next morning Stiff Arm, Grey Owl and Lame Buffalo were called to the council.

"None of you three have walked within the People's Way." The speaker was Grey Mouse. Grey Mouse was the youngest of the Pledgers, and a Dog Soldier. "Today we have all learned because of your actions. You are our brothers and we are your brothers. What are your pledges?"

Stiff Arm spoke first. "I have never loved Grey Owl, but I promise this day to understand him. I have acted shamefully and as a child. I also pledge postponement of my marriage for one year to collect robes for the family of White Shield. And I pledge my life to protect that of Grey Owl." There was not a sound in the camp, even the dogs were still.

Grey Owl spoke second. "I was driven to madness with jealousy, like a rabid mouse. I too have never loved my cousin Stiff Arm. I pledge all of my power that I receive in this Sun Dance to Lame Buffalo and Stiff Arm. And I pledge the care and protection of every child of Lame Buffalo's until each child is a grown man or woman. And then I pledge him my bow. From this day forward, I pledge myself a Dog Soldier to the Brother People, and also to my own People, the Painted Arrows."

The pledging was translated into sign language for Lame Buffalo. After the young men had finished their speech, Lame Buffalo spoke.

"I too acted as a child. And I pledge this Sun Dance to my brothers the Cheyennes, the Painted Arrow People. And I pledge myself a Dog Soldier for both the People."

There was a feast later that same day for the People. Stiff Arm, Lame Buffalo, and Grey Owl were inseparable. A few days before the Sun Dance, Lame Buffalo married Dancing Water.

CRAIG KEY STRETE

Every World With a
String Attached

I don't see what you see. I see what I see. You see the city and your lips put that name to it. It is a CITY. I see a severed insect mound.

Your green earth is my ocean. My eyes are my body. The ability to see is a viral infection. Do you have the cure?

The CITY is an architectural ring of disease with sex at its center. The CITY. The genitals of the angry CITY have been sedated with suburbs. But let us suppose a journey, let us bring forth one of the diseased creatures from a dollar hotel. Let us bring him forth and send him to the edge of the city where he shall discover muddied dreams and zones of sophisticated boredom. We will point the eyes of the city through his eyes and we shall hear the city speaking. It will say, "Look where we worship. Look where we worship."

I am the diseased creature from a dollar hotel. I have fulfilled the premises inherent in life. I have predicted the future. Cancel my subscription to the RESURRECTION. I have predicted the future.

Suppose I saw a foot cut off from its body. Suppose I saw it. If I looked downward, immediately realizing that it was not my foot, if I looked downward and discovered the foot belonged to someone else, would I not be curious?

Curiosity is the greatest single impregnator of mothers in the universe. Even a person of my ability is not immune to it. I would tap the foot lightly. It would seem inanimate. It would seem reluctant to strike up a conversation. It would be dead.

Perhaps it will be severed from a visually unpleasing pulp which lies beneath the bed of an overturned truck. Perhaps.

By itself, the foot will have a curiously appealing quality to it. It will give off an aura of continental largesse that will please me greatly. I will immediately desire its acquaintance.

That is my prediction of the future. It came true. I did see just such a foot. I think I saw it on Tuesday.

Using one of my less desirable skills, I animated the foot and gave it the power of speech. The foot took it quite well. It wiggled its toes experimentally, opened its arches and cleared its metatarsals, preparatory to speaking. Outwardly, it seemed quite pleased with my ministrations.

"Shall we walk and talk?" I began.

"Let's," said the foot. "But keep in mind that neither of us should smile or light up a cigarette."

"I accept your limitations," I said and I began walking briskly down the long hot highway. The foot fell into step with me and we continued along in thoughtful silence.

"I suppose you've walked this way before?" I finally asked.

"Yes and no," said the foot, somewhat cryptically.

"I am a former sky swallower," I said, by way of introduction.

"And I am a foot," said the foot, arching its toes in a little bow, bending stiffly at the joints. "I am still employed as such, although bereft of my employer. It seems, thanks to you, I am yet a foot but am now, thankfully, self-employed."

"It was my pleasure," I replied. "It seemed the least I could do."

Without warning, the foot suddenly rammed into an object, stubbing all of its toes. It cried out in pain and hopped up and down.

"Perhaps I should have given you eyes too," I observed. "This could have been avoided."

"What the hell did I trip over?"

I bent over, as moved by curiosity as the foot seemed to be, and immediately noted that it seemed to be a string made out of rock. It was either that or a rock made out of string.

"It seems to be a string."

"And to what is it attached?" inquired the foot. "To what does it lead?"

"To those questions, I am afraid I draw a blank. It seems to be of indeterminate length, stretching off as far as the eye can see."

"Perhaps we should follow it," suggested the foot.

The suggestion was agreeable to me and we set out to follow the string. Let us suppose a journey.

We journeyed many days and nights. It seemed to stretch out undiminished before us like a fat man climbing a light-year. The string stretched ahead of us, turning, twisting like a nightmare, and we followed patiently.

In Germany, it led through a large oven, as big as a house, that reeked faintly of gas. The string was coiled around a factory that made walls in Berlin. In France, the string covered the ground in cobwebs beneath guillotines.

In America, the string was used to tie the knots that held the doors of slaughterhouses closed against the public. In America, the string tied itself into colored worlds that said, "You can't eat here. You can't sleep here. You can't marry my sister."

We diligently followed the string. In Georgia, the string was a tightrope that political candidates swallowed and unswallowed with arthritic grace.

In Canada, the string was woven up in tuberculous-infected blankets that the Hudson Bay Company passed out to Indians.

In South Dakota, the string was a lynch rope that kept the mice from seeing the cat.

In South America, the string became a highway that mowed down the grass that hid tiny statues made out of wind and night. In South America, the string was a ribbon that rich people cut that let the first car drive across the broken bodies of dying animals, dying dreams.

Patiently, we followed the string.

In Spain, the string was a cure for venereal disease the natives called the INQUISITION. Everyone the string touched was ultimately cured when the grass grew back over their bodies.

In Florida, the string was a roll of tickets to the alligator farm where the last of the Seminoles lived off tips tourists gave him when he put his head inside of an alligator's jaws. He put his head inside and prayed the alligator would swallow.

In Nebraska, the string was a rosary that a Catholic priest tied to a dead Indian baby. In Nebraska, the string was a rosary that built two churches for every child, with the financial support of a God who ultimately said, "I can't see your face in my mind."

We followed the string, ceaselessly. It weaved its way through the bloodstreams of men and women, carelessly draped around their loins in curling spirals of mistrust and doubt. We followed the string. In some men, it entered their eyes and filled the empty sockets with frayed rope. In some women, it entered their bellies as umbilical cords that fed them, that took nourishment from the blood of the children.

As we traveled, we felt less inclined toward conversation, for stretched before us were the visual puppets of the world that danced on string.

It was endlessly fascinating, and we were speechless before the vast panorama of the never-ending string. How it curled like a twisted whore, screaming and thrashing like a child—a small child in nightmare alley! And the string touched all things and beauty and death and hate and love were all knots on the endless surface of the string, all there from the cruelty of children to the kindness of men who killed cattle with hammers in slaughterhouses.

We grew weary. We had seen too much and, perhaps, felt too little.

"I grow weary," I said and I looked with longing once more at the sky and dreamed of the days when I once held it like candy in my mouth.

"I too am weary," said the foot. "I have walked too far and feel that I have blisters that make my mortality significant and valuable."

"Blisters in themselves are no sign of accomplishment," I admonished the foot. "There has yet to be a world that did not have a string attached. There has yet to be a world, but one can hope for it. Until then, we must pay attention that we see more clearly the string so that we may someday touch people without tying them to us like beaded souvenirs on a necklace."

The foot thought this over carefully for a little while, as I once more aimed myself like an arrow of longing at the sky. All my thoughts had turned to the change of seasons, to the harmony of the sky and the four winds of the creation.

"What do you think of Western Civilization?" asked the foot.

I pulled the edge of a cloud out of my mouth long enough to shout back down at him, "I think it would be a very good idea!"

◆◆◆

A Wounded Knee Fairy Tale

He was hustle-looking, hustle-hungry. Sitting there in the doorway of the cut-rate record shop watching the Sunday afternoon in New York scene. Eyes scanning the freaks and the lunch-hour ladies, the alarm-clock, time-card–punching cowboys. Sunday afternoon and Johnny on the record store steps looking for a new boy. He could always tell the new ones, almost smell them. He just sat there, looking for a home in every face.

This boy coming down the street. Some kind of Indian costume. God! Authentic-looking, maybe even real deerskin and wood-and-bone chokers, the whole trip. In New York City, and looking out of place in this authentic suit right down to the moccasins. That whole thing there, he added that up. It had a smell to it of money. Those kinds of costumes are strictly heavy paper over the counter. This boy coming down the street.

Johnny looked at the boy's face and knew he had a mark. A freak, a face-painted freak on Sunday afternoon in New York. The boy was out-of-town action, hick-town, he looked out of place. Strictly a stranger, lost, bewildered, looking like he just got off the boat and everything is new to him.

When that boy went by, Johnny moved out behind him, stalking him like a cat. He kept close, planning, figuring angles, figuring how to take him before the other hustlers moved in. When the boy stopped to look at his reflection in a store window, Johnny moved up and touched him on the shoulder, touched him softly, caressingly.

"You're going to need a guide. Someone to show you the city. Show you the sights. Huh, boy? You're new, boy, you're new here and you need someone to take care of you." Johnny grinned, mixing threat and invitation in his voice. The marks liked Johnny. He had full, soft lips, he talked his hustles nice. He wore old clothes but they were always clean and he had that little-boy look. The little-boy look, the curly hair, the clean, hairless face, the soft neuter movements that made the marks go for him.

"I show you real nice. You're going to like how I show you." Johnny said it right, said it dirty.

But that face-painted freak, that costumed crazy, he was like a million miles away. He just stared at his reflection in the window. Then he spoke, a language of lilting polysyllables, strange inflections. He seemed to speak as much to himself, as much to his reflection, as to the hustler.

"Hell!" muttered Johnny. "I shoulda known you'd be a damn foreigner." The hustler smiled again and gave it another try. "Habla español?"

Behind the boy, Valdez was coming along, coming up behind the boy. Valdez with that empty walk when he's empty, hungry for himself, hungry for that next best mark. Johnny saw him coming, saw that high-pressure hype with the big chest and overmuscled arms, and his face went black with rage. Valdez came up quick, nose out like a fish nibbling bait.

Johnny grabbed the boy, spun him around, tried to pull him away. There was a hiss like animal fat burning in a cook fire and the space where Johnny stood was empty. There was a stench, an odor of scorched hair. Valdez had frozen in place, one arm extended, reaching for Johnny's new boy.

The strange boy turned and looked at Valdez, turned and looked. Valdez was paralyzed The strange boy's face was changing color, going from brown to blood red, and then he was gone. So gone. It was a goddamn trip. He was there and then nothing. It was like a light bulb going out. Sunday afternoon in New York and there was this freak in this damn Indian costume, and two hustlers had tried to take him and one had disappeared like out of some goddamn fairy tale and the other hustler had watched them both disappear. Man, it could only happen in New York City on a Sunday afternoon.

❖❖❖

It wasn't a question of security. It didn't matter if you cut your teeth on the hammer and sickle or on the stars and stripes. It was a gathering of frightened children, a hodgepodge of military and government personnel. There was a full crew of university eggheads, linguists, chiropodists, Russian spies, anyone who might know something, anyone willing to go. Quacks, religious fanatics, candy-ass liberals going to cheer, librarians, intelligence agents from everywhere, militiamen, army men, sailors in white suits, marines shaved bald like smart monkeys, Indian experts with long knives and CARE packages from the state liquor stores, Indian experts with degrees in Pawnee sex practices, phony Indians with hairy knuckles and raised eyebrow ridges, mouth breathers. Ambassadors and diplomats, senators and state governors, painted ladies and the criminally insane, an indistinct group, an inseparable aggregation, all moving together, all running like thunder-frightened cattle.

It began when someone reported that all the tribes were gathering, some FBI informer in a position to know, a reformed Indian with his pants down, waiting for government aid. Some sort of big powwow. Not unusual, not unheard of. That's what the informer said, several tribes had gathered together before, had had their little powwows. But this was different. Before the information could get out on the difference, the reformed Indian fell asleep with a knife in his back.

It *was* different. Suddenly, with no reason given, leaving possessions and homes abandoned, all the tribes began marching toward Wounded Knee. Cars, boats, airplanes, every imaginable type of vehicle was full of Indians moving toward Wounded Knee. A ceremony at the place where the hoop of the nations was broken. A civil disorder. Like Kent State, like Vietnam, like Korea, one civil disorder pretty much like any other. They could handle it. They told everyone they could handle it.

But on the morning of the day the tribes began moving, at 10:45 Eastern Standard time, the lights went out in New York, the dynamos at Niagara froze solid. At Oak Ridge, the powerful atomic reactors fell silent. In Russia, the great bear in night was plunged into a deeper night and confusion. The clocks of the world stopped at 10:45. All over the world, there was the nonsound of things stopped, of machines falling silent.

At 11:30 Eastern Standard time, the only movement, the only sounds made by machines were made by vehicles moving toward Wounded Knee. Cars full of Indians speeding down the highways long after they had run out of gas. A twin-engine plane with two Mohawk families, gliding silently westward over Chicago, both engines feathered, pulled at a speed that strained the wings, pulled forward with both engines silenced while the pilot shouted into a dead headset.

It was a selective madness. Nothing worked that had moving metal parts. Guns, cars, bicycles, garbage disposals, electric garage door openers, all the metal parts frozen solid, fused together, worthless. Only Indians moved freely, their cars worked, their planes, everything they touched, worked. Only Indians had guns that worked. It was stranger than New York City on a Sunday afternoon. Only Indians had guns that worked. And they moved toward Wounded Knee over the bodies of the obstacle course between them and Wounded Knee.

Ten days it took them to gather, ten days for the South American peoples to float up the rivers, to come out of the jungles and hidden places where white men had never been. Ten days to reach the ports and catch the airplanes and boats that waited for them there. Waited there to take them to Wounded Knee.

And the other people of the world, they went crazy. Aliens? An invasion from another planet? A warning from God?

The grasshopper people, government people, military replicas of people, they all danced to the same questions. They came running, crawling on knees suspiciously like helpless fists. Moving like old age toward Wounded Knee. They walked and rode horses. The more important of them rode in hastily built wooden carriages that broke down frequently. In growing numbers, they marched, moved, and crawled. In their path they found only emptiness and stillness, as if a storm had passed leaving the air cleaned and purified. Like hungry junkies with needle intensity, with one goal, one vein, they too moved on Wounded Knee.

The group mind, the briefcase mentality, the committee of single-minded purpose found him. They found him dancing with the Rosebud Sioux. They found him dancing with the Ojibway, the Cherokees, the Seminoles, the Kiowas, all the tribes of creation spread out over the land like the buffalo. Marching and dancing, moving in the wind like the leaves of corn, moving in one vast hoop that stretched across the flat land like one all-encircling snake. They found him dancing with the bird people, dancing with the animal people. They found him dancing with the fox people, the bear people, the wind river people. All around like soft blankets, the spirits of the dead circled the dancers, circled above, moving through the scattered bodies of their children, moving in the shadow and light.

They saw him and he was unlike any man that had ever walked their earth. His face was fire, his shoulders were feathered with black eagle wings, and when he laughed it was thunder and when he smiled it was lightning.

One of the generals, too long accustomed to a desk, too long gone from the world of men, moved forward among the watchers, pushed his way through the rapidly forming committees and study groups. He elbowed his way past the religious bleat, the organic cheering section, he broke through and marched forcefully toward the dancers.

As he moved toward the path of the great circle, the dancers began falling silently to the ground. The women, the children, the old ones, the fierce young men, the proud young women, they all fell back to rest. To rest.

They rested, surrounded by whites held at bay by guns that worked, guarded by tall warriors at the edge of the hoop, fierce-eyed men with rifles. The bodies of those who had come too close kept the others away. Every so often, a liberal believing all men were brothers would add his body to the piles of the dead.

The general was undeterred. The old general walked past the guard who kept the gun pointed at his chest. For some reason, no one made a move to shoot him. The old general walked up to one of the old men.

"How!" the general said, and he put his hand up, open-palmed, like a demented John Wayne. "On behalf of your President, I—"

There was a hiss like animal fat burning in the cook fire and the general and the rest of his sentence were gone.

And the white people moved back as if a spring had snapped within them. And they fled in one flowing wave. The one who fell from the sun stood at the top of the great Hoop of the Nations, and as they rose up, all the peoples of the creation, they rose up. They danced, the old and the young and the sick and the lame, all whole now, all one.

And they danced in clouds of ghosts, whirling around and around, and as they passed beneath the winged man, there was the sound of a thousand things moving in darkness and light, shaking, a thousand things moving and breaking in the time of the going away. And gently, like the stroke of soft-feathered birds, the eyes of the man of thunder and lightning fell upon the people, his eyes touched them and they moved quietly like dying angels, floating like memories to the sun.

Faster and faster, the drums, the drums that went faster and faded and faster and faded and then stopped, each note like a monument, each note rising into the air like a flight of birds. And then they were gone. Gone. The Hoop, the spirits of the dead, the dancers, the drums of the people, all fallen into the sun.

And the being who fell from the sun stood alone. Alone. He spread his wings and let the sun spin above him. And the spin of the sun filled his wings and he left the earth. He left the earth.

Behind him on the plain, in the silence, in the dust, a general and a New York City hustler materialized, embraced in each other's arms. Embraced in each other's arms on sterile ground in a world that would never grow up.

Sterile children in a world that would never grow up.

Red Beauty

"Blood is man's most alarming treasure," said Dr. Vada.

The corpse did not reply.

The white-coated medical students stirred restlessly in their seats. A green-faced freshman in the second row was already having difficulty and Dr. Vada had just barely begun.

Dr. Vada took a scalpel from a tray at his side. He turned and watched the faces of the students in the auditorium. Good. All eyes were on him. He placed the sharpened point on the chest of the corpse.

"What is the only thriving wildlife as yet relatively untouched by man?" he asked.

It was not meant to be answered. He meant to supply the answer himself.

Bellamy, in the first row, could not resist.

"The Dean's wife, Dr. Vada. I don't know about her thriving, but they say she's wild all right!"

There was a roar of laughter from the students at his back. Bellamy turned and faced his audience, bowing slightly. He was enormously pleased with himself.

Dr. Vada's face burned with fury. "That is the last time I will have my class interrupted by . . . by a . . ."

Bellamy spread his hands. "My most humble apologies." He laughed. "Don't forget who I am, Dr. Vada. My father is president of the university and . . ."

"And his son is a fool. Sit down, Bellamy." Dr. Vada's hands trembled and the scalpel bit into the flesh of the corpse. His eyes burned with rage. The hostility between himself and young Bellamy was bitter and of long standing.

"As I was saying," he continued, "the wildlife I referred to that has barely been touched by man is the hot, poorly lit world within himself. We have never learned to admire the absolute beauty of the blood."

Dr. Vada licked his lips. His eyes flashed with excitement. "Blood is misunderstood. We hate the pain that always appears with it and that pain has taught us to hate it, to hate the sight of blood."

Dr. Vada stared at his students. "And thereby, man blinds himself to one of the most beautiful things in creation. Our own rich, red, human blood."

"Taking hematology from a lunatic!" muttered Bellamy to the girl in the seat next to him. Dr. Vada heard him, as he was meant to. Except for a certain tightening of the muscles in his face, he chose to ignore it.

The scalpel was again pressed to the chest of the corpse.

"I'm a nature lover but the only scenery I prefer is inside the body." The doctor's arm flexed. The knife bit into cold flesh, slashing a deep cavity across the cadaver's chest. Sightless eyes stared blankly up at the smile of pleasure that spread across Dr. Vada's face.

"How can one not admire the wondrous shape of the glands, the fragile transparent lungs, the world within worlds of the infinitely complex brain cell mass. And through it all and always, streams the blood."

Dr. Vada made rapid lateral incisions. Dropping the scalpel on the tray, he grabbed the edges of the incision with both hands and laid back the skin with one quick tearing motion, exposing the entire chest cavity of the corpse.

The green-faced freshman in the second row doubled over in his seat. Dr. Vada glared at him. The freshman tried to lift his head, to pretend that nothing was wrong, but it was too much for him. He fainted.

Someone at the back of the room rose to his feet, dropping his books with a crash. He exited at great speed with one hand clamped over his mouth. The sound of someone vomiting in the hall outside came back clearly.

Dr. Vada scowled. "Why must I be plagued with constant interruptions?"

Several students moved to help the one who had fainted.

"Leave him alone!" snapped Dr. Vada, hands still holding the split halves of the chest. "The fool isn't hurt and we've no time to waste on his kind." The students returned to their seats.

"Ah, the blood," said Dr. Vada, almost worshipfully. "And this, the poor, flawed repository in which it streams." He moved so they could get a better view.

Bellamy muttered something else to the girl in the seat beside him. Dr. Vada caught some of it, a fragment of a particularly dirty joke. The girl blushed but did not seem overly offended.

This Dr. Vada could not ignore. It almost amounted to sacrilege.

"Bellamy." Dr. Vada's voice crashed through the hall. "Come here, Bellamy."

Reluctantly, Bellamy rose to his feet.

Dr. Vada kicked a chair in the first row, turning it so it faced the students in the auditorium.

Vada motioned at the chair. "Sit."

"But, Dr. Vada, I was only . . ." began Bellamy with a smirk.

"Sit down and shut up." Bellamy did both.

Dr. Vada nodded to his class, almost apologetically. "Young Bellamy here is in his usual form today. And because he is"—Dr. Vada's hands clamped on Bellamy's neck, pushing him against the back of the chair—"our Mr. Bellamy is going to provide us with a special treat."

Bellamy winced. The old doctor's hands were surprisingly strong.

"I don't want . . ."

"Silence."

Dr. Vada took his hands away and moved to the trays beside the dissection table. He returned with a large syringe and a length of thin rubber tubing.

"Thank you for volunteering to give a blood sample." Dr. Vada's smile could have dispensed ice.

"I'm not volunteering for . . ."

A hand on his shoulder cut him off. Bellamy shuddered. The strength in the old man's hands was really quite incredible. The look in the old man's eyes was something else again. He resisted the impulse to stand up, to take a swing at Vada. How can you hit an old man?

"Roll up your sleeve." Dr. Vada hovered over him, as if daring Bellamy to defy him. I'll get you later, you bastard, thought Bellamy as he rolled his sleeve up past the elbow. You're going to regret you ever laid a hand on me.

"Pay careful attention, class," said Dr. Vada, resuming the role of professor. "Observe as I tie this length of rubber tubing around his upper arm." He did so.

Dr. Vada unwrapped a sterile glass syringe, sunk its plunger into its barrel, placed a sterile needle on the end, and turned to face Bellamy with it.

"Make a fist."

Bellamy did.

The needle got closer. "Aren't you supposed to swab it with alcohol first?" asked Bellamy.

"Only if one wants to lessen the pain," said Dr. Vada, jabbing the needle into Bellamy's outstretched arm. "Notice how smoothly I inserted the needle," he said, once again speaking to his class. "Many of you will find this part difficult. Sticking a needle into someone's skin, like dying, must be done quickly or it becomes a rather messy experience."

When the syringe was full, Dr. Vada pulled it free of Bellamy's arm with a jerk. Bellamy cried out in pain.

Dr. Vada turned to his class with a smile. He held up the syringe for all to see.

"And now we have it. One of the unsung beauties of man. Blood."

Dr. Vada had a look of rapturous contentment on his face. "But does this fragile beauty last?"

Dr. Vada held up a small glass beaker. He emptied the syringe into it, holding it carefully in front of him so that all might see what he had trapped there.

"No. It does not last. Within five minutes, surely no longer than ten, this beautiful ruby-red liquid will change into a solid brown mass. If I were a fool"—he glanced significantly at Bellamy, who was rubbing a sore arm—"and not a scientist, perhaps I might think that this wonderful bit of living matter I have removed from a human body could now blindly live on as if it had never left its home. If I were a fool."

Dr. Vada's face became melancholy. "If only there was a way to keep it as you see it now, in its pure uncoagulated state."

Dr. Vada stared off into space as if he had forgotten where he was and to whom he spoke. "For thirty-five years I have sought the answer to this mystery. I have spent my life trying to stay this coarsening, this destroyer of natural beauty . . . for it was my dream . . . my dream always . . . that my own blood should flow eternally . . . that even at my death the red liquid would . . ." Dr. Vada jumped. He looked around him uncertainly. The puzzled, almost frightened rows of faces stared back at him. At his back, Bellamy silently mouthed the word "lunatic."

Dr. Vada turned pale, licking his lips nervously. He passed his hand across his face, as if wiping it clean of expression.

"Class dismissed," said Dr. Vada. Students sat and stared at each other. Class dismissed an hour early? The doctor set the glass beaker down on his desk and stalked out of the room. At the bottom of the container lay a thick brown mass of coagulated blood.

Bellamy rose with a look of pure malice on his face and followed Dr. Vada. He caught up to him as Dr. Vada prepared to enter his office in the basement of Steiner Hall.

"Yes? What is it?" snapped Dr. Vada. "I want to be alone." The old men opened his door and tried to enter, but Bellamy blocked him.

"I wanna talk to you," said Bellamy. "Now!"

"Another day! I must be alone with my . . ."

Bellamy pushed Dr. Vada through the door and stepped inside behind him. Dr. Vada staggered, recovered his balance, and turned and stared coldly at the angry young man in front of him. The old man seemed neither surprised nor particularly upset.

"Do you intend to beat me?" asked Dr. Vada. "If that is your intention, I cannot defend myself. I have a weak heart."

"You're not going to get off that easily, you old bastard. What's the idea of using me for a guinea pig anyway!" Bellamy rubbed the spot on his arm where the needle had gone in. "You think you can get away with that kind of crap around me? You're going to be sorry you ever . . ."

"And what do you intend to do about it?"

"I mean to see you fired. Not only that, I intend to see to it that you never get a university position anywhere else either."

"Your father is not that powerful, I think," said Dr. Vada calmly. "Besides, how do I know he would do anything to me anyway? Surely your word cannot be all that honorable even in your father's eyes."

"Gloat, you miserable bastard," said Bellamy. "Do you remember Dr. Saygers?"

The old man nodded. "A pity. A very old and dear colleague of mine. His suicide was a very great shock to me."

"He did it because I got him canned," said Bellamy with a note of triumph in his voice. "I shagged him. Just like I'm going to shag you."

Dr. Vada went to his desk and sat down. "You sit here and brag that you are responsible for the death of Dr. Saygers?"

Bellamy laughed.

Dr. Vada stared at the top of his desk. There was no expression on his face. He simply looked tired.

Bellamy leaned on the edge of his desk. "What's the matter, pops, all your stuffing leak out?"

Dr. Vada opened a cigar box on his desk. His hand was hidden by the box lid. "Does the perfect anticoagulant interest you, Mr. Bellamy?"

"Only your disappearance from the university interests me," said Bellamy. "You're senile and should have been put out to pasture a long time ago."

"A pity," said Dr. Vada. "Quite a fascinating subject. After blood leaves the body, prothrombin becomes converted to thrombin. When enough thrombin has formed, it converts fibrinogen to fibrin. I've tested hundreds of serums, perhaps thousands. I've never discovered anything that could reverse or totally inhibit that process." Dr. Vada sighed. He seemed abstracted, almost dreamy.

"You're mad, you know that? Still rattling on about your failures." Bellamy smiled. "Hasn't it sunk into that decrepit brain of yours that you're finished here?"

"Of course it has," said Dr. Vada. "Did you think I did not take you seriously? I assure you I do."

Bellamy stood up. "You'd better. Maybe you should resign. It'll look better than being booted out."

Dr. Vada just smiled. "Resign? I have no intention of resigning. I still have a new serum to try. Not much hope of success, I'm afraid. The proteins involved are impure. Always my greatest problem."

Angrily Bellamy leaned over the desk, opened his mouth to speak.

Dr. Vada struck. His hand came up from the inside of the cigar box. The hypodermic stabbed into the young man's chest.

Bellamy staggered back, eyes wide open with horror. He stumbled on a fold in the carpet and fell. The hypo was jolted free by the impact of the fall and landed in his lap.

"Help!" screamed Bellamy. "Help!"

Dr. Vada consulted the battered timepiece in his vest pocket. "Well, I underestimated the dose. Bit cramped and awkward doing it one-handed. I had hoped you wouldn't be able to scream."

Bellamy tried to rise. His arms and legs stiffened, refusing to obey. He was numb from the neck down. Paralysis was slowly creeping upward. Already his jaws and face felt heavy. His eyes rolled in terror, veins in his neck bulging horribly as he tried to move himself.

"Eleven seconds," said Dr. Vada. "Not a poison, Mr. Bellamy, so you needn't look so horrified. I wouldn't poison anyone. That would be inhuman."

"What are . . . you . . . doing to me?" The words came thickly from Bellamy's throat.

"You are in your usual form today, Mr. Bellamy," said Dr. Vada. He held a scalpel in one hand. "And because you are"—he moved to Bellamy's side—"you are going to provide me with a special treat."

"No! No!" whispered Bellamy.

"Our Mr. Bellamy has volunteered to participate in an anticoagulant test." Methodically, the old man began slicing through the shirt and pants, cutting away the clothes. He removed socks and shoes, undergarments. With a quick flip of the scalpel he snapped a gold chain that had encircled the young man's neck.

"You . . . can't . . . doesn't work . . you know it won't work . . ." Bellamy was almost inaudible.

"Relax, Mr. Bellamy." Dr. Vada lightly scratched the carotid artery with the sharp point of the scalpel. His hand was sure. "Trust me. I know my serum probably won't work, but don't let it concern you. I won't let it discourage me. Like all scientists, I'll just keep trying."

"You . . . please . . . I won't . . . pleeeeeeasssseee." Bellamy could no longer control his vocal cords.

"A very effective drug, is it not, young Mr. Bellamy? Are you comfortable?" Dr. Vada smiled solicitously. "I know you are paralyzed. But you can still hear, still see, Mr. Bellamy. You'll be aware at all times. I find that a rather nice touch."

Bellamy neither moved nor spoke. A tear trickled down one cheek.

Producing another hypo, the old man injected 20 cc's of anticoagulant.

"Keep your fingers crossed," said Dr. Vada with a laugh. "Can't cross them? Pity." He took the scalpel, held it gently to Bellamy's neck. With a firm, decisive stroke, he severed the carotid artery.

A bright arterial flow of blood gushed forth to pool on the floor at Dr. Vada's feet.

"Beautiful! Absolutely beautiful! Oh, beautiful, alarming treasure!" There was a look of pure delight on Dr. Vada's face.

"Do you hear it, my boy? Can you see the great rushing red glory of it?" Dr. Vada sighed. "But of course you can. At least for a little while."

There was silence in the room. Bellamy on the floor in a bright red pool of blood. Dr. Vada back at his desk, dreamily eyeing the red area. If only the beauty could last.

Ten minutes crept by. Bellamy had passed hearing and seeing. Forever.

"Alas," said Dr. Vada.

The beautiful red pool had thickened and turned brown.

Dr. Vada sighed, filled with a great sorrow. Something beautiful had passed out of his life.

◆◆◆

White Brothers From the Place Where No Man Walks

One evening Old Coat sat down in the fire. He did not wince or move his face. After a while the fire burned low. No one spoke.

Old Coat's daughter sat in the cornfield. Within her belly her sorrowing boy-child knew it would be born dead.

Uzmea the conjuror came in the night. Uzmea, the throat spreader, killed her and put her head in a red clay pot. Now the story begins.

Uzmea the taker of sacrifices lived in a cave of no color. No warrior went seeking Uzmea. He lived in the mountains among the strange gods and devices of his race.

One day of blackness and ground clouds, Uzmea came into Chota and stood silently by the village house. Warriors, women, and small ones gathered around him. No one dared move too close, for it was rumored that arms would drop from hands that touched Uzmea.

Uzmea had lived in the place of no color longer than the memory of the pretty women. He had been with our people from back into the time of the big cold land. He was not of our way. He wore strange plates of yellow metal around his chest. Upon his head was a strange metal shield with a tall bird plume. Around his neck was a string of glass stones that were red and blue and glitter. He worshipped strange gods. Gods of the sky and another more powerful, a snake god with feathers.

Twice had Uzmea come into Chota. Twice had the ground shaken the roots of houses and trees down. Twice water in the river had risen and fallen like the tide of the big water, the bottoms of lakes became hills, the earth cracked with the great wounds, and the hot foul breath of demons went into the air.

And each time Uzmea had spoken in a strange tongue to the sun. And then to us he spoke of this world-shake. It was a warning that the land would have new masters, Uzmea said.

Now Uzmea stood in the village again. Many hearts were tight with fear. Uzmea spoke to the sun in his strange tongue. Then he turned to the real people and said in our tongue:

"Listen and I shall tell you of a time long ago. I am the not-alive and the not-dead. I came to this place many animal ages ago. I made prophecy that the great white brothers would come. For the Delawares were upon you and your fires had sunk low. I told your oldest fathers of this place and of the coming of the white brothers who would keep your fires high. And I took blood that my prophecy would grow.

"It was many lifetimes before the whites came. They were not the white brothers I had prophesied. These white men came in ships across the big water. Uzmea sat in his cave dreaming and waiting. The real people had forgotten him except in fire talk but Uzmea did not forget.

"These white men became your brothers but they were not the white brothers of the time of need. Once again I spoke to the oldest of your fathers. I said: The white man will take your land. He will point you to the West, but there is no home for you there. He will make you become like him. He will say your way is no good. He will make roads across your heart so that he may come and look at you. He will teach you his tongue and the strange markings that are his you will learn. He will teach your people to spin and weave clothes that cover what you are not. He will teach you not to hunt and not to fight but to take food out of the ground. By these means he will destroy. He will marry your women and the children will be born boneless and bloodless.

"Some believed Uzmea and some did not. Hide, my children. Go to sleep, I said. Those who believed Uzmea hid in the caves and the high places. They stayed pure. Today I have come to this gathering place for the last time.

"In the eyes of the whites, you are outlaws, the ones who did not move West. Your bones are strong and your blood sings. I have seen the clearness, the vision. I shall speak this once and go to the cave of my race for all time. I have seen the white brother who is yet to come. Perhaps they will come quickly or not in your breathing time. Time has no feeling to them. Years are days to these white brothers. But come now or for your children, they will know your need. He will look upon your bodies that are thin with hair. He will look at the blood of your children and it shall be his blood.

"Their ways are strange but that which has taken from you the white brother will give back. They are mighty. They come across the place where no man walks. Give them the strange things of the ground so that your brothers may live and breed in his home far from this place. This is my prophecy."

Then Uzmea beckoned with his hand to Old Coat.

Old Coat did not show fear as he walked toward Uzmea. He was walking to his death, he knew.

Uzmea stared at Old Coat with ugly prophecy eyes and raised his hands in front of his unsleeping eyes. Old Coat stood before Uzmea. He looked straight into Uzmea's eyes, his back straight. Uzmea's hands fell upon Old Coat's face and Old Coat became as one dead. His eyes were dead fish-eyes in his head.

"Do you see?" asked Uzmea.

Old Coat's voice came from the faraway of the grave. "I see."

Uzmea drew his robe about him. "Three deaths will feed this dream. Three blood lives will grow my prophecy."

As swift as hawk shadow, Uzmea went away from them and disappeared into the hill trees.

Old Coat stood on his dead legs. He began walking with stiffness and the real people parted and let him pass. He went to his house and called his daughter's name. She lay within, heavy with child. She came out and many were the people who gave moan. For she was dead too.

Old Coat and his dead daughter stood in front of the council fire. Old Coat lifted his arms and pointed at the lights in the sky. "They are there," his voice said. "The home of the white brothers is in the sky. The stars are their home. They shall come in round pots through the place where no man walks. They shall give the false white brother the sickness and he will wither as in winter. We will live as we did before. The prophecy is spoken. We must fall asleep and wait and watch the sky."

That night Old Coat sat down in the fire. He did not wince or move his face. After a while the fire burned out. No one spoke.

Old Coat's daughter sat in the cornfield. Within her belly her sorrowing boy-child knew it would be born dead.

Uzmea the conjuror came in the night and killed her and put her head in a red clay pot. He set the pot high in the mountains. Her eyes were pointed to the stars to guide the white brothers through the place where no man walks. No one speaks of this. They are all asleep. Uzmea alone is awake. Uzmea waits and watches beneath the stars.

The story has begun.

JAMES WELCH

◆◆◆

FROM
Winter in the Blood

EDITOR'S NOTE: The thirty-two-year-old narrator of *Winter in the Blood* lives on a cattle ranch run by his stepfather. His life consists of endless days of ranchwork and binges in the Montana towns where he periodically escapes to drink and find women. His sense of dispossession is so profound that he is indifferent to almost everything in his life. What is shattered in this intelligent and sensitive young hero of this novel becomes subtly connected to the shattered heritage of Indians. By the final scene the tragedy of the young man and that of his people have become one.

1

In the tall weeds of the borrow pit, I took a leak and watched the sorrel mare, her colt beside her, walk through burnt grass to the shady side of the log-and-mud cabin. It was called the Earthboy place, although no one by that name (or any other) had lived in it for twenty years. The roof had fallen in and the mud between the logs had fallen out in chunks, leaving a bare gray skeleton, home only to mice and insects. Tumbleweeds, stark as bone, rocked in a hot wind against the west wall. On the hill behind the cabin, a rectangle of barbed wire held the graves of all the Earthboys, except for a daughter who had married a man from Lodgepole. She could be anywhere, but the Earthboys were gone.

The fence hummed in the sun behind my back as I climbed up to the highway. My right eye was swollen up, but I couldn't remember how or why, just the white man, loose with his wife and buying drinks, his raging tongue a flame above the music and my eyes. She was wild, from Rocky Boy. He was white. He swore at his money, at her breasts, at my hair.

Coming home was not easy anymore. It was never a cinch, but it had become a torture. My throat ached, my bad knee ached and my head ached in the even heat.

The mare and her colt were out of sight behind the cabin. Beyond the graveyard and the prairie hills, the Little Rockies looked black and furry in the heat haze.

Coming home to a mother and an old lady who was my grandmother. And the girl who was thought to be my wife. But she didn't really count. For that matter none of them counted; not one meant anything to me. And for no reason. I felt no hatred, no love, no guilt, no conscience, nothing but a distance that had grown through the years.

It could have been the country, the burnt prairie beneath a blazing sun, the pale green of the Milk River valley, the milky waters of the river, the sagebrush and cottonwoods, the dry, cracked gumbo flats. The country had created a distance as deep as it was empty, and the people accepted and treated each other with distance.

But the distance I felt came not from country or people; it came from within me. I was as distant from myself as a hawk from the moon. And that was why I had no particular feelings toward my mother and grandmother. Or the girl who had come to live with me.

I dropped down on the other side of the highway, slid through the barbed-wire fence and began the last two miles home. My throat ached with a terrible thirst.

2

"She left three days ago, just after you went to town."

"It doesn't matter," I said.

"She took your gun and electric razor."

The room was bright. Although it was early afternoon, the kitchen light was burning.

"What did you expect me to do? I have your grandmother to look after, I have no strength, and she is young—Cree!"

"Don't worry," I said.

"At least get your gun back." My mother swept potato peels off the counter into a paper sack at her feet. "You know she'd sell it for a drink."

The gun, an old .30–30, had once been important to me. Like my father before me, I had killed plenty of deer with it, but I hadn't used it since the day I killed Buster Cutfinger's dog for no reason except that I was drunk and it was moving. That was four years ago.

I heard a clucking in the living room. The rocking chair squeaked twice and was silent.

"How is she?" I asked

"Hot cereal and pudding—how would you expect her to be?"

"What, no radishes?"

My mother ignored me as she sliced the potatoes into thin wafers.

"Why don't we butcher one of those heifers? She could eat steak for the rest of her life and then some."

"She'll be gone soon enough without you rushing things. Here, put this on that eye—it'll draw out the poison." She handed me a slice of potato.

"How's Lame Bull?"

She stopped slicing. "What do you mean by that?"

"How's Lame Bull?"

"He'll be here this evening; you can find out then. Now get me another bucket of water."

"How's the water?" I asked.

"It'll do. It never rains anymore." She dumped the slices into a pan. "It never rains around here when you need it."

I thought how warm and flat the water would taste. No rain since mid-June and the tarred barrels under the eaves of the house were empty. The cistern would be low and the water silty.

A fly buzzed into the house as I opened the door. The yard was patched with weeds and foxtail, sagebrush beyond the fence. The earth crumbled into powder under my feet; beneath the sun which settled into afternoon heat over the slough, two pintail ducks beat frantically above the cottonwoods and out of sight. As I lowered the bucket into the cistern, a meadowlark sang from the shade behind the house. The rope was crusty in my hands. Twice I lifted and dropped the bucket, watching the water flow in over the lip until the bucket grew heavy enough to sink.

The girl was no matter. She was a Cree from Havre, scorned by the reservation people. I had brought her home with me three weeks ago. My mother thought we were married and treated her with politeness. My mother was a Catholic and sprinkled holy water in the corners of her house before lightning storms. She drank with the priest from Harlem, a round man with distant eyes, who refused to set foot on the reservation. He never buried Indians in their family graveyards; instead, he made them come to him, to his church, his saints and holy water, his feuding eyes. My mother drank with him in his shingle house beside the yellow plaster church. She thought I had married the girl and tried to welcome her, and the girl sat sullen in the living room across from the old lady, my grandmother, who filled her stone pipe with cuts of tobacco mixed with dried crushed chokecherries. She sat across from the girl, and the girl read movie magazines and imagined that she looked like Raquel Welch.

The old lady imagined that the girl was Cree and enemy and plotted ways to slit her throat. One day the flint striker would do; another day she favored the paring knife she kept hidden in her legging. Day after day, these two sat across from each other until the pile of movie magazines spread halfway across the room and the paring knife grew heavy in the old lady's eyes.

I slid down the riverbank behind the house. After a half-hour search in the heat of the granary, I had found a red and white spoon in my father's toolbox. The treble hook was rusty and the paint on the spoon flecked with rust. I cast across the water just short of the opposite bank. There was almost no current. As I retrieved the lure, three mallards whirred across my line of vision and were gone upriver.

The sugar beet factory up by Chinook had died seven years before. Everybody had thought the factory caused the river to be milky but the water never cleared. The white men from the fish department came in their green trucks and stocked the river with pike. They were enthusiastic and dumped thousands of pike of all sizes into the river. But the river ignored the fish and the fish ignored the river; they refused even to die there. They simply vanished. The white men made tests; they stuck electric rods into the water; they scraped muck from the bottom; they even collected bugs from the fields next to the river; they dumped other kinds of fish in the river. Nothing worked. The fish disappeared. Then the men from the fish department disappeared, and the Indians put away their new fishing poles. But every now and then, a report would trickle down the valley that someone, an irrigator perhaps, had seen an ash-colored swirl suck in a muskrat, and out would come the fishing gear. Nobody ever caught one of these swirls, but it was always worth a try.

I cast the spoon again, this time retrieving faster.

The toolbox had held my father's tools and it was said in those days that he could fix anything made of iron. He overhauled machinery in the fall. It was said that when the leaves turned, First Raise's yard was full of iron; when they fell, the yard was full of leaves. He drank with the white men of Dodson. Not a quiet man, he told them stories and made them laugh. He charged them plenty for fixing their machines. Twenty dollars to kick a baler awake—one dollar for the kick and nineteen for knowing where to kick. He made them laugh until the thirty-below morning ten years ago we found him sleeping in the borrow pit across from Earthboy's place.

He had had dreams. Every fall, before the first cold wind, he dreamed of taking elk in Glacier Park. He planned. He figured out the mileage and the time it would take him to reach the park, and the time it would take to kill an elk and drag it back across the boundary to his waiting pickup. He made a list of food and supplies. He inquired around, trying to find out what the penalty would be if they caught him. He wasn't crafty like Lame Bull or the white men of Dodson, so he had to know the penalty, almost as though the penalty would be the inevitable result of his hunt.

He never got caught because he never made the trip. The dream, the planning and preparation were all part of a ritual—something to be done when the haying was over and the cattle brought down from the hills. In the evening, as he oiled his .30–30, he explained that it was better to shoot a cow elk because the bulls were tough and stringy. He had everything figured out, but he never made the trip.

My lure caught a windfall trunk and the brittle nylon line snapped. A magpie squawked from deep in the woods on the other side of the river.

4

"Ho, you are fishing, I see. Any good bites?" Lame Bull skittered down the bank amid swirls of dust. He stopped just short of the water.

"I lost my lure," I said.

"You should try bacon," he said, watching my line float limp on the surface. "I know these fish."

It was getting on toward evening. A mosquito lit on Lame Bull's face. I brought in the line and tied it to the reel handle. The calf bawled in the corral. Its mother, an old roan with one wild eye, answered from somewhere in the bend of the horseshoe slough.

"You should try bacon. First you cook it, then dump the grease into the river. First cast, you'll catch a good one."

"Are the fish any good?" I asked.

"Muddy. The flesh is not firm. It's been a poor season." He swatted a cloud of dust from his rump. "I haven't seen such a poor year since the flood. Ask your mother. She'll tell you."

We climbed the bank and started for the house. I remembered the flood. Almost twelve years ago, the whole valley from Chinook on down was under water. We moved up to the agency and stayed in an empty garage. They gave us typhoid shots.

"You, of course, are too young."

"I was almost twenty," I said.

"Your old man tried to ride in from the highway but his horse was shy of water. You were not much more than a baby in Teresa's arms. His horse threw him about halfway in."

"I remember that. I was almost twenty."

"Ho." Lame Bull laughed. "You were not much more than a gleam in your old man's eye."

"His stirrup broke—that's how come the horse threw him. I saw his saddle. It was a weakness in the leather."

"Ho."

"He could outride you any day."

"Ho."

Lame Bull filled the width of the doorframe as he entered the kitchen. He wasn't tall, but broad as a bull from shoulders to butt.

"Ah, Teresa! Your son tells me you are ready to marry me."

"My son tells lies that would make a weasel think twice. He was cut from the same mold as you." Her voice was clear and bitter.

"But why not? We could make music in the sack. We could make those old sheets sing."

"Fool . . . you talk as though my mother had no ears," Teresa said.

Two squeaks came from the living room.

"Old woman! How goes the rocking?" Lame Bull moved past my mother to the living room. "Do you make hay yet?"

The rocking chair squeaked again.

"She has gone to seed," I said. "There is no fertilizer in her bones."

"I seem to find myself surrounded by fools today." Teresa turned on the burner beneath the pan filled with potatoes. "Maybe one of you fools could bring yourself to feed that calf. He'll be bawling all night."

Evening now and the sky had changed to pink reflected off the high western clouds. A pheasant gabbled from a field to the south. A lone cock, he would be stepping from the wild rose along an irrigation ditch to the sweet alfalfa field, perhaps to graze with other cocks and hens, perhaps alone. It is difficult to tell what cocks will do when they grow old. They are like men, full of twists.

The calf was snugged against the fence, its head between the poles, sucking its mother.

"Hi! Get out of here, you bitch!"

She jumped straight back from the fence, skittered sideways a few feet, then stood, tensed. Her tongue hung a thread of saliva almost to the ground and the one wild eye, rimmed white, looked nowhere in particular.

"Don't you know we're trying to wean this fool?"

I moved slowly toward the calf, backing it into a corner where the horse shed met the corral fence, talking to it, holding out my hand. Before it could move I grabbed it by the ear and whirled around so that I could pin its shoulder against the fence. I slapped a mosquito from my face and the calf bawled; then it was silent.

Feeling the firmness of its thigh, I remembered how my brother, Mose, and I used to ride calves, holding them for each other, buckling on the old chaps we found hanging in the horse shed, then the tense "Turn him out!" and all hell busted loose. Hour after hour we rode calves until First Raise caught us.

The calf erupted under my arm, first backing up into the corner, then lunging forward, throwing me up against the horse shed. A hind hoof grazed the front of my shirt.

I pitched some hay into the corral, then filled the washtub with slough water. Tiny bugs darted through the muck. They looked like ladybugs with long hind legs. A tadpole lay motionless at the bottom of the tub. I scooped it out and laid it on a flat chunk of manure. It didn't move. I prodded it with a a piece of straw. Against the rough texture of the manure it glistened like a dark teardrop. I returned it to the tub, where it drifted to the bottom with a slight wriggle of its tail.

The evening was warm and pleasant, the high pink clouds taking on a purple tint. I chased the cow back up into the bend of the slough. But she would be back. Her bag was full of milk.

5

After supper, my mother cleared the table. Lame Bull finished his coffee and stood up.

"I must remember to get some more mosquito dope." Teresa emptied the last drops into the palm of her hand. She smeared it on her face and neck. "If your grandmother wants anything, you see that she gets it." She rested her hand on Lame Bull's forearm and they walked out the door.

I poured myself another cup of coffee. The sound of the pickup motor surprised me. But maybe they were going after groceries. I went into the living room.

"Old woman, do you want some music?" I leaned on the arms of her rocker, my face not more than six inches from hers.

She looked at my mouth. Her eyes were flat and filmy. From beneath the black scarf, a rim of coarse hair, parted in the middle, framed her gray face.

"Music," I commanded, louder this time.

"Ai, ai," she cackled, nodding her head, rocking just a bit under the weight of my arms.

I switched on the big wooden radio and waited for it to warm up. The glass on the face of the dial was cracked, and the dial itself was missing. A low hum filled the room. Then the music of a thousand violins. The rocking chair squeaked.

"Tobacco," I said.

The old woman looked at me.

I filled her pipe and stuck it between her lips. The kitchen match flared up, revealing the black mole on her upper lip. Three black hairs moved up and down as she sucked the smoke into her mouth.

The chair surrounded by movie magazines was uncomfortable, so I sat on the floor with my back resting against the radio. The violins vibrated through my body. The cover of the *Sports Afield* was missing and the pages were dog-eared, but I thumbed through it, looking for a story I hadn't read. I stopped at an advertisement for a fishing lure that called to fish in their own language. I tore the coupon out. Maybe that was the secret.

I had read all the stories, so I reread the one about three men in Africa who tracked a man-eating lion for four days from the scene of his latest kill—a pregnant black woman. They managed to save the baby, who, they were surprised to learn, would one day be king of the tribe. They tracked the lion's spoor until the fourth day, when they found that he'd been tracking them all along. They were going in a giant four-day circle. It was very dangerous, said McLeod, a Pepsi dealer from Atlanta, Georgia. They killed the lion that night as he tried to rip a hole in their tent.

I looked at the pictures again. One showed McLeod and Henderson kneeling behind the dead lion; they were surrounded by a group of grinning black men. The third man, Enright, wasn't in the picture.

I looked up. The old lady was watching me.

6

Lame Bull and my mother were gone for three days. When they came back, he was wearing a new pair of boots, the fancy kind with walking heels, and she had on a shimmery turquoise dress. They were both sweaty and hung over. Teresa told me that they had gotten married in Malta.

That night we got drunk around the kitchen table.

7

Lame Bull had married 360 acres of hay land, all irrigated, leveled, some of the best land in the valley, as well as a 2000-acre grazing lease. And he had married a T-Y brand stamped high on the left ribs of every beef on the place. And, of course, he had married Teresa, my mother. At forty-seven, he was eight years younger than she, and a success. A prosperous cattleman.

The next day, Lame Bull and I were up early. He cursed as he swung the flywheel on the little John Deere. He opened up the petcock on the gas line, swung the flywheel again, and the motor chugged twice, caught its rhythm and smoothed out. We hitched the hay wagon behind the tractor and drove slowly past the corral and slough. We followed the footpath upriver, through patches of wild rose, across a field of sagebrush and down into a grove of dead white cottonwoods. A deer jumped up from its willow bed and bounded away, its white tail waving goodbye.

The cabin, log and mud, was tucked away in a bend of the river. A rusty wire ran from the only window up to the top of the roof. It was connected to a car aerial, always a mystery to me, as Lame Bull had no electricity. He gathered up his possessions—a chain saw, a portable radio, two boxes of clothes, a sheepherder's coat and the high rubber boots he wore when he irrigated.

"I must remember to get some more tire patches," he said, sticking a finger through a hole in one of the boots.

We padlocked the cabin, covered the pump with an old piece of tarp and started back, Lame Bull sniffing the sweet beautiful land that had been so good to him.

Later, as we drove past the corral, I saw the wildeyed cow and a small calf head between the poles. The cow was licking the head. A meadowlark sang from a post above them. The morning remained cool, the sun shining from an angle above the horse shed. Behind the sliding door of the shed, bats would be hanging from the cracks.

Old Bird shuddered, standing with his hindquarters in the dark of the shed. He lifted his great white head and parted his lips. Even from such a distance I could see his yellow teeth clenched together as though he were straining to grin at us. Although he no longer worked, he still preferred the cool dark of the horse shed to the pasture up behind the slough. Perhaps he still felt important and wished to be consulted when we saddled up the red horse and Nig on those occasions when it was necessary to ride through the herd. No matter what season, what weather, he was always there. Perhaps he felt he had as much right to this place as we had, for even now he was whinnying out a welcome. He was old and had seen most of everything.

8

Teresa sat on the edge of the concrete cistern.

"Your father won Amos pitching pennies at the fair. He was so drunk he couldn't even see the plates."

"Amos used to follow us out to the highway every morning," I said. "We used to have to throw rocks at him."

"The others drowned because you didn't keep the tub full of water. You boys were like that."

Her fingers, resting on her thighs, were long, the skin stretched over the bone as taut as a drumhead. We could see Lame Bull down by the granary, which doubled as a toolshed. He was sharpening a mower sickle.

"We went to town that day for groceries. I remember we went to the show."

"Yes, and when we came back, all the ducks were drowned. Except Amos. He was perched on the edge of the tub."

"But he never went in. He must have been smarter than the others," I said.

Lame Bull's legs pumped faster. He poured some water on the spinning grindstone.

"He was lucky. One duck can't be smarter than another. They're like Indians."

"Then why didn't he go in with the other ducks?"

"Don't you remember how gray and bitter it was?"

"But the other ducks . . ."

". . . were crazy. You boys were told to keep that tub full." She said this gently, perhaps to ease my guilt, if I still felt any, or perhaps because ducks do not matter. Especially those you win at the fair in Dodson.

We had brought the ducks home in a cardboard box. There were five of them, counting Amos. We dug a hole in the ground big enough for the washtub to fit, and deep enough so that its lip would be even with the ground level. Then we filled the tub to the lip so that the ducks could climb in and out as they chose. But we hadn't counted on the ducks drinking the water and splashing it out as they ruffled their wings. That late afternoon, several days later, the water level had dropped to less than an inch below the rim of the tub. But it was enough. That one inch of galvanized steel could have been the wall of the Grand Canyon to the tiny yellow ducks.

The calf in the corral bawled suddenly.

The day the ducks drowned remained fresh in my mind. The slight smell of muskrat pelts coming from the shed, the wind blowing my straw hat away, the wind whipping the glassine window of the shed door; above, the gray slide of clouds as we stood for what seemed like hours beside the car glaring at the washtub beyond the fence. And the ducks floating with their heads deep in the water as though they searched the bottom for food. And Amos perched on the rim of the tub, looking at them with great curiosity.

My mother talked on about Amos. Not more than six feet away was the spot where the ducks had drowned. The weeds grew more abundant there, as though their spirits had nourished the soil.

"And what happened to Amos?" I said.

"We had him for Christmas. Don't you remember what a handsome bird he was?"

"But I thought that was the turkey."

"Not at all. A bobcat got that turkey. Don't you remember how your brother found feathers all the way from the toolshed to the corral?"

"That was a hateful bird!"

"Oh." She laughted. "He used to chase you kids every time you stepped out the door. We had a baseball bat by the washstand, you remember? You kids had to take it with you every time you went to the outhouse."

"He never attacked you," I said.

"I should say not! I'd have wrung his damn neck for him."

Lame Bull sat on the wooden frame, the big gray grindstone spinning faster and faster as his legs pumped. Sparks flew from the sickle.

It was a question I had not wanted to ask: "Who . . . which one of us . . ."

Teresa read my hesitation. ". . . killed Amos? Who else? You kids had no stomach for it. You always talked big enough, Lord knows you could talk up a storm in those days, and your father . . ."

"First Raise killed him?"

"Your father wasn't even around!" Her fine bitter voice rang in the afternoon heat. "But I'll tell you one thing—I've never seen a sorrier sight when he did come back."

Now I was confused. The turkey was of little importance. I could remember his great wings crashing about my head as he dug his spurs into my sides, his weight bearing me down to the ground until I cried out. Then the yelling and the flailing baseball bat and the curses, and finally the quiet. It was always my father bending over me: "He's all right, Teresa, he's all right . . ." It was he, I thought, who had killed the turkey. But now it was my mother who had killed the turkey while First Raise was in town making the white men laugh. But he always carried me up to the house and laid me on the bed and sat with me until the burning in my head went away. Now the bobcat killed Amos . . .

"No! The bobcat killed the big turkey," she said, then added quietly, as though Lame Bull might hear over the grinding of steel, as though Bird might hear over the sound of the bawling calf, as though the fish that were never in the river might hear: "I killed Amos."

9

"Why did he stay away so much?" I said.

"What? Your father?" The question caught her off-guard.

"Why would he stay away so much?"

"He didn't. He was around enough. When he was around he got things accomplished."

"But you yourself said he was never around."

"You must have him mixed up with yourself. He always accomplished what he set out to do."

We were sitting on the edge of the cistern. Teresa was rubbing Mazola oil into the surface of a wooden salad bowl. It had been a gift from the priest in Harlem, but she never used it.

"Who do you think built the extra bedroom onto the house?" she said. She rubbed her glistening fingers together. "He was around enough—he was on his way home when they found him, too."

"How do you know that?" But I knew the answer.

"He was pointing toward home. They told me that."

I shook my head.

"What of it?" she demanded.

"Memory fails," I said.

It was always "they" who had found him, yet I had a memory as timeless as the blowing snow that we had found him ourselves, that we had gone searching for him after the third day, or the fourth day, or the fifth, cruising the white level of highway raised between the blue-white of the borrow pits. I could almost remember going into the bar in Dodson and being told that he had left for home the night before; so we must have been searching the borrow pits. How could we have spotted him? Was it a shoe sticking up, or a hand, or just a blue-white lump in the endless skittering whiteness? I had no memory of detail until we dug his grave, yet I was sure we had come upon him first. Winters were always timeless and without detail, but I remembered no other faces, no other voices.

My mother stood and massaged the backs of her thighs. "He was a foolish man," she said.

"Is that why he stayed away?"

"Yes, I believe that was it." She was looking toward the toolshed. Three freshly sharpened mower sickles leaned against the granary, their triangular teeth glistening like ice in the sun. "You know how it is."

"He wasn't satisfied," I said.

"He accomplished any number of things."

"But none of them satisfied him."

Teresa whirled around, her eyes large and dark with outrage. "And why not?"

"He wasn't happy . . ."

"Do you suppose he was happy lying in that ditch with his eyes frozen shut, stinking with beer . . ."

But that was a different figure in the ditch, not First Raise, not the man who fixed machinery, who planned his hunt with such care that he never made it. Unlike Teresa, I didn't know the man who froze in the borrow pit. Maybe that's why I felt nothing until after the funeral.

"He was satisfied," she said. "He was just restless. He could never settle down."

A sonic boom rattled the shed door, then died in the distance. Teresa looked up at the sky, her hand over her eyes. The airplane was invisible. She looked down at me. "Do you blame me?"

I scratched a mosquito bite on the back of my hand and considered.

"He was a wanderer—just like you, just like all these damned Indians." Her voice became confident and bitter again. "You I don't understand. When you went to Tacoma for that second operation, they wanted you to stay on. You could have become something."

"I don't blame you," I said.

"You're too sensitive. There's nothing wrong with being an Indian. If you can do the job, what difference does it make?"

"I stayed almost two years."

"Two years!" she said disgustedly. "One would be more like it—and then you spent all your time up in Seattle, barhopping with those other derelicts."

"They didn't fix my knee."

"I see: it's supposed to heal by itself. You don't need to do the exercises they prescribed." She picked up the salad bowl. She was through with that part of my life. A dandelion parachute had stuck to the rim. "What about your wife?" She blew the parachute away. "Your grandmother doesn't like her."

I never expected much from Teresa and I never got it. But neither did anybody else. Maybe that's why First Raise stayed away so much. Maybe that's why he stayed in town and made the white men laugh. Despite their mocking way they respected his ability to fix things; they gave more than his wife. I wondered why he stuck it out so long. He could have moved out altogether. The ranch belonged to Teresa, so there was no danger of us starving to death. He probably stayed because of my brother, Mose, and me. We meant something to him, although he would never say it. It was apparent that he enjoyed the way we grew up and learned to do things, drive tractor, ride calves, clean rabbits and pheasants. He would never say it, though, and after Mose got killed, he never showed it. He stayed away more than ever then, a week or two at a time. Sometimes we would go after him; other times he would show up in the yard, looking ruined and fearful. After a time, a month, maybe, of feverish work, he would go off to overhaul a tractor and it would begin again. He never really stayed and he never left altogether. He was always in transit.

Ten years had passed since that winter day his wandering ended, but nothing of any consequence had happened to me. I had had my opportunity, a chance to work in the rehabilitation clinic in Tacoma. They liked me because I was smarter than practically anybody they had ever seen. That's what they said and I believed them. It took a nurse who hated Indians to tell me the truth, that they needed a grant to build another wing and I was to be the first of the male Indians they needed to employ in order to get the grant. She turned out to be my benefactor. So I came home.

"I think your grandmother deserves to be here more than your wife, don't you?"

"She's been here plenty long already," I agreed.

"Your wife wasn't happy here," Teresa said, then added: "She belongs in town."

In the bars, I thought. That's what you mean, but it's not important anymore. Just a girl I picked up and brought home, a fish for dinner, nothing more. Yet it surprised me, those nights alone, when I saw her standing in the moon by the window and I was the moon on the tops of her breasts and the slight darkness under each rib. The memory was more real than the experience.

Lame Bull had finished his work and was walking toward us. He slapped his gloves against his thigh and looked back at the bank of glistening sickles. He seemed pleased.

"There isn't enough for you here," said my mother. "You would do well to start looking around."

◆◆◆

Magic Fox

They shook the green leaves down,
those men that rattled
in their sleep. Truth became
a nightmare to their fox.
He turned their horses into fish,
or was it horses strung
like fish, or fish like fish
hung naked in the wind?

Stars fell upon their catch.
A girl, not yet twenty-four
but blonde as morning birds, began
a dance that drew the men in
green around her skirts.
In dust her magic jangled memories
of dawn, till fox and grief
turned nightmare in their sleep.

And this: fish not fish but stars
that fell into their dreams.

The Man From Washington

The end came easy for most of us.
Packed away in our crude beginnings
in some far corner of a flat world,
we didn't expect much more
than firewood and buffalo robes
to keep us warm. The man came down,
a slouching dwarf with rainwater eyes,
and spoke to us. He promised
that life would go on as usual,
that treaties would be signed, and everyone—
man, woman and child—would be inoculated
against a world in which we had no part,
a world of money, promise and disease.

❖❖❖

Arizona Highways

I see her seventeen,
a lady dark, turquoise
on her wrists. The land
astounded by a sweeping rain
becomes her skin. Clouds
begin to mend my broken eyes.

I see her singing by a broken shack,
eyes so black it must be dawn.
I hum along, act sober,
tell her I could love her
if she dressed better, if her father
got a job and beat her more.
Eulynda. There's a name
I could live with. I could
thrash away the nuns, tell them
I adopt this girl, dark,
seventeen, silver on her fingers,
in the name of the father, son,
and me, the holy ghost.
Why not? Mormons do less
with less. Didn't her ancestors

live in cliffs, no plumbing,
just a lot of love and corn?
Me, that's corn, pollen
in her hair. East, south, west, north—
now I see my role—religious.

The Indian politician made her laugh.
Her silver jingled in her throat,
those songs, her fingers busy
on her sleeve. Fathers, forgive me.
She knows me in her Tchindii dream,
always a little pale, too much
bourbon in my nose, my shoes
too clean, belly soft as hers.

I'll move on. My schedule
says Many Farms tomorrow, then
on to Window Rock, and finally home,
that weathered nude, distant
as the cloud I came in on.

LESLIE MARMON SILKO

Ceremony

EDITOR'S NOTE: *Ceremony* is about Tayo, an American Indian veteran of World War II who returns home in a state of exhaustion, depression, and shock. In the South Pacific he watched his white friends die. He also saw the execution of many Japanese prisoners of war who, to Tayo, looked very much like his own people. Gradually he came to see that these Japanese people represent a "hated Asian population" not unlike the Indians at home. Silko does not simply make this emotional and haunting global analogy in discursive language, she also develops a strong metaphor connecting the atom bomb dropped on Hiroshima with the first tests of that weapon in New Mexico, near Los Almos, on the very land taken from the Indian people of the Pueblo of Cochiti (very near Silko's home pueblo of Laguna). The focus of the novel is on Tayo's search for the sanity he lost in the white man's war. He goes to Gallup, that tough and racist little town near the Arizona/New Mexico border. There Tayo encounters Old Betonie, a man who knows Indian curative medicine and who therefore attempts to exorcise the evil of Tayo's traumatic military experiences. The central ceremony involves the use of sandpainting and prayer sticks—a very ancient healing ritual in the Southwest of the U.S.

◆◆◆

Black pebbles and the ancient gray cinders the mountain had thrown poked into his backbone. He closed his eyes but did not sleep. He felt cold gusts of wind scattering dry oak leaves in the grass. He listened to the cowboy collect tobacco juice in his mouth and the squirting liquid sound when he spat. He was aware of the center beneath him; it soaked into his body from the ground through the torn skin on his hands, covered with powdery black dirt. The magnetism of the center spread over him smoothly like rainwater down his neck and shoulders; the vacant cool sensation glided over the pain like feather-down wings. It was pulling him back, close to the earth, where the core was cool and silent as mountain stone, and even with the noise and pain in his head he knew how it would be: a returning rather than a separation. He was relieved because he feared leaving people he loved. But lying above the center that pulled him down closer felt more familiar to him than any embrace he could remember; and he was sinking into the elemental arms of mountain silence. Only his skull resisted; and the resistance increased the pain to a shrill whine. He visualized each piece of his own skull, fingering each curve, each hollow, testing its thickness for a final thin membrane worn thin by time and the witchery of dead ash and mushroomed bullets. He searched thin walls, weak sutures of spindle bones above the ear for thresholds. He knew if he left his skull unguarded, if he let himself sleep, it would happen: the resistance would leak out and take with it all barriers, all boundaries; he would seep into the earth and rest with the center, where the voice of the silence was familiar and the density of the dark earth loved him. He could secure the thresholds with molten pain and remain; or he could let go and flow back. It was up to him.

◇◇◇

He heard the truck motor stop and doors slam. The voices were muffled by the distance, but the Texan had not come back alone.

"Hey! I found something! Remember those lion tracks we found last spring? Well there's fresh ones all over the place! Around the number twelve windmill. A big son of a bitch! Tracks the size of my palm!" The new voice was high pitched with excitement.

The cowboy got up from the boulder stiffly and spat out the last of the tobacco wad.

"Well, what about this guy?" he said. "I thought you wanted to take him in."

The Texan cleared his throat. "Shit," he said, "greasers and Indians— we can run them down anytime. But it's been a couple of years since anybody up here got a mountain lion."

"Okay, okay. You were the one that wanted to mess with him, not me."

"Shit, by the time we got him back, the lion would be long gone."

"Just leave him where he is and let's go get the lion hounds before it gets dark."

"Yeah, we taught him a lesson," the Texan said, his voice fading in and out with the wind. "These goddamn Indians got to learn whose property this is!"

◇◇◇

When he woke up again they were gone, and the wind had calmed down; but the air was heavy and damp. The sky was full of storm clouds. The pain and the pounding inside his head were gone, but when he sat up he had to move slowly to avoid jarring the soreness inside his skull. His feet and hands were numb from the cold, and his legs were stiff from lying still so long. He sat rubbing his legs and feet, with a cold breeze at his back. If he went a few yards over the top of the ridge, he would be in the scrub oaks, out of the storm.

The oaks grew thick and close to the ground. He knelt at the edge of the thicket, looking until he found a narrow winding trail through the fringes of oak. The deer made trails through every thicket, and some of the big thickets had two or three trails running parallel to the top of the ridge; they moved into the thickets after sunrise and spent their days in the thickets, sleeping and feeding on acorns, crossing a clearing only to reach another stand of scrub oak. The leaves accumulated in deep layers of years, and his feet sank under the new copper leaves that had already fallen this year. The deer made beds in shallow niches deep within the thickets where the oaks grew tall and made canopies of limbs and branches.

He lay in a shallow depression and heaped piles of dry leaves over himself until he felt warm again. He looked up through the branches and the leaves, which were yellow and soft, ready to fall; the sky was heavy and dark, and purple veins striated the gray swollen clouds dragging their bellies full of snow over the mountaintop. The smell of snow had a cold damp edge, and a clarity that summer rain never had. The scent touched him deep behind his belly, and he could feel the old anticipation stirring as it had when he was a child waiting for the first snowflakes to fall.

❖❖❖

He lay there and hated them. Not for what they wanted to do with him, but for what they did to the earth with their machines, and to the animals with their packs of dogs and their guns. It happened again and again, and the people had to watch, unable to save or to protect any of the things that were so important to them. He ground his teeth together; there must be something he could do to still the vague, constant fear unraveling inside him: the earth and the animals might not know; they might not understand that he was not one of them; he was not one of the destroyers. He wanted to kick the soft white bodies into the Atlantic Ocean; he wanted to scream to all of them that they were trespassers and thieves. He wanted to follow them as they hunted the mountain lion, to shoot them and their howling dogs with their own guns. The destroyers had sent them to ruin this world, and day by day they were doing it. He wanted to scream at Indians like Harley and Helen Jean and Emo that the white things they admired and desired so much—the bright city lights and loud music, the soft sweet food and the cars—all these things had been stolen, torn out of Indian land: raw living materials for their ck'o'yo manipulation. The people had been taught to despise themselves because they were left with barren land and dry rivers. But they were wrong. It was the white people who had nothing; it was the white people who were suffering as thieves do, never able to forget that their pride was wrapped in something stolen, something that had never been, and could never be, theirs. The destroyers had tricked the white people as completely as they had fooled the Indians, and now only a few people understood how the filthy deception worked; only a few people knew that the lie was destroying the white people faster than it was destroying Indian people. But the effects were hidden, evident only in the sterility of their art, which continued to feed off the vitality of other cultures, and in the dissolution of their consciousnesss into dead objects; the plastic and neon, the concrete and steel. Hollow and lifeless as a witchery clay figure. And what little still remained to white people was shriveled like a seed hoarded too long, shrunken past its time, and split open now, to expose a fragile, pale leaf stem, perfectly formed and dead.

◈◈◈

It was still dark when he woke up, and he could feel flakes of snow blowing in the wind. He couldn't see if the sky in the east was getting light yet, because the storm clouds were still dense and low. He shook the snow off his hair; the oak leaves had held a shell of snow around him. He stood up and brushed the leaf dust away and pissed a yellow steaming slash through the snow.

He walked southeast. He went slowly because his whole body was sore and because the snow was rapidly covering the ground, even the big rocks, making it difficult to follow the trail even as the darkness dissolved into gray light. The sky was dense and gray; it was difficult to estimate distances. He turned and looked back in the direction of the mountain, but it was hidden in a swirling mass of wet clouds. He ate a handful of snow, blinking the flakes off his eyelashes as he tried to face the direction the storm was coming from, because the cowboys had gone that way. A gust of wind brought the center of the storm down, and big flakes fluttered around his head like summer moths crowding the sky, rising high over the edges of wet black lava and the tips of yellow grass.

The snow was covering everything, burying the mountain lion's tracks and obliterating his scent. The white men and their lion hounds could never track the lion now. He walked with the wind at his back. It would cover all signs of the cattle too; the wet flakes would cling to the fence wire and freeze into a white crust; and the wire he had cut away and the gaping hole in the fence would be lost in the whiteout, hidden in snow on snow. Under his feet the dark mountain clay was saturated, making it slippery and soft; the ranch roads would be impassable with sticky mud, and it would be days before the cowboys could patrol the fences again. He smiled. Inside, his belly was smooth and soft, following the contours of the hills and holding the silence of the snow. He looked back at the way he had come: the snowflakes were swirling in tall chimneys of wind, filling his tracks like pollen sprinkled in the mountain lion's footprints. He shook his head the way the deer shook snow away and yelled out "ahooouuuh!" Then he ran across the last wide flat to the plateau rim.

The snow packed under his feet with a hollow sound. The big snowflakes still crowded behind him like the gauzy curtains in the woman's house. He stood on the rimrock and looked over the edge, down on the dark evergreens and piñon trees growing thick on the steep canyon slopes. He had to walk about a hundred yards north to find the place where the trail went down between two big piñon trees. He pulled a piñon cone from the snowy branches and shook the fat brown piñons into his hand. He ate them as he walked, cracking the shells one by one, working the nut meat loose with his tongue. He spit the shells into the snow below the trail and tried to see into the distance below the mesa, over the edge of the steep trail where her house was. Then behind him he heard someone singing. A man singing a chant. He stopped and listened. His stomach froze tight, and sweat ran down his ribs. His heart was pounding, but he was more startled than afraid.

> Hey-ya-ah-na-ah! Hey-ya-ah-na-ah!
> Ku-ru-tsu-eh-ah-eh-na! Ku-ru-tsu-eh-ah-eh-na!
> to the east below
> to the south below
> the winter people come.

> Hey-ya-ah-na-ah! He-ya-ah-na-ah!
> Ku-ru-tsu-eh-ah-eh-na! Ku-ru-tsu-eh-ah-eh-na!
> from the west above
> from the north above
> the winter people come.

> eh-ah-na-ah!
> eh-ah-na-ah!

> antlers of wind
> hooves of snow
> eyes glitter ice
> eyes glitter ice
> eh-ah-na-ah!
> eh-ah-na-ah!
> antlers of wind
> antlers of wind
> eh-ah-na-ah! eh-ah-na-ah!

The voice faded in and out, sometimes muffled or lost in the wind. He recognized phrases of the song; he had heard the hunters sing it, late in October, while they waited for the deer to be driven down from the high slopes by the cold winds and the snow. He waited until the hunter saw him before he spoke. He was carrying a small fork-horned buck across his shoulders, steadying the load by gripping the antlers in one hand and the hind legs in the other. He smiled when he saw Tayo.

He wore his hair long, tied back with white cotton string in the old style the men used to wear. He had long strings of sky-blue turquoise in his ears, and silver rings on four fingers of each hand. His face was wide and brown, and the skin was smooth and soft like an old woman's. Instead of a jacket, he was wearing a long fur vest sewn with gray rabbit pelts. The fur was old, and there were small bald patches where the bare skin showed through. The elbows of the brown flannel shirt were worn thin, as if his elbow bone might poke through anytime. But the cap he wore over his ears was made from tawny thick fur which shone when the wind ruffled through it; it looked like mountain-lion skin.

"You been hunting?" he asked, sliding the carcass down from his shoulders into the snow. Tayo noticed that he had already tied delicate blue feathers to the tips of the antlers.

"I was looking for some cattle."

"They are probably down below by now," he said, gesturing at the snow around them and the flakes still falling from the sky. Tayo nodded; he was looking at the old rifle slung across the hunter's back.

"That's an old one," he said, helping the hunter lift the deer up on his shoulders again.

"But it works good," he answered, starting down the trail ahead of Tayo, "it works real good. That's the main thing." He started singing again, this time it wasn't a Laguna song; it sounded like a Jemez song or maybe one from Zuni. He didn't want to interrupt the hunter to ask, but he was wondering where he was from, and where he had learned the Laguna song.

All he could see as he walked down the trail was snow, blurring the boundaries between the earth and the sky. At the bottom of the trail he stopped and kicked away the snow until wet sand was exposed. He was looking for some trace of the cattle, manure or some sign they had been there. The hunter shook his head.

"You better come inside first and have something to eat. You can look for them later." Tayo followed him to the yard. The leaves of the apricot tree were solid with snow. He looked toward the corral for the mare and the cattle, but it was snowing too hard to see anything. He smelled piñon smoke. The hunter motioned for him to step inside.

They stood side by side in front of the corner fireplace. The flames crackled and hissed when they shook the snow from their clothes. The wet leather of Tayo's boots and the hunter's elkskin leggings made steam rise around them like mountain fog after a storm. Tayo looked into the flames for a long time, feeling stronger and more calm as he got dry. When he finally turned around, they were together, the hunter kneeling beside the woman, placing pinches of cornmeal on the deer's nose, whispering to it.

They sat cross from him at the table. When they had finished eating, the hunter stood up and pointed out the window.

"The tree," he said to her, "you better fold up the blanket before the snow breaks the branches."

"I'm going out. I'll shake the snow off the branches," Tayo said, remembering how one spring when a late snow fell he had helped Josiah and Rocky shake the budded apple trees. She nodded, and walked into the bedroom. The black storm-pattern blanket was spread open across the gray flagstone. He watched her fold it.

He walked to the tree. It was a dome of snow with only the edges and tips of the leaves scattered green across the white. The early storm had caught the tree vulnerable with leaves that caught the snow and held it in drifts until the branches dragged the ground. He slipped his gloves out of his jacket pocket and took hold of the boughs gently, remembering that it was an old tree and the limbs were brittle. He shook the snow off carefully, moving around the tree from the east to the south, and from the west to the north, his breath steaming out in front of him. By the time he had shaken a circle of snow in a pile around the tree, the storm had passed. The mesas to the east were obscured by veils of falling snow, and the sky above them was dark blue. But overhead the snowflakes became sparse and floated down slowly of their own weight, now that the wind was gone. To the west the sky was opening into a high gray overcast, and where the clouds were rubbed thin, the streaks of sky were almost blue.

The mare whinnied, and he smiled at the way horses remember those who feed them. She was leaning against the corral gate with her ears pointed at him, alert. She pawed the snow impatiently and pushed her warm nose into his hands. There was a brown crust of blood on the raw skin of her forelegs where she had fallen. Tayo walked her to see how she moved, if she was lame. She followed him eagerly.

"Do you expect me to feed you after the way you dumped me up there?" He scratched her neck, feeling the thick winter hair; a few days before, it had been a summer coat and now suddenly the winter preparations had been made. He pushed her back from the gate and closed it.

She was combing her hair by the window, watching the sky. He watched her take sections of long hair in her hand and comb it with a crude wooden comb. There was something about the way she moved her arms around her head, and the soft shift of her breasts with each stroke of the comb, even her breathing, which was intimate. His face felt hot, and he looked away quickly before the hunter walked in.

"Aren't you going to ask me?"

"About what?" He tried to keep his voice calm and soft, but he was afraid she was referring to the night they slept together.

"You didn't even ask me what I thought when your horse came back to the corral without you."

"Oh."

"You haven't asked me about your spotted cattle either." She was smiling at him now, as if she had guessed the source of his embarrassment.

"I was going to ask you, but I didn't know if—ah, I mean, I wasn't sure if your husband—" She dropped the comb in her lap and clapped her hands together, laughing. The hunter came in from the back room.

"She's giving you a bad time, huh?" he said. He smiled too, but Tayo felt sweat between each of his fingers.

"She's got your cattle, you know." Tayo nodded and glanced at her; she was grinning at him and watching his face while the hunter spoke.

"Which way did they come down?"

He wanted to sound casual, but all he could think about was how the hunter seemed to know that he and the woman had met before.

"Yesterday afternoon," she said, "early. They came running down the big arroyo which comes down from the high canyon."

"But how did you catch them?"

"They went just like the run-off goes after a rainstorm, running right down the middle of the arroyo into the trap. That's why it's there. Livestock come down off the mountain that way. All I had to do was go down and close the gate behind them." She twisted her hair around her fingers and pinned it into a knot again. "We catch our horses the same way." She stood up.

"Come on. I'll show you."

He followed her down the steep trail into the big arroyo. He traced it back into the canyon with his eyes; the gray banks cut a winding track, its curves and twists the print of a snake's belly across the sand. It was only a continuation of the deep canyon orifice that revealed the interior layers of the mountain plateau. The gray clay was slippery, and it stuck to the soles of his boots. The trap for livestock was simple. The people had made such traps for a long time because they were easy to build and because they enable one or two people alone to corral many horses or cattle. The trap took advantage of the way horses and cattle, once they had been driven into a dry arroyo bed, would usually continue following the course of the arroyo because the sides of the banks were steep and difficult to escape; they could be driven deep into an arroyo that way until the banks were fifteen or twenty feet high, making it impossible for horses or cattle to escape. Arroyos might be dry for years, but when heavy rains did come, the run-off carried boulders and logs down the arroyo, where they snagged weeds and sticks and other debris. With a little work the debris could be shifted, small logs and dry limbs placed between boulders to form a barrier that only flood water could pour through.

He couldn't see the barrier to this trap, because it had been carefully built around a curve in the bank where the animals could not see it until after they had gone through the opening. Almost anything could be used for a gate, but, here, unskinned juniper poles had been strung together with baling wire, making them almost indistinguishable from the other driftwood and dry brush collected around the boulders and logs on either side of the gate. Once the animals were inside the trap, it was easy to drag the gate across the opening.

The storm left the sky thin and dappled gray, like a molted snakeskin. "An early snow," he said, "maybe it will be a wet winter. A good year next year."

She didn't say anything; she was stepping carefully over the snow, which had drifted in some places deeper than the tops of her moccasins. The clay and snow were churned into a muddy trench along the gate where the cattle had milled around, pushing their bony heads against the juniper poles, working for another escape.

He followed her inside and pulled the gate closed behind them. She walked close to the arroyo bank to avoid the manure and mud. The cattle backed into the far left corner of the barrier; their eyes were wide and frightened, and some were pawing the mud. Their breathing formed a single cloud of steam that drifted up, floating away over the banks of the arroyo. As they walked closer, the cows crowded closer together, and some of them lowered their heads and snorted as if they were fending off coyotes. He didn't like being on foot in the corral with them, because he suspected that human beings mattered very little to them, and it was only the size of the horse, not the rider, which they respected. But the woman was not afraid. She stepped closer to the cattle, bending down to inspect their bellies and legs, walking a half circle in the muddy snow, looking at all of them. They watched her tensely.

The snow had melted into their hides, washing out the dirt and manure, leaving them silky white; the spots were golden brown. The butterfly brand and Auntie's rafter 4 were barely visible through the heavy new growth of winter hair. Josiah had wanted something more than the stupid drooling Herefords the white ranchers had, something more than animals that had to be driven to water like sheep, and whose bellies shrank around their ribs before they would eat cactus or climb the ridges for brush and bark.

"My uncle was looking for cattle that could survive drought and hard years."

She stepped back from them and nodded her head. Her moccasins were muddy.

"It's a wonder you got this many back again," she said. "Look." She pointed at the necks of the cows closest to her. Rope burns left dark scabby welts in half circles. Strips of hide were missing around their fetlocks.

"Texas roping," she said. "They wanted these Mexican cattle because they are fast and tough. And no loss to them when they happen to break the legs or the neck."

He had never heard it called Texas roping before; he knew it as steer roping, because they used old stringy Mexican steers rather than more expensive cows or calves. It had come from Texas with the cowboys, and it was almost too simple: they rode massive powerful roping horses that were capable of jerking down a steer running full speed, knocking the animal unconscious and frequently injuring or killing it. It was the sport of aging cowboys, too slow and heavy to dismount to wrestle down and tie the animal as they did in calf roping and team tying. He had seen it only once. At the rodeo grounds in Grants. The steer had to stay down for ten seconds before the roper's time could be recorded. The jackpot had been three hundred dollars that day, and the red-faced white man who took it turned in a record time: six seconds; but when the men loosened the rope on the steer's neck, it did not move. They dragged it away behind two horses, one of the forelegs dangling in the hide, shattered. The anger made him lightheaded, but he did not talk about this other dimension of their perversion which, like the hunting of the mountain lion, was their idea of "sport" and fun.

They walked back to the corral. She watched him shake the snow off the saddle blanket and lead the mare to drink at the spring. He looked up at the sky; the sun was in the center of the south sky, covered with high gray clouds.

"I wonder if they'll come looking for the cattle?"

She shrugged her shoulders, unconcerned.

"They won't come down here," she said.

"Why not?"

She gave him a look that chilled him. She must have seen his fear because she smiled and said, "Because of all the snow up there. What else?" She was teasing again. He shook his head.

"I'll get back here and get them as soon as I can," he told her. He took a long time tightening the cinch and checking the leather lacing in the stirrups. He wanted to say something to let her know how good it felt to have her standing close to him. But the hunter was still in the house, so he said nothing. As he stepped over to tie the bedroll behind the saddle, he brushed against her side gently, and she smiled. She knew. She walked close to him as he led the mare out of the corral gate. She pointed at the dusky clouds in the northeast sky.

"It will be cold tonight. The mud and snow will freeze."

"I hope so," he said, "otherwise, the truck will get stuck so deep we won't be able to get it out until next spring." She laughed and nodded.

"Good-bye," he said.

"I'll be seeing you," she said.

When he turned to wave at her, she was gone.

❖❖❖

Humaweepi, the Warrior Priest

The old man didn't really teach him much; mostly they just lived. Occasionally Humaweepi would meet friends his own age who still lived with their families in the pueblo, and they would ask him what he was doing; they seemed disappointed when he told them.

"That's nothing," they would say.

Once this had made Humaweepi sad and his uncle noticed. "Oh," he said when Humaweepi told him, "that shows you how little they know."

They returned to the pueblo for the ceremonials and special days. His uncle stayed in the kiva with the other priests, and Humaweepi usually stayed with clan members because his mother and father had been very old when he was born and now they were gone. Sometimes during these stays, when the pueblo was full of the activity and excitement of the dances or the fiesta when the Christians paraded out of the pueblo church carrying the saint, Humaweepi would wonder why he was living out in the hills with the old man. When he was twelve he thought he had it all figured out: the old man just wanted someone to live with him and help him with the goat and to chop wood and carry water. But it was peaceful in this place, and Humaweepi discovered that after all these years of sitting beside his uncle in the evenings, he knew the songs and chants for all the seasons, and he was beginning to learn the prayers for the trees and plants and animals. "Oh," Humaweepi said to himself, "I have been learning all this time and I didn't even know it."

Once the old man told Humaweepi to prepare for a long trip.

"Overnight?"

The old man nodded.

So Humaweepi got out a white cotton sack and started filling it with jerked venison, piki bread, and dried apples. But the old man shook his head sternly. It was late June then, so Humaweepi didn't bother to bring the blankets; he had learned to sleep on the ground like the old man did.

"Human beings are special," his uncle had told him once, "which means they can do anything. They can sleep on the ground like the doe and fawn."

And so Humaweepi had learned how to find the places in the scrub-oak thickets where the deer had slept, where the dry oak leaves were arranged into nests. This is where he and his uncle slept, even in the autumn when the nights were cold and Humaweepi could hear the leaves snap in the middle of the night and drift to the ground.

Sometimes they carried food from home, but often they went without food or blankets. When Humaweepi asked him what they would eat, the old man had waved his hand at the sky and earth around them. "I am a human being, Humaweepi," he said; "I eat anything." On these trips they had gathered grass roots and washed them in little sandstone basins made by the wind to catch rain water. The roots had a rich, mealy taste. Then they left the desert below and climbed into the mesa country, and the old man had led Humaweepi to green leafy vines hanging from crevasses in the face of the sandstone cliffs. "Wild grapes," he said as he dropped some tiny dark-purple berries into Humaweepi's open palms. And in the high mountains there were wild iris roots and the bulbs from wild tulips which grew among the lacy ferns and green grass beside the mountain streams. They had gone out like this in each season. Summer and fall, and finally, spring and winter. "Winter isn't easy," the old man had said. "All the animals are hungry—not just you."

So this time, when his uncle shook his head at the food, Humaweepi left it behind as he had many times before. His uncle took the special leather pouch off the nail on the wall, and Humaweepi pulled his own buckskin bundle out from under his mattress. Inside he had a few objects of his own. A dried blossom. Fragile and yellow. A smooth pink quartz crystal in the shape of a star. Tiny turquoise beads the color of a summer sky. And a black obsidian arrowhead, shiny and sharp. They each had special meaning to him, and the old man had instructed him to assemble these things with special meaning. "Someday maybe you will derive strength from these things." That's what the old man had said.

They walked west toward the distant blue images of the mountain peaks. The water in the Rio Grande was still cold. Humaweepi was aware of the dampness on his feet: when he got back from his journey he decided he would make sandals for himself because it took hours for his boots to dry out again. His uncle wore old sandals woven from twisted yucca fiber and they dried out almost immediately. The old man didn't approve of boots and shoes—bad for you, he said. In the winter he wore buckskin moccasins and in the warm months, these yucca sandals.

They walked all day, steadily, stopping occasionally when the old man found a flower or herb or stone that he wanted Humaweepi to see. And it seemed to Humaweepi that he had learned the names of everything, and he said so to his uncle.

The old man frowned and poked at a small blue flower with his walking stick. "That's what a priest must know," he said and walked rapidly, then, pointing at stones and shrubs. "How old are you?" he demanded.

"Nineteen," Humaweepi answered.

"All your life," he said, "every day, I have been teaching you."

After that they walked along in silence, and Humaweepi began to feel anxious; all of a sudden he knew that something was going to happen on this journey. That night they reached the white sandstone cliffs at the foot of the mountain foothills. At the base of these cliffs were shallow overhangs with sandy floors. They slept in the sand under the rock overhang; in the night Humaweepi woke up to the call of a young owl; the sky was bright with stars and a half-moon. The smell of the night air made him shiver and he buried himself more deeply in the cliff sand.

In the morning they gathered tumbleweed sprouts that were succulent and tender. As they climbed the cliffs there were wild grapevines, and under the fallen leaves around the vine roots, the old man uncovered dried grapes shrunken into tiny sweet raisins. By noon they had reached the first of the mountain streams. There they washed and drank water and rested.

The old man frowned and pointed at Humaweepi's boots. "Take them off," he told Humaweepi; "leave them here until we come back."

So Humaweepi pulled off his cowboy boots and put them under a lichen-covered boulder near a big oak tree where he could find them. Then Humaweepi relaxed, feeling the coolness of air on his bare feet. He watched his uncle, dozing in the sun with his back against a big pine. The old man's hair had been white and long ever since Humaweepi could remember; but the old face was changing, and Humaweepi could see the weariness there—a weariness not from their little journey but from a much longer time in this world. Someday he will die, Humaweepi was thinking. He will be gone and I will be by myself. I will have to do the things he did. I will have to take care of things.

Humaweepi had never seen the lake before. It appeared suddenly as they reached the top of a hill covered with aspen trees. Humaweepi looked at his uncle and was going to ask him about the lake, but the old man was singing and feeding corn pollen from his leather pouch to the mountain winds. Humaweepi stared at the lake and listened to the songs. The songs were snowstorms with sounds as soft and cold as snowflakes; the songs were spring rain and wild ducks returning. Humaweepi could hear this; he could hear his uncle's voice become the night wind—high-pitched and whining in the trees. Time was lost and there was only the space, the depth, the distance of the lake surrounded by the mountain peaks.

When Humaweepi looked up from the lake he noticed that the sun had moved down into the western part of the sky. He looked around to find his uncle. The old man was below him, kneeling on the edge of the lake, touching a big gray boulder and singing softly. Humaweepi made his way down the narrow rocky trail to the edge of the lake. The water was crystal and clear like air; Humaweepi could see the golden rainbow colors of the trout that lived there. Finally the old man motioned for Humaweepi to come to him. He pointed at the gray boulder that lay half in the lake and half on the shore. It was then that Humaweepi saw what it was. The bear. Magic creature of the mountains, powerful ally to men. Humaweepi unrolled his buckskin bundle and picked up the tiny beads—sky-blue turquoise and coral that was dark red. He sang the bear song and stepped into the icy, clear water to lay the beads on bear's head, gray granite rock, resting above the lake, facing west.

> "Bear
> resting in the mountains
> sleeping by the lake
> Bear
> I come to you, a man,
> to ask you:
> Stand beside us in our battles
> walk with us in peace.
> Bear
> I ask you for your power
> I am the warrior priest.
> I ask you for your power
> I am the warrior priest."

It wasn't until he had finished singing the song that Humaweepi realized what the words said. He turned his head toward the old man. He smiled at Humaweepi and nodded his head. Humaweepi nodded back.

Humaweepi and his friend were silent for a long time. Finally Humaweepi said, "I'll tell you what my uncle told me, one winter, before he left. We took a trip to the mountain. It was early January, but the sun was warm and down here the snow was gone. We left early in the morning when the sky in the east was dark gray and the brightest star was still shining low in the western sky. I remember he didn't wear his ceremonial moccasins; he wore his old yucca sandals. I asked him about that.

"He said, 'Oh, you know the badger and the squirrel. Same shoes summer and winter,' but I think he was making that up, because when we got to the sandstone cliffs he buried the sandals in the sandy bottom of the cave where we slept and after that he walked on bare feet—up the cliff and along the mountain trail.

"There was snow on the shady side of the trees and big rocks, but the path we followed was in the sun and it was dry. I could hear melting snow—the icy water trickling down into the little streams and the little streams flowing into the big sream in the canyon where yellow bee flowers grow all summer. The sun felt warm on my body, touching me, but my breath still made steam in the cold mountain air.

"'Aren't your feet cold?' I asked him.

"He stopped and looked at me for a long time, then shook his head. 'Look at these old feet,' he said. 'Do you see any corns or bunions?'

"I shook my head.

"'That's right,' he said, 'my feet are beautiful. No one has feet like these. Especially you people who wear shoes and boots.' He walked on ahead before he said anything else. 'You have seen babies, haven't you?' he asked.

"I nodded, but I was wondering what this had to do with the old man's feet.

"'Well, then you've noticed their grandmothers and their mothers, always worried about keeping the feet warm. But have you watched the babies? Do they care? No!' the old man said triumphantly, 'they do not care. They play outside on a cold winter day, no shoes, no jacket, because they aren't cold.' He hiked on, moving rapidly, excited by his own words; then he stopped at the stream. 'But human beings are what they are. It's not long before they are taught to be cold and they cry for their shoes.'

"The old man started digging around the edge of a stream, using a crooked, dry branch to poke through the melting snow. 'Here,' he said as he gave me a fat, round root, 'try this.'

"I squatted at the edge off the rushing, swirling water, full of mountain dirt, churning, swelling, and rolling—rich and brown and muddy with ice pieces flashing in the sun. I held the root motionless under the force of the stream water; the ice coldness of the water felt pure and clear as the ice that clung to the rocks in midstream. When I pulled my hand back it was stiff. I shook it and the root and lifted them high toward the sky.

"The old man laughed, and his mouth was full of the milky fibers of the root. He walked up the hill, away from the sound of the muddy stream surging through the snowbanks. At the top of the hill there was a grove of big aspens; it was colder, and the snow hadn't melted much.

"'Your feet,' I said to him. 'They'll freeze.'

"The snow was up to my ankles now. He was sitting on a fallen aspen, with his feet stretched out in front of him and his eyes half closed, facing into the sun.

"'Does the wolf freeze his feet?' the old man asked me.

"I shook my head.

"'Well, then,' he said.

"'But you aren't a wolf,' I started to say.

"The old man's eyes opened wide and then looked at me narrowly, sharply, squinting and shining. He gave a long, wailing, wolf cry with his head raised toward the winter sky.

"It was all white—pale white—the sky, the aspens bare white, smooth and white as the snow frozen on the ground. The wolf cry echoed off the rocky mountain slopes around us; in the distance I thought I heard a wailing answer."

◆◆◆

Yellow Woman

ONE

My thigh clung to his with dampness, and I watched the sun rising up through the tamaracks and willows. The small brown water birds came to the river and hopped across the mud, leaving brown scratches in the alkali-white crust They bathed in the river silently. I could hear the water, almost at our feet where the narrow fast channel bubbled and washed green ragged moss and fern leaves. I looked at him beside me, rolled in the red blanket on the white river sand. I cleaned the sand out of the cracks between my toes, squinting because the sun was above the willow trees. I looked at him for the last time, sleeping on the white river sand.

I felt hungry and followed the river south the way we had come the afternoon before, following our footprints that were already blurred by lizard tracks and bug trails. The horses were still lying down, and the black one whinnied when he saw me but he did not get up—maybe it was because the corral was made out of thick cedar branches and the horses had not yet felt the sun like I had. I tried to look beyond the pale red mesas to the pueblo. I knew it was there, even if I could not see it, on the sandrock hill above the river, the same river that moved past me now and had reflected the moon last night.

The horse felt warm underneath me. He shook his head and pawed the sand. The bay whinnied and leaned against the gate trying to follow, and I remembered him asleep in the red blanket beside the river. I slid off the horse and tied him close to the other horse. I walked north with the river again, and the white sand broke loose in footprints over footprints.

"Wake up."

He moved in the blanket and turned his face to me with his eyes still closed. I knelt down to touch him.

"I'm leaving."

He smiled now, eyes still closed. "You are coming with me, remember?" He sat up now with his bare dark chest and belly in the sun.

"Where?"

"To my place."

"And will I come back?"

He pulled his pants on. I walked away from him, feeling him behind me and smelling the willows.

"Yellow Woman," he said.

I turned to face him. "Who are you?" I asked.

He laughed and knelt on the low, sandy bank, washing his face in the river. "Last night you guessed my name, and you knew why I had come."

I stared past him at the shallow moving water and tried to remember the night, but I could only see the moon in the water and remember his warmth around me.

"But I only said that you were him and that I was Yellow Woman—I'm not really her—I have my own name and I come from the pueblo on the other side of the mesa. Your name is Silva and you are a stranger I met by the river yesterday afternoon."

He laughed softly. "What happened yesterday has nothing to do with what you will do today, Yellow Woman."

"I know—that's what I'm saying—the old stories about the ka'tsina spirit and Yellow Woman can't mean us."

My old grandpa liked to tell those stories best. There is one about Badger and Coyote who went hunting and were gone all day and when the sun was going down they found a house. There was a girl living there alone, and she had light hair and eyes and she told them that they could sleep with her. Coyote wanted to be with her all night so he sent Badger into a prairie-dog hole, telling him he thought he saw something in it. As soon as Badger crawled in, Coyote blocked up the entrance with rocks and hurried back to Yellow Woman.

"Come here," he said gently.

He touched my neck and I moved close to him to feel his breathing and to hear his heart. I was wondering if Yellow Woman had known who she was—if she knew that she would become part of the stories. Maybe she'd had another name that her husband and relatives called her so that only the ka'tsina from the north and the storytellers would know her as Yellow Woman. But I didn't go on; I felt him all around me, pushing me down into the white river sand.

Yellow Woman went away with the spirit from the north and lived with him and his relatives She was gone for a long time, but then one day she came back and she brought twin boys.

"Do you know the story?"

"What story?" He smiled and pulled me close to him as he said this. I was afraid lying there on the red blanket. All I could know was the way he felt, warm, damp, his body beside me. This is the way it happens in the stories, I was thinking, with no thought beyond the moment she meets the ka'tsina spirit and they go.

"I don't have to go. What they tell in stories was real only then, back in time immemorial, like they say."

He stood up and pointed at my clothes tangled in the blanket. "Let's go," he said.

I walked beside him, breathing hard becaue he walked fast, his hand around my wrist. I had stopped to pull away from him, because his hand felt cool and the sun was high, drying the river bed into alkali. I will see someone, eventually I will see someone, and then I will be certain that he is only a man—some man from nearby—and I will be sure that I am not Yellow Woman. Because she is from out of time past and I live now and I've been to school and there are highways and pickup trucks that Yellow Woman never saw.

It was an easy ride north on horseback. I watched the change from the cottonwood trees along the river to the junipers that brushed past us in the foothills, and finally there were only piñons, and when I looked up at the rim of the mountain plateau I could see pine trees growing on the edge. Once I stopped to look down, but the pale sandstone had disappeared and the river was gone and the dark lava hills were all around. He touched my hand, not speaking, but always singing softly a mountain song and looking into my eyes.

I felt hungry and wondered what they were doing at home now—my mother, my grandmother, my husband, and the baby. Cooking breakfast, saying, "Where did she go?—maybe kidnaped," and Al going to the tribal police with the details: "She went walking along the river."

The house was made with black lava rock and red mud. It was high above the spreading miles of arroyos and long mesas. I smelled a mountain smell of pitch and buck brush. I stood there beside the black horse, looking down on the small, dim country we had passed, and I shivered.

"Yellow Woman, come inside where it's warm."

TWO

He lit a fire in the stove. It was an old stove with a round belly and an enamel coffeepot on top. There was only the stove, some faded Navajo blankets, and a bedroll and cardboard box. The floor was made of smooth adobe plaster, and there was one small window facing east. He pointed at the box.

"There's some potatoes and the frying pan." He sat on the floor with his arms around his knees pulling them close to his chest and he watched me fry the potatoes. I didn't mind him watching me because he was always watching me—he had been watching me since I came upon him sitting on the river bank trimming leaves from a willow twig with his knife. We ate from the pan and he wiped the grease from his fingers on his Levis.

"Have you brought women here before?" He smiled and kept chewing, so I said, "Do you always use the same tricks?"

"What tricks?" He looked at me like he didn't understand.

"The story about being a ka'tsina from the mountains. The story about Yellow Woman."

Silva was silent; his face was calm.

"I don't believe it. Those stories couldn't happen now," I said.

He shook his head and said softly, "But someday they will talk about us, and they will say, 'Those two lived long ago when things like this happened.'"

He stood up and went out. I ate the rest of the potatoes and thought about things—about the noise the stove was making and the sound of the mountain wind outside. I remembered yesterday and the day before, and then I went outside.

I walked past the corral to the edge where the narrow trail cut through the black rim rock. I was standing in the sky with nothing around me but the wind that came down from the blue mountain peak behind me. I could see faint mountain images in the distance miles across the vast spread of mesas and valleys and plains. I wondered who was over there to feel the mountain wind on those sheer blue edges—who walks on the pine needles in those blue mountains.

"Can you see the pueblo?" Silva was standing behind me.

I shook my head. "We're too far away."

"From here I can see the world." He stepped out on the edge. "The Navajo reservation begins over there." He pointed to the east. "The Pueblo boundaries are over here." He looked below us to the south, where the narrow trail seemed to come from. "The Texans have their ranches over there, starting with that valley, the Concho Valley. The Mexicans run some cattle over there too."

"Do you ever work for them?"

"I steal from them," Silva answered. The sun was dropping behind us and shadows were filling the land below. I turned away from the edge that dropped forever into the valleys below.

"I'm cold," I said; "I'm going inside." I started wondering about this man who could speak the Pueblo language so well but who lived on a mountain and rustled cattle. I decided that this man Silva must be Navajo, because Pueblo men didn't do things like that.

"You must be a Navajo."

Silva shook his head gently. "Little Yellow Woman," he said, "you never give up, do you? I have told you who I am. The Navajo people know me, too." He knelt down and unrolled the bedroll and spread the extra blankets out on a piece of canvas. The sun was down, and the only light in the house came from outside—the dim orange light from sundown.

I stood there and waited for him to crawl under the blankets.

"What are you waiting for?" he said, and I lay down beside him. He undressed me slowly like the night before beside the river—kissing my face gently and running his hands up and down my belly and legs. He took off my pants and then he laughed.

"Why are you laughing?"

"You are breathing so hard."

I pulled away from him and turned my back to him.

He pulled me around and pinned me down with his arms and chest. "You don't understand, do you, little Yellow Woman? You will do what I want."

And again he was all around me with his skin slippery against mine, and I was afraid because I understood that his strength could hurt me. I lay underneath him and I knew that he could destroy me. But later, while he slept beside me, I touched his face and I had a feeling—the kind of feeling for him that overcame me that morning along the river. I kissed him on the forehead and he reached out for me.

When I woke up in the morning he was gone. It gave me a strange feeling because for a long time I sat there on the blankets and looked around the little house for some object of his—some proof that he had been there or maybe that he was coming back. Only the blankets and the cardboard box remained. The .30–30 that had been leaning in the corner was gone, and so was the knife I had used the night before. He was gone, and I had my chance to go now. But first I had to eat, because I knew it would be a long walk home.

I found some dried apricots in the cardboard box, and I sat down on a rock at the edge of the plateau rim. There was no wind and the sun warmed me. I was surrounded by silence. I drowsed with apricots in my mouth, and I didn't believe that there were highways or railroads or cattle to steal.

When I woke up, I stared down at my feet in the black mountain dirt. Little black ants werre swarming over the pine needles around my foot. They must have smelled the apricots. I thought about my family far below me. They would be wondering about me, because this had never happened to me before. The tribal police would file a report. But if old Grandpa weren't dead he would tell them what happened—he would laugh and say, "Stolen by a ka'tsina, a mountain spirit. She'll come home—they usually do." There are enough of them to handle things. My mother and grandmother will raise the baby like they raised me. Al will find someone else, and they will go on like before, except that there will be a story about the day I disappeared while I was walking along the river. Silva had come for me; he said he had. I did not decide to go. I just went. Moonflowers blossom in the sand hills before dawn, just as I followed him. That's what I was thinking as I wandered along the trail through the pine trees.

It was noon when I got back. When I saw the stone house I remembered that I had meant to go home. But that didn't seem important any more, maybe because there were little blue flowers growing in the meadow behind the stone house and the gray squirrels were playing in the pines next to the house. The horses were standing in the corral, and there was a beef carcass hanging on the shady side of a big pine in front of the house. Flies buzzed around the clotted blood that hung from the carcass. Silva was washing his hands in a bucket full of water. He must have heard me coming because he spoke to me without turning to face me.

"I've been waiting for you."

"I went walking in the big pine trees."

I looked into the bucket full of bloody water with brown-and-white animal hairs floating in it. Silva stood there letting his hand drip, examining me intently.

"Are you coming with me?"

"Where?" I asked him.

"To sell the mat in Marquez."

"If you're sure it's O.K."

"I wouldn't ask you if it wasn't," he answered.

He sloshed the water around in the bucket before he dumped it out and set the bucket upside down near the door. I followed him to the corral and watched him saddle the horses. Even beside the horses he looked tall, and I asked him again if he wasn't Navajo. He didn't say anything; he just shook his head and kept cinching up the saddle.

"But Navajos are tall."

"Get on the horse," he said, "and let's go."

The last thing he did before we started down the steep trail was to grab the .30–30 from the corner. He slid the rifle into the scabbard that hung from his saddle.

"Do they ever try to catch you?" I asked.

"They don't know who I am."

"Then why did you bring the rifle?"

"Because we are going to Marquez where the Mexicans live."

THREE

The trail leveled out on a narrow ridge that was steep on both sides like an animal spine. On one side I could see where the trail went around the rocky gray hills and disappeared into the southeast where the pale sand-rock mesas stood in the distance near my home. On the other side was a trail that went west, and as I looked far into the distance I thought I saw the little town. But Silva said no, that I was looking in the wrong place, that I just thought I saw houses. After that I quit looking off into the distance; it was hot and the wildflowers were closing up their deep-yellow petals. Only the waxy cactus flowers bloomed in the bright sun, and I saw every color that a cactus blossom can be; the white ones and the red ones were still buds, but the purple and the yellow were blossoms, open full and the most beautiful of all.

Silva saw him before I did. The white man was riding a big gray horse, coming up the trail toward us. He ws traveling fast and the gray horse's feet sent rocks rolling off the trail into the dry tumbleweeds. Silva motioned for me to stop and we watched the white man. He didn't see us right away, but finally his horse whinnied at our horses and he stopped. He looked at us briefly before he loped the gray horse across the three hundred yards that separated us. He stopped his horse in front of Silva, and his young fat face was shadowed by the brim of his hat. He didn't look mad, but his small, pale eyes moved from the blood-soaked gunny sacks hanging from my saddle to Silva's face and then back to my face.

"Where did you get the fresh meat?" the white man asked.

"I've been hunting," Silva said, and when he shifted his weight in the saddle the leather creaked.

"The hell you have, Indian. You've been rustling cattle. We've been looking for the thief for a long time."

The rancher was fat, and sweat began to soak through his white cowboy shirt and the wet cloth stuck to the thick rolls of belly fat. He almost seemed to be panting from the exertion of talking, and he smelled rancid, maybe because Silva scared him.

Silva turned to me and smiled. "Go back up the mountain, Yellow Woman."

The white man got angry when he heard Silva speak in a language he couldn't understand. "Don't try anything, Indian. Just keep riding to Marquez. We'll call the state police from there."

The rancher must have been unarmed because he was very frightened and if he had a gun he would have pulled it out then. I turned my horse around and the rancher yelled, "Stop!" I looked at Silva for an instant and there was something ancient and dark—something I could feel in my stomach—in his eyes, and when I glanced at his hand I saw his finger on the trigger of the .30–30 that was still in the saddle scabbard. I slapped my horse across the flank and the sacks of raw meat swung against my knees as the horse leaped up the trail. It was hard to keep my balance, and once I thought I felt the saddle slipping backward; it was because of this that I could not look back.

I didn't stop until I reached the ridge where the trail forked. The horse was breathing deep gasps and there was a dark film of sweat on its neck. I looked down in the direction I had come from, but I couldn't see the place. I waited. The wind came up and pushed warm air past me. I looked up at the sky, pale blue and full of thin clouds and fading vapor trails left by jets.

I think four shots were fired—I remember hearing four hollow explosions that reminded me of deer hunting. There could have been more shots after that, but I couldn't have heard them because my horse was running again and the loose rocks were making too much noise as they scattered around his feet.

Horses have a hard time running downhill, but I went that way instead of uphill to the mountain because I thought it was safer. I felt better with the horse running southeast past the round gray hills that were covered with cedar trees and black lava rock. When I got to the plain in the distance I could see the dark green patches of tamaracks that grew along the river; and beyond the river I could see the beginning of the pale sandrock mesas. I stopped the horse and looked back to see if anyone was coming; then I got off the horse and turned the horse around, wondering if it would go back to its corral under the pines on the mountain. It looked back at me for a moment and then plucked a mouthful of green tumbleweeds before it trotted back up the trail with its ears pointed forward, carrying its head daintily to one side to avoid stepping on the dragging reins. When the horse disappeared over the last hill, the gunny sacks full of meat were still swinging and bouncing.

FOUR

I walked toward the river on a wood-hauler's road that I knew would eventually lead to the paved road. I was thinking about waiting beside the road for someone to drive by, but by the time I got to the pavement I had decided it wasn't very far to walk if I followed the river back the way Silva and I had come.

The river water tasted good, and I sat in the shade under a cluster of silvery willows. I thought about Silva, and I felt sad at leaving him; still, there was something strange about him, and I tried to figure it out all the way back home.

I came back to the place on the river bank where he had been sitting the first time I saw him. The green willow leaves that he had trimmed from the branch were still lying there, wilted in the sand. I saw the leaves and I wanted to go back to him—to kiss him and to touch him—but the mountains were too far away now. And I told myself, because I believe it, he will come back sometime and be waiting again by the river.

I followed the path up from the river into the village. The sun was getting low, and I could smell supper cooking when I got to the screen door of my house. I could hear their voices inside—my mother was telling my grandmother how to fix the Jell-o and my husband, Al, was playing with the baby. I decided to tell them that some Navajo had kidnaped me, but I was sorry that old Grandpa wasn't alive to hear my story because it was the Yellow Woman stories he liked to tell best.

◇◇◇

Tony's Story

ONE

It happened one summer when the sky was wide and hot and the summer rains did not come; the sheep were thin, and the tumbleweeds turned brown and died. Leon came back from the army. I saw him standing by the Ferris wheel across from the people who came to sell melons and chili on San Lorenzo's Day. He yelled at me, "Hey Tony—over here!" I was embarrassed to hear him yell so loud, but then I saw the wine bottle with the brown-paper sack crushed around it.

"How's it going, buddy?"

He grabbed my hand and held it tight like a white man. He was smiling. "It's good to be home again. They asked me to dance tomorrow—it's only the Corn Dance, but I hope I haven't forgotten what to do."

"You'll remember—it will all come back to you when you hear the drum." I was happy, because I knew that Leon was once more a part of the pueblo. The sun was dusty and low in the west, and the procession passed by us, carrying San Lorenzo back to his niche in the church.

"Do you want to get something to eat?" I asked.

Leon laughed and patted the bottle. "No, you're the only one who

needs to eat. Take this dollar—they're selling hamburgers over there."
He pointed past the merry-go-round to a stand with cotton candy and a
snow-cone machine.

It was then that I saw the cop pushing his way through the crowds of
people gathered around the hamburger stand and bingo-game tent; he
came steadily toward us. I remembered Leon's wine and looked to see if
the cop was watching us; but he was wearing dark glasses and I couldn't
see his eyes.

He never said anything before he hit Leon in the face with his fist.
Leon collapsed into the dust, and the paper sack floated in the wine and
pieces of glass. He didn't move and blood kept bubbling out of his mouth
and nose. I could hear a siren. People crowded around Leon and kept
pushing me away. The tribal policemen knelt over Leon, and one of them
looked up at the state cop and asked what was going on. The big cop
didn't answer. He was staring at the little patterns of blood in the dust
near Leon's mouth. The dust soaked up the blood almost before it
dripped to the ground—it had been a very dry summer. The cop didn't
leave until they laid Leon in the back of the paddy wagon.

The moon was already high when we got to the hospital in Albuquerque. We waited a long time outside the emergency room with Leon
propped between us. Siow and Gaisthea kept asking me, "What happened, what did Leon say to the cop?" and I told them how we were just
standing there, ready to buy hamburgers—we'd never even seen him before. They put stitches around Leon's mouth and gave him a shot; he was
lucky, they said—it could've been a broken jaw instead of broken teeth.

TWO

They dropped me off near my house. The moon had moved lower into
the west and left the close rows of houses in long shadows. Stillness
breathed around me, and I wanted to run from the feeling behind me in
the dark; the stories about witches ran with me. That night I had a
dream—the big cop was pointing a long bone at me—they always use
human bones, and the whiteness flashed silver in the moonlight where
he stood. He didn't have a human face—only little, round, white-rimmed
eyes on a black ceremonial mask.

Leon was better in a few days. But he was bitter, and all he could talk
about was the cop. "I'll kill the big bastard if he comes around here
again," Leon kept saying.

With something like the cop it is better to forget, and I tried to make
Leon understand. "It's over now. There's nothing you can do."

I wondered why men who came back from the army were troublemakers on the reservation. Leon even took it before the pueblo meeting. They discussed it, and the old men decided that Leon shouldn't have been drinking. The interpreter read a passage out of the revised pueblo law-and-order code about possessing intoxicants on the reservation, so we got up and left.

Then Leon asked me to go with him to Grants to buy a roll of barbed wire for his uncle. On the way we stopped at Cerritos for gas, and I went into the store for some pop. He was inside. I stopped in the doorway and turned around before he saw me, but if he really was what I feared, then he would not need to see me—he already knew we were there. Leon was waiting with the truck engine running almost like he knew what I would say.

"Let's go—the big cop's inside."

Leon gunned it and the pickup skidded back on the highway. He glanced back in the rearview mirror. "I didn't see his car."

"Hidden," I said.

Leon shook his head. "He can't do it again. We are just as good as them."

The guys who came back always talked like that.

THREE

The sky was hot and empty. The half-grown tumbleweeds were dried-up flat and brown beside the highway, and across the valley heat shimmered above wilted fields of corn. Even the mountains high beyond the pale sandrock mesas were dusty blue. I was afraid to fall asleep so I kept my eyes on the blue mountains—not letting them close—soaking in the heat; and then I knew why the drought had come that summer.

Leon shook me. "He's behind us—the cop's following us!"

I looked back and saw the red light on top of the car whirling around, and I could make out the dark image of a man, but where the face should have been there were only the silvery lenses of the dark glasses he wore.

"Stop, Leon! He wants us to stop!"

Leon pulled over and stopped on the narrow gravel shoulder.

"What in the hell does he want?" Leon's hands were shaking.

Suddenly the cop was standing beside the truck, gesturing for Leon to roll down his window. He pushed his head inside, grinding the gum in his mouth; the smell of Doublemint was all around us.

"Get out. Both of you."

I stood beside Leon in the dry weeds and tall yellow grass that broke through the asphalt and rattled in the wind. The cop studied Leon's driver's license. I avoided his face—I knew that I couldn't look at his eyes, so I stared at his black half-Wellingtons, with the black uniform cuffs pulled over them; but my eyes kept moving, upward past the black gun belt. My legs were quivering and I tried to keep my eyes away from his. But it was like the time when I was very little and my parents warned me not to look into the masked dancers' eyes because they would grab me, and my eyes would not stop.

"What's your name?" His voice was high-pitched and it distracted me from the meaning of the words.

I remember Leon said, "He doesn't understand English so good," and finally I said that I was Antonio Sousea, while my eyes strained to look beyond the silver frosted glasses that he wore; but only my distorted face and squinting eyes reflected back.

And then the cop stared at us for a while, silent; finally he laughed and chewed his gum some more slowly. "Where were you going?"

"To Grants." Leon spoke English very clearly. "Can we go now?"

Leon was twisting the key chain around his fingers, and I felt the sun everywhere. Heat swelled up from the asphalt and when cars went by, hot air and motor smell rushed past us.

"I don't like smart guys, Indian. It's because of you bastards that I'm here. They transferred me here because of Indians. They thought there wouldn't be as many for me here. But I find them." He spit his gum into the weeds near my foot and walked back to the patrol car. It kicked up gravel and dust when he left.

We got back in the pickup, and I could taste sweat in my mouth, so I told Leon that we might as well go home since he would be waiting for us up ahead.

"He can't do this," Leon said. "We've got a right to be on this highway."

I couldn't understand why Leon kept talking about "rights," because it wasn't "rights" that he was after, but Leon didn't seem to understand; he couldn't remember the stories that old Teofilo told.

I didn't feel safe until we turned off the highway and I could see the pueblo and my own house. It was noon, and everybody was eating—the village seemed empty—even the dogs had crawled away from the heat. The door was open, but there was only silence, and I was afraid that something had happened to all of them. Then as soon as I opened the screen door the little kids started crying for more Kool-Aid, and my mother said "no," and it was noisy again like always. Grandfather commented that it had been a fast trip to Grants, and I said "yeah" and didn't explain because it would've only worried them.

"Leon goes looking for trouble—I wish you wouldn't hang around with him." My father didn't like trouble. But I knew that the cop was something terrible, and even to speak about it risked bringing it close to all of us; so I didn't say anything.

That afternoon Leon spoke with the Governor, and he promised to send letters to the Bureau of Indian Affairs and to the State Police Chief. Leon seemed satisfied with that. I reached into my pocket for the arrowhead on the piece of string.

"What's that for?"

I held it out to him. "Here, wear it around your neck—like mine. See? Just in case," I said, "for protection."

"You don't believe in *that*, do you?" He pointed to a .30–30 leaning against the wall. "I'll take this with me whenever I'm in the pickup."

"But you can't be sure that it will kill one of them."

Leon looked at me and laughed. "What's the matter," he said, "have they brainwashed you into believing that a .30–30 won't kill a white man?" He handed back the arrowhead. "Here, you wear two of them."

FOUR

Leon's uncle asked me if I wanted to stay at the sheep camp for a while. The lambs were big, and there wouldn't be much for me to do, so I told him I would. We left early, while the sun was still low and red in the sky. The highway was empty, and I sat there beside Leon imagining what it was like before there were highways or even horses. Leon turned off the highway onto the sheep-camp road that climbs around the sandstone mesas until suddenly all the trees are piñons.

Leon glanced in the rear-view mirror. "He's following us!"

My body began to shake and I wasn't sure if I would be able to speak. "There's no place left to hide. It follows us everywhere."

Leon looked at me like he didn't understand what I'd said. Then I looked past Leon and saw that the patrol car had pulled up beside us; the piñon branches were whipping and scraping the side of the truck as it tried to force us off the road. Leon kept driving with the two right wheels in the rut—bumping and scraping the trees. Leon never looked over at it so he couldn't have known how the reflections kept moving across the mirror-lenses of the dark glasses. We were in the narrow canyon with pale sandstone close on either side—the canyon that ended with a spring where willows and grass and tiny blue flowers grow.

"We've got to kill it, Leon. We must burn the body to be sure."

Leon didn't seem to be listening. I kept wishing that old Teofilo could have been there to chant the proper words while we did it. Leon stopped the truck and got out—he still didn't understand what it was. I sat in the pickup with the .30–30 acrosss my lap, and my hands were slippery.

The big cop was standing in front of the pickup, facing Leon. "You made your mistake, Indian. I'm going to beat the shit out of you." He raised the billy club slowly. "I like to beat Indians with this."

He moved toward Leon with the stick raised high, and it was like the long bone in my dream when he pointed it at me—a human bone painted brown to look like wood, to hide what it really was; they'll do that, you know—carve the bone into a spoon and use it around the house until the victim comes within range.

The shot sounded far away and I couldn't remember aiming. But he was motionless on the ground and the bone wand lay near his feet. The tumbleweeds and tall yellow grass were sprayed with glossy, bright blood. He was on his back, and the sand between his legs and along his left side was soaking up the dark, heavy blood—it had not rained for a long time, and even the tumbleweeds were dying.

"Tony! You killed him—you killed the cop!"

"Help me! We'll set the car on fire."

Leon acted strange, and he kept looking at me like he wanted to run. The head wobbled and swung back and forth, and the left hand and the legs left individual trails in the sand. The face was the same. The dark glasses hadn't fallen off and they blinded me with their hot-sun reflections until I pushed the body into the front seat.

The gas tank exploded and the flames spread along the underbelly of the car. The tires filled the wide sky with spirals of thick black smoke.

"My God, Tony. What's wrong with you? That's a state cop you killed." Leon was pale and shaking.

I wiped my hands on my Levis. "Don't worry, everything is O.K. now, Leon. It's killed. They sometimes take on strange forms."

The tumbleweeds around the car caught fire, and little heatwaves shimmered up toward the sky; in the west, rain clouds were gathering.

WILLIAM LEAST HEAT MOON

FROM
Blue Highways

EDITOR'S NOTE: *Blue Highways* is William Least Heat Moon's account of his three-month trip over the backroads of America.

◆◆◆

Dirty and hard, the morning light could have been old concrete. Twenty-nine degrees inside. I tried to figure a way to drive down the mountain without leaving the sleeping bag. I was stiff—not from the cold so much as from having slept coiled like a grub. Creaking open and pinching toes and fingers to check for frostbite, I counted to ten (twice) before shouting and leaping for my clothes. Shouting distracts the agony. Underwear, trousers, and shirt so cold they felt wet.

I went outside to relieve myself. In the snow, with the hot stream, I spelled out *alive*. Then to work chipping clear the windows. Somewhere off this mountain, people still lay warm in their blankets and not yet ready to get up to a hot breakfast. So what if they spent the day selling imprinted ballpoint pens? Weren't they down off the mountains?

Down. I had to try it. And down it was. Utah 14 a complication of twists and drops descending the west side more precipitately than the east. A good thing I hadn't attempted it in the dark. After a mile, snow on the pavement became slush, then water, and finally at six thousand feet, dry and sunny blacktop.

Cedar City, a tidy Mormon town, lay at the base of the mountains on the edge of the Escalante Desert. Ah, desert! I pulled in for gas, snow still melting off my rig. "See you spent the night in the Breaks," the attendant said. "You people never believe the sign at the bottom."

"I believed, but it said something about winter months. May isn't winter."

"It is up there. You Easterners just don't know what a mountain is."

I didn't say anything, but I knew what a mountain was: a high pile of windy rocks with its own weather.

In the cafeteria of Southern Utah State College, I bought a breakfast of scrambled eggs, pancakes, bacon, oatmeal, grapefruit, orange juice, milk, and a cinnamon roll. A celebration of being alive. I was full of victory.

Across the table sat an Indian student named Kendrick Fritz, who was studying chemistry and wanted to become a physician. He had grown up in Moenkopi, Arizona, just across the highway from Tuba City. I said, "Are you Navajo or Hopi?"

"Hopi. You can tell by my size. Hopis are smaller than Navajos."

His voice was gentle, his words considered, and smile timid. He seemed open to questions. "Fritz doesn't sound like a Hopi name."

"My father took it when he was in the Army in the Second World War. Hopis usually have Anglo first names and long Hopi last names that are hard for other people to pronounce."

I told him of my difficulty in rousing a conversation in Tuba City. He said, "I can't speak for Navajos about prejudice, but I know Hopis who believe we survived Spaniards, missionaries, a thousand years of other Indians, even the BIA. But tourists?" He smiled. "Smallpox would be better."

"Do you—yourself—think most whites are prejudiced against Indians?"

"About fifty-fifty. Half show contempt because they saw a drunk squaw at the Circle K. Another half think we're noble savages—they may be worse because if an Indian makes a mistake they hate him for being human. Who wants to be somebody's ideal myth?"

"My grandfather used to say the Big Vision made the Indian, but the white man invented him."

"Relations are okay here, but I wouldn't call them good, and I'm not one to go around looking for prejudice. I try not to."

"Maybe you're more tolerant of Anglo ways than some others."

"Could be. I mean, I *am* studying to be a doctor and not a medicine man. But I'm no apple Indian—red outside and white underneath. I lived up in Brigham City, Utah, when I went to the Intermountain School run by the BIA. It was too easy though. Too much time to goof around. So I switched to Box Elder—that's a public school. I learned there. And I lived in Dallas a few months. What I'm saying is that I've lived on Hopi land and I've lived away. I hear Indians talk about being red all the way through criticizing others for acting like Anglos, and all the time they're sitting in a pickup at a drive-in. But don't tell them to trade the truck for a horse."

"The Spanish brought the horse."

He nodded. "To me, being Indian means being responsible to my people. Helping with the best tools. Who invented penicillin doesn't matter."

"What happens after you finish school?"

"I used to want out of Tuba, but since I've been away, I've come to see how our land really is our Sacred Circle—it's our strength. Now, I want to go back and practice general medicine. At the Indian hospital in Tuba where my mother and sister are nurse's aides, there aren't any Indian M.D.'s, and that's no good. I don't respect people who don't help themselves. Hopi land is no place to make big money, but I'm not interested anyway."

"You don't use the word *reservation*."

"We don't think of it as a reservation since we were never ordered there. We found it through Hopi prophecies. We're unusual because we've always held onto our original land—most of it anyway. One time my grandfather pointed out the old boundaries to me. We were way up on a mesa. I've forgotten what they are except for the San Francisco Peaks. But in the last eighty years, the government's given a lot of our land to Navajos, and now we're in a hard spot—eight thousand Hopis are surrounded and outnumbered twenty-five to one. I don't begrudge the Navajo anything, but I think Hopis should be in on making the decisions. Maybe you know that Congress didn't even admit Indians to citizenship until about nineteen twenty. Incredible—live someplace a thousand years and then find out you're a foreigner."

"I know an Osage who says, 'Don't Americanize me and I won't Americanize you.' He means everybody in the country came from someplace else."

"Hopi legends are full of migrations."

"Will other Hopis be suspicious of you when you go home as a doctor?"

"Some might be, but not my family. But for a lot of Hopis, the worst thing to call a man is *kahopi*, 'not Hopi.' Nowadays, though, we all have to choose either the new ways or the Hopi way, and it's split up whole villages A lot of us try to find the best in both places. We've always learned from other people. If we hadn't, we'd be extinct like some other tribes."

"Medicine's a pretty good survival technique."

"Sure, but I also like Jethro Tull and the Moody Blues. That's not survival."

"Is the old religion a survival technique?"

"If you live it."

"Do you?"

"Most Hopis follow our religion, at least in some ways, because it reminds us who we are and it's part of the land. I'll tell you, in the rainy season when the desert turns green, it's beautiful there. The land is medicine too."

"If you don't mind telling me, what's the religion like?"

"Like any religion in one way—different clans believe different things."

"There must be something they all share, something common."

"That's hard to say."

"Could you try?"

He thought a moment. "Maybe the idea of harmony. And the way a Hopi prays. A good life, a harmonious life, is a prayer. We don't just pray for ourselves, we pray for all things. We're famous for the Snake Dances, but a lot of people don't realize those ceremonies are prayers for rain and crops, prayers for life. We also pray for rain by sitting and thinking about rain. We sit and picture wet things like streams and clouds. It's sitting in pictures."

He picked up his tray to go. "I could give you a taste of the old Hopi Way. But maybe you're too full after that breakfast. You always eat so much?"

"The mountain caused that." I got up. "What do you mean by 'taste'?"

"I'll show you."

We went to his dormitory room. Other than several Kachina dolls he had carved from cottonwood and a picture of a Sioux warrior, it was just another collegiate dorm room—maybe cleaner than most. He pulled a shoebox from under his bed and opened it carefully. I must have been watching a little wide-eyed because he said, "It isn't live rattlesnakes." From the box he took a long cylinder wrapped in waxed paper and held it as if trying not to touch it. "Will you eat this? It's very special." He was smiling. "If you won't, I can't share the old Hopi Way with you."

"Okay, but if it's dried scorpions, I'm going to speak with a forked tongue."

"Open your hands." He unwrapped the cylinder and ever so gently laid across my palms an airy tube the color of a thunderhead. It was about ten inches long and an inch in diameter. "There you go," he said.

"You first."

"I'm not having any right now."

So I bit the end off the blue-gray tube. It was many intricately rolled layers of something with less substance than butterfly wings. The bite crumbled to flakes that stuck to my lips. "Now tell me what I'm eating."

"Do you like it?"

"I think so. Except it disappears like cotton candy just as I get ready to chew. But I think I taste corn and maybe ashes."

"Hopis were eating that before horses came to America. It's piki. Hopi bread you might say. Made from blue-corn flour and ashes from grease-wood or sagebrush. Baked on an oiled stone by my mother. She sends piki every so often. It takes time and great skill to make. We call it Hopi cornflakes."

"Unbelievably thin." I laid a piece on a page of his chemistry book. The words showed through.

"We consider corn our mother. The blue variety is what you might call our compass—wherever it grows, we can go. Blue corn directed our migrations. Navajos cultivate a yellow species that's soft and easy to grind, but ours is hard. You plant it much deeper than other corns, and it survives where they would die. It's a genetic variant the Hopi developed."

"Why is it blue? That must be symbolic."

"We like the color blue. Corn's our most important ritual ingredient."

"The piki's good, but it's making me thirsty. Where's a water fountain?"

When I came back from the fountain, Fritz said, "I'll tell you what I think the heart of our religion is—it's the Four Worlds."

Over the next hour, he talked about the Hopi Way, and showed pictures and passages from *Book of the Hopi*. The key seemed to be emergence. Carved in a rock near the village of Shipolovi is the ancient symbol for it:

With variations, the symbol appears among other Indians of the Americas. Its lines represent the course a person follows on his "road of life" as he passes through birth, death, rebirth. Human existence is essentially a series of journeys, and the emergence symbol is a kind of map of the wandering soul, an image of a process; but it is also, like most Hopi symbols and ceremonies, a reminder of cosmic patterns that all human beings move in.

The Hopi believes mankind has evolved through four worlds: the first a shadowy realm of contentment; the second a place so comfortable the people forgot where they had come from and began worshipping material goods. The third world was a pleasant land too, but the people, bewildered by their past and fearful for their future, thought only of their own earthly plans. At last, the Spider Grandmother, who oversees the emergences, told them: "You have forgotten what you should have remembered, and now you have to leave this place. Things will be harder." In the fourth and present world, life is difficult for mankind, and he struggles to remember his source because materialism and selfishness block a greater vision. The newly born infant comes into the fourth world with the door of his mind open (evident in the cranial soft spot), but as he ages, the door closes and he must work at remaining receptive to the great forces. A human being's grandest task is to keep from breaking with things outside himself.

"A Hopi learns that he belongs to two families," Fritz said, "his natural clan and that of all things. As he gets older, he's supposed to move closer to the greater family. In the Hopi Way, each person tries to recognize his part in the whole."

"At breakfast you said you hunted rabbits and pigeons and robins, but I don't see how you can shoot a bird if you believe in the union of life."

"A Hopi hunter asks the animal to forgive him for killing it. Only life can feed life. The robin knows that."

"How does robin taste, by the way?"

"Tastes good."

"The religion doesn't seem to have much of an ethical code."

"It's there. We watch what the Kachinas say and do. But the Spider Grandmother did give two rules. To all men, not just Hopis. If you look at them, they cover everything. She said, 'Don't go around hurting each other,' and she said, 'Try to understand things.'"

"I like them. I like them very much."

"Our religion keeps reminding us that we aren't just will and thoughts. We're also sand and wind and thunder. Rain. The seasons. All those things. You learn to respect everything because you *are* everything. If you respect yourself, you respect all things. That's why we have so many songs of creation to remind us where we came from. If the fourth world forgets that, we'll disappear in the wilderness like the third world, where people decided they had created themselves."

"Pride's the deadliest of the Seven Deadly Sins in old Christian theology."

"It's *kahopi* to set yourself above things. It causes divisions."

Fritz had to go to class. As we walked across campus, I said, "I guess it's hard to be a Hopi in Cedar City—especially if you're studying biochemistry."

"It's hard to be a Hopi anywhere."

"I mean, difficult to carry your Hopi heritage into a world as technological as medicine is."

"Heritage? My heritage is the Hopi Way, and that's a way of the spirit. Spirit can go anywhere. In fact, it has to go places so it can change and emerge like in the migrations. That's the whole idea."

GERALD VIZENOR

The Psychotaxidermist

Colonel Clement Beaulieu, the old mixed-blood fur trader and teller of
fine tales, leaned forward into the autumn wind as he walked down the
hard earth trail to Saint Benedict Catholic Mission on the White Earth
Reservation. His white hair wagged on the wind, and while he walked
behind three tribal mongrels he turned over in his mind, like sun-
warmed stones, the stories he could tell the old nuns and priests during
their evening meal.

Colonel Clement smiles on his uncommon memories. The wrinkles
on his slim face purl from interior humors. The mongrels pitch their
heads back, tongues swerving to the side, when he clears his throat four
times and gestures with his lips in the tribal manner—his ceremonial
preparation in the oral tradition that stories are about to be told.

◆◆◆

District Court Judge Silas Bandied snapped his ceramic teeth in the
hollow downtown courtroom, Colonel Clement said in his mind, remembering the strange tale about a tribal shaman psychotaxidermist,
and cleared his throat three times, his religious trine, like a cormorant,
before reading the sentence:

"Shaman Newcrows, alias Random New Crows, alias The Crow, alias
The Psychotaxidermist, we have reviewed the charges and evidence here
and find you this fine morning full of guilt without a doubt. . . . This
court sentences you now and forever to serve ten years at hard labor for
the crime of wild animule molestation, indecent liberties with dead animules in public places; to wit, a four-hole golf course, the first in the
state, might we add here, and then . . ."

"Evidence?" questioned Newcrows.

"Silence," commanded Bandied. "The evidence is clear that you were
dressed in a bear animule mask, rapacious sight that it must have been
that night, and . . ."

"Ceremonial bear," explained Newcrows, who was leaning back in his

124

chair at a comfortable escape distance from the judge and the prosecutor, dressed in a red velvet suit with a bear-claw necklace. He was smiling like a human, but his head shifted from side to side, the morning motion of the bear in him, and his distance, his powerful energies dancing through the memories of oak and cedar and summer ponds in the courtroom.

"Nothing more than a circus bear mask, leaning over dead animules at the golf course, which you admitted stuffing—"

"Take care with what you tell here," warned Newcrows. "The animals and birds are listening."

"Rubbish," sneered the judge. "Dead is dead, and no man, not to mention animules, has ever come back from the dead. . . . No sane man that is—"

"What dead animals?"

"Indian evildoer," snapped the judge and his teeth. "Savage, how dare you defile this courtroom with your word trickeries? You are beyond contempt; you are pitiable and must remain silent here."

"But, Your Honor, please," pleaded the prosecutor whose face and neck was covered with brown tick bites. "Your Honor, consider this: We have dropped the charges on this man because we lost the dead evidence—"

"You lost dead animules?"

"Yes, Your Honor," the tall prosecutor responded, scratching at his chest and arms. "We had the dead evidence on the fourth green, but it up and disappeared during a thunderstorm."

"Mister Prosecutor," said Judge Bandied, stretching his thin cormorant neck over his dark bench, "let me warn you now, this crime took place on our new four-hole course, and this is no time for you to misplace the evidence, dead or alive. We will recess a few minutes now for you to gather your wits and find the dead evidence."

Judge Bandied was a charter member of the new four-hole golf course at the Town and Country Club of Saint Paul, and he boasts that it was he who dropped the first official putt with a green ball through the snow and cold on February 11, 1888, when the course first opened. Now, during the first full season, the fourth hole was fouled forever, so the judge reasoned, because of "some strange dead animule exorcism by a damned circus clown in a bear mask."

Shaman Newcrows, born on the shores of Bad Medicine on the White Earth Reservation, was blessed with animal spirits and avian visions. He traveled in magical flight through four levels of consciousness and the underworld. During the summer when he was twelve, lightning flashed from the eyes of seven crows in his dreams, from whom he took his spirit name, and from bears, ursine shivers from the darkness, and he took from the woods for the first time the languages of animals and birds and flowers and trees. He listened to the languages of the living earth.

Newcrows heard the wise crows curse the evil in men, which was traditional in most human minds but unimaginative. His vision revealed that crows lust for attractive women, white women, their opposite in tone, and their raucous conversations, crow to crow between trees, is seldom more than prurient gossip.

Newcrows heard his own voice rumbling from the heart of a bear. Standing down at the treeline near the water, slow and certain in his movements, he laughed from his solitude and darkness, from the interior of his sacred maw. He listened to secret languages from the darkness, the bears spoke, and he heard animal languages that humans once understood.

Newcrows saw in his vision, from the lightning flashing all around him, the auras and shadows of trees towering over their stumps. The cedar- and white-pine spirits spoke to him from their sacred places on the earth, from the places where trees were cut, and together each tree, cut but not dead, recited the names of the cutters and the places in the cities where their bodies were sold as beams and fence posts.

Newcrows listened to the animals and trees tell him that all who have died will return to the earth. Under a full moon, said an otter, his brothers and sisters will return in face and breath and spirit from the land of the dead. The trees told about the coming fires when their ashes will return to the earth together with their woodland auras.

Newcrows dreamed that strokes of lightning would resurrect all dead animals and those who praised and celebrated their lives. Whenever he passed beneath a tree, or watched a bird in flight, wolves on the run, beaver, insects turning in the morning sun, the crows when their stories were not prurient, he heard them all whisper: *There is one who carries our dream to return to the living earth.* His vision was to deliver the dead to the great spirit during a thunderstorm.

But on the outside Newcrows was neither tree nor otter, he was in his manner three parts fool with humans. His head rolled on the run, and he dropped words in simple phrases, lost his references to time, and the colonial agents on the reservation solicited his signature, his precious mark, five times for federal treaties with the tired tribes because he could remember but one line at one place at one time. His memories were episodic, his form was his content, and he did not perceive his world in grammatical models, cumulatives, generalizations, and plurals.

When he was three years old he walked into the woods alone while his mother was gathering wild rice. He was missing for three days when his mother feared the spirits had taken him to the underworld, but on the morning of the fourth day he walked out of the woods smiling, with bear hair on his face and clothes.

Newcrows did not speak the language of humans for several years, but when he did speak again, when he was twelve, he spoke from his vision with animals and trees returning to the earth. He tossed his head, followed bears into the woods, laughed and shivered with the trees, and never thought about possessions until he found a woman undressing.

"Stop drooling and open the door," said Sister Isolde to the peeping stranger she saw stuck between the logs. Her white breasts wambled in the light from the fire.

Newcrows blinked twice and turned to the darkness, but before he disappeared, she leaped through the door and stopped him at the dark treeline.

Sister Isolde lived with several mongrels and an affectionate fox, in a small cabin she had built from scraps, near Mallard on the White Earth Reservation, which was an abandoned sawmill town. Little remained of the town but her cabin and huge piles of sawdust. She was abandoned, too, at age ten, the lone daughter of a skidder and a timber-town prostitute.

Newcrows drooled and drank and laughed too much at the animal in him until his new woman and her animals were bored with his cabin weaknesses. It was the affectionate fox, snapping at his bare feet at night, who turned him back to the woods and his vision. Months later, when his blood was clean, he was reminded of his vision to return the animal dead to the earth.

Near his birthplace at Bad Medicine, Newcrows collected the dead, from natural and unnatural causes, for the coming storm. He perched and poised thousands of birds and animals near the shore of the lake. But without the lightning he saw in his vision, the animals decomposed. Not one bird or animal came back to the living. The fetid smell burned in the nostrils of the tribe, but it was not his familial nonfluences that lead to his banishment, not the tribe, but the white colonial officers who ordered him to leave the reservation, banished at last from his place on the earth for remembering the earth.

Newcrows traveled from reservation to reservation, but the word was out about his strange habits, and he was asked to leave. He was seeking the secret of preserving the dead, not knowing how long the dead should wait for the coming lightning. He asked white people. A mortician taught him the art of taxidermy, but stuffing animals transformed their images and separated their bones and blood from their spirit without ceremonies. He listened to tribal prophets, the new ones, speak of the new gods and resurrection, but not until he listened to an old shaman woman who lived at La Pointe on Madeline Island in Lake Superior did he understand the secret of holding the dead for the coming of the great spirit and the balance of the earth. The secret was imagination, imagining the spirit and shape of the earth in animals and birds and trees. She taught him to travel with the dead, and it was the dead who told him how to hold the dead and their spirits in his imagination. Imagination, he was told, will hold the earth in balance, our bones having been separated and defiled and our languages seldom spoken now in the hearts of humans. The spirits from the underworld told him to prepare for the storm and the fires to come.

◆◆◆

"Your Honor," pleaded the prosecutor, scratching his neck and shoulders, "if it pleases the court, permit me to continue with this explanation . . ."

"Remember this, Mister Prosecutor, our fourth hole has been defiled forever with these strange animules," Bandied warned, his neck extended over his bench. "We must not permit this crime to pass without punishment, fitting punishment."

"Yes, Your Honor. Now, permit me this review: We found the accused man, New Crows—"

"Newcrows."

"What?"

"Newcrows, one word, one consciousness, one time in all to live on the earth as a bird and animal," explained Newcrows.

"Newcrows, we found Newcrows on the fourth hole under a full moon dressed in a bear costume and dancing around hundreds of dead birds and animals which he explained were his friends. . . . Now, we arrested him then and there, but because the evidence was so strange, we left it in situ and called the zoo. The animals were dead but somehow appeared to be still living, and, forgive the contradictions, Your Honor, asleep, motionless, but with their eyes open, alert, awake, and poised. . . . More like creatures waiting to attack or be attacked. The experience was too strange to move, but before the zoo people could get there, a thunderstorm blew up from nowhere and when lightning struck all around the fourth green, the animals and birds let out this horrible primal scream, loud and clear, and then, sure as you see me here before you now, the dead evidence walked, some ran, loped and leaped, and flew with the storm. Not even a feather or a claw remained on the fourth hole as evidence."

"Damn your evidence," wailed Bandied. "There must be evidence, charge him with something as an evil-doer then. Lock him up somehow."

"But we have no statute for evil."

"Psychotic and dangerous to the living, then," demanded Bandied, clearing his cormorant throat three times and stacking his stout white fingers on the bench with pride.

"Dangerous to whom?"

"Not to whom."

"Dangerous to what then?"

"To the fourth green, to the human spirit," Bandied snapped, "dangerous to civilization, men and women who take pleasure in outdoor exercise and a good game."

"But Your Honor—"

"How did he do it?" asked the judge. He seemed more calm. "How did he do it with all those animals, what was the trick?"

"Never a trick," said Newcrows.

"Close your evil mouth in this courtroom," snapped the judge, changing his mood. "The accused is not permitted to speak here to me. . . . No telling what evil could come from your mouth."

"My words from the dead," said Newcrows.

"Silence," demanded Bandied.

"Silence," mocked Newcrows.

"Silence that evildoer."

"Silence that evildoer."

"Officer, remove him now."

"Officer, remove me now."

"Please continue, Mister Prosecutor."

"With what, Your Honor?"

"How does he do it, fool?"

"Yes, yes, Your Honor, if it pleases the court, we have a letter from Samuel Mitchell, a medical doctor, to one Samuel Burnside, which was published in a recent edition of a book entitled *Study of Mortuary Customs Among the North American Indians* by H. C. Yarrow. This letter bears on your question, Your Honor, in that the letter and the female described in the letter are both held in the American Antiquarian Society.

"Mitchell writes, after examining a female corpse, that 'it is a human body found in one of the limestone caverns of Kentucky. . . . The skin, bones, and other firm parts are in a state of entire preservation. . . . The heart was in situ.'"

"What does that mean?" asked the judge.

"In situ, Your Honor, means the pagans did not eat her heart out like they do the animals; bears, for example," explained the prosecutor while he scratched harder at his chest and stomach.

"What is all this scratching?"

"Tribal ticks—"

"What, if anything, can this evildoer know about bears or animules?" asked the judge. He leaned over behind his massive dark bench to scratch his ankles and did not hear the prosecutor read from *Bear Ceremonialism in the Northern Hemisphere*, a University of Pennsylvania dissertation written by A. Irving Hallowell:

"'The categories of rational thought, by which we are accustomed to separate human life from animal life and the supernatural from the natural, are drawn upon lines which the facts of primitive cultures do not fit.

"'Animals are believed to have essentially the same sort of animating agency which man possesses. They have a language of their own, can understand what human beings say and do, have forms of social or tribal organization, and live a life which is parallel in other respects to that of human societies.

"'Magical or supernatural powers are also at the disposal of certain species; they may metamorphosize themselves into other creatures or, upon occasion, into human form. . . . Dreams may become a specialized means of communication between man and animals.'"

"Where did those ticks come from?" the judge asked as he emerged from behind his bench. He pulled his black robe off and scratched at his thighs and crotch.

"From the bears," explained the prosecutor, scratching at his cheeks. "Bear ticks trained to disrupt our system of justice . . ."

"That evildoer did this to us—"

"Drop the charges," wailed the prosecutor while he scratched. "Drop the goddamn charges and call the ticks off Your Honor."

"Charges dismissed!" screamed the judge from the floor behind his bench where he was scratching and scratching like a reservation mongrel on a tick mound. In seconds the bear ticks were gone and the prosecutor and the judge were back at their benches and chairs with their forms and robes and pencils and plurals.

Gathering his papers and charge sheets, the prosecutor looked up at the judge and said: "Hallowell was told by an old Indian that a bear—"

"Hollowill who?" asked Bandied.

"No, Your Honor, not Hollowill but Hallowell, the author of *Bear Ceremonialism*, which we read into the record," explained the prosecutor. "Hallowell was told by an old Indian that a bear is wiser than a man because a man does not know how to live all winter without eating anything."

Judge Bandied stretched his cormorant neck over his dark bench one more time and said, in a patronizing tone of voice, "But bears suck their paws and masturbate."

◆◆◆

Colonel Clement rounded the last curve down the hill to Saint Benedict Mission. He pulled back his white hair, gestured to the mongrels with his lips in the tribal manner, cleared his throat four times, pushed the door open, and started his stories during the evening meal with the nuns and priests.

"This is a true tale from the reservation," Colonel Clement began, "about Sister Isolde, an old white shaman woman from Mallard who lived in an abandoned scapehouse that lightning struck four times each summer. The crows gossiped about her because she loved a bear who had a vision that he was human. Sister Isolde learned from the bear how to preserve the dead and how to train ticks to disrupt the evildoers in the white world.

"In Saint Paul, one summer before the turn of the century, when the first golf course was opened there, Sister Isolde followed her bear to the fourth green for a bear ceremonial with the dead, with thousands of dead birds and animals dancing under the full moon and waiting for the lightning to return them to the earth . . ."

The mongrels pitched their heads back and waited outside for the stories to end on the inside. The mongrels waited for their master to lead them back through the dark before the storm. The animals were honored by his preparation.

◆◆◆

Rattling Hail Ceremonial: Cultural Word Wars Downtown on the Reservation

> "Artists are the Indians of the white world. They are called dreamers who live in the clouds, improvident people who can't hold onto their money . . . They say the same things about Indians."
> —John Lame Deer, *Lame Deer Seeker of Visions*

Rattling Hail, he said in a harsh voice, was his whole name in all languages. He was a veteran from a recent war. For his patriotic service as an enlisted man, representing the reservation prairie tribes, he was awarded several ribbons, which he wore on the suit coat he was given at a church clothing sale; service-connected dental care; educational benefits; and, for losing one leg on a land mine, he was awarded a small pension as a disabled veteran.

Clement Beaulieu, mixed-blood director of the American Indian Employment and Guidance Center when it was first opened in Minneapolis, encountered Rattling Hail four times in four months, as in a new urban ceremonial downtown on the reservation. On the first morning the center opened in a northside settlement house, Rattling Hail appeared the first time, hobbling across the hard tile floor on one crutch with one pant leg tucked under his belt, folded and creased in a military manner. Beaulieu was moving a desk when the decorated veteran halted at the office door and stood at parade rest.

"Did you bastards open this place?"

"Not the bastards . . . ."

"Who are you?" asked Rattling Hail.

"Beaulieu is the name," he said with a forced smile. "My people come from the White Earth Reservation . . . who are you?"

"Remember Rattling Hail."

"Sacred name?" asked Beaulieu, referring to the tradition of giving sacred dream names to tribal children. Missionaries and colonial government officials translated, with indifference to tribal cultures, familiar descriptive names and nicknames of tribal people as last names. Some missionaries thought that tribal descriptive names were sacred, but sacred names were seldom revealed to strangers.

In his book *The American Indian*, about tribal people on reservations at the turn of the last century, Warren Moorehead writes about the problem of familiar names entered on official tribal rolls. "Many years ago the employees at White Earth Agency made a roll of the Chippewa Indians. One would suppose that so important a document as a register of all the Indians would be accurate. But the original roll, as on file at the White Earth office, bristled with inaccuracies. For instance, the name Mah-geed is the Ojibwa pronunciation of Maggie. Many of the Indian girls were named Mah-geed by the priests and missionaries. Those who made the Government roll apparently thought that Mah-geed was a distinguished Indian name, so they had entered up quite a number of Mah-geeds. No other name is added.

"The Ojibwa name for old woman is Min-de-moi-yen. To the clerks who made the roll this sounded like the name of an Indian, so they solemnly set down many such names. Having assembled as our witnesses the most reliable old Indians, we were able to check up the many errors in the government roll. Frequently there would be as many as forty or fifty Ojibwa assembled in the schoolroom where our hearings were held. When the interpreter called out such a name as Min-de-moi-yen or Mah-geed, the other Indians would shout with laughter and, when they recovered sufficiently, they would state that they did now know what individual Indian was named as there were a score who might respond to that appellation."

Rattling Hail waited at the door.

"Or is your name a translation?" asked Beaulieu.

"Rattling Hail is Rattling Hail," said Rattling Hail, stressing over and over, with his lips drawn tight over his teeth, the word *hail*. "Rattling Hail is the whole name, all the name, that sound in the world is me here, in all languages and tongues for all times. Remember Rattling Hail."

"Standing Rock in North Dakota?" asked Beaulieu. He was interested in locating his name on a reservation, the place for his name. Where one comes from is a cultural signature in the tribal world, a special sign, the casual diction of identities. Some reservations have had little contact with outsiders while others, the White Earth Reservation for example, about which Warren Moorehead writes, have been virtual bicultural centers for intermarriage and cultural diffusion. Some reservations have mixed-blood roots to black and white, social and genetic evidence that black soldiers and white traders did more with the tribes than contain them on colonial exclaves. Mixed-bloods who hate white and black must hate that place and time in themselves.

"No reservation on me . . . no mixed-blood should ask me about that," said Rattling Hail, grinding his teeth together. "What are you white bloods doing here, what is this place?"

"We are setting up an employment and social services center, a new idea for urban centers for tribal people," Beaulieu explained. "You, believe it or not, are the first person through the door. We moved the desks in this morning."

"White blood liars . . ."

"Tell me about it," said Beaulieu.

Rattling Hail raised his crutch and hobbled around the desk toward Beaulieu. His lips spread, like a cornered animal with no escape distance, exposing his clean, white, perfect teeth. Check out the teeth, Beaulieu once told his friends, because perfect teeth in a tribal mouth means a government child or dental care in a foster home. Most poor people have poor teeth to prove it.

"Down with the crutch general," said Beaulieu, moving counterclockwise around the room and keeping the desk between them. "We opened the doors this morning, and here you are, the first one in the door. What is it you want here? Work, or a little abusement?"

"White blood liars . . ." he said again and again as he hobbled around and around the desk, swinging one crutch. "No one ever helped us with nothing. . . . White blood liars."

"Now look, general, put down the crutch and walk out of here the same way you came in. This is not a good way to start anything," said Beaulieu. He stopped near the door to the office and waited. "This is no morning watering hole or abusement park and no one needs you here to blame the world. Come back again when you are sober."

Rattling Hail lowered his crutch and hobbled toward the door. He stopped at attention in front of Beaulieu, face-to-face, staring from his interior darkness and grinding his perfect teeth together. Then he turned and hobbled from the building on a warm morning in late summer.

Rattling Hail appeared the second time while he was exercising his new service-connected plastic limb. He was marching, tapping at the cement with his new cane, down Vineland Place past the Walker Art Center and the Guthrie Theater in Minneapolis. Near the entrance to the theater he stopped on the sidewalk, tapped his cane one final time, and then raised his arm and saluted with his left hand, the wrong hand, several actors and actresses leaving the building. His teeth flashed under the street lamp when he turned in a military manner, lowered his arm, and continued walking on his plastic leg.

Rattling Hail, the warrior veteran on one leg, wounded in the white wars, saluted the theater, places in make-believe. He saluted the blond children dressed in purple tapestries—back from building imaginative castles with sacred cedar and barricades on stage with reservation plans—with the wrong hand. He must have heard the new world rehearsing overscreams from Sand Creek where Colonel John Chivington said, "I have come to kill Indians, and believe it is right and honorable to use any means." He saluted the voices imitating five hundred dead at Mystic River in Connecticut, millions dead in the path of white progress, dead with the earth.

Rattling Hail flashed his teeth and listened as he passed; he must have heard old tribal voices on the wind, from the oral tradition down the mountains, from the woodland and across the prairie. He saluted the voices from his past, the voices remembered in his blood.

Black Hawk tells that the "white men are bad schoolmasters. They carry false looks and deal in false actions. The white men do not scalp the head, they do worse. They poison the heart. It is not pure with them. . . ."

Chief Joseph tells that "good words will not give my people good health and stop them from dying. I am tired of talk that comes to nothing. It makes my heart sick when I remember all the good words and all the broken promises. There has been too much talking by men who had no right to talk. . . ."

Yellow Robe tells that the "coming of the white man is no different for us than dissension, cruelty, or loneliness. It is a learning for us. . . ."

Kicking Bird tells that he is a "stone, broken and thrown away. One part thrown this way and one part thrown that way. I am grieved at the ruin of my people; they will go back to the old road and I must follow them. They will not let me live with the white people. . . ."

Black Elk tells that the white soldiers killed Crazy Horse. "He was brave and good and wise. He never wanted anything but to save his people, and he fought the *wasichus* only when they came to kill us in our own country. He was only thirty years old. They could not kill him in battle. They had to lie to him and kill him that way. The old people never would tell where they took the body of their son. It does not matter where his body lies, for it is grass; but where his spirit is, it will be good to be."

Tribal people were hanged then, children were starved with their heads shaved for the missionaries. Tribal women were dismembered by white soldiers for souvenirs and the earth turned to crust and the water rushed through the stumps down to the sea. Buffalo skulls and tree phantoms howl and scream on the wind.

Rattling Hail disappeared in the darkness.

When the theater rehearsals were over, the actors and actresses mounted their wheels for new parties under the blood-soaked beams in the urban hills. Rattling Hail had saluted their passing in the night while other tribes enacted their cultural suicides downtown on the reservations.

Rattling Hail appeared the third time, as in a new urban ceremonial, standing behind a park bench watching the ducks feed in the autumn on the shores of the pond in Loring Park near downtown Minneapolis. He flashed his teeth, moved toward the birds, and then lifted his face and his arms in flight.

Rattling Hail appeared the last time walking through the new snow without his cane. Four months from the time he first hobbled into the American Indian Employment and Guidance Center, which was moved from the northside to a corner storefront location more convenient to tribal people on Chicago Avenue near Franklin in Minneapolis, he was walking with ease on his new plastic leg.

Clement Beaulieu and several volunteer workers at the center were watching the first winter snow from the storefront window. Night fell with the fresh snow while they talked in the growing darkness about the problems tribal people encountered in urban centers. The urban reservations were no better than colonial reservations for services, and the heartless federal government passed tribal people back and forth like crippled beasts of burden.

The Last Lecture, a tribal watering hole for broken warriors, was located catercorner from the center. The corner door opened at the bar and out stepped Rattling Hail, unbroken, on his new tribal, flesh-tone plastic leg. He stood at attention for a few minutes at the entrance to the Last Lecture, marking his place on the fantastic battle line, his perfect teeth flashing across the street through the falling snow, and then he began marching without a can into battle toward the center on the opposite corner.

Bealieu and his friends were sitting inside in the darkness watching Rattling Hail walk toward them. He passed beneath the streetlight, marching in a straight line across the street, leaving distinctive footprints. The heel on his plastic leg skimmed over the fresh snow.

Rattling Hail opened the front door of the center without hesitation, stepped inside, shook the snow from his coat, and spread his lips like an animal, flashing his perfect teeth once more. The illumination in the room came through the windows from the streetlight outside.

Then, in silence, Rattling Hail faced each person in the storefront, as if he were an officer inspecting his troops on the battle line. He stared at them, his black eyes rolling from an interior darkness, darkness out of the past, rolling under tribal secrets, ground his teeth together, and then he marched out of the building without closing the door. No words were spoken.

Rattling Hail, wagging his elbows on his march in the manner of a trickster, disappeared in the fresh snow. The new urban ceremonial had ended.

◆◆◆

Land Fill Meditation

Clement Beaulieu conducts seminars on Native American philosophies and tribal meditation, environmental fantasies, animal languages, and talking and walking backward, one night each week at Shaman High, a transcendental college, in Marin County.

The teaching trickster was late last week, and when he entered the classroom, conversations stopped in the middle of sentences. He removed his leather coat with unusual caution, walked backward moving his head from side to side like an animal at the shoreline, smiled, turned out the overhead fluorescent lights, and then waited near the open window in silence. There, in his visions, he followed the water moons backward over the mountains on familiar tribal faces. Traffic over the Golden Gate Bridge roared down the word maps and sacred place names in the distance.

Beaulieu told stories backward about the four directions and the four tribal characters who traveled with him that night from the window: Martin Bear Charme, the forward meditator; Happie Comes Last, the demure gossiper; Oh Shinnah Fast Wolf, the metatribal moralist; and Belladonna Winter Catcher, the roadwoman with terminal creeds.

This is a translation from the drawkcab or backward patois in which these stories were first told and recorded.

Martin Bear Charme owns a reservation, the teaching trickster told backward from the darkness, teaches a seminar on refuse meditation, and circumscribes his own unusual images in the material world.

Charme commands us to understand that imaginative meditation is walking backward through the refuse and telling visual stories to writers who never take notes but not speaking to be recorded or smiling to be photographed.

Words are rituals in the oral tradition, from the knowledge of creation, little visions on the winds, said the old tribal scavenger to his students, not electronic sounds separating the tellers from the listeners. Land fill meditation restores the connection between refuse and the refuser.

Charme, mixed-blood master meditator who tells that he walked backward down from the Turtle Mountain Reservation in North Dakota, is much more vain than astute about his photogenic face and emulsion visage. He has an enormous nose, and his stare has the power of the bear.

Last month in Berkeley, onstage at the Unitarian Church, Oh Shinnah Fast Wolf, autonomous mistress of metatribal ceremonies, started sighing, under the sounds of automobile traffic, about the guardians at the heart of mother earth, while a disciple, bearing a pacific smile, held open the double doors for one more cash contribution to balance the earth.

Happie Comes Last, reservation-born nurse, public health graduate student, and columnist for the *Mountain Meditator*, a critical tabloid on meditation and holistic healing, would have been the last cash donor, but there at the double doors, sorting through the cards and letters in her leather pouch like a marsupial, she found a free press ticket and a caricature of the refuse meditation leader. Flashing the ticket and caricature, she asked the disciple as she moved beneath his outstretched arms, Where was the refuse meditator sitting?

Charme sits over there, the disciple said as he pointed with his blond head. He is in the white pants, the one with oil on his nose, in the back near the window.

Comes Last leaned back to gossip with the disciple, did you know that he walks and talks backward and he never answers interviews but in public places like this?

No, he whispered back over his shoulder. Where are his private places?

Martin Bear Charme, founder of the Land Fill Meditation Reservation and the seminar with the same name, scooped the oil from his outsize nose with his dark middle finger, his habit once or twice an hour, and spread the viscid mounds over his cuticles. Sitting near the window, one would never know, watching his smooth hands in backward speech, that the refuse meditator was reservation-born, once poor and undereducated for urban survival.

Nose Charmer, his tribal pet name on the reservation, hitchhiked to San Francisco when he was sixteen, settled in a waterfront hotel and studied welding. But scrap connections bored him, so he turned his attention to scavenging and made his fortune hauling and filling wet lands with urban swill and solid waste. His meditation reservation was once a worthless mud flat which he bought and covered with waste. Now his lush refuse reservation on South San Francisco Bay near Mountain View is worth millions. Charme has petitioned the federal government for recognition as a sovereign meditation nation.

There was never refuse like this on reservations, he told his seminar, because, he said walking backward to the window, on the old reservations *we* were the refuse, *we* were the waste, solid and swill on the run, telling stories from a discarded culture to amuse the colonial refusers. . . . Over here now, on the other end of the wasted world, we meditate in peace on this land fill reservation.

The blond disciple dropped his arms, and his smile and the double doors wagged closed on the traffic sounds. Oh Shinnah, her hair bound back in tight braids, cut countershapes around her head in abstruse hand rituals and then snapped two match heads together four times, igniting a small cedar bundle in front of her on the floor.

Comes Last, smiling and nodding with embarrassment, broke through the silent aisles while the little chapel filled with thick, sweet smoke. Down the back row she cleared her throat twice and then perched on the last chair, not knowing that the old scavenger commanded the last place near the window.

Charme scooped his nose oil once more while Oh Shinnah focused on the visions in her crystal ball and then in perfect tribal trickster time he rolled with his chair past Comes Last in magical flight toward the window, a movement she later described in her column as *soaring backward on a shaman chair*.

Startled from his soaring, Comes Last dropped her pouch and properties. Bending over to retrieve her press ticket and the caricature of the meditator, she snorted with shame and snapped at him from the wooden floor, who the hell is this *wanaki wanaki?* She remembered the first time she called on the refuse meditator at his urban reservation. When she asked him about his education and his theories on meditation, while he sat in a room filled with trash, he said nothing more than *wanaki nin wanaki*. Her loud and nervous voice broke the cedar silence.

Martin Bear Charme smiled, nodded four times backward, and then laughed, throwing his nose back like a bear at the tree line, ha ha ha haaaa.

Looking up from her ball and turtle fetish, Oh Shinnah stopped her invocation on mother earth between the words *intuitive* and *compassion* to explain that she had serious business on her mind and in her heart, to which the blond disciple nodded his head in agreement, about mineral companies and progressive reservation governments, and, she said, we *will* compete with children for attention during these ceremonies, but we will *not* compete with adults and animals. Send the animals out now, this is not a pound.

Wanaki nin wanaki ha ha ha haaaa, Charme chanted, throwing his voice backward from his escape distance near the window.

Who would believe you were a meditator, Comes Last whispered out of the side of her mouth. She shifted from side to side on her perch. She was a bird who appeared perched wherever and on whatever she sat.

What does it mean?

What does *it* mean?

Wanaki nin wanaki over and over.

Thank god we are pagans ha ha ha haaaa.

Not pagan, she said through tense lips, not pagan, tell the truth, what does it mean?

Wanaki peaceful place, *nin wanaki* in me lives a peaceful place ha ha ha haaaa.

Where?

Land fill and summer swill.

Talk sense, she demanded, opening her leather-bound notebook. How are those words spelled? she asked.

D-R-A-W-K-C-A-B N-A-M-A-H-S

Mister Charme, she said, shifting her head to the side to see his nose, what does it mean, land fill meditation? Please, in a phrase or two, speak slow now.

Unstable.

Unstable what?

Unstable in an earthquake.

Be serious, please.

Stable.

Stable what?

Stable in a mind swell.

Never mind, she said, closing her leather notebook. Damn fool, what do you know about meditation? Nothing!

Refuse meditation cures cancer with visions. Some people clean their kitchens better than others, too, said the solid waste magnate.

Mister Charme, please, you are speaking to a registered nurse, she said brushing lumps of leather from her black dress, not one of your meditation victims.

Charme scooped the oil from his nose and continued. Clean minds and clean kitchens are delusions. When our visions are clean we seem to feel much better, but no less insecure.

Comes Last turned her head, avoiding the meditator, pretending not to be interested. Stop talking at me, she said.

But you listen so much better when you are not listening to me ha ha ha haaaa.

Damn fool.

Once upon a time taking out the garbage was an event in our lives, a state of being connected to action. We were part of the rituals connecting us to the earth, from the places food grew through the house and our bodies, and then back to the earth. Garbage was real, part of creation, not an objective invasion of cans and cartons.

Refuse meditation turns the mind back to the earth through the visions of real waste, the trash meditator continued. His voice distracted the celebrants sitting in the next row. Faces turned and scowled. The old scavenger smiled back and resumed his stories.

We are the garbage, the waste, we make it and dump it, to be separated from it is a cancer causing delusion, he said, but with some doubt in the tone of his voice. We cannot separate ourselves clean and perfect when we dump something out back in the trash can. Clean is a vision of internal trash, not a mere separation.

Stop this now, Comes Last insisted. You made your fortune on trash and now you are making me sick with it. Leave me sit here now and not listen to you.

Sickness is one of the best meditation experiences. Think about being sick, focus on your stuffed nose, make your mind an unclean kitchen. Now, said the old scavenger, rather than hating to clean up the kitchen, making it smell different, get right down there with the odors. Focus on the odors in the corners, take the odors in, you know the same way we smell our underarms, because *we* are the bad smells we smell, separated from our own real kitchens in the mind.

What was that?

Never mind . . . and the clean words that part us from the real smells, leave us defensive victims of fetid swill and cancer. Did you understand that part? Ha ha ha haaaa.

You are sick, what you need are some clean words in your head, said Comes Last, moving two chairs down the back row out of his bad-breath range.

Cancer is first a word, a separation without vision, he said, following her down the row. We are culture-bound to be clean, but being clean is a delusion and a separation from the visual energies of the earth. Holistic health is a harmonious vision, not an aromatic word prison.

Listen, we are the dreamers for the earth, he said in a deep voice. Turning down the dreams with clean words, defensive terminal creeds, earth separations, denies odors and death and causes cancer.

The celebrants turned toward the old scavenger in the back row and told him to be silent. One woman wagged her hand at him, warning him not to speak about diseases during sacred ceremonies.

We *are* death, said the refuse meditator to the woman in the next row. Unabashed, he stood and spoke in a loud voice to all the celebrants in the chapel. *We are rituals, not perfect words, we are the ceremonies, not the witnesses, which connect us to the earth. We are the earth dreamers, the holistic waste, not the detached nose pinchers between the refuse and the refusers.*

Go to a place in the waste to meditate, chanted the refuse meditator. Come to our reservation on the land fill to focus on waste and transcend the ideal word worlds, clean talk and terminal creeds, and the disunion between the mind and the earth. Come meditate on trash and swill odors and become the waste that connects us from the earth.

Pipe down in the back.

Oh Shinnah raised an eagle feather and told the mother earth celebrants that her feather made her tell the truth; should I not speak straight the feather will tremble. Now, listen, we live in a retarded country . . . we vote for a peanut picker looking for a way to freedom and look where we have come. People are tearing up our land without examining it.

Hang with mother earth, she said, raising her fist, if the four corners tribal land is destroyed, then purification comes with a closed fist. If the electromagnetic pole at the four corners is upset, the earth will slip in space, causing the death of two thirds of the population, no matter where you go to hide.

Oh Shinnah makes more sense with cedar smoke and fetishes than you do with all that double backtalk about meditation, Comes Last declared, raising her chin.

Silence.

The lights flickered several times, and then out. The celebrants whispered in the darkness until the smell of cedar smoke in the chapel turned to the odor of land fill swill, or what Comes Last described in her column as a mixture of human excrement and dead animals. At first whiff the celebrants took cover in clean words, thinking the person next in row had passed bad air. But later when the chapel filled with the scent of wild flowers one celebrant allowed how terrible was the smell. While the others praised the passing of the bad odors, Comes Last, whose nose had not separated from the world of animals, smelled a bear in the darkness.

Listen ha ha ha haaaa.

Martin Bear Charme moved around the chapel in the darkness, from row to row and chair to chair, telling stories about terminal creeds. His voice seemed to rise and waver from the four directions. Words dropped from the beams, sounds came from under the chairs, and several celebrants were certain that the stories he told that night were told inside their own heads.

Listen ha ha ha haaaa.

Orion was framed in a great wall of red earthen bricks, said the refuse meditator. Within the red walls lived several families who were descendants of famous hunters and western bucking horse breeders. Like good horses, the sign outside the walls said, proud people keep to themselves and their own breed, but from time to time we invite others to share food and conversation.

Belladonna Winter Catcher, who was born and conceived at Wounded Knee, her traveling companion Catholic Bishop Omax Parasimo, and several other tribal pilgrims, knocked at the gate. We are tribal mixedbloods with good stories and memories from thousands of good listeners. Open the gate and let us in or we will blow your house down.

Listen to this, said Belladonna who was reading the sign on the red wall: Terminal Creeds are Terminal Diseases. . . . The Mind is the Perfect Hunter, and Narcissism is a Form of Isolation.

The metal portcullis opened, and several guards dressed in uniforms escorted the pilgrims through the red wall. The pilgrims were examined. Information about birthplaces, education and experiences, travels and diseases, attitudes on women and politics, was recorded. The hunters and breeders welcomed the visitors to tell stories about what was happening in the world outside the walls.

The pilgrims followed the hunters and breeders through the small town to one of the large houses where dozens of people were waiting on the front steps. Introductions and questions about political views were repeated again and again.

Thousands of questions were asked before dinner was served in the church dining room. Bishop Parasimo was the first to shift the flow of conversations. He asked the hunters and breeders sitting at his table to discuss the meaning of the messages on the outside walls. What does it mean, narcissism is a form of isolation? Please explain how the mind is the perfect hunter.

Narcissism rules the possessor, said a breeder with a deep scar on the side of his forehead. Narcissism is the fine art that turns the dreamer into paste and ashes.

The perfect hunter leaves himself and becomes the animal or bird he is hunting, said a hunter on the other side of the table. He touched his ear with his curled trigger finger as he spoke. The perfect hunter turns on himself, hunts himself in his mind. He lives on the edge of his own meaning, the edge of his own humor. He is the hunter and the hunted at the same time.

The breeders and hunters at the table smiled and nodded and then turned toward the head table where the bald banker-breeder was tapping his water glass. Belladonna was sitting next to the banker. Her nervous fingers fumbled with the two beaded necklaces around her neck.

The families applauded when the banker spoke of their mission against terminal creeds. Depersonalize the work in the world of terminal believers, and we can all share the good side of humor. . . . Terminal believers must be changed or driven from our dreams.

Belladonna could feel the moisture from his hand resting on her shoulder. He referred to her as the good spirited speaker who has traveled through the world of savage lust on the interstates, this serious tribal woman, our speaker from the outside world, who once carried with her a tame white bird.

Belladonna leaned back in her chair. Her thighs twitched from his words about the tame white bird. The banker did not explain how he knew that she once lived with a dove. The medicine man told her it was an evil white witch, so she turned the dove loose in the woods, but the bird returned. She cursed the bird and locked it out of her house, but the white dove soared in crude domestic circles and hit the windows. The dove would not leave. One night, when she was alone, she squeezed the bird in both hands; the dove was content in her hands. She shook the dove. Behind the house, against a red pine tree, she severed the head of the white dove with an axe. Blood spurted in her face. The headless dove flopped backward into the dark woods.

We are waiting, said the banker.

Belladonna shivered near her chair, staring to chase the dove from her memories. She fumbled with her neck beads. Tribal values and dreams is what I will talk about.

Speak up . . . speak up!

Tribal values is the subject of my talk, she said in a louder voice. She dropped her hands from her beads. We are raised with values that shape our world in a different light. . . . We are tribal, and that means that we are children of dreams and visions. Our bodies are connected to mother earth, and our minds are the clouds. Our voices are the living breath of the wilderness.

My grandfathers were hunters, said the hunter with the trigger finger at his ear. They said the same thing about the hunt that you said is tribal, so what does that mean?

I am different than a white man because of my values, she said. I would not be white.

Do tell me, said an old woman breeder in the back of the room. We can see that you are different from a man, but tell us how you are so different from white people.

We are different because we are raised with different values, Belladonna explained. She was fumbling with her beads again. Our parents treat us different as children. We are not punished. We live in larger families and never send our old people to homes to be alone. These are some things that make us different.

More, more.

Tribal people seldom touch each other, said Belladonna. She folded her hands over her breasts. We do not invade the personal bodies of others and we do not stare at people when we are talking. . . . Indians have more magic in their lives.

Wait a minute, hold on there, said a hunter with an orange beard. Let me find something out here before you make me so different from the rest of the world. . . . Tell me about this word *Indian* you use, tell me which Indians are you talking about, or for, or are you talking for all Indians? And if you are speaking for all Indians, then how can there be truth in what you say?

Indians have their religion in common.

What does *Indian* mean?

Are you so stupid that you cannot figure out what and who Indians are? An Indian is a member of a tribe and a person who has Indian blood.

But what is Indian blood?

Indian blood is not white blood.

Indians are an invention, said the hunter with the beard. You tell me that the invention is different than the rest of the world when it was the rest of the world that invented the Indian. An Indian is an Indian because he speaks and thinks and believes he is an Indian. . . . The invention must not be too bad because the tribes have taken it up for keeps.

Mister, does it make much difference what the word *Indian* means when I tell you that I have always been proud that I am an Indian? said Belladonna. Proud to speak the voice of mother earth.

Please continue.

Well, as I was explaining, tribal people are closer to the earth, to the meaning and energies of the woodlands and mountains and plains. . . . We are not a competitive people like the whites who competed this nation into corruption and failure.

When you use the collective pronoun, asked a woman hunter with short silver hair, does that mean that you are talking for all tribal people?

Most of them.

How about the western fishing tribes, the old tribes, the tribes that burned down their own houses in potlatch ceremonies?

Exceptions are not the rule.

Fools never make rules, said the woman with silver hair. You speak from terminal creeds, not a person of real experience and critical substance.

Thank you for the meal, said Belladonna. She smirked and turned in disgust from the hunters and breeders. The banker placed his moist hand on her shoulder. Now, now, she will speak in good faith, said the banker, if you will listen with less critical ears. She does not want a debate. Give her another good hand. The hunters and breeders applauded. She smiled, accepted apologies, and started again.

The tribal past, our religion and dreams and the concept of mother earth, is precious to me. Living is not important if it is turned into competition and material gain. . . . Living is hearing the wind and speaking the languages of animals and soaring with eagles in magical flight. When I speak about these experiences it makes me feel powerful, the power of tribal religion and spiritual beliefs gives me protection. My tribal blood is like the great red wall you have around you. . . . My blood moves in the circles of mother earth and through dreams without time. My tribal blood is timeless and it gives me strength to live and deal with evil.

Right on, sister, right on, said the hunter with the trigger finger on his ear. He leaped to his feet and cheered for her views. .

Powerful speech, said a breeder.

She deserves her favorite dessert, said a hunter in a deep voice. The hunters and breeders do not trust those narcissistic persons who accept personal praise.

Shall we offer our special dessert to this innocent child? asked the breeder banker. Let me hear it now, those who think she deserves her dessert, and those who think she does not deserve her dessert for her excellent speech.

No dessert please, said Belladonna.

Now, now, how could you turn down the enthusiasm of the hunters and breeders who listened to your thoughts here? How could you turn down their vote for your dessert?

The hunters and breeders cheered and whistled when the cookies were served. The circus pilgrims were not comfortable with the shift in moods, the excessive enthusiasm.

The energies here are strange, said Bishop Parasimo up his sleeve. What does all this cheering mean?

Quite simple, said the breeder with the scar. You see, when questions are unanswered and there is no humor, the messages become terminal creeds, and the good hunters and breeders here seek nothing that is terminal. Terminal creeds are terminal diseases, and we celebrate when death is inevitable.

The families smiled when she stood to tell them how much she loved their enthusiasm. In your smiling faces I can see myself, she said. This is a good place to be, you care for the living. The hunters and breeders cheered again.

But you applaud her narcissism, said the bishop to the breeder with the scar. His hands were folded in a neat pile on the table.

She has demanded that we see her narcissism, said the breeder. You heard her tell us that she did not like questions, different views, she is her own victim, a terminal believer.

But we are all victims.

The histories of tribal cultures have been terminal creeds and narcissistic revisionism, said the breeder. The tribes were perfect victims; if they had more humor and less false pride, then the families would not have collapsed under so little pressure from the white man. . . . Show me a solid culture that disintegrates under the plow and the saw.

Your views are terminal.

Who is serious about the perfections of the past? Who gathers around them the frail hopes and febrile dreams and tarnished mother earth words? asked the hunter with the scar. Surviving in the present means giving up on the burdens of the past and the cultures of tribal narcissism.

Belladonna nibbled at her sugar cookie like a proud rodent. Her cheeks were filled and flushed. Her tongue tingled from the tartness of the cookie. In the kitchen the cooks had covered her cookie with a granulated time-release alkaloid poison that would soon dissolve. The poison cookie was the special dessert for narcissists and believers in terminal creeds. She was her own perfect victim. The hunters and breeders have poisoned dozens of terminal believers in the past few months. Most of them were tribal people.

Belladonna nibbled at the poison dessert cookie, her polite response to the enthusiasm of the people who lived behind the wall. She smiled and nodded to the hunters and breeders who all watched her eat the last crumb.

The sun dropped beneath the great red earthen wall when the pilgrims passed through the gate. The pilgrims were silent, walking through the shadows. Seven crows circled until it was dark.

My father took me into the sacred hills, chanted Belladonna. We started when the sun was setting because Old Winter Catcher had to know what the setting sun looked like before he climbed into the hills for the night. The sun was beautiful, it spread great beams of orange-and-rose colors across the heavens. My father said it was a good sunset. No haze to hide the stars. He said it was good and we climbed into the hills. It feels that time now, I feel like we are climbing into the hills for the visions of the morning.

We walked up part of the hill backward, Belladonna said with her head turned backward. Then he told me that the world is not as it appears to be frontward, not then, not now. To leave the world and see the power of the spirit on the hills we had to walk out of the known world backward. We had to walk backward so nothing would follow us up the hill.

My father said that things that follow are things that demand attention. Do you think we are being followed now?

No, said Bishop Parasimo, looking behind.

When I do this, we are walking and talking into the morning with Old Winter Catcher, she said, walking and talking backward down the road. .noitnetta ruo no sdnamed on htiw gninrom otni emoc ot tsrif ehT   The first to come into morning with no demands on our attention.

Shaman High smelled of wild flowers and bears and land fill swill when the teaching trickster ended his stories. Clement Beaulieu soared backward out the window in the darkness and laughed ha ha ha haaaa over the mountains and familiar tribal faces on the water moons.

SIMON J. ORTIZ

Three Women

"I'm gonna kill him," Rowena said. She wrenched the wheel sharply from the street into the lot by the launderette. "That son of a bitch!" Her teeth ground down on her words.

Annie braced her hand on the dashboard; she didn't say anything.

The pickup truck tires spun gravel to the side as tires turned and they parked abruptly.

"That's the last stupid time he's gonna do that, the last." And then Rowena gripped the wheel hard for a half moment, let go, and jumped out of the truck.

Annie closed the door on her side and began to get their baskets of washing out of the truck bed. "We have so much laundry this time," she said.

Her sister threw her a glare that Annie could feel on her face. She almost dropped the bleach.

Rowena took the heaviest basket of clothes and lunged with its weight against the launderette door, almost knocking over the manager, who was moving to open it for her. Annie murmured, "Sorry." Rowena didn't even notice.

They went back out one more time to get two more basket loads, and then they began to stuff empty washers. It was hot and steamy in the launderette. Rowena didn't say anything as she threw Ray's oil-and-grease—grimed work clothes into a separate washer. As Annie put the checkered and stripes into another, she could see her sister's jaw muscles tensing and untensing.

"There," Annie said with a sigh when all the clothes were in. She was sweating, and she could feel the biting odor of Clorox at her nostrils. She knew she would feel nauseated soon, and she would fight it as she always did.

When putting the detergent into the top-loading washers, Annie asked, "Do you want a Coke? I've going to have one; it's so hot in here."

Rowena didn't seem to hear at first, but she finally said, "Yeah, I guess so," and sank down in a metal chair propped against the dull green wall. Annie brought back the cans of Coke and handed one to her sister. They sat in silence.

The din was always the same in the launderette. Sloshing water, the change in cycles, wash spin rinse, the whir of the dryers. Tin doors slamming, kids stamping their shoes on the cement floor, Okie and Navajo women talking. Annie could feel the nausea coming on. She sipped on her Coke, trying to keep the sickly feeling down.

"You know I married that man because I loved him," Rowena said suddenly. She looked at Annie and then across the room. "I sure as hell did; I don't remember why, but I did."

Annie nodded. She remembered how proud her sister had acted riding around in Ray's car. She sometimes went with them to the movies or to the store, and she always rode in the backseat.

"We were doing it all the way before we got married—did you know that?—because I loved him. The son of a bitch." It was a matter of fact, the way Rowena said it.

Annie didn't know if it was a real question she was being asked, but when Rowena looked at her, she said, "No, I didn't know." Her voice was even smaller than usual.

"It wasn't any great shakes," Rowena said, shrugging her shoulders, "and it wasn't going to make any difference because I wanted to get married. Now it doesn't make any difference because I want to get out!" Her latter words were grim and final.

Not knowing if she should say anything, if there was anything to say, Annie found herself saying, "He loved you, too. He told me."

"That bastard couldn't love anybody," Rowena said and then asked directly, "Did he say that?"

Annie hesitated and then said, "Yes." It was twice he had said so, and she felt uneasy remembering the second time. She wished she hadn't mentioned it and feebly hoped Rowena would not ask for details.

The noise in the launderette seemed to ebb and then immediately rise. Annie tried to think around the knot of nausea in her stomach, and, out of the corner of her eyes, she was relieved to see Rowena staring far away to the other side of the launderette.

❖❖❖

Ray had been drinking that weekend and fighting with Rowena. He'd been working on something that was wrong with the truck they had. Annie, who lived nearby with their mother, was watering Rowena's garden as a favor; Rowena had taken the kids to a church youth picnic that afternoon.

She knew they had been fighting. She could feel it when they did; she had heard yelling and then the car engine racing away. A half-hour later, after lunch, she had started to water the garden. She was almost through when Ray turned from the truck and spoke to her.

"Your sister is nuts. No offense, but she's nuts," he said.

Annie had to giggle at that. Sometimes she said and felt the same as Ray had said about Rowena. But she didn't say anything.

"She wanted me to go to a picnic with her and the kids, and she got mad because I said I couldn't because I have to work on the truck so I can go to work in it tomorrow." Ray wiped his hands on a rag from an old T-shirt. And he lit a cigarette.

"The boys said you were all going to go," Annie said. Her nephews, who liked to talk with her, had been excited about the picnic.

"Well, shoot, yeah, I was going to go, but then I couldn't. I can't help it if this old thing needs working on." He slammed his hand on the truck fender.

"I guess they'll be gone all afternoon," Annie said.

"I was going to go," Ray repeated, "but then I couldn't. Rowena said I was just making it up. I told her, 'You take that truck then and see how far it'll take you.' She said, 'Yeah, it'll take you as far as the bar, I know that much! It always does.' 'It takes me to work,' I said."

He threw away his cigarette and said, "She started yelling about my drinking. I told her not to yell so much. Shoot, you probably heard her over at your mother's." He looked at Annie.

"Yes. I heard both of you," she said, feeling a stir in herself for her sister. Rowena had talked, though not a lot, about Ray's drinking. It seemed to be other things besides the drinking, but drinking had some to do with the other things also.

"I drink, sure, but I work steady, and we manage to get things. Sometimes she wants to get things that we can't afford, and we get into hassles about that, too. Like that color TV, you know? I don't even like TV that much, but she wanted to get it."

Rowena had been proud of the new console when they first bought it. She brought Annie and Mother over to see it, and she kept putting lemony smelling polish on it although it didn't seem to need it. Lately though, Annie noticed that dust was gathering on the console top.

"Hassles," Ray said, and shrugged, "but that's married life, I guess. Annie, I love her, but something's not there. I don't even know if its love anymore. Maybe it's just a used-to-be love. What do you think about that." And he laughed in the boyish manner he had. He could tease, and Annie remembered before the marriage she used to laugh at his teasing. They all did. She couldn't help giggling now.

"I don't need used-to-be love, I need some right-now loving," Ray said, and, laughing, he suddenly took Annie's hand and squeezed it. For a split second, Annie felt a surge of sensual energy—and then she tried to withdraw her hand. Ray's handhold was strong and she had to jerk her hand from his. His laughter cut short and he looked startled.

Annie turned back to watering the rest of the lettuce and carrots. After she turned off the water and coiled the plastic hose, she walked to Ray, who was cleaning parts in a can. She told him, "Rowena loves you, too, Ray. It's not a used-to-be, either. She wories; that's why she gets mad—crazy, like you say."

She had spoken without thinking much about what she said. She didn't know if Rowena loved him. If she had paused in thought she might not have said it. It was certain, though, that Rowena worried about their sons and herself and Ray.

Ray didn't say anything.

◆◆◆

Rowena got up from the metal chair and threw the empty Coke can into a trash container with a loud clatter. Annie could see that two of the top-loading washers they had filled were in the rinse cycle. And then she looked at Rowena, who was standing, staring at a woman who had just come in with a large cardboard box overflowing with clothes.

Rowena kept staring at the woman, who held her gaze down as she found an empty washer right next to them. All other washers were full. The woman lifted her face and seemed to look frantically around the launderette, but there were no other washers empty.

The woman sat her cardboard box down heavily, and Rowena sat back in the metal chair, watching the woman go out the door. After a moment, the woman came back through the launderette door with a pillow sack and, still keeping her head down, she began to put clothes into the single empty washer.

Annie noticed then the purple puffiness of the woman's white face. The dark swelling was mostly visible around her eyes and on the side of her neck. Annie sucked in her breath suddenly, and Rowena looked at her. Annie said, "That woman, her face."

"I saw," Rowena said gruffly, just above her breath.

Without wanting to, trying at the same time not to, the sisters watched the woman. She looked totally wearied. Annie felt a shiver in her own bones and muscles. She noticed that some pieces of clothing the woman was stuffing into the washer seemed to have dark stains. The woman's upper lip glistened with sweat. She seemed to be near collapse, and she stumbled as she reached into the cardboard box. Rowena jumped up and walked over.

"Let me help you," she said.

The woman had one hand on the edge of the washer; her knuckles were white. "No, that's all right," she said, stammering. "I'll get it done." And she pushed Rowena's hand away, almost slapping it.

"Okay," Rowena said, shrugged, and started to walk away. She turned and said gently, "We'll be finished with these four washers soon." The woman lifted her face an instant and nodded. Rowena sat down.

Not looking at Annie, she said, "She must have a bastard of an old man, too." And then she spoke to herself, "I think I'm gonna get out of it. I know it'll upset Mother, but she doesn't know what I've gone through."

Annie didn't say anything right away, and then she said, "She knows some. And she'll understand." She was trying to keep the muscles in her stomach from tensing with nausea, but the more she tried, the more it wanted to come.

Rowena turned to her. Very directly, she asked, "Do you understand?"

Feeling defensively small, Annie said, "No, not a lot." She glanced at the woman by the washer.

"To tell you the truth, I don't, either," Rowena said. "I told you I loved—or did—Ray, but I want to get out. I'm convinced of that. It doesn't feel good anymore. Maybe it hasn't for a long time, and it's not safe for me anymore, nor for the boys. I don't know what he's going to do from one day to the next." She let her voice drift away.

The sisters were silent for several minutes, each in their own minds. Annie's thoughts were mixed with the constant noise of the launderette and her nausea. She wondered, almost doing so aloud, if Rowena had the same sickening feelings. She had to get up and move around. "This one is just about to finish," she said. The spin light was on.

For several minutes, the woman had been standing by the washer she had started. She looked dazed, as if she did not know where she was. Annie couldn't help it as she said, "Please, won't you sit down." She pointed to the metal chair she had been sitting in.

The woman's red-tinged eyes locked on Annie's, and Annie was about to feel an automatic wish that she hadn't said anything when the woman said, "Yes, I think I will." She took the few steps over to the chair and unsteadily sat down beside Rowena.

The first top loader finished spinning. Annie brought a wheeled basket over from the corner, and she began to take the heavy, wet clothes out. As she pulled handfuls out of the washer, Rowena came up beside her and said, "I can't stand it. It's done. I feel like I'm going nuts, and I know I'm not nuts. It's done. That woman just decided for me."

Annie looked at her sister's face and saw she had made a decision. She looked at the woman, sitting tired and slumped on the metal chair. Her face was down again, and Annie could see her lips moving. She was talking to herself or praying, and it could have been both.

The other washers stopped almost all at the same time and Rowena started to empty the one nearest the washer the woman had filled. When she finished, she turned and told the woman, "This one is free now, and I'll be done with this other real quick." She pointed to the one with Ray's clothes in it. The woman turned to Rowena. "Thank you," she said.

Before Rowena turned back to empty the washer, she said, "It'll be all right." Annie heard her say that, and when she looked at the woman rising from the metal chair and at Rowena, she found a shared, faint smile on their faces.

◆◆◆

The Panther Waits

*"That people will continue longest in the enjoy-
ment of peace who timely prepare to vindicate
themselves and manifest a determination to protect themselves whenever they are wronged."*
Tecumseh, 1811

Tahlequah is cold in November, and Sam, Billy, and Jay sat underneath a lusterless sun. They had been drinking all afternoon. Beer. Wine. They were talking, trying not to feel the cold.

Maybe we need another vision, Billy.

Ah shoot, vision. I had one last night and it was pretty awful—got run over by a train and somebody stole my wife.

He he he. Have another beer, Billy.

Maybe, though, you know. It might work.

Forget it, huh. Cold beer vision, that's what I like.

No, Sam, I mean I've been thinking about that old man that used to be drunk all the time.

Your old man, he he he, he was drunk all the time.

Yeah, but not him. He was just a plain old drunk. I mean Harry Brown, that guy that sat out by the courthouse a lot. He used to have this paper with him.

Harry J. Brown, you mean? He was a kook, a real kookie kook, that one?

Yeah. Well, one time me and my brother, Taft, before he died in that car wreck down by Sulphur, well, me and him we asked Harry to buy us some beer at Sophie's Grill, you know, and he did. And then he wanted a can and sure, we said, but we had to go down by the bridge before we would give him one. We did and sat down by the bushes there and gave him a beer.

Yeah, we used to, too. He'd do anything for a beer, old Harry J. Brown. And your brother, he was a hell of a drinker, too, he he he.

We sat and drank beer for a while, just sitting, talking a bit about fishing or something, getting up once in a while to pee, and just bullshitting around. And then we finished all the beer and was wishing we had more, but we had no money, and we said to Harry, Harry, we gotta go now.

He was kind of fallen asleep, you know, just laid his head on his shoulder like he did sometimes on the cement courthouse steps. We shook his shoulder.

Uh, uh yeah, he said. And then he sort of shook his head and sort of like cleared his eyes with his hand, you know, like he was seeing kind of far and almost like we were strangers to him, like he didn't know us, although we'd been together all afternoon.

We said we was leaving, and he looked straight up into Taft's eyes and then over to me and then back to Taft. And then he rubbed his old brown hand over his eyes again and said, Get this. He said, Yes, kinda slow in his voice and careful, Yes, it's true, and it will come true.

I just realized, Harry Brown said slowly but clearly then, not like later on when you'd hardly understand what he was saying at the courthouse.

Realized, he repeated, you're the two. Looking straight into Taft's and my eyes. And then he kind of smiled and made a small laugh and then he shook and started to cry.

Harry, Taft said, you old fool, what the hell you talking about. C'mon, get a hold of yourself, shape up, old buddy. Taft always liked to talk to old guys. Sometimes nobody else would talk to them or make fun of them, remember? But Taft was always buddies with them.

Yeah, they gave him wine, that wino, Sam giggled. He knew how to hit them up.

Anyway, Harry sat up then and didn't look at us no more, but he said, Sit down, I want to show you something. And then he pulled out this paper.

It was just a old piece of paper, sort of browned and folded, soft-looking, like he'd carried it a long time. Listen, he said, and then he didn't say anything. And we said again, We gotta go soon, Harry.

Wait. Wait, he said, you just wait. It's time to wait. And so we kept sitting there, wondering what in the world he was up to. The way Harry Brown was, his eyes sort of closed and thinking, made us interested.

Finally, he cleared his throat and spit some beer foam out and then he said, I just remembered something I thought I forgot. It's not from a long time ago, I don't think but longer than a man's age, anyway. I'm maybe seventy years along and that's not too long and what I remembered is longer than that. I carry this with me all the time. Once I thought I lost it, but then it had got thrown in the washing machine by Amy, my daughter, and she pulled it out of my pants, and you can't tell what it says clearly, but it's there, and it will always be there. I can still see it.

And then Harry opened up the paper. There was nothing on it, just a brown piece of wrinkled paper. There's nothing there, Harry, I said, nothing but a piece of paper.

There's something there, he said, serious and solemn. There's something there. It's clear in my mind.

I looked over at Taft, who was on his knees staring at the paper and he caught my eye. I kind of shrugged, but Taft didn't say anything. I knew old Harry Brown's mind probably wasn't all that clear anymore with his old age and all the wine he drank all the time. But you know, he spoke clearly, and the way he was talking was serious and sure.

He said, They traveled all over. They went south, west, north, east, all those states now that you learn about in books. Even Florida, even Mississippi, even Missouri, all over they did.

Who did? Taft asked. I was wondering myself.

The two brothers. Look, you can see their marks and their roads. He was pointing with his shaky old scarred finger. That old man had thick fingers. I've seen him lift a beer cap off the old kind of beer bottle with his thumb. The scar was from when the state police slammed his hand some years ago.

Taft was looking at the paper with a curious look on his face. I mean curious and serious, too. I still couldn't see anything. Nothing. I thought maybe there was a faint picture of something, but there didn't seem to be anything—just paper.

Taft looked over at me then and made a motion with his chin, and I looked at the paper again and listened.

They tried to tell all the people. They said, You Indians—they meant all the Indians wherever they went and even us now I'm sure—you Indians must be together and be one people. You are all together on this land. This land is your home and you must see yourself as all together. You people, you gotta understand this. There is no other way we're gonna be able to save our land and our people unless we decide to be all together.

The brothers traveled all over. Alabama, Canada, Kentucky, Georgia, all those states now on the map. Some places people said to them, We don't want to be together. We're always fighting with those other people. They don't like us and we don't like them. They steal and they're not trustworthy.

But the brothers insisted, We are all different people, that's for sure, but we are all human people, all humankind, all sisters and brothers, and this is all our land. We have to settle with each other. No more fighting, no more arguing, because it is the land and our home we have to fight for. That is what we have come to convince you about.

The brothers said, We will all have to fight before it's too late. They are coming. They keep coming and they want to take our land and our people. We have told them, No, we cannot sell our mother earth, we cannot sell the ocean, we cannot sell the air, we cannot give our lives away. We will have to defend them, and we must do it all together. We must do it, the brothers said. Listen.

Taft just kept looking at the paper and the brown finger of Harry Brown moving over the paper, and I kept looking, too. I still didn't see anything except the wrinkles and folds of the paper, but what Harry was saying with his serious-story voice put something there I think, and I looked over at Taft again. He was nodding his head like he understood perfectly what the old man was saying.

They were talking about the Americans coming and they wanted the Indians to be all together so they could help each other fight them off. So they could save their land and their families. That's what I remembered just awhile ago. I thought I'd forgotten, but I don't think I'll ever forget. It's as close to me as you two are.

Harry paused and then he went on. They were two brothers like you are. One of them, the older, was called Tecumtha. I've heard it means *the panther in waiting*. And the other was one who had old drunk problems like me, but he saved himself and helped his people. Maybe the vision they said he had came from his sickness of drinking, but it happened and they tried to do something about it. That's what is on here, look.

And Taft and I looked again, but I still couldn't see anything. But I didn't say so, and Taft said, Yeah, Harry, I see.

And then we had to go. We was supposed to pick up some bailing wire from Stokes' Store and take it back to our old man. Before we left, Harry looked up at us again, straight into our faces. His eyes had cleared, you know, and he said, They were two brothers.

Taft and I talked some about it and then later on somebody—you know Ron and Jimmy, the two brothers from up by Pryor?

Yeah, Jimmy the all-state fullback? Boy, was he something. Yeah, I know them.

Yeah. Well, Ron told me old Harry Brown told them that same story, too. but they couldn't see nothing on the paper, either. They said it was kind of blue not brownish like I'd seen. I told Taft and he said, Well those two guys are too dumb and ignorant to see anything if it was right in front of their nose.

Jimmy got a scholarship to college and works for an oil company down in Houston, and Ron, I think, he's at the tribal office, desk job and all that, doing pretty good. I said to Taft, You didn't see anything, either. And he looked at me kind of pissed and said, Maybe not, but I know what Harry meant.

Geesus, that Taft could drink. He coulda been something, too, but he sure could drink like a hurricane, he he he. Tell us again what happened, Jay.

No, Sam, it was just a car wreck.

Maybe we need another vision, Billy said.

❖❖❖

A Day at Tsaile Lake

From a distance,
the lake looks small.
But I had to walk far
to the south around the edge
of a channel filled with algae.
Climb on clay banks, hot stone.
A Navajo man and three sons
are fishing.
When I got to them,
I could see I had come a ways.
This lake is as large
as an eye looking into the sky.

The Navajo man's son
fumbles with his fishing hook.
Corn for bait keeps falling
off his fingers.
The lake is very deep here.
I learned to dive
in Vietnam, he says.
His eyes are jaded and flat
from the beer at his side,
from the fierce light
of the hot afternoon sun.
You can do thirty feet
without gear, he said,
but after that you can't.
His words stumble.
Once, he said, I did fifty feet.
His laugh halts.
Finally, he baits his hook
and throws it into the water.
This part of the lake is deep.

A woman with a hat,
a man with a Budweiser T-shirt,
and a little girl
sit by the lakeshore
on aluminum chairs.
Fishing lines are languid
in the lake.
The water barely laps.
Little bits of light,
like mica, jump about.
I wonder about a memory
that it signals.
The man looks me over,
suspicious, from under his hat,
and then at his pickup truck.
Across the back window
is a deer rifle.
I want to tell him
I'm not a stranger.
The litttle mica lights jump
on the lake.

I like it where I'm alone

I climb through brush
standing on a clay cliff
and slide down to Tsaile Creek
where it is muddy.
Maybe I pretend
to be a mountain lion
stopping to drink,
crossing one mountain range
to another, maybe.
I leave my pawprints.

A horse has walked here, too,
gingerly, making sure
there is no sudden quicksand.

Here the creek seeps
to the surface barely
and forms a little pool
behind an old piñon log.

I stop on the log and cross.

There are a man's footprints
of several days before.
He was walking alone.

The bird flew from right
in front of me.
From a green clump of plants
tipped with yellow flowers.
I looked down,
and there it was.
A perfect circle
of skinny sticks, strands
of wool, dark horsehair.

Parting the stems
of the plants,
I saw them,
mottled blue and white
in the soft bowl
of sticks, wool, and hair.
My blood, my blood halts
for just an instant.

Never before
have I wished so much
I had been more gentle
in my life.

Horses fleet away
from me
like heartbeats.
They cross a barley field
and race toward a hill.

There is a barn
built of railroad ties
and pine logs.
Carefully and with great task,
I am sure of that.
An old hayrake rusts
and sags nearby.
A wheel from something
leans on an old fence.

Shadows peer at me
from the spaces
between the ties and logs.

I cross the barley field.

The horses have stopped
at the foot of the hill,
waiting to make sure I am gone.

I see two children
on the northeast shore
as I walk.
They are almost hidden
by a tall gray bush.
Leaning into a bit of wind,
I hear them murmuring.

I think of a storyteller
who listens for the wind
to bring things.

When I get to the children
I say, Hello.
And nothing else.
I sit on the ground
listening to their silence,
listening to the wind.

They have nylon lines
wrapped around beer cans.
They are catching nothing.
The afternoon has been hot.
The shadow from the bush
is beginning to lean
into the lake.
Maybe soon.
I say nothing more
and they say nothing more.

I want to tell them things,
and I think they would understand
I am the father of two children.
I smoke a cigarette
and carefully put it out
in the sand, and then I get up
and say, Good-bye.
And they say, Good-bye.
And I leave.

When I leave and angle away
from the lake,
the shadows of sage and juniper
are long.
I think of a story, listening.

HANAY GEIOGAMAH

◈◈

FROM
49

EDITOR'S NOTE: The play, *49*, from which scenes three and four are drawn, is the most theatrically sophisticated and the most direct of Geiogamah's works. At the same time, though conventionally Anglo-American in its form, *49* has a strong traditional Indian atmosphere. In this play, which was first performed at the University of Oklahoma in 1975, the playwright links the past with the present and points toward an Indian future. *49* celebrates the continuity and tenacity of Indian life.

SCENE 3

Lights reveal Night Walker, whose body is making the motions of a journey through rugged terrain. Odd flashes of light illuminate his progress, which is being observed by masks and faces of humans and animals. The 49 group are in their hiding positions throughout the scene. Night Walker reaches a clearing, composes himself, and delivers a prayer that is directed as much to himself as to the power spirits.

NIGHT WALKER
  I heed as unto those I call.
  I heed as unto those I call.
  Send to me thy potent aid.

  Help us, the tribe, our people, oh, holy place around. Help us, our friends, our brothers and sisters. We heed as unto thee we call.

  I come to visit with my brothers and sisters.
  Will you hear my voice?

  Will you hear my voice? The voice of a friend who has honor and respect deep in his heart for you?

  I am the oldest man of the tribe, our people. You, my brothers and sisters, have given me this honor of life.

162

The masks and faces and supernatural activities become larger.

You know my voice. We sing together. You were at my birth. You know my father. You know my father's father, and you know his father. You are kind and generous to all of us, the tribe, our people.

Will I sing for you now? I will tell you a story of a bear who comes to watch the dancing of the tribe, our people. *(pause)* Some of the people say the bear is learning our songs.

I have brought food for my friends. I will make a meal for us. I will make a fire. I will spread my blankets.

He does these things.

I have tobacco with me. It is good tobacco.

I have sage that was brought to the tribe our people from a place far away from our home. I will burn it for you.

He waits, then lights the sage.

I saw a young man and a young girl of the tribe our people the other day. *(pause)* They both were smiling and happy. I looked at them for a long time. I watched them walk about. I saw in their smiles the signs of a family of wonderful hunters and weavers.

I had a feeling to speak with them, but I . . . did . . . not.

The faces move closer.

The faces of these two young ones appear before me now. I bring their smiles here for my friends to see.

I am made sad . . . by . . . these smiles. My friends!

I am the youngest man of the tribe, our people. You, my brothers and sisters have given me this honor.

Haw!
Haw!
I know.
I hope.
I pray.

He has established communication.

I dream.
I smile.
I do.

Haw!
I know the smiles.
I see.
I am the oldest man of the tribe. Haw! Haw!
The young ones' smiles are my smiles.
It is I who am smiling.
I am the girl.
I am the boy.
Yes.
They will both know that I am they.

A longer pause. A jew's harp and Apache violin* are heard.

The men chiefs of the tribe, our people, do not look to me when they talk with me of the things that concern the good of the tribe, our people.

They do not tell me all that they want me to know.

When they return to the tribe, our people, after fighting with the enemies. I must talk more and more to Brother Death.

I must ask Brother Death . . . to . . . take the spirits . . . of the young men . . . who have stopped living . . . with us.

Haw! I wait.
Haw!
I see.
I see. Brother Death sees too. How long? How far?

He lights more sage, then the young people begin, with soft voices, the Sioux Medicine Chant, and sing it as a counterpoint to Night Walker's prayer.

I have come here for the young man whose smiles I see.
I have come here for the young woman, who is so pretty.
I have come here for the warrior chiefs who will not look at me.
I am the oldest man of the tribe.
I have come here as two smiles who cannot see into the darkness that I see, gathering ahead on our road.

Must Brother Death direct their eyes? (*very firmly*)

Must all life be taken from us?
My friends know.

* An Apache violin is a one-string instrument that produces a monotone similar to a running single note repeated on a violin.

I do not know about the smiling faces of the young man and the young woman of the tribe, our people.

I do not know how long the young people will know the smell of the sage and the cedar.

I sing. Will they sing? Many beautiful songs?
I dance. How will they know to dance?
I make pictures of color. Will they see this beauty?

I conduct the ceremonies of our journey. Which one of them will follow me to lead?

I heal my siser's child. Will they know the medicine of the tribe, our people?

I have learned the way of Brother Winter and I talk with our brothers in the grass and trees and in the sky. Will they know these friends?

I am the oldest man of the tribe, our people, and I give help to my brothers and sisters in our journey.

The answer is completed.

They will hear my voice. They will hear your voices.
They will look to me. They will look to you.

We live a very long time. They will live a very long time. I am not afraid. I will not stop walking. I will not stop singing. I will not stop dancing. I will talk to all of my friends for a very long time. We will walk through the dark that *has* passed us, the tribe, our people. A-ho! A-ho, pah-bes. A-ho.

We will live and walk together for a long time. All of us will live and walk together for a long time.

He bows deeply and remains in the position as the Sioux Medicine Chant builds, then fades to end the scene. His exit is like a disappearance.

SCENE 4

In the darkness a youth strikes a match and draws it slowly toward his face, illuminating his features until he whistles softly, blowing it out.

Other matches and whistles begin to dot the scene.

The 49 group one by one come out of their hiding positions and begin circling in an effort to find each other.

The Water-whistles Song is heard as this night ballet unfolds.

They find their friends and partners, stand together in small groups, check the night air for a feeling of safety.

When the group has re-formed, the song, which has no words, ends. All lights go to a blue shading to complete the scene.

RAY A. YOUNG BEAR

The Significance of a Water Animal

Since then I was
the North.
Since then I was
the Northwind.
Since then I was nobody.
Since then I was alone.

The color of my black eyes
inside the color of King-
fisher's hunting eye
weakens me, but sunlight
glancing off the rocks
and vegetation strengthens me.
As my hands and fingertips
extend and meet,
they frame the serene
beauty of bubbles and grain—
once a summer rainpool.

A certain voice of *Reassurance*
tells me a story of a water animal
diving to make land available.
Next, from the Creator's
own heart and flesh
Ukimau was made:
the progeny of divine
leaders. And then
from the Red Earth
came the rest of us.

"To believe otherwise,"
as my grandmother tells me,
"or to simply be ignorant,
Belief and what we were given
to take care of,
is on the verge
of ending. . ."

◆◆◆

The Personification of a Name

Our geodesic dome-shaped lodge
redirects the drifting snow.

Above us, through the momentary
skylight, an immature eagle
stops in its turbulent flight
to gaze into our woodland
sanctuary.

Easily outstared, we rest our eyes
on the bright floor. He reminds us
further of his presence through
the shadow movement of his wings:
Portrait of a hunter
during first blizzard.

Black Eagle Child.

All-Star's Thanksgiving/1965

At midnight
when we finally signaled for
and received permission
to go outside and relieve
ourselves, I stepped off
the porch onto a steep cliff.
Immediately, I dropped
to the ground for fear
I would tumble down
the mountainside.
"Get up," said Facepaint,
the trickster who brought
me to his relatives's *amanita*
congregation.
"There are no mountains
in the Midwest."
Later, after he got me upright,
we went back inside.
Comforted by people,
I sat back against
the log cabin wall
and closed my watery eyes.
Suddenly, I was sitting on
a tropical beach with my legs
in the vibrant surf. In the breeze
I felt the sun's warmth. I became
sleepy, and when my head sank
into the wall, I woke up.
I soon discovered that
my left leg was missing.
I truly thought I had
sacrificed it as a brake
to keep me from falling.
My inquiry made a spectable
until an old man directly
across from me theorized
the leg probably became numb
under my weight. When I looked,

it was there. But the missing-leg
dream was a minor problem compared
to the disconcertion of thinking
oneself in a state of religious
purpose: bilingual songs
and cigarette-smoking
constellations

◆◆◆

The Last Time They Were Here

In between the deafening locust-shrill
on the apple trees the locusts pause
at their own noise and then
to a silent signal they drop down
to another leaf or branch,
stopping when the chorus
starts again.

The last time they were here
this is what I remember:

I see my grandfather kneeling before
rolls of our delicately tied belongings.
He instructs, "It will always be important
as you travel in life to tie protection
as I have just done."

As we move without him now, I think
about my belongings spread apart
in three different houses. No matter
how powerful my sinew star-symbols
over my writings, they are defenseless
without my actual presence.

The Song Taught to Joseph

I was born unto this snowy-red earth
with the aura and name of the Black Lynx.
When we simply think of each other,
night begins. My twin the Heron
is on a perpetual flight northward,
familiarizing himself with the landscape
of afterlife, but he never gets there . . .
because the Missouri River descends
from the Northern Plains
into the Morning Star.

One certain thing though,
he sings the song of the fish
below him in the mirror
of Milky Way.

It goes:

In this confrontation,
the gills of the predator
overtake me in the daylight toward home;
In this confrontation,
he hinders my progress with a cloud of mud he stirs.
Crying, I ask that I not feel each painful part
he takes, at least not until I can grasp
in the darkness the entrance
of home.

◆◆◆

The Reason Why I Am Afraid
Even Though I Am a Fisherman

Who is there
to witness the ice
as it gradually forms itself
from the cold rock-hard banks
to the middle of the river?
Is the wind chill a factor?
Does the water at some point
negotiate and agree to stop
moving and become frozen?
When you do not know the answers
to these immediately you are afraid,
and to even think in this inquisitive
manner is contrary to the precept
that life is in everything.
Me, I am not a man;
I respect the river
for not knowing its secret,
for answers have nothing
to do with cause and occurence.
It doesn't matter how early
I wake to see the sun shine
through the ice-hole;
only the ice along
with my foolishness
decides when
to break.

THREE POEMS/1979

1.

The high uncut grass was covered
with a cool sheen of dew.
Grasshoppers sat quietly
in the shadows—oblivious
to the fact that the price
of gasoline was the reason
for their August bed
and comfort.
The sun was beginning
to filter and mix into
the new green-colored forest,
all of which made for ritualistic
morning.
There was never any indication
as to what made the Nicotines
decide to gather frogs
from their yard for bait.
First, the wife would merely
suggest the catching of sha-qua-ma-qwa'
when the humidity decreased,
how in the bank-pole evening
they would throw out their lines,
sensing by the firm splash
over the river's depth that they
were about, just by that sound
alone.
Unconsciously, the husband
would bring out the bait bucket.
Together they would talk,
reassuring each other if
they could find at least six frogs
before the sun rose,
tomorrow would mean fried flathead,
boiled potatoes, wild onions,
and Canadian ale.

Further, it would be an opportunity
to set aside portions of their catch
and to supplicate *those who have passed*,
implanting within them this doubt
and reverence for existence.

2.

Everything is arranged for us
when we arrive in the small Norwegian town
for the poetry reading. To welcome us,
they release the Styrofoam snow
and restaurants list the food
we like in their menus:
spaghetti for Selene
and chili for me.
Although we whisper
to each other as to what
we should drink, the waiter
with extraordinary hearing
orders milk and Pepsi from
a distance. On our drive
to the cliffs where the ancient
glaciers supposedly stopped,
we observe caucasians who dress
and act like Indians: three middle-
aged men sit on a car hood and drink
their whiskey in public; an old lady
walks to town in a strong, even pace.
Jokingly, I sometimes tell friends
they have white opposites, but when
I finally meet mine, it isn't comical.
But through him, we are here.
Contrary to what is written
on the dust jacket of his poems,
I have never seen Michael B.
on or near the tribal settlement.
To say you are *a part* is no easy
matter. Before I question other
people's lives, there is my own
to consider. Together we read
from our work. I am sure the freshman
students do not understand my life
as well as his. However, they are
amused when I tell them of my ms.
rejections from elite east coast
publications (anything east
of the Mississippi), and why
I am beyond the listless primitive
who tracks the extinct wolf.

After classes, a bearded professor
invites us to his country house—
a remodeled mental institute.
During lunch, adopted Chinese
children dash in and the professor's wife plunges a spoon
with peanut butter into their
mouths. I suddenly realize
when I touch the Chinese girl's
warped head that this place isn't real,
that it was arranged in haste.
They are fascinated by the cutbead
barrettes on my wife's hair and I am
puzzled why they have invited us.

Before graph paper existed,
you planned the first series of geometric
communiques.
Although I can't decipher
the signals or the code,
I know from having seen computers
there is something reaching me.
The Czechoslovakian cutbeads
which decorate the barrettes
in your hair
flash synchronously
by the candlelight: U.F.O.
I discuss the plight
of the grasshopper who had chosen
me the morning previous (on my way
to the university) to oblige
his planned suicide by jumping
onto my path.
In Indian I told him:
it's simple to end yourself,
but me I am in the human snowdrift already
in need of money, excitement and guaranteed
warmth.
Venison takes the space in my freezer;
otherwise, I would take you there
as a favor, to let you sleep until
the Iowa River freezes and lower you
on hook in exchange for prehistoric-
looking fish.

◆◆◆

From the Spotted Night

In the blizzard
while chopping wood
the mystical whistler
beckons my attention.
Once there were longhouses
here. A village.
In the abrupt spring floods,
swimmers retrieved our belief.
So their spirit remains.
From the spotted night
distant jets transform
into fireflies who float
towards me like incandescent
snowflakes.
The leather shirt
which is suspended
on a wire hanger
above the bed's headboard
is humanless; yet when one
stands outside the house,
the strenuous sounds
of dressers and boxes
being moved can be heard.
We believe someone wears
the shirt and rearranges
the heavy furniture,
although nothing
is actually changed.
Unlike the Plains Indian shirts
which repelled lead bullets,
richocheting from them
in fiery sparks,
this shirt is the means;
this shirt *is* the bullet.

The Language of Weather

The summer rain isn't here yet,
but I hear and see the approaching
shadow of its initial messenger:
Thunder.
The earth's bright horizon
sends a final sunbeam directly
towards me, skimming across the tops
of clouds and hilly woodland.
All in one moment, in spite
of my austerity, everything
is aligned: part sun, part cloud,
part sky, part sun and part self.
I am the only one to witness
this renascence.
Before darkness replaces the light
in my eyes, I think about the *Factors*
which make my existence possible
and the absence of importunity.
My parents, who are hurrying
to overturn the reddish-brown dirt
around the potato plants, begin
to talk above the rumbling din.
"See that everyone in the house
releases parts of ourselves . . ."
While raindrops begin to cool
my face and arms, lightning
breaks a faraway cottonwood
in half; small clouds of red
garden dust are kicked into
the frantic air by grasshoppers
in retreat.

I think of the time I stood
on this same spot years ago,
but it was under moonlight,
and I was watching this beautiful
electrical force dance above
another valley.
In the daylight distance,
a stray spirit whose guise
is a Whirlwind spins and attempts
to communicate from its ethereal
loneliness.

WENDY ROSE

Sipapu

Hand by hand
bone by bone
dancing on the ladder
like mosquitoes
climbing
foot by foot
heel hanging in space
impressions of spruce
cut into our flesh
hand by hand
thumbs wrapped
in daylight
we   emerge
we   emerge
like wind
like dust
we travel a life time
each moment climbing
we handle time
like something
fragile
we fulfill
what we say
in the songs
we name
the landscape
of our skin
the map on the backs
of our hands
bone by bone
one people
bleeding
leading on
to a trail
our ancestors knew

what we do
at night
in the scent
of spruce
and clay
we   emerge
we   emerge
Anasazi throats
Anasazi feet
at the top
of the world
in the taste
of daylight
a sound
of birth
a whirl
of blood
a spin
of song

* Anasazi: ancient cliff-
dwelling people ancestral
to the Hopi

Comparison of Hands
One Day Late Summer

My hand
at the flame
is white clay
unchipped, unshaped,
the parched earth,
the empty ravine,
horizontal cracks
that trace the bone
and fat of me
reluctant or angry,
dodging the droughts,
a configuration of colors
mixed up and unsettled.

Solid on mine and so strong
your hand contains
summer thunder,
the moist dark belly
in which seeds sprout,
the beginning of laughter,
a child's voice,
the promise perhaps
of tomorrow,
the wash
edges deepending into night
sculpted by blood,
tumbling end over end
everyone's names.

And myself jealous
of the bones you hold so well,
their proper shapes,
precision of length,
those old songs

whirling from your throat
easy and hot
for the dancers.
You and your memories
of berries picked ripe,
late summer days like this one
with tongue turning black
and teeth blue, loosely made basket
on your elbow.
Your people stretched you
til one day you woke up
and you probably just knew
who you were.

I would mention
my own recollections
but would you want to hear
of afternoons alone
and cold nights on Eagle Hill
being a wild horse
among the oats, the willow,
eucalyptus trees
and sunset-colored spirit women?
Or would you want to listen
that I who sing so much
of family and blood
grew alone and cold
on those silent foothills?
Would you want to hear
the sound of being tough,
or the hollow high winds
in my mother's closet?
Would you want to count
the handfuls of pills
or touch the fingers
that tighten my soul?

Who would want to know
where all the words went
when the trails narrowed
into drought,

the sky dipped
to the empty river,
the birds never nested
but judged and condemned.
What is a ghost after all
but dryness
years, apples, memories,
dry berries, clouds,
dry skin, words,
not enough blackbirds
           to quarrel for the seeds . . .

Dream About Poetry and the Mask

You
lie still.

Lying
still.

Careful.

Being
careful.

Keep
those eyes closed,
those lips
together
now   beware
there may be someday
the light
tumble
of foreign hair.

Beware.
Eyes are closed,
lips together.

Okay now
be ready.

Ready.

Slowly so slowly
I'll let it down.
Cover your throat
and don't move
even if it feels
hard or warm
or smells still
of the tree.

Lying still.
Upturned my face
waiting.
Throat is covered.

                        A word first. You know
                        this is just the beginning.

Beginning.
                        Do you believe that?

I believe
what begins.

                        The beginning, yes
                        how the dream
                        sits on paper,
                        how the song rattles
                        the fingers that write it
                        or the fingers that try.
                        And the dream
                        binds the tongue
                        that tries to sing it.

The dream—
write it.
The song—
write it.
Keep
some songs
silent,
others
tied up.

                        Oh, you know that.
                        You have always known.
                        Okay, now, the mask
                        is coming at you.
                        Easy now, it's coming.

I feel my breath
fog back to my cheeks
so hot so close
my forehead
may erupt
splinters

                        now I'm securing it
                        a second . now

I hear the whisper
of leather ties,
shuffle of spruce
needles and the pain
in my shoulder
where they stick me

nothing you weren't
in need of
or prepared for

no nothing
I have needed this
prepared
waited
waited for you

it fits just right
hey you knew it would fit
even with your
mixed proportions

it is good
how it weighs me
how it presses my skin
into proper folds
into Hopi folds

oh, yes it had to fold you
you know it's always
been your blind ancestor
the one that gave you
his mountain-brown eyes

the one who was
reaching for me
just there I saw him
til now we merge
he and she

well that's it
that's enough
I will take the mask
let you dream it
from time to time
so long as you don't forget

I will not forget
I will not forget

                                what did I tell you
                                it was the word
                                the beginning

maatsiwa
how could I forget
now you have tied it to me
I must sing
I must begin it
again and again

                                and again and again

cold air startles
my forehead sweat
the wind is gone
that swept me home

                                another time
                                I'll return
                                I'll bring it back
                                I keep the mask

I wear the mask
                                I keep the mask

I wear the mask
                                I keep the mask

I wear the mask
                                I keep the mask

I wear the mask

      * maatsiwa: Hopi for the act of being named formally

                        ◆◆◆

Alfalfa Dance

Warm afternoons
smell of alfalfa
green in the air
            I pretend
            I am graceful
            and thin
            tie my hair
with wool ribbons
squash blooms
a Hopi ballerina
whose hands flutter

into fiddles and flutes,
step from room to room
curtains closed

walking
through knee-high thistle
of San Francisco
prance and bow
        elk doe
        waiting for her buck
        or for applause
or for the stones to move
beetles skittering
from beneath
        or fragrant with the earth
        mist and steam
        in the sun
        lift one obsidian hoof
nose directly
into the wind
dance away
from humanity.

◆◆◆

For a Poet Named Thatcher
Who Makes Much of Grains & Grasses

(for *Hale Thatcher*)

The house is built
above us, the bricks are layered
and the floor danced hard,
the ceiling of sticks and mud
clicked into place and pressed.
The humid air is fragrant
with a thousand fogs.

A poet named Thatcher laces
the grass and reeds, patiently crossing

stem to stem, seed to seed,
below and above, around and through
clay and straw a tangle of words,
a knot, a sky, a planet
to shed the vision
that dropped on our hands,
encircled our heads
from far away
and would wreck our technique,
our humble sleep, our breath,
our heartbeat, would wake us
to the sound
of small finches
and their twigs.

Thatcher
our ancestors know
who we are.

◆◆◆

Passover Rules
April 1981

Passover approaches
this cold morning
to cities and mountains
with a muted song,
whispers pulled from our throats
stiff as the white and gold lilies
on altars from coast to coast.

In a Brooklyn churchyard
magnolias birth from crooked limbs
and in Berkeley the cherry-plum trees
grow pink snow.
Dakota skies cloud over
to end the drought,
heifers find the youth of green shoots
and geese honk north
to the prairie.

In the desert
a spaceship settles
in the shimmering red dust
and two whitemen walk out
healthy and wise
smelling still from the smolder
of re-entry.

The wind dances
from Chicago to Dallas,
hats fly and old men bend double
over their walking sticks,
mumble in their beards
and compare the ancient succulence
of their scars.

Everywhere in the country there are
crossed over our hearts green ribbons.
On every door the blood
of the Passover Lamb.

* spaceship: the space shuttle Columbia
* green ribbons: commemoration/protest of the murder of
young Black people in Atlanta and elsewhere
* Passover Lamb: the eternal sacrifice

Robert

the lines of your arteries
begin to glow   making maps
finger follows afraid &
firm   pale like the alamagordo sky
the white lizards in the sand

are you humming or is it
a wayward insect or the tremble
of your deepest bones, los alamos
trinity alamagordo frail robert
jornada del muerto   you crouch
your light grey business suit
loosened tie   speaking to
transparent friends or to no one
in particular
"It's amazing how
the tools, the technology
trap one."
& you were amazed at the welts
so wide on your wrists, those chains
enormous from your belt.

not even your wife was awake
morning pivot of your life
the radio groaned   you twisted
the knob feeling for
an end to feeling   but the voice
said anyway how your kids went screaming
from the crotch of the plane
mouth-first onto play yard & rooftops
& gardens & temples, onto hair & flesh
onto steel & clay   leaving you
leaving you in shreds your own fingerprints
in the ashes   your vomit your tears

"I am death, the destroyer of worlds . . . The physicists
have known sin and this is a knowledge they cannot lose."
—J. Robert Oppenheimer

◆◆◆

Evening Ceremony Dream

We are turned to the sun
looking west, the petals of our eyes
wrinkled into slits sidewise.
We imagine antelope feet
making hesitant drumbeats,
they are so light
they approach and spin
become fawns again
and we leap in the circle and out,
running hard to our childhood
to later emerge
dancers masked
and painted priests,
women encircling
the full baskets,
grandmothers bent
under blankets and squash.

Along the narrow tall buttes
smoke lays low, blue,
and choke cherries gossip
rustling each other ripe.
Songs rumble up
from underground men
keeping like a robe
around them the kiva.*
Shoulder to shoulder
we who wait are the mesa edge
tipping into space or tumbling
down to ruins
among buried bones.

The man walks
across ancient words,
peeling the masks

* kiva: underground ceremonial room

and the shields away,
his hard fingertips
carving blood-red faces,
his bare feet flexing
the clay into mud,
mother-flesh into water.

He says "I've been tricked,"
his cheeks gold with fever,
death flowering
in his bowels.
"It is you," he mumbles
"Who came dancing
like a mosquito
to my hand.
You are the bile
of my afternoon sleep,
the convulsions
of my pale morning.
You are the wall
I am forgetting to climb,
the witch I forgot
to reckon with."

And then I knew who he was,
could name every bone
in his blue-black feathers.

Look how the people
push down the sun,

pull the stars
out with their teeth.

◆◆◆

Loo-wit

The way they do
this old woman
no longer cares
what others think
but spits
her black tobacco
any which way
stretching full length
from her bumpy bed.
Finally up
she sprinkles ash
on the snow,
cold and rocky ribs
promising nothing
but that winter is gone.
Centuries of berries
have bound her to earth,
huckleberry ropes
about her neck.
Her children play games
(no sense of tomorrow);
her eyes covered with bark
she wakes at night
and fears she is blind.
Nothing but tricks
left in this world,
nothing to keep
an old woman home.
Around her
machinery growls,
snarls and ploughs
great patches
of green-gray skin.
She crouches
in the north,
the source of the trembling
dawn appearing

* Loo-wit: Mount Saint Helens

with the shudder
of her slopes.
Blackberries unravel,
stones dislodge;
it's not as if
they weren't warned.
She was sleeping
but she heard the boot scrape,
the creaking floor,
felt the pull of the blanket
from her thin shoulder.
With one free hand
she finds her weapons
and raises them high,
clearing the twigs
from her throat
she sings, she sings,
shaking the sky
like a blanket about her
Loo-wit sings and sings and sings.

◆◆◆

Hanabi-ko [Koko]

"A visitor recently stopped by to see Koko. On greeting the 180-pound gorilla, the visitor pointed to her and then made a small circle with her open hand in the air in front of her own face, signing You're pretty. *Koko digested this comment for a moment and then stroked her finger across her nose; her reply meant* false *or* fake."
—Francine Patterson, Koko's teacher
in American Sign Language, 1981

With her voice
she is grooming me

◆　　◆　　◆　　◆

sounds
like falling rain,
like wind, like something
I don't remember

◆　　◆　　◆　　◆

touch me here and here
on the underside
of my thigh, the back of my hand,
all over the top
of my head

❖   ❖   ❖   ❖❖

little sounds
mouth was warm
good   taste
of hair flesh salt
mother
          this one went away
          and this one returned

❖   ❖   ❖   ❖

is this my mother
rain wind touch of sound?

❖❖❖

Julia

AUTHOR'S NOTE: Julia Pastrana, 1832–1860, was a singer and dancer who
was billed in the circus as "The World's Ugliest Woman" or "Lion Lady"
because of her deformed face and the hair that grew from all over her
body and face. She was a Mexican-Indian woman with a delicately beautiful singing voice. Her manager, in an attempt to maintain control over
her life on the midway, married her. She believed what he told her and,
on her wedding day, was heard to remark, "I know he loves me for my
own sake." A year later, she gave birth to a boy who inherited her defor-
mities, looking just like her, but who died six hours after he was born. A
few days later, Julia also died. Her husband, in whom she had such great
trust, was unwilling to sacrifice his investment. Through a special European process, he had Julia and her infant son preserved and mounted in a
glass-and-wood case so he could continue exhibiting them. As recently
as 1975, Julia Pastrana and her baby boy were exhibited at locations in
the United States and in Europe. Where they are now is unknown.

◆◆◆

Tell me it was just a dream,
my husband, a clever trick
made by some tin-faced village god
or ghost-coyote pretending to frighten me
with his claim that our marriage
is made of malice and money.
Oh tell me again
how you admire my hands,
how my jasmine tea is rich and strong,
my singing sweet, my eyes so dark
you would lose yourself swimming
man into fish
as you mapped the pond
you would own.
That was not all.
The room grew cold as if to joke
with these warm days.
The curtains blew out and fell back
against the moon-painted sill.
I rose from my bed like a spirit,
and not a spirit at all
floated slowly to my great glass oval
to see myself reflected
as the burnished bronze woman,
skin smooth and tender,
I know myself to be in the dark
above the confusion of French perfumes
and I was there in the mirror
and I was not.
I had grown hard
as the temple stones of Otomi,
hair grown over my ancient face
like black moss, gray as jungle fog
soaking green the tallest tree tops.
I was frail
as the breaking dry branches
of my winter sand canyons
standing so still
as if to stand
forever.

198   WENDY ROSE

Oh such a small room!
No bigger than my elbows outstretched
and just as tall as my head,
a small room
from which to sing open the doors
with my cold graceful mouth,
my rigid lips, my silences
dead as yesterday,
cruel as what the children say,
cold
as the coins
that glitter in your pink fist.
And another terrifying magic
in the cold of that tall box:
in my arms or standing next to me
on a tall table by my right shoulder
a tiny doll
that looked
like me.
Oh my husband,
tell me again
this is only a dream
I wake from warm
and today is still today,
summer sun and quick rain;
tell me, husband,
how you love me for myself
one more time.
It scares me so
to be with child,
lioness with
cub.

◈◈◈

I Was a Centaur, Remember

Between earth nipples
water is rushing,
grasses release white flowers
from their heads;

treefrogs climb, call
from twisted madrone
and acorns are cracking
underfoot.
I will go
dissolving all my caution
about talking to strangers.

But remember
remember remember

the peeling red trees,
a little of my blood
on the round brown leaves;
hoofprints big as postholes
in the riverbank,
wind a mumble and braiding of mane
along human spine, horse withers;
and the sun circling
from that side
to that side.
Points of grain surround me
fetlock-high,
ancient wheat is gathered
by mice and gophers.
Oh the lobster smell
of the morning harbor,
the shadow-mint
of my mountain cave,
the beat pause and echo
of my sandstone songs,
the manzanita's
enduring stone skin.
Please
remember it all
this way

remember
the lift of my tail,
my noble ancestry,
my perfect scheme.
Remember both
the whinny
and the words.

◆◆◆

The Halfbreed Chronicles: Maurice

"The healthiest Indians are those behind bars."
—The Native People, Sept. 17, 1982

I suppose Coyote's laughing upstairs.
Down here my fingers are frozen
into the shape of Bigfoot's corpse
twisted to the earth at Wounded Knee.
Autumn caught me ordering the dust
but your eastern wind has scattered it
and my broom is defeated from its single sweep.
The heavy heart is genuine enough—
              no metaphor, there is suspended
              between my ribs a small stone
              big as your fist
self-contained, solid, almost still.
Your fingertips are embedded there
my ribs unevenly growing half-round
to protect the stone from further assaults.

The bars of this prison
merge with my bones.
The floor is my flesh on which cockroaches feed;
the dribble of water in the toilet is blood
that winter freezes, rats quickly lap.
The guards have been bribed, my brother,
and there is not even a biscuit
              nor gravy nor meat
              especially not the touch
              of a comforting hand.

Nothing fancy to tell you
except I survived after all.
The last apple leaf is beaten from the branch
by the sudden shout of male rain;
the tiny creek beside my house
has covered the road with black silt.
Things go on.
Coyote has done well polishing this wall

and my image is thin, not like me
but small like you: my hair fades
from black to wispy white and thins
into a pencil of a pony tail;
my eyes become transparent;
my nose grows Mohawk-high,
my voice New York fast.

Strawberries unpicked rot around me
the vines tangling my wrists.
Hawks cackle down from the scaffold
appearing in the dawn drizzle
like vampires you have called.
Your name is burned on the rope;
my blood carries your spies.
You will want to display my skull
with the other bones in your bed.
Coyote is laughing upstairs.

HAROLD LITTLEBIRD

Independence Pass

mountains snow covered and glowing
in the afternoon's brilliance
air thick of pine and pitch
springs erupting from cracks
in the sides of rough granite land flows
gushing and pumping the life-blood of the earth mother
far to the valleys below
and the peak towering like sentries
high into the clouds and further
and the fullness and wonder and serene beauty
this pass called Independence
surrounded in awe, wide-eyed and reverent
like the time in Utah, at sweat, with Bruce and Adrianna
the all-mother came and washed me
blessing with air and cold and I sang in solemn laughter
and my thoughts were of home
and my dad's father and his father before him
the language to describe this wholeness and being a part of it
one part in many
my heart was pounding mountain summer
asking to breathe, taste and share
like dancing and the cottonwood drum
every muscle and vein was taut and swollen
intent on moving without strain, bursting forth
for the people in harmony and song
the wind gusting, trees swaying
springs running, grasses growing
snow covering, the earth living . . .
these and more I know my father and his father
and his father's father danced
and my father has let it be known to me

up there is prayer without words
surrounded by spirits of caring
and the tears in my eyes were for knowing
that's from where I come
and that's where song and motion and language is born and re-
born
and the sound from any one person is re-called and,
should be held in deepest respect and mystery
for it is sacred like breath itself

DUANE NIATUM

Old Tillicum

(for Francis Patsy, my grandfather)

A timber blue haze dissolves
on chokecherry leaves, black caps, and the ants'
footprints at the beginning of the thicket.
Pebbles of water leap before the salmon
in the current; the brush keeps the secret
steps of elk kicking dirt down the canyon.
The sky lifts my alder-smoked frame
like an unbroken impulse of the mountain's,
to pause with goldenrod, willow, and blue jay
gazing across the river of my people.
An old Klallam, I sit with my grandson
while from the fern distances, the Elwah
rushes seaward. I wait for the voices
of the river to compose my son's manhood,
strengthen the green awkwardness of youth,
flush his cheek with spruce light,
and promise my brittle bones a future.

Memp-ch-ton, mirrored in the rapids,
magnified by the falling sun,
dwarfs the white firs enclosed in
the luminous gatherings of sap and lichen.
Pitch-dry with age, I am here to see
my daughter's son start the long journey
into the clearing of Old Patsy's.
Old Patsy's story of a seal hunt, a net
full of herring, pulls him on like a tide.
Once frightened of the surf's crack
below the pine, our evening walks by lantern
to the circle of Young and Lucy Patsy's,
he now disappears happily beyond the edge
of the mountain's hide; fox running shadows.

Muted by the dusk and roosting quail,
the ridge above the ravine, he remembers
the legend of the seven brothers
that named the village long burned to ash,
how they danced into the fire to forget.
And like their forgotten totem,
the moon drifts full height into the next horizon,
returning to its birth.
Perhaps wanting us all to touch earth
through spring, the dawn carries
the water drum away.

As his grandfather, I rise too late
to walk with little crow. Instead, I hear
his first jump through chance's hoop.

❖❖❖

At the International Poetry Festival

I awoke to the flight of a tern skimming the canal,
to cars swerving round a packed and portly trolley.
Thriving, the city rides the morning rail.
Street voices dangle in the present, coffeed and busy.
Rotterdam's all commerce, bustling and concentric—
gulls and peddlers give birth and die on water,
pass under, over bridges, while the traffic
collides at the market, fades to a ship's blurr.
The light's a balcony, Vermeer's or van Gogh's—
June palette of window boxes: geraniums and pansies.
I almost touch the Rembrandt-sky, grey-orange,
the corner-stalls, the red and yellow poppies.
In Holland, my pain's a skull, void of face;
like the cypress, I leave shadows to their surface.

◆◆◆

To My Coast Salish Ancestors

In the late evening, rain and fog.
Who sends dancers with elk-teeth rattles
to roam the alley next to my cottage?
Their song enters the window,
a Swinomish chorus: each step
that brings them closer forms
another mask of the moon,
another color of the Northwest sea.

I open the door and follow;
they toss legends I must find in the dark.
In their honor I cross knives with them;
our union is a force the wind receives.
I am of this coast and its keeper.

◆◆◆

Tess One Winter in the Fields

She glances round to see snow settle on the hill.
feels a flake melt against her palm, coarsen her mood.
All day she shudders at the ghostly blizzard,
its drifts that cannot fill the emptiness of pails.

Ice tufts cup the hedgerow's thorns;
grow to four times their actual size.
The terrain flows crystal in her blood.
The men are brooding: something must be wrong.

Cobwebs hang here and there along stonewalls;
reveal lines where they are usually concealed.
A haze leaves the land birch white; falls
like loops of silk on barn and plough.

Because the snow now curdles into slush,
a scarecrow tips his hat to sheep and cow.
Suddenly, birds circle from the frozen North;
huge shabby birds whose eyes are bright and black.

She wonders, do these creatures carry a nightmare
the farm of Flintcomb-Ash will soon imagine?
When the sky is struck by these brazen birds,
she and another maid under their beating wings

dismiss their feathered strangeness with a shrug.
They want only to abandon the digging and the cold,
sing again the old harvest songs of youth,
block the wind burying the cow's bell in the mud.

◆◆◆

For the People Who Came From the Moon

They stalked deer for generations
down the mountain to the meadows
where the wind settles in our city's
mushroom heart. We called them
old friends and traded salmon
for their trophies. They were
the Snoqualmie and the river willow
echo their chants to children chasing
quail into the afternoon.

As carriers of the dream wheel
we sing of rain and thunder to the strangers
from our longhouses rising from the sea.
And when the evening logs burn down to masks
the hunters from the sky
will sleep as our guests in a light
that mutes both snowpeak and fern.
Circling the lake for the dawn
we enter the dream's spruce canyons
and see blue mallards land on the bow
of a lost canoe.

Our grandfathers with family buried
under clouds drifting from here to the waterfall,
by morning will put their ears against
the rotting cedar to hear the hoofbeats
of deer and elk pound tributes in our veins
the pulse of a new fire-winged season.

The Art of Clay

The years in the blood keep us naked to the bone.
So many hours of darkness we fail to sublimate.
Light breaks down the days to printless stone.

I sing what I sang before, it's the dream alone.
We fall like the sun when the moon's our fate.
The years in the blood keep us naked to the bone.

I wouldn't reach your hand, if I feared the dark alone;
My heart's a river, but is not chilled with hate.
Light breaks down the days to printless stone.

We dance for memory because it's here on loan.
And as the music stops, nothing's lost but the date.
The years in the blood keep us naked to the bone.

How round the sky, how the planets drink the unknown.
I gently touch; your eyes show it isn't late.
Light breaks down the days to printless stone.

What figures in this clay? Gives a sharper hone?
What turns the spirit white? Wanting to abbreviate?
The years in the blood keep us naked to the bone.
Light breaks down the days to printless stone.

JOY HARJO

I Give You Back

I release you, my beautiful and terrible
fear. I release you. You were my beloved
and hated twin, but now, I don't know you
as myself. I release you with all the
pain I would know at the death of
my daughters

You are not my blood anymore.

I give you back to the white soldiers
who burned down my house, beheaded my children,
raped and sodomized my brothers and sisters.
I give you back to those who stole the
food from our plates when we were starving.

I release you, fear, because you hold
these scenes in front of me and I was born
with eyes that can never close.

I release you, fear, so you can no longer
keep me naked and frozen in the winter,
or smothered under blankets in the summer.

I release you
I release you
I release you
I release you

I am not afraid to be angry.
I am not afraid to rejoice.
I am not afraid to be black.

I am not afraid to be white.
I am not afraid to be hungry.
I am not afraid to be full.
I am not afraid to be hated.
I am not afraid to be loved.
to be loved, to be loved, fear.

Oh, you have choked me, but I gave you the leash.
You have gutted me but I gave you the knife.
You have devoured me, but I laid myself across the fire.
You held my mother down and raped her,
but I gave you the heated thing.

I take myself back, fear.
You are not my shadow any longer.
I won't hold you in my hands.
You can't live in my eyes, my ears, my voice
my belly, or in my heart my heart
my heart   my heart

But come here, fear
I am alive and you are so afraid
of dying.

❖❖❖

New Orleans

This is the south. I look for evidence
of other Creeks, for remnants of voices,
or for tobacco brown bones to come wandering
down Conti Street, Royale, or Decatur.
Near the French Market I see a blue horse
caught frozen in stone in the middle of
a square. Brought in by the Spanish on
an endless ocean voyage he became mad
and crazy. They caught him in blue
rock, said
            don't talk.

I know it wasn't just a horse
                        that went crazy.

Nearby is a shop with ivory and knives.
There are red rocks. The man behind the
counter has no idea that he is inside
magic stones. He should find out before
they destroy him. These things
have memory,
                    you know.

I have a memory.
                    It swims deep in blood,
a delta in the skin. It swims out of Oklahoma,
deep the Mississippi River. It carries my
feet to these places: the French Quarter,
stale rooms, the sun behind thick and moist
clouds, and I hear boats hauling themsleves up
and down the river.

My spirit comes here to drink.
My spirit comes here to drink.
Blood is the undercurrent.

There are voices buried in the Mississippi
mud. There are ancestors and future children
buried beneath the currents stirred up by
pleasure boats going up and down.
There are stories here made of memory.

I remember DeSoto. He is buried somewhere in
this river, his bones sunk like the golden
treasure he traveled half the earth to find,
came looking for gold cities, for shining streets
of beaten gold to dance on with silk ladies.

He should have stayed home.

                    (Creeks knew of him for miles
                        before he came into town.
                            Dreamed of silver blades
                            and crosses.)
And knew he was one of the ones who yearned
for something his heart wasn't big enough
to handle.
                    (And DeSoto thought it was gold.)

The Creeks lived in earth towns,
                                    not gold,
               spun children, not gold.
That's not what DeSoto thought he wanted to see.
The Creeks knew it, and drowned him in
               the Mississippi River
                              so he wouldn't have to drown himself.

❖❖❖

For Alva Benson, and for Those Who Have Learned to Speak

And the ground spoke when she was born.
Her mother heard it. In Navajo she answered
as she squatted down against the earth
to give birth. It was now when it happened,
now giving birth to itself again and again
between the legs of women.

Or maybe it was the Indian Hospital
in Gallup. The ground still spoke beneath
mortar and concrete. She strained against the
metal stirrups, and they tied her hands down
because she still spoke with them when they
muffled her screams. But her body went on
talking and the child was born into their
hands, and the child learned to speak
both voices.

She grew up talking in Navajo, in English
and watched the earth around her shift and change
with the people in the town and in the cities
learning not to hear the ground as it spun around
beneath them. She learned to speak for the ground,
the voice coming through her like roots that
have long hungered for water. Her own daughter
was born, like she had been, in either place
or all places, so she could leave, leap
into the sound she had always heard,
a voice like water, like the gods weaving
against sundown in a scarlet light.

WORDS IN THE BLOOD   213

The child now hears names in her sleep.
They change into other names, and into others.
It is the ground murmuring, and Mt. St. Helens
erupts as the harmonic motion of a child turning
inside her mother's belly waiting to be born
to begin another time.

And we go on, keep giving birth and watch
ourselves die, over and over.
And the ground spinning beneath us
goes on talking.

◈◈◈

Anchorage

(For Andre Lorde)

This city is made of stone, of blood, and fish.
There are Chugatch Mountains to the east
and whale and seal to the west.
It hasn't always been this way, because glaciers
who are ice ghosts create oceans, carve earth
and shape this city here, by the sound.
They swim backwards in time.

Once a storm of boiling earth cracked open
the streets, threw open the town.
It's quiet now, but underneath the concrete
is the cooking earth,
                           and above that, air
which is another ocean, where spirits we can't see
are dancing   joking   getting full
on roasted caribou, and the praying
goes on, extends out.

Nora and I go walking down 4th Avenue
and know it is all happening.
On a park bench we see someone's Athabascan
grandmother, folded up, smelling like 200 years
of blood and piss, her eyes closed against some
unimagined darkness, where she is buried in an ache
in which nothing makes
                           sense.

We keep on breathing, walking, but softer now,
the clouds whirling in the air above us.
What can we say that would make us understand
better than we do already?
Except to speak of her home and claim her
as our own history, and know that our dreams
don't end here, two blocks away from the ocean
where our hearts still batter away at the muddy shore.

And I think of the 6th Avenue jail, of mostly Native
and Black men, where Henry told about being shot at
eight times outside a liquor store in L.A., but when
the car sped away he was surprised he was alive.
no bullet holes, man, and eight cartridges strewn
on the sidewalk
           all around him.

Everyone laughed at the impossibility of it.
but also the truth. Because who would believe
the fantastic and terrible story of all of our survival
those who were never meant
                     to survive?

❖❖❖

She Had Some Horses

She had some horses.

She had horses who were bodies of sand.
She had horses who were maps drawn of blood.
She had horses who were skins of clean water.
She had horses who were the blue air of sky.
She had horses who were fur and teeth.
She had horses who were clay and would break.
She had horses who were splintered red cliff.

She had some horses.

She had horses with long, pointed breasts.
She had horses with full, brown thighs.
She had horses who laughed too much.
She had horses who threw rocks at glass houses.
She had horses who licked razor blades.

She had some horses.

She had horses who danced in their mothers' arms.
She had horses who thought they were the sun and their
bodies shone and burned like stars.
She had horses who waltzed nightly on the moon.
She had horses who were much too shy, and kept quiet
in stalls of their own making.

She had some horses.

She had horses who liked Creek Stomp Dance songs.
She had horses who cried in their beer.
She had horses who spit at male queens who made
them afraid of themselves.
She had horses who said they weren't afraid.
She had horses who lied.
She had horses who told the truth, who were stripped
bare of their tongues.

She had some horses.

She had horses who called themselves. "horse."
She had horses who called themselves, "spirit," and kept
their voices secret and to themselves.
She had horses who had no names.
She had horses who had books of names.

She had some horses.

She had horses who whispered in the dark, who were afraid
to speak.
She had horses who screamed out of fear of the silence, who
carried knives to protect themselves from ghosts.
She had horses who waited for destruction.
She had horses who waited for resurrection.

She had some horses.

She had horses who got down on their knees for any saviour.
She had horses who thought their high price had saved them.
She had horses who tried to save her, who climbed in her
bed at night and prayed as they raped her.

She had some horses.

She had some horses she loved.
She had some horses she hated.

These were the same horses.

MAURICE KENNY

When in Reality

I wrote in my journal
I had eaten only an orange
and some cheese this morning,
and drunk a pot of coffee dry.
When in truth, at dawn, I had eaten
lizards, coyotes, silver and cactus,
and a lone laborer in the desert.
I drank sky, sun and clouds;
my eyes consumed plains, mountains,
countries, continents;
worlds rumbled in my belly.
Tonight I slice and fork the western moon,
crunch on stars,
and drink the whine of wolves.

◆◆◆

Wild Strawberry

(For Helene)

And I rode the Greyhound down to Brooklyn
where I sit now eating woody strawberries
grown on the backs of Mexican farmers
imported from the fields of their hands,
juices without color or sweetness

    my wild blood berries of spring meadows
    sucked by June bees and protected by hawks

have stained my face and honeyed
my tongue . . . healed the sorrow in my flesh

vines crawl across the grassy floor
of the north, scatter to the world
seeking the light of the sun and innocent
tap of the rain to feed the roots
and bud small white flowers that in June
will burst fruit and announce spring
when wolf will drop winter fur
and wrens will break the egg

my blood, blood berries that brought laughter
and the ache in the stooped back that vied
with dandelions for the plucking,
and the wines nourished our youth and heralded
iris, corn and summer melon

we fought bluebirds for the seeds
armed against garter snakes, field mice;
won the battle with the burning sun
which blinded our eyes and froze our hands
to the vines and the earth where knees knelt
and we laughed in the morning dew like worms
and grubs; we scented age and wisdom

my mother wrapped the wounds of the world
with a sassafras poultice and we ate
wild berries with their juices running
down the roots of our mouths and our joy

I sit here in Brooklyn eating Mexican
berries which I did not pick, nor do
I know the hands which did, nor their stories . . .
January snow falls, listen . . .

LANCE HENSON

evening song
at my grandfathers house

outside a whisper moves windlike
through the trees
sunlight drifts across the yard

a slow circumference the world is green

a white bird flies through the light of someone
missing

all that i have lost is here
the world fills with its presence

dusk this evening
prairie light through a red shawl

◆◆◆

in the house of my childhood

quiet grows out of the long path the sun has made
the radio plays slow familiar songs
across fields of cotton and alfalfa
a triangle of crows

i look from my coffee cup to a wasp against the window
and beyond
toward the settling mist of early autumn
i reach for something to carry forward
against the days immovable portions
the way heat waits beyond the porch
the solemnity of daylight
in unlit rooms

ANITA ENDREZZE-DANIELSON

The North People

They live where the stars are
jagged badger claws
in the thick black-furred night.
And where the mountains sleep
like humped blue bears.
Their skin is a pattern of snowflakes;
their eyes are round stones
tumbled in milky rivers.
Too cold to touch each other
without losing
parts of themselves,
they guard nameless summits,
their voices swords of ice.
Their laughter is a hollow tooth.
They have as many souls as death
allows: the lost hunter, a starved elk,
the winter-broken cedar whose soul
is a prayer of sun and rain.

Sometimes they walk among us,
on our cold journeys
away from ourselves,
licking the salt from our wounds,
envying our secret hearts full
of silence, sadness, or love.
Through the paths lined with snowy trees
or littered with silver leaves,
they walk forever in our footsteps,
alone, alone.

What We Believe

We believe in a land where sweating horses
kick up the dust, forming clay ponies
that sigh with red and yellow breaths.

We believe in a grass-weaver,
whose fingers make gentle blankets,
trusting in green, yellow, and brown.

We believe the horses will wear our blankets,
will drift forever past our campfires,
listening to us telling stories of long ago.

We believe that long ago we were horses
and grass, that our stories are our children's
dreams. We are waiting for the sound of hoof-beats

to rise from our throats and for the tall grasses
to stamp and snort in the wind. What we believe
will always be—and always be true.

◆◆◆

Amber Moon
"You don't look like an Indian"

I am the aspen remembering the fire
that burned my heart into the legends of owls.

I am the smoky wolves whose eyes
reveal the mystery of my loss.

I am the fish whose crystal fin sings
in a vine-threaded pool.

I am the earth-drum of the kiva,
the seven adobe villages that surround
the sun like a shield,
the ghost song of all hunted deer.

I am the snowy pheasant
rolling the red bear berry into my throat.

I am the reed flutes that water plays
in its joyous dreaming.

I am the stars that prickle like cactus.
I am grass shaking my green feathers.

I look like myself and every self
I've ever been. I am season's wings
and earth's ringing. I am half an amber moon,
my spirit the ancestor of light.

PETER BLUE CLOUD

Of All Tomorrows

Time flies away on the wings
of yesterday, he said,
spreading out a night blanket.

He emptied his sack of bones
at the feet of bent saplings
white-haired with snow.

The brittle music of cracked
bones splintered the night
with puffs of frost.

He reached further into his sack
pulling out an obsidian ball
which was the sleeping moon.

Look, he said, this globe
is the owl's own dreaming
etched in forgotten charcoal.

He reached again into his sack
and drew forth a necklace
of star fingers;

When dawn washes all this away,
he said, we will have long since
departed this desolate place.

Then from his sack he took
a flute of newly polished bone
fashioned from my thigh.

And
they
played

a
lonely
farewell

as
we
departed.

And
they
forgot

and
forgot
again

all
the
pain

of
their
birth.

And
he
smiled

He played a shower of seeds   and
which fell upon the snow   told
as tiny, blue children.   me

He folded the blanket of night   that
about their naked bodies   a
and continued to play.   promise

And now the flute was crying   had
of dreams the raven's wings   been
enfold thru all eternities.   given

He smiled a breath of stars   us
which fell around us softly,   this
giving substance to the night.   night.

Then he played dawn's own song,   And
and maybe had changed his mind,   the
for we had not departed.   promise

He smiled again, and said okay,   is
let us together call the sun   that
to witness our first meeting.   life

And the sun found a nation of   born
golden children playing flutes   of
which were Creation songs.   youth

And each and every note was   thru
a plant, or insect, or bird   old
spreading out from their circle.   teachings

Now, he said, let us leave   is
and let night be a part   the
of all their dreaming: fabric

we, after all, are but myths   of
etched on old bones and boulders   all
like memories of all tomorrow.   tomorrows.

For a Dog-Killed Doe

They say she cried her agony for a long time
as dog fangs tore her body apart,
                                      trapped
at the corner of a fence, too swollen with
an unborn fawn to leap and run any further.

The neighbor had her in a wheelbarrow,
ready to take her body outside the fence
and dump her in a gully. "She's no more
good," he said, not looking at me.

"She's still all right," I said, meaning
much more as I looked into her eyes,
still so alive seeming.
                              There were two
deaths standing close by.

                              When I cut
her belly open, that which was dead
tumbled out as if to mimic birth.
Many nations passed thru my mind as
I began skinning the body of her clan.

I sit eating the flesh of her youth,
taking the strength of her never-to-be
motherhood. I feast solemnly,
                                      wishing
sadly that I could take her back
        to winter.

ROBERTA HILL WHITEMAN

They Mention a Word Like "Welcome"

Early morning shadows arrive
in the southwest corner of the porch.
They jangle the lilies of the valley,
creating a lithe breeze. Perched
on a wire, the sparrow hardly feels
its shadow, low in the gravel,
lifts a wing feather for flight.

In a squinting noon,
shadows nestle in thickets,
spangle the deep limbs of elms,
hover in crickets' crazy eyes.
Only curs call to those shadows
of the sun which rove every
eleven years over the full moon.

Shadows watch what no one else does,
then wade into our lives.
The friendly ones
stretch rocks under a sloshing wave,
or spin a dizzy pattern
in the school yard's din.
One shadow alone
can lengthen the haze on a river,
or hold the heavy peony
prisoner to its stem.

Our shadows arrive before we do.
If we could touch them, they'd flutter
like moths caught in a fist.
As we die, they mention
a word like 'welcome,'
leading us into oak groves

where the hopeful ones
gather our aging sins.
Only then do they ease us up
until we glide without them
inside the essential world,
like the dandelion seed,
blown across midsummer meadows.

◆◆◆

The Man Who Blessed
the Telephone Poles

Whispering his riddles, the man came up Christiana.
She cut across the yard. Her friends scattered home
to avoid him. He must have walked around the earth.
Exiled from daylight, his coat endured its shadow.
His shoes curl now and forever
from street salt and his kingdom's claim.
When he came, the street grew so much longer
in the winter dusk that where the walks converged
to one bright spot, summer slept
in a cup of emerald trees.

He'd stand beneath the streetlight's halo,
waiting its light to embrace him.
From the stairwell, she'd see him
bless each pitted shaft.
His cuffs would move
and as he passed, snow burned bluer
and dusk settled in.

Oh magic country shaped by blood and sighs,
was he the one meant to be free?
Were the elders dispersed to fashion from defeat
blessings for this arc of man-made light?

Her father's shirt smelled of pickles.
As they crossed the track, she and her sister
bounced in the back past the drop forge
with its desperate clang, the brick and barbed wire
of Port Forward, smoldering its mill dirt downriver,
a bomb in slow motion, partially blown.

They parked where the wind snapped at each plastic flag.
"Bill and Myra's" hung beneath the "Schlitz."
An itch danced down her part as they walked
to a corner near the parrot's cage.
Runnels of laughter flowed over her skin.
Fish fry night. They climbed in the booth.
"Is this the Silver Whale?"

"Junior, you're too much. I'll tell sister
Jonah wants a ride." The waitress got a beer,
slipped the girls some chips.
Runnels of laughter. Itch, itch, itch.
She better not scratch or someone will come
to fry them chicken before too long.

The bartender's face caught the dim winter light.
His eyes, like spring puddles, had enough space
for birds to bathe and popsicle sticks
to unload their cargo of black ant slaves.
Perhaps they came on an albatross
skimming indigo waves.

Those on shore watched it become
a boat manned by bewildered men,
hugging iron and glass beads.
The rats were all eaten. Their pants water-worn.
Spiral on spiral, no time is the same.
The moment they landed, seeds from a maple
whirled through the sunlight and someone,
astonished, offered them corn.

Woolgathering, the girl smelled
tide break against islands, ripple
in pineknots. How many died?
Plagues introduced them. Carved from the forest,
the faces kept watch, chafed at the bonepile,
and wished they could blister.

Invitations overlapped like waves in high wind.
The French—The English are at it again.
The Dutch exchange prisoners: 'Come to our meeting.'
The French claim they're sovereign: 'Come here to trade.'
Only English have wanted peace in this decade.
'Come hear our greeting. Come for the bleeding.
Come take these pots and accept our kind king.'

Up from the earth, we stood the same height.
The parrot broods in the smoky light.
What catches the web of the child's ear?
The blizzard wind of 1650
glutting itself on the weapons of war.
No one has had to endure this before.

Huddled together on St. Joseph's Island,
Hurons moan through their frozen dreams.
Her knees growing numb, one child whispers,
'Watch. Snowgeese fly from my thumb.'
Their backbones split like cold-blasted trees.
They no longer care,
for winter has gripped these refugees
running, running, running,
refugees running away from those wars.

Warm New Yorkers ask for more corn.
The lamplighter calls out. 'Dusk has come in.'

◆◆◆

Four Girls and One Toad

Two shoved a brown sack
under him and squealed.
One in skates held her chest,
as if afraid to breathe,

then clapped, shuffling closer
to the road. The youngest
squat in sympathy, then
hopped to show him how.

"I got him." Cheryl screamed,
the pride of the block,
stretching the crumbled sack
before her, wishing a lock

could secure her treasure.
They crossed the street.
Two more girls peered inside
at toad, a stone mottled

in taupe, dusty pink
and beryl. "He's got blood
on his eye." Crystal whispered
Her sister in a diaper

ran away, afraid.
They pondered what to do.
Kiss him? Make him spit?
One could take him home,

give him a glass jar
to live in and dead flies.
Watch out. His warts
can travel up your arm

and make your teeth fall out.
They dumped him deep in grass
under a quaking aspen.
His one good eye

will ward off poison for them
and his throat will bubble
with songs through the twilight
of this coming winter.

❖❖❖

One Toad and Four Girls

Stifled by sun, I tumbled earth over me
and heard the eye gliding where
spurge and milkweed flower.

Snug in a pit, I dreamed myself the toad
that helped create a continent, diving up
and down through murky seas

to give a goddess eight globs of dirt.
She breathed on them until a storm
transformed them into mountain chain,

shore, valley, plain, ocean floor and desert.
Can the eye see how far I've come?
This day's too dry, too windless for someone.

Beyond the barricades we know, a thousand wounds,
a thousand melodies spring from rocks,
leaves, bog and riverbed.

Searching a song, I skittered across the tar.
Night hurled its whole weight on my head
and ripped out half my world.

Shoved in a hot abyss, I wasn't kissed by goddesses.
They joggled me so hard, I ate my skin
and relinquished every poison.

Yet when they spilled this earth heart into clover,
I gleamed with song and throbbed in light
that played continuously like

pale butterflies in a field of purple asters.
An oblique rain has numbed my happy half a world,
and in the softer shade,

a whirlpool of stars uncoils, humming
the low note of the universe. Split tongue,
you ask if I'm afraid?

◆◆◆

In the Summer After "Issue Year" Winter (1873)

AUTHOR'S NOTE: I based the incidents in the poem on Batiste Good's Winter Count, which marks the years for the Brule Lakota between 1700–1880. One of the incidents mentioned is the 1856 capture of Little Thunder and Batiste Good and one hundred and thirty Lakota at Ash Hollow. The U.S. policy was to imprison Indian people, steal their horses and weapons, arrest or kill the chiefs in order to force them into signing agreements which allowed for railroad construction, improvement of the Bozeman Trail, and the establishment of military posts. The Dog Soldiers are one of the Warrior Societies that vowed to stake themselves to the ground and fight to the death defending their people. Reference is also made to Chivington's bloody spree at Sand Creek in 1864.

Another incident mentioned is the death of High Back Bone, a chief who was shot at long range by Crows and Shoshones around 1870–1871. Shooting from a great distance was contrary to plains warfare because a *brave* warrior touched his enemy with a coupe stick instead of firing from a safe distance. During the years mentioned in the poem, the Lakota, and their allies, the Arapahoe and the Cheyenne, confronted white diseases, decreasing buffalo herds, starvation, the further reduction of their lands by treaty agreements, which were then broken and resulted in battles with white soldiers. "Issue Year" refers to blankets and goods given to the Lakotas in 1873–74. Incidently, after the first "Issue Year" of 1858–59, a smallpox epidemic is listed two years after and in the year following 1873, another epidemic marks the year—"Measles and Sickness Used Up the People Winter."

◇◇◇

I scratch earth around timpsila
on this hill while below me,
hanging in still air, a hawk
searches the creekbed for my brothers.
Squat leaves, I'll braid your roots
into such long ropes, they'll cover
the rump of my stallion.
Withered flower, feed us now
buffalo rot in the waist-high grass.

Hear my sisters laugh?
They dream of feasts, of warriors
to owl dance with them
when this war is over. They don't see
our children eating treebark, cornstalks,
these roots. Their eyes gleam
in shallow cheeks. The wagon people
do not think relationship is wealth.

Sisters, last night the wind
returned my prayer, allowing me to hear
Dog Soldiers singing at Ash Hollow.
I threw away my blanket
stained with lies.
Above the wings of my tipi,
I heard the old woman in Maka Sica
sigh for us. Then I knew
the distance of High Back Bone's death—

fire from another world away. Even they
may never stop its motion.

Yesterday at noon, I heard
my Cheyenne sister moan as she waded
through deep snow before soldiers
cut up her corpse to sell
as souvenirs. Are my brothers
here? Ghosts bring all my joy.
I walk this good road between rock
and sky. They dare not threaten with death
one already dead.

◆◆◆

At Alma on the Mississippi

I was detached, watching bugs mate
in the grass when she passed by,
one light shy hand framing her forehead.
So pale the pale children wouldn't play,

she walked to where three dark children
seesawed up and down. On the path,
her parents begged her back, but
swallows hid their words along the cliff.

While buffalo treehoppers wisely tucked
their next generation into a twig,
the one who spun beyond Mendel's Law
now skipped by the swings.

A phoebe's song rumpled hair
against each forehead, then all four stopped
silent in a ripening shaft of sun.
Even the boy hung gallant

in mid-air. How many people
to people such a moment?
Below the cliff, a million ripples
are whipped down a distant current.

Hear their rattles in the windblast?
This ledge I often run in dreams,
tasting the blood of the fallen
as it careens into sunlight

and smoke confuses the horizon.
I kneel with foreboding into the grass.
Those three dark ones begin to laugh,
gently signaling with open hands.

◆◆◆

Reaching Yellow River

"It isn't a game for girls,"
he said, grabbing a fifth
with his right hand,
the wind with his left.

"For six days
I raced Jack Daniel's.
He cheated, told jokes.
Some weren't even funny.

That's how come he won.
It took a long time
to reach this Yellow River.
I'm not yet thirty,

or is it thirty-one?
Figured all my years
carried the same hard thaw.
Out here, houselights hid

deep inside the trees.
For a while I believed this road
cut across to Spring Creek
and I was trucking home.

I could kid you now,
say I ran it clean,
gasping on one lung,
loaded by a knapsack

of distrust and hesitation.
I never got the tone
in all the talk of cure.
I sang Honor Songs, crawled

the railroad bridge to Canada.
Dizzy from the ties,
I hung between both worlds.
Clans of blackbirds circled

the nearby maple trees.
The dark heart of me said
no days more than these.
As sundown kindled the sumacs,

stunned by the river's smile,
I had no need for heat,
no need to feel ashamed.
Inside me then the sound

of burning leaves. Tell them
I tumbled through a gap on the horizon.
No, say I stumbled through a hummock
and fell in a pit of stars.

When rain weakened my stride,
I hear them singing
in a burl of white ash,
took a few more days to rave

at them in this wood.
Then their appaloosas nickered
in the dawn and they came
riding down a close ravine.

Though the bottle was empty,
I still hung on. Foxtails beat
the grimace from my brow
until I took off my pain

like a pair of old boots.
I became a hollow horn filled
with rain, reflecting everything.
The wind in my hand

burned cold as hoarfrost
when my grandfather nudged me
and called out
my Lakota name."

In memory of Matò Hehlog eca's grandson

CESAR VALLEJO

Down to the Dregs

This afternoon it rains as never before; and I
don't feel like staying alive, heart.

The afternoon is pleasant. Why shouldn't it be?
It is wearing grace and pain; it is dressed like a woman.

This afternoon in Lima it is raining. And I remember
the cruel caverns of my ingratitude;
my block of ice laid on her poppy,
stronger than her crying "Don't be this way!"

My violent black flowers; and the barbarous
and staggering blow with a stone; and the glacial pause.
And the silence of her dignity will pour
scalding oils on the end of the sentence.

Therefore, this afternoon, as never before, I walk
with this owl, with this heart.

And other women go past; and seeing me sullen,
they sip a little of you
in the abrupt furrow of my deep grief.

This afternoon it rains, rains endlessly. And I
don't feel like staying alive, heart.

Translated by James Wright

The Black Riders

There are blows in life so violent—I can't answer!
Blows as if from the hatred of God; as if before them,
the deep waters of everything lived through
were backed up in the soul . . . I can't answer!

Not many; but they exist . . . They open dark ravines
in the most ferocious face and in the most bull-like back.
Perhaps they are the horses of that heathen Attila,
or the black riders sent to us by Death.

They are the slips backward made by the Christs of the
        soul,
away from some holy faith that is sneered at by Events.
These blows that are bloody are the crackling sounds
from some bread that burns at the oven door.

And man . . . poor man! . . . poor man! He swings
        his eyes, as
when a man behind us calls us by clapping his hands;
swings his crazy eyes, and everything alive
is backed up, like a pool of guilt, in that glance.

There are blows in life so violent . . . I can't answer!

                    Translated by Robert Bly

◆◆◆

The Spider

It is a huge spider, which can no longer move;
a spider which is colorless, whose body,
a head and an abdomen, is bleeding.

Today I watched it with great care. With what tremen-
        dous energy
to every side
it was stretching out its many feet.
And I have been thinking of its invisible eyes,
the death-bringing pilots of the spider.

It is a spider which was shivering, fixed
on the sharp ridge of a stone;
the abdomen on one side,
and on the other, the head.

With so many feet the poor thing, and still it cannot
solve it! And seeing it
confused in such great danger,
what a strange pain that traveler has given me today!

It is a huge spider, whose abdomen
prevents him from following his head.
And I have been thinking of his eyes
and of his many, many feet . . .
And what a strange pain that traveler has given me!

Translated by Robert Bly

◆◆◆

Twilight

I have dreamed of flight. And I have dreamed
of your laces strewn in the bedroom.
I have dreamed of some mother walking the length of a
        wharf
and at fifteen nursing the hour.

I have dreamed of flight. A "forever"
sighed at a fo'c'sle ladder.
I have dreamed of a mother,
of fresh sprigs of table-greens,
and the stars stitched in bridals of the dawn.

            The length of a wharf . . .
the length of a drowning throat!

Translated by John Knoepfle

Agape

Today no one has come to inquire,
nor have they wanted anything from me this afternoon.

I have not seen a single cemetery flower
in so happy a procession of lights.
Forgive me, Lord! I have died so little!

This afternoon everyone, everyone goes by
without asking or begging me anything.

And I do not know what it is they forget, and it is
heavy in my hands like something stolen.

I have come to the door,
and I want to shout at everyone:
—If you miss something, here it is!

Because in all the afternoons of this life,
I do not know how many doors are slammed on a face,
and my soul takes something that belongs to another.

Today nobody has come;
and today I have died so little in the afternoon!

Translated by John Knoepfle

Have You Anything to Say
in Your Defense?

Well, on the day I was born,
God was sick.

They all know that I'm alive,
that I'm vicious; and they don't know
the December that follows from that January.
Well, on the day I was born,
God was sick.

There is an empty place
in my metaphysical shape
that no one can reach:
a cloister of silence
that spoke with the fire of its voice muffled.

On the day I was born,
God was sick.

Brother, listen to me, Listen . . .
Oh, all right. Don't worry, I won't leave
without taking my Decembers along,
without leaving my Januaries behind.
Well, on the day I was born,
God was sick.

They all know that I'm alive,
that I chew my food . . . and they don't know
why harsh winds whistle in my poems,
the narrow uneasiness of a coffin,
winds untangled from the Sphinx
who holds the desert for routine questioning.
Yes, they all know . . . Well, they don't know
that the light gets skinny
and the darkness gets bloated . . .
and they don't know that the Mystery joins things
    together . . .

that he is the hunchback
musical and sad who stands a little way off and foretells
the dazzling progression from the limits to the Limits.

On the day I was born,
God was sick,
gravely.

Translated by James Wright

❖❖❖

FROM
Trilce (1922)

XV

In that corner, where we slept together
so many nights, I've sat down now
to take a walk. The bedstead of the dead lovers
has been taken away, or what could have happened.

You came early for other things,
but you're gone now. This is the corner
where I read one night, by your side,
between your tender breasts,
a story by Daudet. It is the corner
we loved. Don't confuse it with any other.

I've started to think about those days
of summer gone, with you entering and leaving,
little and fed up, pale through the rooms.

On this rainy night,
already far from both of us, all at once I jump . . .
There are two doors, swinging open, shut,
two doors in the wind, back, and forth,
shadow   to   shadow.

Translated by James Wright

PABLO NERUDA

The Word

The word
was born in the blood,
grew in the dark body, beating,
and flew through the lips and the mouth.

Farther away and nearer
still, still it came
from dead fathers and from wandering races,
from lands that had returned to stone
weary of their poor tribes,
because when pain took to the roads
the settlements set out and arrived
and new lands and water reunited
to sow their word anew.

And so, this is the inheritance—
this is the wavelength which connects us
with the dead man and the dawn
of new beings not yet come to light.

Still the atmosphere quivers
with the initial word
dressed up
in terror and sighing.
It emerged
from the darkness
and until now there is no thunder
that rumbles yet with all the iron
of that word,
the first
word uttered—
perhaps it was only a ripple, a drop,
and yet its great cataract falls and falls.

Later on, the word fills with meaning.
It remained gravid and it filled up with lives.
Everything had to do with births and sounds—
affirmation, clarity, strength,
negation, destruction, death—
the verb took over all the power
and blended existence with essence
in the electricity of its beauty.

Human word, syllable, combination
of spread light and the fine art of the silversmith,
hereditary goblet which gathers
the communications of the blood—
here is where silence was gathered up
in the completeness of the human word
and, for human beings, not to speak is to die—
language extends even to the hair,
the mouth speaks without the lips moving—
all of a sudden the eyes are words.

I take the word and go over it
as though it were nothing more than a human shape,
its arrangements awe me and I find my way
through each variation in the spoken word—
I utter and I am and without speaking I approach
the limit of words and the silence.

I drink to the word, raising
a word or a shining cup,
in it I drink
the pure wine of language
or inexhaustible water,
maternal source of words,
and cup and water and wine
give rise to my song
because the verb is the source
and vivid life—it is blood,
blood which expresses its substance
and so implies its own unwinding—
words give glass-quality to glass, blood to blood,
and life to life itself.

Translated by Alastair Reid

◆◆◆

The Night in Isla Negra

The ancient night and the unruly salt
beat at the walls of my house;
lonely is the shadow, the sky
by now is a beat of the ocean,
and sky and shadow explode
in the fray of unequal combat;
all night long they struggle,
nobody knows the weight
of the harsh clarity that will go on opening
like a languid fruit;
thus is born on the coast,
out of turbulent shadow, the hard dawn,
nibbled by the salt in movement,
swept up by the weight of night,
bloodstained in its marine crater.

Translated by Alastair Reid

◆◆◆

Poetry

And it was at that age . . . Poetry arrived
in search of me. I don't know, I don't know where
it came from, from winter or a river.
I don't know how or when,
no, they were not voices, they were not
words, nor silence,
but from a street I was summoned,
from the branches of night,
abruptly from the others,
among violent fires
or returning alone,
there I was without a face
and it touched me.

WORDS IN THE BLOOD 247

I did not know what to say, my mouth
had no way
with names,
my eyes were blind,
and something started in my soul.
fever or forgotten wings,
and I made my own way,
deciphering
that fire,
and I wrote the first faint line,
faint, without substance, pure
nonsense,
pure wisdom
of someone who knows nothing,
and suddenly I saw
the heavens
unfastened
and open,
planets,
palpitating plantations,
shadow perforated,
riddled
with arrows, fire and flowers,
the winding night, the universe.

And I, infinitesimal being,
drunk with the great starry
void,
likeness, image of
mystery,
felt myself a pure part
of the abyss,
I wheeled with the stars,
my heart broke loose on the wind.

Translated by Alastair Reid

We Are Many

Of the many men whom I am, whom we are,
I cannot settle on a single one.
They are lost to me under the cover of clothing.
They have departed for another city.

When everything seems to be set
to show me off as a man of intelligence,
the fool I keep concealed in my person
takes over my talk and occupies my mouth.

On other occasions, I am dozing in the midst
of people of some distinction,
and when I summon my courageous self,
a coward completely unknown to me
swaddles my poor skeleton
in a thousand tiny reservations.

When a stately home bursts into flames,
instead of the fireman I summon,
an arsonist bursts on the scene,
and he is I. There is nothing I can do.
What must I do to single out myself?
How can I put myself together?

All the books I read
lionize dazzling hero figures,
always brimming with self-assurance.
I die with envy of them;
and, in films where bullets fly on the wind,
I am left in envy of the cowboys,
left admiring even the horses.

But when I call upon my dashing being,
out comes the same old lazy self,
and so I never know just who I am,
nor how many I am, nor who we will be being.
I would like to be able to touch a bell
and call up my real self, the truly me,
because if I really need my proper self,
I must not allow myself to disappear.

While I am writing, I am far away;
and when I come back, I have already left.
I should like to see if the same thing happens
to other people as it does to me,
to see if as many people are as I am,
and if they seem the same way to themselves.
When this problem has been thoroughly explored,
I am going to school myself so well in things
that, when I try to explain my problems,
I shall speak, not of self, but of geography.

Translated by Alastair Reid

❖❖❖

To the Foot From Its Child

The child's foot is not yet aware it's a foot,
and wants to be a butterfly or an apple.

But later, stones and glass shards,
streets, ladders,
and the paths in the rough earth
go on teaching the foot it cannot fly,
cannot be a fruit swollen on the branch.
Then, the child's foot
was defeated, fell
in the battle,
was a prisoner
condemned to live in a shoe.

Bit by bit, in that dark
it grew to know the world in its own way,
out of touch with its fellow, enclosed,
feeling out life like a blind man.

These soft nails
of quartz, bunched together,
grew hard, and changed themselves
into opaque substance, hard as horn,
and the tiny, petaled toes of the child
grew bunched and out of trim,
took on the form of eyeless reptiles
with triangular heads, like worms.
Later, they grew calloused
and were covered
with the faint volcanoes of death,
a coarsening hard to accept.

But this blind thing walked
without respite, never stopping
for hour after hour,
the one foot, the other,
now the man's,
now the woman's,
up above,
down below,
through fields, mines,
markets and ministries,
backward,
far afield, inward,
forward,
this foot toiled in its shoe,
scarcely taking time
to bare itself in love or sleep;
it walked, they walked,
until the whole man chose to stop.

And then it descended
to earth, and knew nothing,
for there, everything everywhere was dark.
It did not know it had ceased to be a foot,
or if they were burying it so that it might fly,
or so that it might become
an apple.

MIGUEL ANGEL ASTURIAS

Gaspar Ilóm
FROM
Men of Maize

EDITOR'S NOTE: Asturias's second novel was called *Men of Maize* (1949), and it is from the opening pages of that book that we have drawn an exceptionally evocative sequence. Composed of a series of interconnected tales about a land in which the ancient Maya myths continue to live as metaphors of contemporary social conflicts, *Men of Maize* was clearly Asturias's masterwork. Although he wrote in many different forms, it is in his folkloric novels that he achieved true mastery.

❖❖❖

I

"Gaspar Ilóm is letting them steal the sleep from the eyes of the land of Ilóm."

"Gaspar Ilóm is letting them hack away the eyelids of the land of Ilóm with axes . . ."

"Gaspar Ilóm is letting them scorch the leafy eyelashes of the land of Ilóm with fires that turn the moon the angry brown of an old ant . . ."

Gaspar Ilóm shook his head from side to side. To deny, to grind the accusation of the soil where he lay sleeping with his reed mat, his shadow and his woman, where he lay buried with his dead ones and his umbilicus, unable to free himself from a serpent of six hundred thousand coils of mud, moon, forests, rainstorms, mountains, birds and echoes he could feel around his body.

"The earth falls dreaming from the stars, but awakens in what once were green mountains, now the barren peaks of Ilóm, where the guarda's song wails out across the ravines, the hawk swoops headlong, the giant ants march, the dove sighs, and where sleeps, with his mat, his shadow and his woman, he who should hack the eyelids of those who fell the trees, singe the eyelashes of those who burn the forest, and chill the bodies of those who dam the waters of the river that sleeps as it flows and sees nothing until trapped in pools it opens its eyes and sees all with its deep water gaze . . ."

Gaspar stretched himself out, curled himself in, and again shook his head from side to side to grind the accusation of the earth, bound in sleep and in death by the snake of six hundred thousand coils of mud, moon, forests, rainstorms, mountains, lakes, birds and echoes that pounded his bones until they turned to a black frijole paste dripping from the depths of the night.

And then he heard, with the hollows of his ears he heard:

"Yellow rabbits in the sky, yellow rabbits in the forest, yellow rabbits in the water will fight with Gaspar. Gaspar Ilóm will go to war, compelled by his blood, his river, the blind knots of his speech . . ."

The word of the earth turned to flame by the sun all but set fire to the maize-leaf ears of the yellow rabbits in the sky, the yellow rabbits in the forest, the yellow rabbits in the water; but Gaspar was once again becoming earth that falls from where the earth falls, which is to say, sleep that finds no shade in which to dream in the soil of Ilóm, and the solar flame of the voice could do nothing, tricked by the yellow rabbits that set to suckling in a papaya grove, turned into forest papayas, that fixed themselves against the sky, turned into stars, and faded into the water like reflections with ears.

Bare earth, wakeful earth, sleepy maize-growing earth, Gaspar falling from where the earth falls, maize-growing earth bathed by rivers of water fetid from being so long awake, water green from the wakefulness of the forests sacrificed by the maize made man the sower of maize. The maize planters beat their way in with their fires and their axes, into forests that were grandmothers of shade, two hundred thousand young silk-cotton trees each a thousand years old.

In the grass was a mule, on the mule was a man, and in the man was a dead man. His eyes were his eyes, his hands were his hands, his voice was his voice, his legs were his legs and his feet were his feet for taking him to war as soon as he could get away from the snake of six hundred thousand coils of mud, moon, forests, rainstorms, mountains, lakes, birds and echoes that had curled itself around his body. But how could he get away, how could he untie himself from the crops, from his woman, the children, the rancho; how could he break free of the cheery companionship of the fields; how was he to drag himself off to war with the half-flowered bean patch about his arms, the warm chayote tips around his neck, and his feet caught in the noose of the daily round.

The air of Ilóm was heavy with the smell of newly felled trees, the ashes of trees burned down to clear the ground.

A whirlwind of mud, moon, forests, rainstorms, mountains, lakes, birds and echoes went round and round and round and round the chief of Ilóm, and as the wind beat against his face and body and as the earth raised by the wind beat against him he was swallowed by a toothless half moon which sucked him from the air, without biting him, like a small fish.

The air of Ilóm was heavy with the smell of newly felled trees, the ashes of trees burned to clear the ground.

Yellow rabbits in the sky, yellow rabbits in the water, yellow rabbits in the forest.

He didn't open his eyes. They were already open, piled up among his eyelashes. He was shaken by the thudding of his heartbeats. He didn't dare move, swallow saliva, touch his naked body, for fear he would find his skin cold and inside his cold skin the deep ravines dribbled in him by the serpent.

The brilliance of the night dripped copal resin between the canes of the rancho. His woman scarcely showed up on her petate. She was breathing face down as though she were blowing on the fire in her sleep.

Gaspar dragged himself off on his hands and knees, full of empty ravines, to search for his bottle gourd, making no sound other than the joints of his bones, which ached as if by an effect of the moon, and in the darkness, striped like a poncho by the firefly light of the night filtering in through the canes of the rancho, his face, that of a thirsty idol, could be seen sucking away at the gourd, drinking down great gulps of cane liquor with the greed of a baby too long deprived of the breast.

A flash of maize-leaf flame caught his face as he finished the gourd. The sun that beats down on the sugar plantations burned him inside: it burned his head till his hair no longer felt like hair, but like a pelt of ashes, and it burned the flittermouse of his tongue in the roof of his mouth, so he couldn't let the words of his dreams escape as he slept, his tongue that no longer felt like a tongue, but like a maguey rope, and it burned his teeth that no longer felt like teeth, but like freshly sharpened machetes.

His half-buried hands clawed at the ground, the ground sticky with cold, his fingers glued to it, deep, hard, without resonance, his fingernails heavy as shotgun slugs.

But the liquor didn't burn his face. The liquor didn't burn his hair. The liquor didn't decapitate him because it was liquor but because it was the water of war. He drank to feel himself burned, buried, beheaded, which is how you have to go to war if you want to go unafraid: no head, no body, no skin.

That is what Gaspar thought. That is what he said, his head separated from his body, babbling, burning, wrapped in a bundle hoary with moonlight. Gaspar grew older as he talked. His head had fallen to the ground like a potsherd broken into fragments of thought. What Gaspar was saying, now that he was old, was forest. What he was thinking was forest remembered, not new hair. His thoughts passed out of his ears to hear the cattle going by above his head. A herd of clouds on hoofs. Hundreds of hoofs. Thousands of hoofs. The booty of the yellow rabbits.

Piojosa Grande struggled beneath Gaspar's body that was damp and warm as young maize shoots. He carried her with him in his pulsations, ever further away. The spasm took them far beyond him, far beyond her, to where he ceased to be just himself and she ceased to be just herself, to become species, tribe, a stream of sensations. Suddenly he held her tight. Piojosa cried out. Shouts, boulders. Her sleep spread over the petate like her matted hair combed by Gaspar's teeth. Her pupils of grieving blood saw nothing. She shrank back like a blind hen. A handful of sunflower seeds in her entrails. The smell of the man. The smell of breath.

And the next day:

"Look, Piojosa, the ruckus'll be starting up any day now. We've got to clear the land of Ilóm of them who knock the trees down with axes, them who scorch the forest with their fires, them who dam the waters of the river that sleeps as it flows and opens its eyes in the pools and rots for wanting to sleep . . . The maizegrowers, them who've done away with the shade, for either the earth that falls from the stars is going to find some place to carry on dreaming its dream in the soil of Ilóm, or they can put me off to sleep forever. Get some old rags together to tie up my things, and don't forget the cold tortillas, and some salt beef, and some chili, all a man needs to go to war."

Gaspar scratched the anthill of his beard with the fingers on his right hand, took down his shotgun, went down to the river and fired on the first maizegrower who passed by, from behind a bush. Name of Igiño. The next day, in another spot, he brought down the second one. Fellow called Domingo. And from one day to another Igiño, Domingo, Cleto, then Bautista and Chalio, until the forest was clear of the planters.

The matapalo is bad, but the maizegrower is worse. The matapalo takes years to dry a tree up. The maizegrower sets fire to the brush and does for the timber in a matter of hours. And what timber. The most priceless of woods. What guerrillas do to men in time of war the maizegrower does to the trees. Smoke, flames, ashes. Different if it was just to eat. It's to make money. Different, too, if it was on their own account, but they go halves with the boss, and sometimes not even halves. The maize impoverishes the earth and makes no one rich. Neither the boss nor the men. Sown to be eaten it is the sacred sustenance of the men who were made of maize. Sown to make money it means famine for the men who were made of maize. The red staff of the Place of Provisions, women with children and men with women, will never take root in the maize plantations, try as they will. The earth will become exhausted and the planter will take his little seeds off somewhere else, until he too begins to waste away like a discolored seed fallen in the midst of fertile lands ripe for planting, lands that could make him a rich man instead of a nobody who wanders around ruining the earth everywhere he goes, always poor and finally losing all pleasure in the good things he could have had: sugar cane on the hot low-lying slopes, where the air grows thick over the banana groves and the cacao trees shoot up like rockets in the sky to explode silently in sprays of almond-colored berries, not to mention the coffee, in rich soils spattered with blood, and the wheatfields ablaze beyond.

Creamy skies and butter rivers running low, turning green, merged together in the first downpour of a winter that was pure wasted water on the barren black fields, and nothing anyone could do about it. It was a crying shame to see all those crystals falling from the sky onto the burning thirst of the abandoned plots. Not a seed, not a furrow, not a planter. Indians with rainwater eyes spied on the houses of the Ladinos from the mountains. There were forty houses in the town. Only rarely did anyone set foot in the cobbled streets in the early morning air, for fear of being killed. Gaspar and his men could make out their forms and if the wind was right they could hear the grackles squabbling in the silk-cotton tree down in the square.

Gaspar is invincible, said the old folk of the town. The rabbits with maize-leaf ears protect Gaspar, and for the yellow rabbits with maize-leaf ears there are no secrets, no dangers, no distances. Gaspar's hide is mamey skin and gold his blood—"great is his strength," "great is his dance"—and his teeth, pumice stones when he laughs and flint stones when he bites or grinds them, are his heart in his mouth, as his heelbone is his heart in his feet as he walks. Only the yellow rabbits know the mark of his teeth in the fruits and the mark of his feet along the paths. Word for word, that is what the old folk of the town said. You can hear them walking when Gaspar walks. You can hear them talking when Gaspar talks. Gaspar walks for all who have walked, all who walk and all who will walk. Gaspar talks for all who have talked, all who talk and all who will talk. That is what the old folk in the town told the maize-growers. The storm beat out its drums in the hall of the blue doves and beneath the sheets of cloud over the savannahs.

But one day after a day, the knotted speech of the old folk announced that the mounted patrol was on its way again. The countryside sown with yellow flowers warned danger to the one protected by the yellow rabbits.

At what hour did the troop enter the town? To the Ladinos under threat of death from the Indians it seemed like a dream. They neither spoke nor moved nor saw anything in the shadow that was as hard as the walls. The horses passed before them like black worms, and they sensed the riders had faces of burned almonds and honey. It had stopped raining, but there was a stupefying smell of sodden earth and the stench of skunk.

Gaspar changed his hiding place. In the deep blue of the night of Ilóm tiny twinkling rabbits hopped from star to star, a sign of danger, and the mountains smelled of yellow marigolds. Gaspar Ilóm changed his hiding place with his gun fully loaded with seeds of darkness—that's what gunpowder is, deathly seeds of darkness—his machete dangling at his waist, a gourd full of liquor, a cloth with his tobacco, his chili and his salt beef, two bay leaves stuck with saliva to the panicky senses, a jar of bitter-almond oil, and a small box of cameline ointment. Great was his strength, great was his dance. His strength was the flowers, his dance was the clouds.

❖❖❖

The balcony of the Council House was up above. Down below the square looked heavy with water. The saddled horses were tossing about in the smoky dampness of their breath, with their bridles tied to the stirrup leathers and their girths loosened. Ever since the troop arrived the air smelled of soaking wet horses.

The leader of the mounted troop wandered in and out of the gallery, a lighted cigar in his mouth, uniform unbuttoned, a white crape kerchief at his neck, and faded trousers hanging over his leggings and combat boots.

By this time the town had eyes only for the forest. Those who had not already fled were decimated by the Indians who came down from the mountains of Ilóm, led by a cunning and treacherous chief, and those who stuck it out in the town stayed holed up in their houses and when they crossed the street they scuttled like lizards.

The news of the proclamation brought all out of their houses. It was read out on every corner. "Colonel Gonzalo Godoy, Leader of the Army Expeditionary Force in the Field, wishes to inform that having regrouped his forces and received orders and supplies, he entered Pisigüilito last night with one hundred and fifty riflemen on horseback and another hundred men on foot armed with machetes, and every one just waiting to throw lead and steel against the Indians up in the mountains."

Shadow of dark clouds. Distant sun. The mountains an olive green. The sky, the air, the houses, everything the color of prickly pear. The man reading the proclamation, the little group of townspeople listening from corner to corner—almost always the same group—the soldiers escorting him with pipe and drum, seemed to be made not of flesh, but of green tomatoes, vegetables, edible things.

After the proclamation the elders of the town paid Colonel Godoy a visit. No sooner was it over than a delegation of them arrived. Don Chalo, without removing the bar from his mouth, sitting in a hammock hanging from one of the beams of the gallery, fixed his round blue eyes on everything about him, except the delegation, until one of them, after much hesitation, took a step forward and made as if to speak.

The colonel looked him over. They had come to offer him a serenade with marimba and guitars to celebrate his arrival in Pisigüilito.

"Seeing as we've butted in on you, colonel," said the one who had spoken, "see what you think of our program. 'Too Much Mustard,' first tune of the first part; 'Black Beer,' second tune of the first part; 'Baby's Died,' third—"

"What about the second part?" the colonel cut him short.

"Ain't no second part," said the oldest of the serenaders, taking a step forward. "Here in Pisigüilito these are the only tunes we've played in a long while, and every one of them my own composition. The last one I wrote was 'Baby's Died,' when our Crisanta's little girl was taken up to heaven, that's its only merit."

"Well, my friend, you'd better start writing a song called 'I Was Born Again,' because if we hadn't arrived here last night the Indians would have come down from the mountains this morning and not one of you slobbering bastards would be alive to tell the tale. They'd have trampled over the lot of you."

The composer, with his skin like old bark, his hair sticking out over his forehead like the tip of a sucked mango, and his eyes scarcely visible between the slits of his lids, stood looking at the colonel in the silence, which was like a spreading creeper through which everyone could feel the Indian bands gliding, the Indians who under Gaspar Ilóm had lost none of their taste for the things they lacked, still hankering after cattle, after liquor, after dogs, and the patchouli in the apothecary's store that would disguise their sweat.

The Indian warrior smells of the animal that protects him and the aroma he puts on: patchouli, aromatic water, magic ointments, fruit juices, help him rub out that magic presence and put those who seek to harm him off the scent.

The warrior who smells of peccary disguises his trail and adorns himself with orrisroot. Heliotrope water hides the odor of the deer and is used by the warrior who gives off little deer-drops of sweat. Still more penetrating is the spikenard, most suitable for those who are protected in war by night birds, frozen and perspiring. Likewise the essence of the gardenia is for those who are shielded by snakes, those who have scarcely any odor at all, those who do not perspire in combat. The fragrance of rosewood conceals the warrior whose smell is of the mockingbird. The morning-glory hides the warrior who smells like the hummingbird. Arabian jasmine he who reeks of kinkajou. Those who give off the sweat of the jaguar must smell of forest lilies. Of rue those who give off the odor of the macaw. Of tobacco those who clothe themselves in parrot cackle as they sweat. The tapir warrior is concealed by the fig leaf. The bird warrior by rosemary. The crab warrior by orange-blossom water.

Gaspar, yellow flower in the wind of time, and his Indian bands, heelbones that were hearts within the stones, continued to pass through the spreading creeper of silence woven between the colonel and the old musician of Pisigüilito.

"Even if they'd murdered the lot of you," the colonel's voice began to rise, "even if they'd trampled all over you there'd have been no loss, and that's a fact. What kind of town is it where you can't even have a horse shod, for Christ's sake?"

The colonel's men, curled up among the horses, jumped to their feet all at once, shooing away a kind of waking dream they had subsided into through crouching for so long on their heels. A dog dyed red with ringworm was running round the square like a firecracker, its tongue hanging out, its eyes staring, snorting and dribbling.

The men lapsed back into their brooding, sitting back on their heels to stay silent for hours and hours in their waking doze. If a dog's after water it ain't got rabies and the wretched animal rolled about in the puddles, then jumped, black with mud, to rub itself against the walls of houses which looked onto the square, against the silk-cotton tree, and the badly worn wood of the straypost.

"What's wrong with that mutt?" asked the colonel from his hammock, the same agave net which seemed to catch him in every town at siesta time.

"Had some kind of accident," said the orderly, without taking his eyes off the dog. He was sitting on the verandah of the Council House with his feet wedged heel to toe against one of the posts by the colonel's hammock. He fell silent and then, without changing position, he said, "I reckon he's eaten a billbug and sent himself crazy."

"Go find out, it could be rabies."

"Where can I find out?"

"In the apothecary's, fuck it, there's nowhere else here."

The orderly put on his rope sandals and ran to the store, just across the square from the Council House. The dog was still raging. Its barks splintered the silence of the horses tossing their long-maned heads, and the half-conscious dozing of the men crouching among them. Suddenly it ran out of steps. It scrabbled at the ground as if it had buried them and was looking for them now that it had to be off again. Then a shake of the head, another, then another, trying to wrench out whatever was stuck in its throat. The animal spat foam, dribble, and a whitish substance which flew from the back of its throat to the ground without touching either tongue or teeth on the way. It wiped its muzzle, barking furiously, and set off on the scent of some medicinal herb which in the snaking confusion of its run became a shadow, a stone, a tree, retching and vomit, mouthfuls of quicklime on the ground. Then off again, running like a jet of water the wind curved up and outwards, then let drop to the ground once more. Urged on by its body, it managed to stand again, eyes flecked, tongue hanging, tail thrashing between rigid legs, shivery and brittle. But in trying to take the first step forward it stumbled, as though it were hobbled, and the death spasm wheeled it round and threw it to the ground with its legs pawing the air, fighting with all its strength not to leave this life.

"It's stopped tearing about at last . . . ," said one of the men crouched among the horses. Their looks were striking. The one who had spoken had a face the color of vinegar scum with a machete scar right on his eyebrow.

The dog shook its teeth into chattering like a wooden rattle and then lay trapped in its own rib cage, ringworm, penis, entrails, anus. Funny how life clings hardest to the basest parts of the body in the desperation of dying, when everything begins to grow dim in the dark pain without pain that is death. Or so thought another of the men curled up among the horses. And he couldn't contain himself and said, "It's still moving a bit. It's even a job to put an end to this goddamn life. Good thing God made us so we could die without beating about the bush—what reason could he have found to make us live forever? It turns my guts over just thinking about it."

"That's why I say it's no great punishment to be shot," added the man with the scar on his eyebrow.

"It ain't a punishment, it's a cure. It'd be a punishment if they could leave you alive forever, just imagine."

"Yes, that would be real hell."

The orderly returned to the gallery of the Council House. Colonel Godoy was still mounted in his hammock, moustachioed, eyes open wide, just like a fish swelling a net.

"Apothecary says he gave it something to eat, colonel, on account of it's filthy with ringworm."

"Didn't you ask him what he gave it to upset it like that?"

"Something to eat, he said—"

"Something to eat, yes, but what did he put in it?"

"Ground glass mixed with poison."

"What sort of poison?"

"Just a moment, I'll go ask him."

"Better do it yourself, Chalo old boy," the colonel muttered to himself, as he climbed out of his hammock, his pale blue eyes like ground glass, and in his thoughts poison for the chief of Ilóm.

"You," Godoy ordered the soldier, "go find me those musicians who came about the serenade and tell them to be here tonight."

The afternoon turned deep yellow. The mountain of the deaf ones was sawing up the great rain clouds soon to be burned by the storm like maize-ear dust. Weeping of the spines on the cactuses. Moans of parrots in the ravines. Ay, and what if the yellow rabbits fall into the trap! Ay, and what if the perfume of the chilca, color of the stars by day, fails to cover Gaspar's smell, the mark of his teeth in the fruits, the mark of his feet along the paths, known only to the yellow rabbits!

The dog kicked out its legs in the death frolic, unable to raise its head, urinating fitfully, swollen belly, bristling backbone, erect penis, foaming muzzle. You could hear the stampeding rainstorms in the distance. The animal closed its eyes and then lay fast against the earth.

◆◆◆

With one violent kick the Leader of the Expeditionary Force knocked over the three bamboo legs holding up an earthenware flowerpot in which someone had just lit a torch pine in front of the Council House, to advertise the serenade. The man who had lit it took part of the blow and the orderly, who was just coming down from the gallery with a lighted paraffin lamp, received a lash on the back. This gave the town elders something to think about. Shouts of "put out that light," "throw earth on it." And once the colonel's goodwill had been retrieved, arms waved about like roots to salute him. They introduced themselves. The one standing nearest to the colonel was Señor Tomás Machojón. Standing between the colonel, the military authority, and his wife, the supreme authority, Vaca Manuela Machojón.

Machojón and the colonel moved off, speaking in low voices. Señor Tomás had formerly been one of Gaspar Ilóm's band. He was an Indian, but his wife, Vaca Manuela Machojón, had turned him into a Ladino. Ladino women have iguana's spittle, which hypnotizes men. Only by hanging them by their ankles can you extract those viscous mouthfuls of flattery and servility which allow them to have their way in everything. That was how Vaca Manuela won Señor Tomás over for the maize-growers.

It was raining. Mountains under the rain in the night give off the smell of dampened embers. The rainstorm thundered on the Council House roof like the lament of all the planters murdered by the Indians, shadowy corpses scattering handfuls of maize down from the sky in torrents of rain which could be heard above the sound of the marimba.

The colonel lifted his voice to call the head musician. "Listen, maestro, that tune of yours, the one you call 'Black Beer,' change its name, will you? Call it 'Holy Remedy' instead. And I'll dance it with Doña Manuelita here."

"If that's what you want, it's agreed, so dance: 'Holy Remedy' coming up."

Vaca Manuela and Colonel Godoy jigged in and out of the darkness to the sound off the marimba, like the ghosts that come up from the rivers when it rains in the night. And in his partner's hand the Leader of the Expeditionary Force in the Field left a small bottle, a holy remedy, he said, for Indian ringworm.

II

The sun let down its hair. The summer was received in the domain of the chieftain of Ilóm with comb honey rubbed on the branches of the fruit trees, so the fruit would be sweet; with headdresses of immortelles on the heads of the women, so the women would be fertile; and with dead raccoons hanging from the doors of the ranchos, so the men would be potent.

The firefly wizards, descendants of the great clashers of flint stones, sowed sparkling lights in the black air of the night to be sure there would be guiding stars in the winter. The firefly wizards with their obsidian sparks. The firefly wizards, who dwelt in tents of virgin doeskin.

Then they lit bonfires, to speak with them of the heat that would parch the earth if it beat down with its yellow might, of the ticks that made the cattle thin, the locusts that dried out the moisture in the sky, the empty streams, where the mud gets more wrinkled year by year, like an aging face.

Around the fires the night was like a dense flight of small birds with black breasts and blue wings, the same ones the warriors took as tribute to the Place of Abundance. Men, crisscrossed with cartridge belts, their haunches pressed against their heels. Without speaking, they were thinking, it's always more difficult for those who live in the mountains to fight in summer than it is for the horse soldiers; but next winter it will be the other way round, and they feed the fires with thorny branches, because in the fire of the warriors, which is the fire of war, even the thorns weep.

Close by the blazing fires other men cleaned their toenails with their machetes, the machete edge inside the nail hardened by long days of mud, and the women counted their beauty spots, laughing and laughing, or counted the stars. The woman with the most beauty spots was the mother of Martín Ilóm, the newborn son of chief Gaspar Ilóm. The one with the most beauty spots and the most fleas. La Piojosa Grande, the Great Fleabag, the nana of Martín Ilóm.

In her lap that was warm as a baking dish, in her rags worn smooth with age, her son slept like a new clay pot and beneath the coxpi, the delicately woven net that covered his head and face to protect him from evil eye, you could hear the sound of his breathing like water falling on porous earth.

Women with children and men with women. Heat and light from the fires. The women far away in the firelight and close by in the shadows. The men close by in the firelight and far away in the shadows. All of them in the roaring tumult of the flames, fire of the warriors, fires of war that will turn even the thorns to weeping.

So said the oldest Indians, with the senile nodding of their heads beneath the wasps. Or they said, without losing their old men's motion: Before they plaited the first maguey rope they plaited the hair of the women. Or again: Before men and women intertwined from the front there were those who were intertwined from the other side. Or: Alvarado ripped the gold rings from the ears of the lords. The lords cringed in the face of such brutality. And precious stones were delivered up to that man who ripped the gold rings from the ears of the lords. Or: They were savages. One man for one woman, they said. One woman for one man, they said. Savages. Beasts were better. Snakes were better. The worst animal was better than the man who denied his seed to the woman who was not his wife and kept his seed cool as the life he denied.

Adolescents with faces like unpainted tortilla gourds played among the old people, among the women, among the men, among the bonfires, among the firefly wizards, among the warriors, among the cooks sinking calabash ladles into great pots of pulique, sancocho, chicken stew and pipian, to fill the glazed earthenware bowls the guests kept passing and passing and passing and passing, without ever confusing the orders, whether pipian, stew or pulique. The women in charge of the red chili sprinkled drops of huaque chili like spots of blood into bowls of tawny soup swimming with spiny chayote halves, skins intact, chunks of meat, pacayas, melting potatoes, and tender guicoy squashes shaped like shells, and handfuls of stringbeans, and strips of root chayote, all with coriander, salt, garlic and tomato to taste. And they sprinkled red chili over bowls of rice and chicken stew, seven chickens, nine white chickens. The tamale-makers, blackened by the smoke, took banana-leaf bundles tied with reed strands out of bubbling earthenware tubs and opened them in a trice. Those who served the open tamales, the ones ready to eat, were sweating as though exposed to the sun, after standing so long taking the blistering steam from the boiled maize dough full in their faces, those brilliant red packages with meat inside, snares set for folk who eat the tamale and end up sucking their fingers and exchanging confidences with their neighbors. Guests are put at their ease as they eat their tamales, so much so they soon have no qualms about trying their companion's or asking for another, like Gaspar's brash guerrillas as they asked the serving women, slipping in a pinch or two, only to have their hands brushed aside or answered with slaps, "Let's have another one, missy . . . !" Large tamales, red ones and black ones, the red ones salted, the black ones filled with turkey, sugar and almonds; and smaller ones like acolytes in white maize-leaf surplices, and others of purple amaranth, pink choreque flowers, loroco seeds, or pita and pumpkin flowers; and tamales with aniseed and tamales with green maize-ears, like the soft unhardened flesh of little maize boys. "Let's have another one, missy . . . !" The women were eating things that looked like roseapples of maize dough brushed in milk, little tamales colored with cochineal and subtly perfumed. "Let's have another one, missy . . . !" The cooks wiped the backs of their hands across their foreheads to push their hair away. Now and then they used their hands to wipe their noses, streaming with the smoke and the tamales. Those serving the roasts savored the first smell of the meat smoking nearby: dried beef seasoned with sour oranges, lots of salt and lots of sun, meat contorted in the fire as though the animal had come back to life and were being burned alive. Other eyes were devouring other dishes. Roasted calabashes. Yucca with cheese. Oxtails with chili sauce, so sweet it seemed like calabash honey. Meat fritters sweating with red-hot chili. Those drinking chilate finished off their gourds as though they were putting them on as masks, so eager were they to taste the last salty dregs. The atole was served in round bowls, slightly mauve, slightly acid. The atole made from whey and maize tasted like eloatole, and the ground atole tasted like cane sugar. The boiling fat made rain bubbles in tortilla dishes steadily losing the glory of fried bananas, served whole and covered in mead to women who were already flocking and twittering to taste the cinnamon-flavored milk and rice, plums in syrup and coyoles in honey.

Vaca Manuela Machojón heaved herself up from the mound of clothes on which she was seated, she wore lots of skirts and lots of petticoats ever since she went down with her husband, Señor Tomás Machojón, to live in Pisigüilito, whence they had traveled to be at Gaspar's celebration. She rose to thank Piojosa Grande for the invitation, Piojosa still with Gaspar Ilóm's son in her lap.

Vaca Manuela Machojón made a slight bow and hung her head as she said, "Beneath my armpit I shall place you, for you have the white heart of a dove. I shall place you on my forehead, where the swallow of my thoughts has flown, and I shall not slay you on the white mat of my fingernail even if I catch you in the black mountain of my hair, because my mouth has eaten and my ears have heard pleasant things in your company of shade and water, of grain-bringing stars, of the tree of life that gives color to our blood."

Beaten in gourd cups you couldn't hold in your fingers, so hot was the liquid smelling of pinole they contained, rose water in tumblers, coffee in small wooden cups, maize beer in chocolate beaters, and cane liquor by the bowlful kept each gullet clear for the chattering conversation and the food.

Vaca Manuela Machojón did not repeat her words of gratitude. Like the outline of a mountain, with her child in her arms, Piojosa Grande disappeared into the night.

"Piojosa's made off with your son," Vaca Manuela Machojón ran to tell Gaspar, who was sitting eating among the firefly wizards, those who dwelt in tents of virgin doeskin and fed on the flesh of the paca.

And the man who saw in the dark better than a forest cat, whose eyes were yellow in the night, got up, and left the conversation of the firefly wizards, which was like a silversmith's tiny hammer, and—

"By your leave," he said to Señor Tomás Machojón and Vaca Manuela Machojón, who had come up to the feast with news of Pisigüilito.

With one bound he caught up with her. Piojosa heard him leaping through the trees like her heart inside her clothes, to drop into her path of black honey with his fingers like arrowheads to put her to death, seeing her closed eyes from whose seams, badly sewn by her eyelashes, butterflies emerged—he was not dead, and her caterpillar tears had turned to butterflies—speaking to her with his silence, possessing her with a tooth and cactus-tree love. He was its tooth and she its cactus-tree gum.

Piojosa Grande made to take the gourd that Gaspar held in his hands. By now the firefly wizards and guerrillas had caught them up. But too late, for her fingers were paralyzed in the air as she saw the chief of Ilóm's mouth wet with that vile liquor, that liquid with the weight of lead in which two white roots were reflected, and she set off again, running like cascading water.

The horror of it extinguished their words. Faces of men and women trembling like the leaves of trees hacked by machetes. Gaspar raised his gun, rested it against his shoulder, took aim—and did not fire.—A hump on his woman's back. His son. Something like a little worm curled on Piojosa's back.

When Vaca Manuela Machojón had come up to declare her affection

Piojosa had remembered a dream, from which she awoke weeping just as she was weeping now that she could wake no more, in which two white roots moving like reflections in troubled waters penetrated from the green earth down to the black earth, from the surface of the sun to the depths of a dark realm. Beneath the earth, in that dark realm, a man seemed to have been invited to a meeting. She could not see the faces of the other guests. They were cracking whips, jingling spurs, spitting. The two white roots dyed the amber liquid the man at the underground feast held in his hands. He did not see the reflection of the white roots and when he drank from it he turned pale, gesticulated, and fell writhing to the ground, feeling as though his intestines were ripping him open, his mouth foaming, his tongue purple, his eyes staring, his nails almost black against his fingers yellow in the moonlight.

Piojosa Grande could not get away fast enough, could not break the paths fast enough, the stalks of the paths, the trunks of the roads stretching out in the heartless night that was already swallowing up the distant glow of the festive fires, the voices of the guests.

Gaspar Ilóm appeared at dawn after drinking down the river to extinguish the thirst of the poison in his intestines. He washed out his entrails, washed his blood, cast off his death, pulled it over his head, away from his arms, like dirty clothing, and let it float away downstream. He vomited, spitting and weeping as he swam, head down among the stones, beneath the water, head up again, recklessly, sobbing. How disgusting was death, his death. The intolerable cold, the paralysis in his stomach, the itching at his ankles, at his wrists, behind his ears, on the slopes of his nostrils, which were like terrible defiles along which the sweat and tears flowed toward the ravines.

Alive, erect, his face of yellow clay, his hair of gleaming black varnish, his teeth of granular white coconut, shirt and breeches clinging to his body, dripping liquid maize-ears of muddy rainwater, river weeds and leaves, Gaspar Ilóm appeared with the dawn, triumphant over death, triumphant over poison, but his men had been taken by surprise and massacred by the soldiers.

In the soft blue glow of the morning, the sleeping moon, the moon of disappearance with the yellow rabbit on its face, father of all the yellow rabbits on the face of the dead moon, the saffron-colored mountains, bathed in turpentine down to the valleys, and the morning star, the Nixtamalero.

The maizegrowers returned to the mountains of Ilóm. Their iron tongues could be heard cutting at the trunks of the trees. Others set fires to clear the ground for planting, little fingers of an obscure will which still struggles, after thousands of years, to free the prisoner of the white hummingbird, the prisoner of man in the stones and in the eyes of maize grains. But the captive can escape from the entrails of the earth in the blazing heat of the clearing fires, or of warfare. The prison is fragile and if the fire escapes, what fearless manly heart can fight against it, if it makes all men flee in terror?

Gaspar, seeing that he had lost, threw himself into the river. The water which gave him life against the poison would give him death against the soldiers who fired on him and missed. Then all that could be heard was the buzzing of the insects.

OCTAVIO PAZ

Two Bodies

Two bodies face to face
are at times two waves
and night is an ocean.

Two bodies face to face
are at times two stones
and night a desert.

Two bodies face to face
are at times two roots
laced into night.

Two bodies face to face
are at times two knives
and night strikes sparks.

Two bodies face to face
are two stars falling
in an empty sky.

Translated by
*   Muriel Rukeyser*

◆◆◆

In Uxmal

1. TEMPLE OF THE TORTOISES

In this court vast as the sun
rests and dances a stone sun,
naked before the sun; he too is naked.

2. NOON

Light unblinking,
time empty of minutes,
a bird stopped short in air.

3. LATER

Light flung down,
the pillars awake
and, without moving, dance.

4. FULL SUN

The time is transparent:
even if the bird is invisible,
let us see the color of his song.

5. RELIEFS

The rain, dancing, long-haired,
ankles slivered by lightning,
descends, to an accompaniment of drums:
the corn opens its eyes, and grows.

6. SERPENT CARVED ON A WALL

The wall in the sun breathes, shivers, ripples,
a live and tattooed fragment of the sky:
a man drinks sun and is water, is earth.
And over all that life the serpent
carrying a head between his jaws:
the gods drink blood, the gods eat man.

Translated by Muriel Rukeyser

◈◈◈

San Ildefonso Nocturne

I

In my window night
                    invents another night,
another space:

in a square yard of blackness.
                              Momentary
confederations of fire,
                        nomadic geometries,
errant numbers
                From yellow to green to red,
the spiral unwinds.
                    Window:
magnetic plate of calls and answers,
high-voltage calligraphy,
false heaven/hell of industry
on the changing skin of the moment.

Sign-seeds:
              the night shoots them off,
they rise,
            bursting above,
                              fall
still burning
              in a cone of shadow,
                                      reappear,
rambling sparks,
                  syllable-clusters,
spinning flames
                that scatter,
                              smithereens once more.
The city invents and erases them.

I am at the entrance to a tunnel.
These phrases puncture time.
Perhaps I am that which waits at the end of the tunnel.

I speak with eyes closed.
                              Someone
has planted
                    a forest of magnetic needles
                    in my eyelids,
                                        someone
guides the thread of these words.
                                        The page
has become an ants' nest.
                                   The void
has settled at the mouth of my stomach.
                                             I fall
endlessly through that void.
                                        I fall without falling.
My hands are cold,
                        my feet cold,
    but the alphabets are burning, burning.
                                               Space
constructs and deconstructs itself.
                                        The night insists,
the night touches my forehead,
                                        touches my thoughts.
What does it want?

2

Empty streets, squinting lights.
                                   On a corner,
the ghost of a dog
                        searches the garbage
for a spectral bone.
                         Uproar in a nearby patio:
cacophonous cockpit.
                              Mexico, circa 1931.
Loitering sparrows,
                        a flock of children
builds a nest
                    of unsold newspapers.
In the desolation
                        the streetlights invent
unreal pools of yellowish light

Apparitions:
time splits open:
                        a lugubrious, lascivious clatter of heels,
beneath *a sky of soot*
                        the flash of a skirt.
C'est la mort—ou la morte . . .
                                    The indifferent wind
pulls torn posters from the walls.
At this hour,
                    the red walls of San Ildefonso
are black, and they breathe:
                                sun turned to time,
time turned to stone,
                        stone turned to body.
These streets were once canals.
                                    In the sun,
the houses were silver:
                        city of mortar and stone,
moon fallen in the lake.
                            Over the filled canals
and the buried idols
                    the Creoles erected
another city
            —not white, but red and gold—
idea turned to space, tangible number.
                                        They placed it
at the crossroads of eight directions,
                                        its doors
open to the invisible:
                        heaven and hell.
Sleeping district.
                    We walk through galleries of echoes,
past broken images:
                        our history.
Hushed nation of stones.
                            Churches,
dome-growths,
                their facades
petrified gardens of symbols.
                                Shipwrecked
in the spiteful proliferation of dwarf houses:
humiliated palaces,
                        fountains without water,

affronted frontispieces. Cumuli,
insubstantial mad repose, accumulate
over the ponderous bulks,
                              conquered
not by the weight of the years
but by the infamy of the present.

                          Zócalo Plaza,
vast as the earth:
                    diaphanous space,
court of echoes.
                    There,
between Alyosha K and Julien S,
                              we devised bolts of lightning
against the century and its cliques.
                              The wind of thought
carried us away,
                    the verbal wind,
the wind that plays with mirrors,
                              master of reflections,
builder of cities of air,
                              geometries
hung from the thread of reason.

Shut down for the night,
                              the yellow trolleys,
giant worms:
              S's and Z's:
a crazed auto, insect with malicious eyes.
                                    Ideas,
fruits within an arm's reach,
                              like stars,
                                    burning.
The girandola is burning,
                          the adolescent dialogue,
the scorched hasty frame.
                          The bronze fist
of the towers beats
              12 times.
                          Night
bursts into pieces,
                    gathers them by itself,
and becomes one, intact.

We disperse,
not there in the plaza with its dead trains,
                              but here,
on this page: petrified letters.

3

The boy who walks through this poem,
between San Ildefonso and the Zócalo,
is the man who writes it:
                              this page too
is a ramble through the night.
                              Here the friendly ghosts
become flesh,
                 ideas dissolve.

Good, we wanted good:
                       to set the world right.
We didn't lack integrity:
                       we lacked humility.
What we wanted was not innocently wanted.
Precepts and concepts,
                       the arrogance of theologians,
to beat with a cross,
                       to institute with blood,
to build the house with bricks of crime,
to declare obligatory communion.
                                   Some
became secretaries to the secretary
to the General Secretary of the Inferno.
                                   Rage
became philosophy,
                    its drivel has covered the planet.
Reason came down to earth,
took the form of a gallows
                       —and is worshiped by millions.
Circular plot:
                 we have all been,
in the Great Flayhouse of the World,
judge, executioner, victim, witness,
                                   we have all
given false testimony
                       against the others
and against ourselves.

                    And the vilest: we
were the public that applauded or yawned in its seats.
The guilt that knows no guilt,
                                innocence
was the greatest guilt.
                    Each year was a mountain of bones.

Conversions, retractions, excommunications,
reconciliations, apostasies, recantations,
the zig-zag of the demonolotries and the androlotries,
bewitchments and aberrations:
my history.
            Are they the histories of an error?
History is the error.
                    Further than dates,
closer than names,
                    truth is that
which history scorns:
                    the everyday
—everyone's anonymous heartbeat,
                            the unique
beat of every one—
                    the unrepeatable
everyday, identical to all days.
                            Truth
is the base of time without history.
                        The weight
of the weightless moment:
                        a few stones in the sun
seen long ago,
            today return,
stones of time that are also stone
beneath this sun of time,
sun that comes from a dateless day,
                            sun
that lights up these words,
                    sun of words
that burn out when they are named.
                        Suns, words, stones,
burn and burn out:
                    the moment burns them
without burning.
            Hidden, immobile, untouchable,
the present—not its presences—is always.

Between seeing and making,
                              contemplation or action,
I chose the act of words:
                              to make them, to inhabit them,
to give eyes to the language.
                              Poetry is not truth:
it is the resurrection of presences,
                              history
transfigured in the truth of undated time.
Poetry,
        like history, is made;
                              poetry,
like truth, is seen.
              Poetry:
                    incarnation
of the-sun-on-the-stones in a name,
                              dissolution
of the name in a beyond of stones.
Poetry,
        suspension bridge between history and truth,
is not a path toward this or that:
                              it is to see
the stillness in motion,
                        change
in stillness.
            History is the path:
it goes nowhere,
                  we all walk it,
truth is to walk it.
                    We neither go nor come:
we are in the hands of time.
                          Truth:
to know ourselves,
                    from the beginning,
                                        hung.
Brotherhood over the void.

4

Ideas scatter,
              the ghosts remain:
truth of the lived and suffered.
An almost empty taste remains:
                              time

—shared fury—
                        time
—shared oblivion—
                                in the end transfigured
in memory and its incarnations.
                                        What remains is
time as portioned body: language.

In the window,
                        battle simulacrum:
the commercial sky of advertisements
                                        flares up, goes out.
Behind,
            barely visible,
                            the true constellations.
Among the water towers, antennas, rooftops,
a liquid column,
                        more mental than corporeal,
a waterfall of silence:
                            the moon.
                                    Neither phantom nor idea:
once a goddess,
                        today an errant clarity.
My wife sleeps.
                    She too is a moon,
a clarity that travels
                        not between the reefs of the clouds,
but between the rocks and wracks of dreams:
she too is a soul.
                        She flows below her closed eyes,
a silent torrent
                    rushing down
from her forehead to her feet,
                                she tumbles within,
bursts out from within,
                            her heartbeats sculpt her,
traveling through herself
                            she invents herself,
inventing herself
                        she copies it,
she is an arm of the sea
                            between the islands of her breasts,
her belly a lagoon
                        where darkness and its foliage

grow pale,
        she flows through her shape,
rises,
    falls,
        scatters in herself,
              ties
herself to her flowing,
           disperses in her form:
she too is a body.
          Truth
is the swell of a breath
and the visions closed eyes see:
the palpable mystery of the person.

The night is at the point of running over.
                   It grows light.
The horizon has become aquatic.
              To rush down
from the heights of this hour:
          will dying
be a falling or a rising,
        a sensation or a cessation?
I close my eyes,
        I hear in my skull
the footsteps of my blood,
           I hear
time pass through my temples.
            I am still alive.
The room is covered with moon.
           Woman:
fountain in the night.
        I am bound to her quiet flowing.

Translated by Eliot Weinberger

JUAN RULFO

Luvina
FROM
The Burning Plain

Of the mountains in the south Luvina is the highest and the rockiest. It's infested with that gray stone they make lime from, but in Luvina they don't make lime from it or get any good out of it. They call it crude stone there, and the hill that climbs up toward Luvina they call the Crude Stone Hill. The sun and the air have taken it on themselves to make it crumble away, so that the earth around there is always white and brilliant, as if it were always sparkling with the morning dew, though this is just pure talk, because in Luvina the days are cold as the nights and the dew thickens in the sky before it can fall to the earth.

And the ground is steep and slashed on all sides by deep barrancas, so deep you can't make out the bottom. They say in Luvina that one's dreams come up from those barrancas; but the only thing I've seen come up out of them was the wind, whistling as if down below they had squeezed it into reed pipes. A wind that doesn't even let the dulcamaras grow: those sad little plants that can live with just a bit of earth, clutching with all their hands at the mountain cliffsides. Only once in a while, where there's a little shade, hidden among the rocks, the chicalote blossoms with its white poppies. But the chicalote soon withers. Then you hear it scratching the air with its spiny branches, making a noise like a knife on a whetstone.

"You'll be seeing that wind that blows over Luvina. It's dark. They say because it's full of volcano sand; anyway, it's a black air. You'll see it. It takes hold of things in Luvina as if it was going to bite them. And there are lots of days when it takes the roofs off the houses as if they were hats, leaving the bare walls uncovered. Then it scratches like it had nails: you hear it morning and night, hour after hour without stopping, scraping the walls, tearing off strips of earth, digging with its sharp shovel under the

279

doors, until you feel it boiling inside of you as if it was going to remove the hinges of your very bones. You'll see."

The man speaking was quiet for a bit, while he looked outside.

The noise of the river reached them, passing its swollen waters through the fig-tree branches, the noise of the air gently rustling the leaves of the almond trees, and the shouts of the children playing in the small space illumined by the light that came from the store.

The flying ants entered and collided with the oil lamp, falling to the ground with scorched wings. And outside night kept on advancing.

"Hey, Camilo, two more beers!" the man said again. Then he added, "There's another thing, mister. You'll never see a blue sky in Luvina. The whole horizon there is always a dingy color always clouded over by a dark stain that never goes away. All the hills are bare and treeless, without one green thing to rest your eyes on; everything is wrapped in an ashy smog. You'll see what it's like—those hills silent as if they were dead and Luvina crowning the highest hill with its white houses like a crown of the dead—"

The children's shouts came closer until they penetrated the store. That made the man get up, go to the door and yell at them, "Go away! Don't bother us! Keep on playing, but without so much racket."

Then, coming back to the table, he sat down and said, "Well, as I was saying, it doesn't rain much there. In the middle of the year they get a few storms that whip the earth and tear it away, just leaving nothing but the rocks floating above the stony crust. It's good to see then how the clouds crawl heavily about, how they march from one hill to another jumping as if they were inflated bladders, crashing and thundering just as if they were breaking on the edge of the barrancas. But after ten or twelve days they go away and don't come back until the next year, and sometimes they don't come back for several years— No, it doesn't rain much. Hardly at all, so that the earth, besides being all dried up and shriveled like old leather, gets filled with cracks and hard clods of earth like sharp stones, that prick your feet as you walk along, as if the earth itself had grown thorns there. That's what it's like."

He downed his beer, until only bubbles of foam remained in the bottle, then he went on: "Wherever you look in Luvina, it's a very sad place. You're going there, so you'll find out. I would say it's the place where sadness nests. Where smiles are unknown as if people's faces had been frozen. And, if you like, you can see that sadness just any time. The breeze that blows there moves it around but never takes it away. It seems like it was born there. And you can almost taste and feel it, because it's always over you, against you, and because it's heavy like a large plaster weighing on the living flesh of the heart.

"The people from there say that when the moon is full they clearly see the figure of the wind sweeping along Luvina's streets, bearing behind it a black blanket; but what I always managed to see when there was a moon in Luvina was the image of despair—always.

"But drink up your beer. I see you haven't even tasted it. Go ahead and drink. Or maybe you don't like it warm like that. But that's the only kind we have here. I know it tastes bad, something like burro's piss. Here you get used to it. I swear that there you won't even get this. When you go to Luvina you'll miss it. There all you can drink is a liquor they make from a plant called hojasé, and after the first swallows your head'll be whirling around like crazy, feeling like you had banged it against something. So better drink your beer. I know what I'm talking about."

You could still hear the struggle of the river from outside. The noise of the air. The children playing. It seemed to be still early in the evening.

The man had gone once more to the door and then returned, saying: "It's easy to see things, brought back by memory, from here where there's nothing like it. But when it's about Luvina I don't have any trouble going right on talking to you about what I know. I lived there. I left my life there— I went to that place full of illusions and returned old and worn out. And now you're going there— All right. I seem to remember the beginning. I'll put myself in your place and think— Look, when I got to Luvina the first time— But will you let me have a drink of your beer first? I see you aren't paying any attention to it. And it helps me a lot. It relieves me, makes me feel like my head had been rubbed with camphor oil— Well, I was telling you that when I reached Luvina the first time, the mule driver who took us didn't even want to let his animals rest. As soon as he let us off, he turned half around. 'I'm going back,' he said.

" 'Wait, aren't you going to let your animals take a rest? They are all worn out.'

" 'They'd be in worse shape here,' he said. 'I'd better go back.'

"And away he went, rushing down Crude Stone Hill, spurring his horses on as if he was leaving some place haunted by the devil.

"My wife, my three children, and I stayed there, standing in the middle of the plaza, with all our belongings in our arms. In the middle of that place where all you could hear was the wind—

"Just a plaza, without a single plant to hold back the wind. There we were.

"Then I asked my wife, 'What country are we in, Agripina?'

"And she shrugged her shoulders.

" 'Well, if you don't care, go look for a place where we can eat and spend the night. We'll wait for you here,' I told her.

"She took the youngest child by the hand and left. But she didn't come back.

"At nightfall, when the sun was lighting up just the tops of the mountains, we went to look for her. We walked along Luvina's narrow streets, until we found her in the church, seated right in the middle of that lonely church, with the child asleep between her legs.

"'What are you doing here, Agripina?'

"'I came to pray,' she told us.

"'Why?' I asked her.

"She shrugged her shoulders.

"Nobody was there to pray to. It was a vacant old shack without any doors, just some open galleries and a roof full of cracks where the air came through like a sieve.

"'Where's the restaurant?'

"'There isn't any restaurant.'

"'And the inn?'

"'There isn't any inn.'

"'Did you se anybody? Does anybody live here?' I asked her.

"'Yes, there across the street— Some women— I can still see them. Look, there behind the cracks in that door I see some eyes shining, watching us— They have been looking over here— Look at them. I see the shining balls of their eyes— But they don't have anything to give us to eat. They told me without sticking out their heads that there was nothing to eat in this town— Then I came in here to pray, to ask God to help us.'

"'Why didn't you go back to the plaza? We were waiting for you.'

"'I came in here to pray. I haven't finished yet.'

"'What country is this, Agripina?'

"And she shrugged her shoulders again.

"That night we settled down to sleep in a corner of the church behind the dismantled altar. Even there the wind reached, but it wasn't quite as strong. We listened to it passing over us with long howls, we listened to it come in and out of the hollow caves of the doors whipping the crosses of the stations of the cross with its hands full of air—large rough crosses of mesquite wood hanging from the walls the length of the church, tied together with wires that twanged with each gust of wind like the gnashing of teeth.

"The children cried because they were too scared to sleep. And my wife, trying to hold all of them in her arms. Embracing her handful of children. And me, I didn't know what to do.

"A little before dawn the wind calmed down. Then it returned. But there was a moment during that morning when everything was still, as if the sky had joined the earth, crushing all noise with its weight— You could hear the breathing of the children, who now were resting. I listened to my wife's heavy breath there at my side.

"'What is it?' she said to me.

"'What's what?' I asked her.

"'That, that noise.'

"'It's the silence. Go to sleep. Rest a little bit anyway, because it's going to be day soon.'

"But soon I heard it too. It was like bats flitting through the darkness very close to us. Bats with big wings that grazed against the ground. I got up and the beating of wings was stronger, as if the flock of bats had been frightened and were flying toward the holes of the doors. Then I walked on tiptoes over there, feeling that dull murmur in front of me. I stopped at the door and saw them. I saw all the women of Luvina with their water jugs on their shoulders, their shawls hanging from their heads and their black figures in the black background of the night.

"'What do you want?' I asked them. 'What are you looking for at this time of night?'

"One of them answered, 'We're going for water.'

"I saw them standing in front of me, looking at me. Then, as if they were shadows, they started walking down the street with their black water jugs.

"No, I'll never forget that first night I spent in Luvina.

"Don't you think this deserves another drink? Even if it's just to take away the bad taste of my memories."

❖❖❖

"It seems to me you asked me how many years I was in Luvina, didn't you? The truth is, I don't know. I lost the notion of time since the fevers got it all mixed up for me, but it must have been an eternity— Time is very long there. Nobody counts the hours and nobody cares how the years go mounting up. The days begin and end. Then night comes. Just day and night until the day of death, which for them is a hope.

"You must think I'm harping on the same idea. And I am, yes, mister— To be sitting at the threshold of the door, watching the rising and the setting of the sun, raising and lowering your head, until the springs go slack and then everything gets still, timeless, as if you had always lived in eternity. That's what the old folks do there.

"Because only real old folks and those who aren't born yet, as they say, live in Luvina—And weak women, so thin they are just skin and bones. The children born there have all gone away— They hardly see the light of day and they're already grown up. As they say, they jump from their mothers' breasts to the hoe and disappear from Luvina. That's the way it is in Luvina.

"There are just old folks left there and lone women, or with a husband who is off God knows where— They appear every now and then when the storms come I was telling you about; you hear a rustling all through the town when they return and something like a grumbling when they go away again— They leave a sack of provisions for the old folks and plant another child in the bellies of their women, and nobody knows anything more of them until the next year, and sometimes never— It's the custom. There they think that's the way the law is, but it's all the same. The children spend their lives working for their parents as their parents worked for theirs and who knows how many generations back performed this obligation—

"Meanwhile, the old people wait for them and for death, seated in their doorways, their arms hanging slack, moved only by the gratitude of their children— Alone, in that lonely Luvina.

"One day I tried to convince them they should go to another place where the land was good. 'Let's leave here!' I said to them. 'We'll manage somehow to settle somewhere. The government will help us.'

"They listened to me without batting an eyelash, gazing at me from the depths of their eyes from which only a little light came.

"'You say the government will help us, teacher? Do you know the government?'

"I told them I did.

"'We know it too. It just happens. But we don't know anything about the government's mother.'

"I told them it was their country. They shook their heads saying no. And they laughed. It was the only time I saw the people of Luvina laugh. They grinned with their toothless mouths and told me no, that the government didn't have a mother.

"And they're right, you know? That lord only remembers them when one of his boys has done something wrong down here. Then he sends to Luvina for him and they kill him. Aside from that, they don't know if the people exist.

"'You're trying to tell us that we should leave Luvina because you think we've had enough of going hungry without reason,' they said to me. 'But if we leave, who'll bring along our dead ones? They live here and we can't leave them alone.'

"So they're still there. You'll see them now that you're going. Munching on dry mesquite pulp and swallowing their own saliva to keep hunger away. You'll see them pass by like shadows, hugging to the walls of the houses, almost dragged along by the wind.

"'Don't you hear that wind?" I finally said to them. 'It will finish you off.'

"'It keeps on blowing as long as it ought to. It's God's will,' they answered me. 'It's bad when it stops blowing. When that happens the sun pours into Luvina and sucks our blood and the little bit of moisture we have in our skin. The wind keeps the sun up above. It's better that way.'

"So I didn't say anything else to them. I left Luvina and I haven't gone back and I don't intend to.

"—But look at the way the world keeps turning. You're going there now in a few hours. Maybe it's been fifteen years since they said the same thing to me: 'You're going to San Juan Luvina.'

"In those days I was strong. I was full of ideas— You know how we're all full of ideas. And one goes with the idea of making something of them everywhere. But it didn't work out in Luvina. I made the experiment and it failed—

"San Juan Luvina. That name sounded to me like a name in the heavens. But it's purgatory. A dying place where even the dogs have died off, so there's not a creature to bark at the silence; for as soon as you get used to the strong wind that blows there all you hear is the silence that reigns in these lonely parts. And that gets you down. Just look at me. What it did to me. You're going there, so you'll soon understand what I mean—

"What do you say we ask this fellow to pour a little mescal? With this beer you have to get up and go all the time and that interrupts our talk a lot. Hey, Camilo, let's have two mescals this time!

"Well, now, as I was telling you—"

But he didn't say anything. He kept staring at a fixed point on the table where the flying ants, now wingless, circled about like naked worms.

Outside you could hear the night advancing. The lap of the water against the fig-tree trunks. The children's shouting, now far away. The stars peering through the small hole of the door.

The man who was staring at the flying ants slumped over the table and fell asleep.

ABOUT THE AUTHORS

Charles Alexander Eastman (Ohiyesa)

Charles Alexander Eastman (1858–1939) was a mixed-blood Sioux (Dakota). He was given the name Ohiyesa when he was four years old. During the Sioux Uprising of 1862, Ohiyesa became separated from his father—his mother had died when he was born—and fled from his reservation in Minnesota to Canada under the protection of his grandmother and uncle, who took charge of his upbringing. In exile in Canada, remote from the culture of white settlers, Ohiyesa was schooled in Indian ways until the age of fifteen when he was suddenly reunited with his father, who had been converted to Christianity while a prisoner-of-war in the United States. Mr. Eastman took his son, Ohiyesa, back to a homestead in Dakota Territory where the young Indian warrior was deprived of his Indian culture, converted to a new faith, and trained in an alien way of life.

Eastman went on to become one of the best-known Indians of his time and was held up as a model of success in the education of Native Americans who were generally considered hopeless students. Receiving a Bachelor of Science degree from Dartmouth in 1887 and a medical degree from Boston University three years later, Eastman devoted his life to Indian education.

"Evening in the Lodge" is drawn from *Indian Boyhood* (1902), one of three autobiographical books by Eastman, including *The Soul of the Indian* (1911), and *From Deep Woods to Civilization* (1916). Charles Alexander Eastman wrote nine other books, all devoted to making visible and significant the traditional life of his people.

"Evening in the Lodge" is typical of the attitude and subject matter of *Indian Boyhood*. It is mild in its pride and inclined to offer glimpses of Indian life with an apologetic tone. Eastman's later works are far less apologetic. "Moreover," as Frederick W. Turner III has noted, "there is an increasingly forthright critique which comes close to an indictment by a man who during his lifetime was often advertised and introduced as a classic example of the viability of the American Dream."

❖❖❖

D'Arcy McNickle

D'Arcy McNickle, a member of the Flathead tribe, grew up on his people's reservation in northwestern Montana. He has been widely recognized as one of the two or three inaugural masters of Native American literature. Born in 1904 at St. Agnatius, Montana, he trained at the University of Montana, Oxford University, and the University of Grenoble. His nonfiction work, *Indian Man,* was nominated for a National Book Award in 1971. His other books include *They Came Here First* (1949), *Runner in the Sun* (1954), *Indians and Other Americans* (with Harold E. Fey, 1959), *Wind From an Enemy Sky* (published posthumously, 1978), and his first published work, *The Surrounded* (1936).

D'Arcy McNickle was revered both as a writer and an Indian organizer, and his political efforts included the co-founding of the National Congress of American Indians. He died in late 1977, shortly after completing *Wind From an Enemy Sky.*

❖❖❖

N. Scott Momaday

N. Scott Momaday, a Kiowa Indian from Oklahoma and son of the artist Al Momaday, won the Pulitzer Prize in 1969 for his first novel *House Made of Dawn* (1968). Born in 1934, he grew up on Indian reservations in the American Southwest where he was graduated in 1958 from the University of New Mexico. He then went to Stanford University in California where he took two further degrees in English. He taught English at the University of California at Santa Barbara and at Berkeley before becoming a professor of English at Stanford University in 1963. He currently teaches in the English Department of the University of Arizona in Tucson. He is the author of a reworking of Kiowa folk tales entitled *The Way to Rainy Mountain* (1969).

Though known essentially as a writer of prose, Momaday has also written splendid poetry. Two works, "Carriers of the Dream Wheel" and "Rainy Mountain Cemetery," convey some of the power of his poetic imagination.

Hyemeyohsts Storm

Hyemeyohsts Storm is a Northern Cheyenne, born and raised on the Cheyenne and Crow reservations in Montana. He taught at the University of Iowa and lectures widely. His books include *Seven Arrows* (1972) and *Song of Heyoehkah* (1981).

Seven Arrows is an innovative book, a combination of highly lyrical writing and romantic graphics and photographs. Its themes are ambiguous and its form is poetic: a testament of the spiritual life of a people; a romance about the Northern Cheyenne and their history. It is also a novel about the Peace Chiefs Hawk, Night Bear, and Green Fire Mouse, and the Brotherhood of the Shields. From their tales we learn Hyemeyohsts Storm's personal interpretation of the symbols of such Plains Indian motifs as the Medicines of the Four Directions as well as the People's Names and Shields. The famed Vision Quest of the Northern Plains tribes is also a theme of this novel. "But at its core *Seven Arrows* is about the Sun Dance, the Medicine Wheel, and the Sacred Hoop of the People. It is about the equality and brotherhood of all the Earth's creatures and the Great Balancing Harmony of the Total Universe" (Storm).

❖❖❖

Craig Kee Strete

Craig Kee Strete was born in Fort Wayne, Indiana, of Indian parents. He has subsequently traveled extensively throughout Europe where his writing is both widely praised and published in numerous foreign editions. His first book, from which one of the stories included in this collection is drawn, was first published in Holland: *If All Else Fails, We Can Whip the Horse's Eyes and Make Him Cry and Sleep*, a title that ideally summarizes Strete's avant-garde mentality and imagination. That title was borrowed from a song by the popular poet and rock star Jim Morrison, an idol whose tragic life means so much to Strete that he recently wrote a semifictional work about Morrison called *Burn Down the Night* (1982). By contrast, Strete has also written several books for children: *Paint Your Face on a Drowning in the River* (1978), *The Bleeding Man and Other Science Fiction Stories* (1974/77), and *When Grandfather Journeys into Winter* (1979). A remarkable tribute came in the form of a preface for the first English edition of *If All Else Fails . . .* (1980). Written by Jorge Luis Borges, the preface stated, ". . . with this book we risk the dangerous power of genius, of one who can construct a universe within the skull, to rival the real." Craig Kee Strete lives in North Hollywood, California, and he is currently writing both for the theater and cinema.

◆◆◆

James Welch

James Welch was born in November 1940, in Browning, Montana. He is Blackfeet on his father's side and his mother was a Gros Ventre Indian. He attended schools on the Blackfeet and Fort Belnap reservations before attending the University of Minnesota. He received his B.A. degree from the University of Montana. His first book, a collection of poems titled *Riding the Earthboy 40* was published in 1971. *Winter in the Blood* was published in 1974. Another novel, *The Death of Jim Loney*, was issued in 1979.

James Welch is currently serving on the Montana State Board of Pardons. A poet and writer of extraordinary skill and imagination, Welch has won praise for his precise language and direct, sparse narrative style.

◆◆◆

Leslie Marmon Silko

Leslie Marmon Silko was born in 1948 in Albuquerque, New Mexico. She was brought up on the Laguna Pueblo reservation and is a mixed-blood: part Laguna, part Mexican, and part white. "I don't apologize for this anymore—not to whites, not to full bloods—[my family's] origin is unlike any other. My poetry, my storytelling rise out of this source," Silko has explained. Her gift of several heritages and languages had produced a brilliance in her prose unique to North American Indian writers. Her conflicts and pain during her search for identity as a half-breed are, as she has said, at the core of her writing.

Silko was graduated from the University of New Mexico and studied for three semesters at that university's American Indian Law Program before leaving to devote herself full-time to writing. For a time she lived in Ketchikan, Alaska, but recently, after winning the prestigious Mac-Arthur Award, she bought a ranch near Tucson, Arizona, where she now lives. She also teaches at the University of Arizona in Tucson.

Silko has published numerous stories and poetry in journals and anthologies. *Storyteller* (1981) recycles some of her best poems and stories in a distinctive style and within an innovative form, combining oral tradition, lyric descriptions, and personal experiences in a complex tapestry of storytelling.

William Least Heat Moon

William Least Heat Moon is the Osage name of William Trogdon, a mixed-blood who lives in Columbia, Missouri. He was born in Kansas City, Missouri, in 1939. When Least Heat Moon lost his job at a college in Missouri, he got a half-ton Ford van, packed a few necessaries including *Leaves of Grass* by Walt Whitman and Neihardt's *Black Elk Speaks*, and set out to follow the track of various ancestors along America's "blue highways"—the backroads printed in blue on maps.

The result of this journey was the nonfiction work, *Blue Highways* (1982), Least Heat Moon's account of his three-month trip over the backroads of America. A much-heralded book which has won both immense popular success and exceptional critical praise, *Blue Highways* propelled Least Heat Moon into a place of importance in the literary world and made him the first Indian to produce a bestseller. In this, his first published book, Least Heat Moon considers the Ghost Dance ceremony the controlling structural element.

◈◈◈

Gerald Vizenor

Gerald Vizenor is a teacher and writer from Minnesota. He divides his time, as a teacher, between the University of Minnesota and the University of California at Berkeley where he teaches American Indian literature, film, and philosophy. Vizenor is an enrolled member of the White Earth Reservation, and is of mixed French and Ojibwe descent.

Vizenor's publications include *Earthdivers: Tribal Narratives on Mixed Descent* (1981); *Summer in the Spring: Ojibwe Lyric Poems and Tribal Stories* (1981); *Wordarrows: Indians and Whites in the New Fur Trade* (1978); and *The Everlasting Sky: New Voices From the People Named the Chippewa* (1972).

◈◈◈

Simon J. Ortiz

Simon J. Ortiz is an Acoma Pueblo Indian, born in Albuquerque, New Mexico, in 1941. He served three years in the U.S. Army and then attended the University of New Mexico and the University of Iowa. He has taught at San Diego State University, the Institute of American Indian

Arts, and Navajo Community College at Chinle (on the Navajo Reservation).

Ortiz's poetry and prose have been widely published in journals and anthologies. His principal publications include *Going For the Rain* (1976), a collection of his poetry; *A Good Journey* (1977), another poetry collection; *Howbah Indians* (1978), a series of short stories; *Fight Back: For the Sake of the People, For the Sake of the Land* (1980), poetry and prose; and the highly acclaimed series of poems entitled *From San Creek* (1981).

❖❖❖

Hanay Geiogamah

Hanay Geiogamah is an active playwright and director in Native American theater. He was the Artistic Director of the Native American Theater Ensemble from 1972 to 1975, touring with the Ensemble throughout the U.S and Europe. Born in Lawton, Oklahoma, of Kiowa parents, Geiogamah studied journalism at the University of Oklahoma before turning to the theater. He and the Native American Theater Ensemble have had an important relationship with both the Institute of American Indian Arts in Santa Fe, New Mexico, and with the La Mama Theatre in New York City. Most of Hanay Geiogamah's plays were written for the Ensemble. Geiogamah has taught native American theater at the University of Washington.

❖❖❖

Ray A. Young Bear

Ray A. Young Bear was born in Tama, Iowa in 1950. His tribe is the Sauk and Fox of Iowa, better known as the Mesquakies. He has been writing with immense success since 1966, and his poetry has appeared in a wide range of major poetry publications and anthologies. He was also an art student at the University of Northern Iowa at Cedar Falls.

A collection of poems, entitled *Winter of the Salamander* (1980), won unlimited critical acclaim. A new collection (to be published shortly and to include all the poems published here for the first time) will be entitled *The Bumblebee Is the Bear-King.*

◈◈◈

Wendy Rose

Wendy Rose was born in Oakland, California, in 1948. She is of Miwok and Hopi ancestry. She was graduated by the University of California at Berkeley, where she taught until 1983. She is a poet of very considerable achievement; the author of *Hopi Roadrunner Dancing* (1973), *Long Division* (1976/1981), *Academic Squaw* (1977), *Builder Kachina: A Home Going Cycle* (1979), *What Happened When the Hopi Hit New York* (1982), and her collected works, *Lost Copper* (1980).

Wendy Rose edits *The American Indian Quarterly* and was the recipient of a 1982 National Endowment of the Arts Fellowship.

◈◈◈

Harold Littlebird

Harold Littlebird, of Santo Domingo and Laguna Pueblos, is a well-known potter. His poetry has been published in numerous anthologies and journals. His first book of poems was entitled *On Mountains' Breath* (1982). He has also co-edited, with Jim Sagel, an issue of *Suntracks, An American Indian Literary Magazine*, published by the University of Arizona at Tucson.

Harold Littlebird is also a performing artist who combines his own poetry and songs with an understanding of Pueblo Indian oral traditions.

◈◈◈

Duane Niatum

Duane Niatum is the author of four volumes of poetry, including *Ascending Red Cedar Moon, Digging Out the Roots,* and *Songs for the Harvester of Dreams,* which won the American Book Award, 1982, from the Before Columbus Foundation. His short fiction and essays have also appeared in magazines, newspapers, and anthologies. He was born in 1938 in Seattle where he makes his home. He is a member of the Klallam tribe, whose ancestral lands are on the Washington State coast, along the Strait of Juan de Fuca. He graduated from the University of Washington with a B.A. in English and later took an M.A. from Johns Hopkins University. In June 1983, he was invited to participate in Rotterdam's International Poetry Festival. His work has been translated into numerous languages. And he distinguished himself in 1975 as the editor of a landmark anthology of contemporary Native American poetry for Harper and Row, entitled *Carriers of the Dream Wheel*.

❖❖❖

Joy Harjo

Joy Harjo was born in Tulsa, Oklahoma, in 1951, and is of the Creek tribe. She left Oklahoma to attend high school at the Institute of American Indian Arts, Santa Fe, and later received her B.A. from the University of New Mexico and her M.F.A. from the Iowa Writers' Workshop. She has taught Native American literature at the Institute of American Indian Arts and at Arizona State University. She also serves on the Board of directors for the National Association of Third World Writers and is on the Policy Panel of the National Endowment for the Arts. She is the author of two previous collections of her poems: *The Last Song* and *What Moon Drove Me to This*.

Most recently she has published a new collection of poetry entitled *She Had Some Horses*, from which we have drawn the poems represented in this anthology.

Besides her very active work as a poet, Harjo is also interested in cinema and is at work on a screenplay, and also contributed poetic narration for a recent PBS film on the life and works of the Indian painter Jaune Quick-to-See Smith.

❖❖❖

Maurice Kenny

Maurice Kenny, born and raised in northern New York State near the St. Lawrence River, has authored numerous books, among them: *North: Poems of Home* (1977); *I Am the Sun* (1976/1979); *Dancing Back Strong the Nation* (1979/1981); *Only as Far as Brooklyn* (1979); *Kneading the Blood 1981)*; and perhaps his most significant collection to date, *Blackrobe: Isaac Jogues* (1982).

Maurice Kenny currently lives in Brooklyn.

He provided the following statement about his poetry: "My deepest belief is that poetry, and especially Native American poetry, is a quick step from prayer. Song, in the old way, was meant to praise and give thanks to the Creator for life itself, and all the creatures and grasses and rocks and waters that all may be sustained. Ceremony was incomplete without song and music, the intense drama of performance, spectacle, meant, of course, to insure the survival of the village, its rites and total culture, and all that shared the environs of the village."

Lance Henson

Lance Henson, a Cheyenne Indian from Calumet, Oklahoma, was born in 1944. He served in the U.S. Marine Corps, after which he attended the Oklahoma College of Liberal Arts in Chicasha. He is a member of the Cheyenne Dog Soldier Society and belongs to the traditional Native American Church. He has also trained in the Graduate Creative Writing Program of Tulsa University in Oklahoma.

Raised by his Cheyenne grandparents in traditional culture, Henson's interest lies in expressing the inner mythic being of the Native American. Poems dealing with this central focus have appeared in several magazines and anthologies. He has published the book entitled *Keeper of Arrows: Poems for the Cheyenne* (1977). He is working on a novel and has composed several poems published in an anthology of writings by Vietnam veterans.

Characteristic of Henson's poetry is a brevity and clarity that approaches the poetic styles of the Orient.

Anita Endrezze-Danielson

Anita Endrezze-Danielson was born in 1952 in Long Beach, California. She has lived in Oregon and Hawaii, but Washington State is her home. She is half-Yaqui (a tribe from the American Southwest and northern Mexico). She is also Yugoslavian (Slovenian) and part Italian, as well as German-Saxon from the Transylvanian region of Rumania.

A 1973 honors graduate of Eastern Washington State College, where she also received an M.A. in creative writing, Anita Endrezze-Danielson now lives in the middle of a broad pine forest with her husband and son; their home is a log house they constructed themselves.

Endrezze-Danielson has published her poetry in numerous magazines and anthologies. She is also the author of a collection of poems entitled *Claiming Lives* (1983).

Peter Blue Cloud

Peter Blue Cloud was born at Kanawake (Caughnawaga Reservation) in 1933. He is a member of the Turtle Clan of the Mohawk Tribe, Six Nations, in New York State. A former ironworker who helped build Manhattan's skyscrapers, Blue Cloud is a prolific writer of prose and poetry. His experiences as part of the Alcatraz militant occupation in the late 1960s were the basis of a book he edited entitled *Alcatraz Is Not an Island.* He has also contributed many poems to the national Native American newspaper, *Akwesasne Notes.*

Peter Blue Cloud has published six books, the most recent being *Elderberry Flute Song* (1982) and the verse-play for voices, *White Corn Sister* (1979).

❖❖❖

Roberta Hill Whiteman

Roberta Hill Whiteman is one of the most accomplished Native American poets working today. She is a Wisconsin Oneida, born in Baraboo, Wisconsin, in 1947. She attended the University of Wisconsin (where she took a B.A. in psychology) and the University of Montana (where she received an M.F.A. in writing). She has taught at Sinte Gleska College on the Rosebud Reservation in South Dakota and currently teaches in the English Department at the University of Wisconsin in Eau Claire.

Though widely published in magazines and anthologies, Roberta Hill Whiteman's first collection of poems was released in 1983, *Star Quilt.*

❖❖❖

Cesar Vallejo

Cesar Vallejo—a half-caste Peruvian born in a small village in 1892—spent more time in Paris during the 1920s and 1930s than any other Latin American poet of his generation; yet he was hardly the urbane expatriate one might suspect. He abhorred the French avant-garde for reason of his proletariat political persuasion. His character and his lifestyle were in conflict in the glittering, innovative Paris of the 1920s, but this peculiar combination of circumstances resulted in his producing some of the best poetry in the Spanish language.

Vallejo's mestizo blood placed him symbolically in the classic colonial predicament—in a no man's land culturally and politically. Nonetheless, he took immense pride in his Indian ancestry, an unusual sentiment for a Latin American of his time. The warm recollections of his childhood infused his poetry with images of a lost paradise, of his Indian grandmothers and his solemn grandfathers, who were both Spanish priests.

His political fervor ran high, and he participated in many socialist meetings, both in France and Spain. But he was already terminally ill, and in 1938 he died in Paris.

Vallejo's poetry has a decided political impulse; yet when viewed in its entirety, the body of his work places him in a central position in the vanguard of the avant-garde of his era. Behind Vallejo's social consciousness was a persistent search for the structure of poems, the effort to twist the Spanish language into new arrangements and meanings: cutting up words and rearranging their component phonemes in unusual and daring ways. He also had an unconventional approach to versification: He took the surrealistic verse of the French avant-garde and imposed its manner on Spanish, freeing it from logical continuity, from the classical and linear progression and realism that dominated late nineteenth-century poetry of Spain and Latin America. Vallejo's poetry was unselfconsciously radical. His work is not only brilliant and daring and profoundly moving, it is also the rarest of combinations: a poetry that is committed both politically and aesthetically.

◆◆◆

Pablo Neruda

Pablo Neruda was a poet of complex and wide-ranging concerns. His reputation, however, as a political poet along with the tragic circumstances of his death at the time of the Chilean army's overthrow of President Allende, will make any effort to read his poetry simply as poetry exceptionally difficult for a long time to come. It is for this reason that this collection gives particular emphasis to his most literary and coloristic writings, rather than the significant but perhaps, for now, overemphasized social aspect of his poetic vision.

Yet Neruda himself would have abhorred any effort to depoliticize his poetry. He was devoted to the defense of socialism as embodied both in the Soviet Union and in Chile's Communist Party. He also befriended the socialists in the Spanish Civil War. His last dictated words were a stern condemnation of the assassination of Chile's Communist President Allende. But despite the devotion of Neruda to his political ideals, we must not overlook the fact that he was one of Latin America's greatest poets, winner of the Nobel Prize in 1971 and honored internationally by literary people of all political persuasions.

Deeply committed to his Indian heritage, Neruda was born in a small town in southern Chile in 1904. His mother died less than two months after his birth, and he was totally in the care of his father and his father's family. It was not an easy childhood.

Neruda was born Ricardo Eliecer Neftali Reyes. But his father, a plain man who was a railroad worker, emphatically did not want his son to become a poet. So Ricardo invented a pseudonym: Pablo Neruda! The first name was taken from Paul Verlaine and the surname from a Czech gothic novelist. Into this invented identity there quickly grew a fine poet.

In 1927, Neruda entered the diplomatic service, which was to preoccupy him during his entire life. He was sent to a variety of places as a representative of Chile: Burma, Rangoon, Ceylon (now Sri Lanka), Java, and Singapore. The life Neruda experienced in the East was horrendous. He was totally alienated from his surroundings. His only means of communication was English, a language with which he had many difficulties. Neruda became obsessed with sex and drugs, and his only contact with reality was his poetry. Out of this hell a friendship developed with Andrew Boyd, a young English poet living in the East. From the influence of this poet came Neruda's intense interest in several masters of English literature: William Blake, T. S. Eliot, D. H. Lawrence, and Walt Whitman. Neruda's familiarity with these writers and his long-standing regard for Baudelaire, Rimbaud, Verlaine, and other French symbolist poets slowly merged with his anguished and isolated life, producing a style and tone in his writing that gives it strength, vividness, and originality.

In 1940, Neruda was appointed Consul General in Mexico. He finally returned to his native Chile in 1943. Stricken with cancer in the last years of his life, Neruda nonetheless retained an active affiliation with the government of President Allende. The violent assassination of Allende in 1973 and the military coup that overturned the Communist regime was the final blow. Neruda died of a heart attack, leaving as his legacy a vast repertoire of books, as well as eight volumes of unpublished poetry and his unfinished memoirs.

If we wonder about the enormity of his creative output or his dedication to political ideals that are not universally admired, we cannot question his position as one of the great poets of the twentieth century.

❖❖❖

Miguel Angel Asturias

Miguel Angel Asturias is the quintessential Latin American writer: deeply rooted in Indian traditions, devoted to social crusades seeking to improve the life of his people. Asturias also won the Nobel Prize in 1967, and was a stylist of grand poetic language as well as earthy concerns. The paradox in the career of this Guatemalan author is the fact that his discovery of his Latin American roots was the result of studies in Paris under the guidance of a French anthropologist who specialized in Central American religions.

That history of Miguel Angel Asturias is not as peculiar as it may first appear. Most Latin American intellectuals of his era were educated in France; most were political liberals interested in social reform; and many of them saw the Indian (even those who were part-Indian themselves) as a perfect metaphor for the tragic colonialism of the Americas. In the work of Asturias all these attitudes and ideals find eloquent expression.

Born in Guatemala in 1899 to a middle-class family of mixed blood (he was always very proud of his Mayan lineage), Asturias spent the first twenty-one years of his life under Estrada Cabrera's dictatorship. Cabrera's fall from power in 1921 did not improve the Guatemalan political situation, and, after receiving his law degree, Asturias moved to London. It was there, at the British Museum, that he first recognized the brilliance of Maya art—a trove of exceptional culture that was largely ignored in his native land. From London, Asturias went on to Paris where he took courses at the Sorbonne in Central American mythology from Professor Georges Raynaud, a specialist in Mayanology.

Asturias also made the acquaintance of a circle of Spanish American writers living in Paris; and through them he encountered a number of French surrealists. The cumulative effect of these experiences profoundly effected Asturias's writing and thinking.

In 1933, Asturias returned to Guatemala. He had already established himself as an interpreter of Maya mythology, producing a translation of the *Popol Vuh*, the sacred book of the Maya (1925), and writing a collection of tales, *Legends of Guatemala* (1930), published with a preface by the famed French poet Paul Valery. After returning to Guatemala he completed a very different kind of novel, *El Señor Presidente* (1946), a political work quickly proclaimed as the best Latin American novel of its time. *Men of Maize* was his second book, one which returned to the folkloric interests of Asturias. Asked in 1972 by Rita Guibert to define his artistic credo, Asturias recalled an idiomatic formula he had learned in France: magic realism. "There are no boundaries between reality and dreams, between reality and fiction, between what is seen and what is imagined. The magic of our climate and light gives our stories a double aspect—from one side they seem dreams, from the other, they are realities."

◆◆◆

Octavio Paz

Octavio Paz was born on the outskirts of Mexico City in 1914. A mestizo with deep pride in his Indian blood, Paz has evolved from a simple background to a person generally considered to be the leading figure of Mexican intellectual life. He is a major poet, and his essays and critical reviews have established him as one of the truly brilliant voices of contemporary Latin American culture. Central to his viewpoint is a pluralistic view of reality that values each and every variation of human culture and personality. It is a premise that has evolved through a series of truly dazzling books that help greatly to define the crisis of our modern world.

Octavio Paz studied at the National Autonomous University, and by 1931, he was actively involved in the cultural life of Mexico City. In 1937, he went to Spain to participate in a literary conference organized by the Spanish government during the devastating civil war. There Paz met both Vallejo and Neruda. On his return to Mexico in 1938, Paz became active within a circle of Marxist writers. But the pact between the Nazis and Soviets that same year totally disenchanted Paz, and he broke with the Stalinists. He concentrated upon the literary world, and by 1943, his little magazine, *Workshop,* had become one of Mexico's most vital literary reviews. In 1943, he visited the United States on a Guggenheim Fellowship and lived in the West and later in New York City for two years. Then, in 1945, Paz returned to his native Mexico and entered the diplomatic service. During World War II he was sent to Paris where he met André Breton and established an affinity for the surrealists. His poetic style began to change rapidly. A new interpretation of Aztec mythology emerged through the surrealistic imagery he had discovered in France. Then in 1952, Paz visited the Far East and became entranced by India and Japan. In 1962, he became Mexican ambassador to New Delhi, returning to Mexico in 1968. For six years, while in the East, Paz studied Buddhism and Tantrism. These eastern concepts infused a new impulse in Octavio Paz's works.

Octavio Paz is a complex blend of numerous influences. At the same time he remains the most distinctive voice of Mexico. In his poetry we find an amalgam of feeling and intellect that is exceptionally difficult to achieve in any art but is particularly elusive in poetry. The density, range, and variety of Paz's writing is not easily illustrated with a few poems. But whichever poems of Octavio Paz we encounter, we are certain to come away with a sense of lucidity and engagement.

◆◇◆

Juan Rulfo

Juan Rulfo was born in 1918 in a small town in Mexico near Jalisco. His birth coincided with a time of great upheaval in Mexico, and the revolution shattered his life. His father was murdered when he was only seven. His grandmother tried to force him into the priesthood; an uncle promised help only on the condition that he drop his family name and assume the anonymous "Perez" (a Spanish equivalent to the American name "Smith") in order for his family to avoid the embarrassment of having a member who was publicly "literary." Enraged by his family, Rulfo went to Mexico City where he survived on menial jobs while he pursued, with painful perfectionism, his literary career. Then in 1953, after the successful publication of his only book of short stories, *The Burning Plain* (from which "Luvina" is drawn), Rulfo received a Rockefeller grant to write a novel: *Pedro Paramo* (1956). These two works represent Rulfo's entire creative output, yet his novel is considered a classic of Mexican fiction and his short stories are greatly admired for their unique atmosphere and style.

Rulfo owes much to several writers, although his own work is strikingly original in its melding of influences. In technique Rulfo draws much from William Faulkner, who has been a major model for many Latin American authors. There is also a decided Kafkaesque mood in Juan Rulfo's best scenes, not to mention the epic qualities found in several Scandinavian writers, such as Knut Hamsun. Rulfo's world is desolate and cruel. It is populated by murderers, perverts, and pathetic peasants caught in a crossfire of dimly perceived political and psychological ferment. The style is spare and bitterly ironic in manner. Rulfo's world is haunted by tragic shadows—a world of the powerless and the too powerful. Beneath every phrase there is a pessimism that is overwhelming in its stifled expression of the bleakest of human feelings.

Juan Rulfo is not a writer of political optimism. He is clearly and unapologetically a writer of despair. His hellish world is an evocation of the Indian nightmare that has persisted for four hundred years. It is from that nightmare that Indian writers are trying to awake, but they cannot do so at the expense of the validity of their depiction of the Native American predicament. For now we must end with the terrifying imagery of Juan Rulfo's "Luvina." Perhaps somewhere beyond the nightmare is a better dream that we have yet to dream.

JAMAKE HIGHWATER is the author of *Journey to the Sky*, a novel about the rediscovery of the Mayan civilization in the nineteenth century; *Anpao: An American Indian Odyssey*, which won the 1978 Newbery Honor Award, the Boston Globe/Horn Book Honor Award, and the ALA Best Book for Young Adults Award; *Many Smokes, Many Moons*, an American Indian Chronology, which won the Jane Addams Peace Book Award for 1979; *The Sun, He Dies*, a novel about the end of the Aztec world, (available in Signet and Meridian editions); *Song from the Earth, North American Indian Painting*, winner of the 1981 Anisfield-Wolf Award; *The Sweet Grass Lives On: Fifty Contemporary North American Indian Artists; Moonsong Lullaby; Dance: Rituals of Experience* and *The Primal Mind* (available in a Meridian edition), the basis of a PBS television documentary. He has also written many reviews and articles for major magazines and journals.